The circus became my ⌐
clowns and music, wire
fortune tellers but pull back the canvas flap, just enough to peer inside. There someone's running a scam, some clown is heading toward a brutal alcoholic abyss, the advance teams are stealing and the lot is strewn with marginal bums and hobos. In the end they took it down and the rag pickers came and stripped the carcass clean. Just like my poker room.

"Xero, circus traveler, poker player and self-reflective intellectual is a fascinating character. Most poker pros are boring. Not Xero. Reber brings this character to life in rich sentences and telling details. Enjoy the ride." Alan Schoonmaker, author of *Anxiety and the Executive* and *The Psychology of Poker*

"A delightfully bumpy on-the-road tale full of characters living on the fringes. Humor and introspection paint bizarre situations in quick and cleverly written brushstrokes." Alan Geik, author of *Glenfiddich Inn*

"If you'd ever wished you'd played in the edgier days of poker, Arthur Reber provides you a glimpse into what it was like. Suffocated by the rules of college, his hero seeks his fortune on the rougher edges of society. A great tour of back rooms and hustles now disappearing." Linda Johnson, First Lady of Poker

"A coming of age novel about a literate poker-playing layabout of Greek descent It's high time to reclaim the phrase "rollicking tale" – and Reber's *Xero to Sixty* is just the book to do it!" Peter Alson, author of *Confessions of an Ivy League Bookie* and *Take Me to the River*

Books by Arthur Reber

Toward a Psychology of Reading (Erlbaum), Ed. with Don Scarborough

Dictionary of Psychology (Penguin Books, Ltd.), 4th Edition (with Rhiannon Allen and Emily Roberts)

Implicit Learning and Tacit Knowledge: An Essay on the Cognitive Unconscious (Oxford)

The New Gambler's Bible (Three Rivers)

Gambling for Dummies (Hungry Minds), with Lou Krieger and Richard Harroch

Poker, Life and Other Confusing Things (ConJelCo)

Xero to Sixty

A NOVEL BY
ARTHUR S. REBER

2226 Sunrise Drive
Point Roberts, WA
98281
(360) 945-5075
areber@brooklyn.cuny.edu

Dedication

To Mike Z and life's stories.

Acknowledgements

Thanks to Anna for guiding me through the process of actually publishing a novel. Thanks to the many whose lives left their mark on me.

Table of Contents

Cast of Characters

<u>Main Characters (in order of appearance)</u>
Xerxes "Xero" Konstantakis — Protagonist, only son of Greek immigrants
Tony Piccolo — Xero's boss/father-surrogate
Henry Shannon — Bar owner, part-time gangster
Armin Harmoninsky — Law professor, advisor, friend of Xero and Lydia
Lydia Demerara — Xero's wife, civil rights lawyer

<u>Secondary Characters (in order of appearance)</u>
Alkaios Konstantakis — Xero's father, professor of linguistics
Hanna Konstantakis — Xero's mother, editor
Frankie Quasimodo — Xero's cousin, auto mechanic
Arianna (Anna) — Xero's sister
Billy — Anna's husband
Maurice Blackmun — Encyclopedia company executive
Bobby Joe Campbell — Redneck salesman, Federal agent impersonator
Joe Friday — FBI agent
Judge Montgomery — Municipal court judge
Doris/Daciana — Gypsy, fortune teller, con artist
Johnny, Cliffy, Connie, Louie the Loser — Xero's co-workers in the boiler room
Ken Karson — Circus owner
Ricco — Ringmaster
Judy — Circus performer
Persephone — Animal trainer
Wispy — Performing pig
Grace and Sal Pirelli — High wire acrobats
Rudy — Hanger on with circus, Doris's go-fer.
Sabato Demerara — Lydia's father, cop
Tessa Demerara — Lydia's mother, homemaker
Luigi Demerara — Lydia's brother, mechanic, bookie

Janice Shannon — Henry's wife, alcoholic
A. P. Bolling — Gynecological surgeon
Bowie Blatinmann — Tattooed, gay music producer
Tommy T-Bird — Professional poker player
Toby, Charlene, Lorenzo, Arnie, Herschel, Sarge, Maury, Barry, Dickless Charlie, Flathead Freddie, No Name, Doc — poker players
Mr. Neat — Chip snatcher, poker cheat
Porkpie — Armed robber
Larry — Security guard in a poker room
Manny — Assistant Head of Security in a poker room
Horst Harmoninsky — Armin's son
Sarah Harmoninsky — Horst's wife
Big George — Mafia enforcer
Artie Mondessini — Mafia hood
Sheldon — Poker room manager
Marty — Poker player, thief
Earl — Unpleasant poker player
Rollie — Con artist and poker player
Idaho Bob — Bouncer
Ranjani Winstone — Armin's test-tube daughter

<u>Peripheral Characters (in order of appearance)</u>
Manfred Housemann — College dean
Patrick Holder — Auto mechanic
Stefan R. — Peripatetic Swede
T.D. — Anna's dog
Harlan — Used car salesman
Sales manager (unnamed) — Used car sales manager
Ralph/Rod Buckley — Encyclopedia sales supervisor
Mr. Pajamas — Undercover cop
Bradley — An Australian
Marvin Burrows — Court bailiff
Chris — Pro bono lawyer
Maxim Karson — Circus clown, alcoholic
Barney Quinn — WW II vet, occasional circus worker

Selma, Rosalie Demerara — Lydia's sisters
Sal — Wannabe hood from Bensonhurst
T.C. — Xero and Lydia's cat
Ninny, Joey Blue Eyes, Maxine, Linda — Poker dealers
Sonny/Eddie G — Minor hood
Julie — Shylock
Bailey — An Australian
Barry — Teacher, poker player

Xero to Sixty

Part I

I. 1959 – December

I am a wretched son of noble Greeks. I'd cheated on exams, plagiarized papers, cribbed lab reports and was still flunking four courses. I sat in front of Manfred Housemann, Dean of Students, whose flaking scalp and awkward hair were the butt of so many jokes. Deans can make you or break you no matter what they look like. Housemann walked around his desk and stared at me sternly, tiny flakes of dandruff like ash from a distant fire falling on his shoulders. It was our third little get-together. I felt he liked me, a conspiracy of opposites perhaps. He knew my dad, which helped. We knew we needed an angle, an honorable one – leaves are for those in good standing; this I was not.

"Couldn't we, sir," I postured diplomatically, "call it a 'psychoneurosis' or a 'mental hygiene problem?'" a phrase that had some currency back then.

Housemann leaned forward, his thighs pressing against his worn desk. He scratched his head sending a cascade of flakes onto his shoulders and smiled. A deal was cut. I was officially determined to be *psychologically unprepared for the university experience*. Blanks were filled in. Papers were signed. Promises were made. Hands shaken. Fingers crossed. "I wish you the very best, Mr. Konstantakis," Housemann smiled at me and for a fleeting second I thought he meant it. "I hope to see you back here soon." That was just for show.

A week passed uncomfortably. My parents couldn't help but notice that I was there, that nothing was happening. I wasn't looking for a job, I wasn't exploring options or writing poetry or doing anything that smacked even remotely of what they regarded as sensible, adult behavior. My mother's face was rich with worry and questioning; my father's flickering glances from papers, books, journals and the many other things he read increased in number, each looking more like an indictment than a query.

I am, alas, the first-born male in an old and honored family. Peloponnesian messiah, my duty is to carry the banner my immigrant parents brought into the new world and I was out of options. I got out my duffle bag, explained that I really had to get away, somewhere, anywhere away. The only away they would accept was Arianna's, my older sister in California. Fine. Why not. Life surely bristles with opportunity there, but my eyes only found floors or chairs, windows, walls, anything but my father's gaze.

The next morning before my folks woke, I stuffed what I could in the bag, sneakers, jeans, T-shirts, lots of underpants, my Young Ivy Leaguer outfit and my prized Rawlings 'Pro,' with the baseball and bottle of neatsfoot oil wrapped with a huge rubber band, snapped the bag shut and headed out. I was in one of those "my-way" moods, though I had no idea what that way was. Willie, my best friend that year, gave me a lift through the Holland tunnel and onto a patch of Jersey highway with a gentle on-ramp. A hug and tap on the cheek and I was alone. I set my bag on the ground, hoping I looked like a soldier just back from some war and angled my thumb westward.

Three vaguely unpleasant days later, marked mainly by cold, sleet, run-down motels and best forgotten, I found myself, miraculously, in the outskirts of Ypsilanti, less than a mile from my cousin Frankie's. Frankie was a bit of a bum, but he was family, only half-Greek but that was good enough and had me feeling almost like I knew what I was doing. The Frankie thing hit me somewhere near the Ohio state line when it began to dawn on me just how big this damn country was.

Our family was dotted across the continent. The first of them, like my folks, left Greece in the '30s; others trickled in over a twenty year period. Most of them aimed high. Some not so. Many made it. Some didn't. All were expected to. Frankie straddled expectations. I'd always liked him, thought he was cool. There was a certain edginess to him, a bit of the nonconformist. His version of the American dream was rehabbing stock cars but my arrival seemed to push him over a line he'd been tip-toeing along. He'd had it with grease and bending steel and grinding valves. He was, he said over hot chocolates Auntie Clara made for us while I tried to thaw out, ready for something new and I made one sweet excuse.

II. 1959 – December

Early the next morning we barged into Frankie's workplace, the fabulously cluttered, grease-spattered home of P. Holder: Auto Body Shop.

"Hey, Pasquale," said Frankie as we walked in and around a dozen or more car doors, fenders, engines, transmissions, naked chassis and random bits of mufflers, windshields and wires.

"It's *Patrick*, you little shit," said the rumpled, grizzled character pulling his head from under the hood of a busted up Buick. "You call me that one more time and I'll cut your nuts off."

"Yeah, yeah, Patrick, Pasquale. Whatever you want. But, hey, man, it don't make any difference 'cause I'm outta here."

"You're what?"

"Outta here. I quit. I am off to Californ-i-a. My cuz here and me are heading west. I will see you some day down the long bumpy road."

"You're what?" repeated Patrick, louder this time.

"Quitting. Jeez, man, how many times do I have to say it? Finished, done, leaving town," Frankie laughed.

"Listen asshole," Patrick sneered. "You can't leave, not with that goddamn Buick engine lying there. You took that sucker apart. You gotta put it back! How the fuck am I going to find someone who knows how to set a valve in this dump?"

"For what you pay me? Sorry, paisan, not my problem anymore. The West coast calls. The beaches beckon and I hate this friggin' job. You're a good Joe, if a bit cheap, so good luck," he taunted as we headed out of the garage, ducking a toxic wave of curses.

"Screw rebuilt engines, fuck Columbia, Xero, my cousin of cousins," he said, smacking me on the back. "California *is* the place to be."

And it was. There were hints in the air that we both could sense. It was the beginning of the time of madness; the world was getting its comeuppance. A new decade was being belched from the maw of the one past. Paranoids need not apply. Marginal young men welcomed.

The next day we called the number we found tacked on the YMCA bulletin board. Stefan R., a peripatetic Swede, was heading where the dying sun falls last into the sea. He's got wheels and needs someone to share the driving. Suddenly he had two. Cool.

Well, maybe not, because when he pulled up at Frankie's place it was in a freakin' Nash Metropolitan – wheelbase shorter than a VW beetle with two small front seats, an apology for a bench in the back and what Frankie said was a four-hamster-power engine.

"Are you out of your mind?" snapped Frankie later that afternoon. We were sitting in a bar nursing cold beers and going over our options. "We can't drive all the way to California in that piece of shit."

"But we do not," I said calmly, "have a lot of choices. You have noticed we're not exactly swimming in loose change. Besides, that baby is cute and cuteness counts for something right? It's two-toned, white and turquoise. This is the future man, this is tomorrow. I'm not lettin' this get away. Besides, I like Stefan and I'm ready to roll. Coming? Or are you gonna slink back to Pasquale?"

That one got Frankie's attention. He slid his glass back and forth across the bar intoning, "Nash-Pasquale? Pasquale-Nash? Nash-Pasquale?" Stopped, downed the last of the beer and laughed, "Is there any doubt, cuz?"

The little Nash wasn't ready for this either. We took turns driving, sitting shotgun and chewing on our kneecaps in the rear. Our bags were roped to a roof rack and the little Nash cornered like a tipsy giraffe. Gravity alternated between villain and savior. We struggled up hills urging on the hamsters; we flew down them with a recklessness fit for the young and stupid.

What a time it was, crashing three to a room in cheap motels, scarfing down chili cheese dogs with cokes made from real syrup and seltzer, drinking coffee so weak you could read your future in the cracks in thick, bottom-heavy porcelain cups.

We took random forks and turns on whims, through mill towns with quiet streets and churches on every other corner. We broke bread with the locals in cattle towns and logging camps, in small cafes and diners. We drove past farms large and small, prosperous and desperate, through open lands dotted with chromatic layers of rock, slate gray, ochre, veins of black from ancient fires, along the buttes and valleys of the high desert plains, under the sun above a land I, poor deprived city boy, barely knew was there.

Just outside of San Francisco Stefan decided that he wanted to see the great Pacific Northwest. Appealing as it was to keep rolling, my sensible side (for which I have always thanked my mother) won the day. I knew, better the sheltering, if likely reluctant, arm of my sister than more of the open road. The trip finished like it began, in the morning on an on-ramp with my thumb. A grizzled trucker picked us up and many hours later we rolled into Santa Monica on a cool, soft January evening.

III. 1960 – January

Arianna wasn't crazy about two of us showing up. She knew I was coming. Frankie was a surprise. But family was family. Besides, as I was to discover to my delight, Arianna wasn't quite the sensible one anymore. She was also now just "Anna" – nothing quite like getting away from home. She's only four years older than me but somehow managed to act like an aunt or mother surrogate, which was both comforting and off-pissing. She and Billy had stepped to the head of the wave of migrants filling up southern California. She'd studied sociology, meaning she didn't know dick and was shuffling papers in a law office. Billy had had a better idea, electrical engineering, and he exuded this "I'm gonna be jes' fine, thank you ma'am" air.

Anna wasn't Arianna and it wasn't just the now unruly hair and baggy sweaters. No longer the tight-assed immigrants' kid, she had become conventionally unconventional, leftist in the growing fashion of the time, feminist before it was a fashion. Their house in Santa Monica had none of the formality we had grown up with. The door was always open and the most unusual parade of people set a feast for us fugitives. Beards, hair, smoke, all kinds of smoke. Suspect philosophy, beat poetry, badly tuned guitars, jug wine and Southern Comfort. Why? I did not know. I hate the damn stuff but there were always bottles of it lying around. Evenings filled with laughter, tears, songs and feelings I couldn't quite get a grip on. Nobody seemed to care how young Frankie and I were and that was cool. Anna and Billy had no kids and no interest in any half-grown ones. We got the basics, a roof, kinly love, a dram or two of support. That was it. After a while an unsubtle but familiar message: Get a job.

Sure, I thought. Why not? This was California, Southern California, on the coast, rich, blossoming, expanding. Opportunity lurked everywhere, right? Well, maybe and maybe not. There were problems. I knew nothing, had no training, no skills, no education, no experience, no résumé, no contacts. My life's vision was warped, hazy, tunneled. The future I spied came through the wrong end of a telescope.

But California was coming into its own, beaches, bohemians, rock and roll and America's great passion, the automobile. I couldn't sing a lick and there wasn't much promise on the beaches. I topped out at five eleven and a stretchy half and on a good day came in, as the Brits would put it, a shade over 'leven stone. I could have been the model for the *before* shot in those ads gracing the back pages of Superman comics, gettin' sand kicked in my bespectacled face. So I reached out to the remaining option, as the ad in the *L.A. Times* announced, salesmen were wanted, immediately.

The Ivy League outfit got dug out of the duffle bag and I learned how to use an iron. Khakis, sports jacket with obligatory elbow patches, penny loafers, argyle socks and Xerxes Theodore Konstantakis, coddled child of the fifties, was ready to stride upon the stage, to audition for his first role in the theater of fools, a grown-up. One quick interview later and I was a used-car salesman. Unfuckingbelievable.

The first week was a blast; I was gliding along on the buoyant residue of our arrival in the land of milk and plastic. It was nutty but wonderful. There I was – the only son of a family that traced its roots to the nobles of Cos – a used-car salesman. This was so insanely improbable that it hardly mattered that at the end of a week I hadn't made a sale. I was working the back end of the showroom with Harlan something or other, an enigmatic journeyman who said he was from Kansas but maybe that was Kentucky, not that it mattered. There was a vague sense of discontent about Harlan that I connected with, like he'd left something, someone, some other life that just wasn't working out. He had this squirrely "only some of me is here right now" thing that I liked. It made me feel sane – and gave me hope. Harlan wasn't very good at the used car game either but he did like a good brew. We would get together with Frankie after what passed for work. We found Venice and a bar near the beach and we knew were ready to be *real* Californians.

Venice, the ultimate urban fraud, all glitz and froth that attracted and repelled like those black and white Scottie dogs on magnets. A cotton candy town, a carnival masquerading as a city – step right up folks, you say you're not satisfied, say you want more for your money, well then, just you take a taste of this seductive pink cloud.

We sipped our beer and watched the *after* shots pose in the sand, dodged the teenagers, the budding hipsters, the starlet hopers and middle-aged usetabes as they whipped up and down the concrete by the sand on skates and bikes. I marveled at each new face, as beguiled with life and its lunacy as the one in the mirror. We found a little Greek diner with a Tuesday special, all the moussaka you can eat for two bucks. It wasn't mom's but it filled the gut.

IV. 1960 – January

"Xero" is my private joke for Xerxes, itself a joke of a name (*ruler of heroes* for God's sake). Being not quite the nillness of my name, I started checking out the old-timers who actually made a living moving used cars. There was a crude but workable art form here built on fragile half-truths, of things we want to be. They didn't exactly lie; it was subtler, like pulling back the corner of a tent flap, letting in just enough light, a hint of something faint but alluring.

I gave it a try and, sum'bitch, I sold my first car, a year-old Caddy convertible, white walls, leather interior, lethal fins. I'd been salivating over it since it hit the lot; its turquoise body and white canvas roof evoked images of hours spent curled up in the back of a motorized Gulag. It was as long as a football field and carried about three hundred weight of chrome trim. It was like driving around in a drop-top living room. It took me an entire afternoon to make the sale. I drove my customer around in it – with the top down of course. I let him have a solo test-drive. I casually tossed the keys to the guy's fiancée for a spin. I even took her rotten little kid around the block in it. I went for the kill. I hit the diner across the street for coffee and apple pie for them both and ice cream for the kid. We haggled on price. I gave him a break because I liked his face. I stuck on a couple of extras that the fiancée "had to have." I worked out a complicated financing scheme. I was fucking brilliant. I slunk home at the end of the day and poured a guilty double-shot of Southern Comfort – and wondered why I did that.

The next week I learned more about why used-car salesman never appears on Johnny's "and-what-do-you-want-to-be-when-you-grow-up?" list. With the rest of the crew I went to pick up my paycheck. I had so far not enjoyed this ritual of the dealership. My pay, being that I was at the bottom of the bottom, consisted solely of commissions on finalized sales. I found that the cupboard was bare. There was nothing for me. No paper, no check, no note, no record of my sale. I fell back on my role of spoiled number one son and started whining. The clerk just snickered and said the predictable, "If you got any complaints kid, take 'em to the sales manager." And so I did.

"Excuse me, sir," I said, after the obligatory tap on the door frame.

He glanced up at me with that why-are-you-bothering-me look that we'd all come to hate. "Yes? What do you want?"

"Today's payday but there wasn't a check for me," I said, trying not to sound petulant.

"Of course not," he replied. "You didn't sell anything."

"I'm sorry, I don't understand."

"What's to understand? You sold no car, you earned no commission."

"But I did," I could feel my voice taking on a testy quality. "I moved that monster of a Cadillac just last Friday."

"Actually, you didn't."

"Look," I said, almost sputtering, "this is just not true. I spent the better part of the day on the deal."

"I'm sorry," he said in an annoyingly calm voice. "There's no record of a sale of a Cadillac by you."

"What the hell are you talking about?" I was on to bleating. "You approved the damn deal."

"Not *that* deal."

"There was only one deal. The two-toned one."

We went on for some time. This, I thought, must be what it's like prying secrets from the FBI. Eventually I discovered that my Cadillac-loving buddy's credit was, well, just not there. At all. He was a poseur. Bankrupt. No credit, no loan, no sale – no commission.

I took a stroll to get my blood pressure down. I wandered about the lot looking to have a chat with my Caddy. It was nowhere to be seen. I headed back to the manager's office.

"Excuse me for interrupting you again," I said, rapping on the door frame, "but I don't see the Cadillac anywhere on our lot."

"Of course not. I sold it."

"You?" I said rising intonation contour, eyebrows ceiling-ward.

"Yup. Would you like to see the papers?"

"Absolutely, yes," I said, curious and confused.

So, I saw them. And didn't like what I saw. The lousy dickhead had whited out my credit-challenged patron's name and penned in the fiancée's, whose credit was fine. My honored Greek name with its implied list of heroes ruled over was similarly excised and the manager's inserted.

I kinda lost it and let fly with a rip much like Pasquale'd thrown our way. The "conversation" ended up the only place it could. I was told to clean out my stuff and get the fuck out of there – the first and only time I've ever been fired. It was a defining moment in how I've lived my life.

V. 1960 – January

That evening I poured myself a beer and tried to dissolve my pissoffedness in it. I was in Anna and Billy's backyard watching the first wisps of mist drift in when Frankie came out. He had a large glass of Southern Comfort on the rocks – what the hell is it with that stuff? – and, to my surprise, was in worse shape than I was. He'd had it with Santa Monica, with Venice, with imported palm trees and cheap moussaka, with beatniks, poetry and dope but mostly with Anna's nagging. A little freedom was trickier than he thought. As he awkwardly explained, maybe he really was a small-town, Ypsilanti guy. He liked tearing engines apart and gritty mid-western mill towns and his girl friend who, he revealed with a smirk, gave good head. "I'm sorry man but I think I gotta go back."

"It's okay, no sweat," I said and I meant it though I realized there was a downside. Anna and Billy would surely focus their growing annoyance on me. "You do what you gotta do. Fuck it, man, I'd pull out too if I had some place to pull to." And we sat there, under the hazy moon, in silence. I knew I had to do something. I had just about run through the money Dad had quietly slipped me and it was starting to feel like back in New York, living rent-free, but paying in other coin.

The next day, I drove Frankie to the airport, hugged him like I loved him, which I did, and then headed to Venice, to the beer joint by the sand where I could sit in relative quiet and contemplate all the things I wasn't. I ordered a draft and, sipped it slowly, pondering my bleakness, diving into misery as only a nineteen year-old, lost, college dropout can and in the quiet of the tavern I heard two guys talking and an oddly familiar phrase wormed through my gloom. ... "The son of bitch took three and fucking drew out on me."

'Drew out on?' my head pivoted ninety degrees.

"No," said his friend, voice rich with feigned sympathy.

"Yeah, I'm pat. Three way pot," said the first guy. "Patsy took three, can you fucking believe it, and the asshole hit a goddamn smooth six."

There was but one speck of the cosmos from which those words could come. I leaned over, nodded at the two guys and, as delicately as I could, inserted myself into the conversation where I was told, like how could I not know, that they play poker in Gardena – wherever the hell that was.

"They play poker in Gardena?" I asked, bewildered, thinking – Legal poker? For money? With real (unmarked?) cards? Apparently they did and it wasn't far though, as I discovered, the cards were occasionally marked.

Perhaps, I thought, my Ivy "education" wasn't wasted. I'd played a lot of poker at Columbia, too much, far too much. Being Greek, I found The Greeks, the frat houses, games at least twice a week. Scrape the dinner table, kick the cats out of the chairs, spread the cards. Zeta Eata Potata was what I dubbed the house with the best game.

What a crew. I often found myself shifting into anthropologist mode, squinting through my glasses. Smart, spoiled kids from wealthy families, pampered, clueless, pathetic. Dickless Charlie sat in his underwear at the table. He'd lift up his hairy gut, scratch his balls and hemorrhage cash. None of us ever saw his dick. We were sure he had one but it was always buried in layers of flab. Flathead Freddie the calling station would phone Poppa up every week or so and complain that he was broke. Poppa never failed his poor baby. No Name Sammy was the local cipher, so boring I never did find a handle for him. These guys had so much money, privilege and pedigree. And, man, could they drink! I spent most of that year walking around with a hunk of cash and two, three "can't-cover-it-now-man-hold-till-next-week" checks in my wallet. Of course, I was paying a price. Folded in with all that paper was the first draft of my academic obit.

I never got over how stupid these future captains of industry were. Maybe it was the privilege. Maybe they just had too much money to care. It was always "dealer's choice" and they loved those off-the-wall games, *anaconda* where you shipped half your hand to the guy on your right, *night baseball* with 3's and 9's wild and 6's got you another card and if you got dealt a 4 you had to toss a shot of vodka – or was that 6's and 4's were wild and…. It didn't matter. Those games are just crap-shoots. I learned to play poker that year – a little bit anyway. I learned about probabilities and position and *draw* became my game 'cause the dealer draws last and bets last – a huge advantage. Those idiots played *night baseball, anaconda, fiery cross*. I chose *draw, jacks or better*, sometimes *lowball*. It was just weird; I almost *had* to win money.

The next day, armed with my revelation, I headed to Gardena with its organized, legal card rooms. Oops. Another of life's little surprises. This wasn't ZEP. No Dickless Charlie, no Flathead Freddie. No dealer's choice. The only games played were draw, mainly jacks or better or, as they called it, "California draw" and lowball. Worse, the rooms were full of tobacco chewing, cigar chompin', hard-edged bastards, honed on the wheel of life. Those guys were nasty. They cussed and insulted newcomers and played so tight. So tight. One guy picked up a quarter in his tar-stained fingers and I swore I could hear the eagle squawk. I remember that first day there, at the legendary Gardena Club. They looked at me, the wheels spinning, "fish, fish, a new fish." I wasn't exactly, but by the third or fourth visit I realized this wasn't going to be an easy way to raise the rent.

But my eye got focused, my ear tuned. I felt like I was moving the dial on an old radio back and forth, trying to get a signal, a clear one to the characters who were slithering through this world. There was something alluring about Gardena. It tugged at me. I could feel the cadence, sense the rhythm, the pulse of the place. But right now everyone seemed to be screaming at me that this was not what my life was supposed to be. Billy finally had that "cheap freeloader" shit-fit that had been brewing since Frankie bailed. He and Anna wanted me to pay for my lodgings. I was slipping down the social ladder and the humor of it seemed lost on all but me.

VI. 1960 – March

I woke one noonish morning after dragging my sorry ass home at an obscene hour. I sat at a vaguely unsanitary kitchen table and sipped hot coffee that had boiled down to syrup. As was my wont during those Gardena days, I hadn't gotten out of bed till TD came and sat on me. TD was Anna's dog. He was some kind of mutt but he was a real trooper and had taken a shine to me, mainly because I was the only one who paid him any attention. I was also the one who named him TD, which stood for "The Dog" because till I got there the poor thing had no name. I cracked open a still-runny boiled egg and hoped that the dysfunctional toaster would banish the stale taste from at least one side of the bread, rummaged through the *LA Times* want ads and there it was.

> Intelligent, independent young man wanted. Represent a major academic publisher. Desire to succeed and an independent style the only requirements.

The odd repetition notwithstanding, "This was meant for me," I said to no one in particular though TD assumed it was him and he wagged his tail and dropped his sorry head in my lap. "I am, if nothing else, *independent*." The Mr. Blackmun the ad instructed me to call was most pleasant and gave me an appointment for the very next morning.

I arrived on a fine, early spring day in what served as *downtown* for the glorious City of Angels. I was on time, back in "hire-me" mode, all gussied up from the BrylCreem on my dark Aegean curls, through the squared-off horn rims, jacket with elbow patches and buffed-up loafers. I stood in front of the offices of a famous encyclopedia firm, looked about and discovered that I'd arrived at the same time as two dozen or so other familiar-looking, intelligent and certainly independent young chaps.

We were herded into a large room with several rows of chairs and a lectern where a slightly older, more polished version of the assembled hopefuls leaned on his elbows. With a smile that is the reason the word *unctuous* is in the English language, he introduced himself as Maurice Blackmun and spun out a pitch that P. T. Barnum would have been proud of. I sat there with what I know was a quizzical tilt to my head – I tend to adopt this pose when my bullshit detector is turned on. The *Blackmun* spieling away was most certainly not the one who answered the phone yesterday. The voice was wrong, the manner different. As he went on, it dawned on me, "Blackmun" was a cover name for any executive who was addressed or approached.

Still, I was fascinated. It was a classic pyramid set-up. The salesmen were the grunts. They slogged away working door-to-door with commissions (or 'commish' as they liked to say) based on individual sales. Each local group of these corporate wannabes had a supervisor, job description: "Draconian Martinet with Simon Legree overtones, to counsel, cajole, exhort, and abuse your charges." These guys got a cut of everything their "boys" sold. One step up were the regional managers who got a piece of the action of everything sold under them. The handsome devil up there who may, or not,

Arthur S. Reber

have been Maurice Blackmun claimed to have cracked the million dollar mark – at the tender age of 31.

But not everybody was buying it. More than a few of the less adventurous quietly made for the door. But, BS twanger or not, I stayed. This kind of shit, I thought, is just the sort of thing that should come rolling down the pike when you're out of options. "What's waiting for me if I leave," I muttered under my breath to the now vacant chair next to me. "Cheap moussaka and tobacco encrusted poker junkies?" I thought I might even be making progress. I was pretty sure that chart from Soc. 101 had door-to-door encyclopedia peddler a tick up the Socio-Economic-Scale from used-car salesman. Then again, maybe not.

I didn't actually get hired. None of the remaining did. We were given the status *observer* and told to prepare to go out into the field with one of the journeymen pros to "observe" the operation. I drew one Bobby Joe Campbell who, it turned out, had his own ideas about the duties of an observer. Mr. Campbell was the first person I'd met who was really named "Bobby Joe." He drawled it out real slow for me, so it's all one name, "Baah-buuh-jo." He was also among the more peculiar characters I'd encountered in my walkabout. He stood about five-five and was built like a deluxe model water cooler. He had tiny hands with small, thick fingers and a knuckle-crushing grip. His smooth baby face was highlighted by wide-set blue eyes and a tiny piggy nose perched above a large mouth with which he smiled surprisingly pleasantly.

"Xero, good buddy," he drawled and snickered, "man, that is one weird name. How the fuck did yo folks ever lay that on you. Zero, nuthin,' fuckin' nada. Sheet, man, I woulda changed that fucker if it was mine." And he laughed with an oddly nasal snicker.

There is, I thought, no way to tell him that I already changed it, so I just smiled and laughed back, hoping I didn't sound like I was mocking him.

"But, fuck it man, it don't make no diff'rence what yo' handle is," he said reaching up to smack me on the arm, obviously not feeling mocked, "'Cause we are gonna make one hell of a team. Ah, suh, am the meanest muthafuckah in the world and the best 'cyclopedia salesman in Californi' and you git to watch me roll. And, check this out, man." And he took off his jacket, peeled back the sleeve of his white, starched, short-sleeve shirt, its pocket adorned with two pens and an automatic pencil, to show off his new prize, an American Bald Eagle tattoo with the full rack of redneck shit, arrows in one claw, rifles in the other, a limp rat hanging from its beak and, yup, there it was, a Confederate flag in the background. The ink was still fresh and the skin not yet healed, and Bahbuhjo beamed at me and I beamed back. After all, we were best buds now.

A few minutes later, settled more or less comfortably in his beat-up Chevy, we headed eastward, to the fertile grounds, the tract houses of Covina. As we wended our way through the rapidly developing outskirts of Los Angeles, through the edges of the urban, into the sub-urban, where cookie-cutter developments were being slapped down on what recently was the edge of a desert, I sensed that this strange, otherworldly place, was – yes, deny it at your peril – where the age to come will be born, the next not very brave new world.

VII. 1960 – March

⁓

The whole continent seemed to have been tilted, migrants obeying the tug of some strange kind of gravity. They needed houses with bassinettes and cribs, they needed cars with fins, had to have Good Housekeeping Seal'ed ranges and fridges and we knew, me an' Bobby Joe, that they also will need words, knowledge, facts, dates and names, to be told of wars, who started 'em, fought 'em, won 'em and got to write the one true history. They need to be linked with Sputnik and the bomb, with Barbie, and the creeping commies, with Fidel and Ike and Khrushchev and de Gaulle and Starkweather and Van Allen and everything new and scary. We were the bringers of the word and we were tooling down the road in a second-hand green Chevy with a wobbly right rear wheel.

Bobby Joe was whooping it up. He went on and on with what felt like manufactured tales of his life, pumped up with his exploits with "white-girls, nigger-girls, chinky-girls" and what he did *to* them. I began to get the feeling that my new best friend was one of those good ol' boys who, if you pass 'em on the highway, gotta pass you back just to show you, you dumb-ass motherfucker, who's boss.

We drove out to a dried-up field on the edge of Covina and met up with Ralph Buckley, our supervisor, who looked like Rod Steiger and sounded like him too and I felt more than a little disoriented. I was a movie buff. Was I in one? Or watching it? I was standing in my Ivy League finest on the edge of a dusty, junk-filled lot holding a huge, square briefcase full of books a punk redneck racist told me I had to carry and one of my favorite faces is sitting in a two-year old Buick talking in a flat Midwestern monotone about encyclopedias. Fucking weird.

Rod/Ralph took us deep into tacky town, row upon row of stucco boxes, pretty little houses, sprinkled lawns of surprising green, stunted chimneys poking above cheap asphalt roofs but, no doubt and as advertised, fertile fields for the likes of us. The place, whether anyone liked it or not, was alive, alive and thriving, working and lower middle class, solid family folks with lots of young kids.

"These," smiled Ralph/Rod as he opened the door for us, "are exactly the folks to pitch encyclopedias to. How can you," he winked at us, "raise the next generation of corporate giants if you don't educate your babies? I'll pick up you guys and the other teams working this area at 5:30. Knock 'em dead."

It was only March but we were, though I hadn't fully grasped it, no longer under the blessed umbrella of the sea. It had warmed up, seriously. Slowly it crept into my brain. This is a desert; deserts want to kill you. The pavement heat came through my soles and the samples gained weight by the minute. We got absolutely nowhere for over an hour, no-one-homes and sorry-we're-not-interesteds in rapid alternation. Not selling books was worse than not selling cars. I was also hungry as Rod/Ralph dropped us lunchless into the field and there was nothing but tract housing as far as we could see. At a house at the end of a cul-de-sac, near the front door, was the first serious tree we'd seen. At least, I thought, this time we'll be told to fuck off in the shade.

Bobby Joe dutifully pushed the plastic cap on the doorbell and waited. And pressed again, twice, and waited. After a minute I turned to leave when Bobby Joe said, "Hold on, man. I think I hear somethin'." The door opened and a large man in slippers and rumpled pajamas stood there looking confused. Bobby Joe flashed his pearly whites, ignored the deeply pissed look on the fellow's face and started into his pitch.

The guy absolutely blew up, a total, full-bore rip. "Books! Fucking books!" he snarled. "You motherless bastards woke me up to sell me books. Get the fuck outta here and take your books with you," – or something to that effect with a fleeting reference about a location for the books.

Chastened, I turned, mumbling an apology when suddenly Bobby Joe stepped up and kicked the door out of the guy's hand, reached into his inside jacket pocket and pulled out his wallet. He flashed a very official looking ID card and badge and introduced himself as "Mr. Robert J. Campbell, Treasury Agent." The guy stood there looking bewildered, like aliens had just landed on his lawn or some nut left the gate to the asylum open.

Bobby Joe laid out this line about the guy being investigated for a variety of crimes including money laundering and tax evasion and would be hearing from us. He told him not to leave town because he was "under surveillance." With a flourish he put back his wallet, turned to me and said, "Let's go file this."

When we reached the sidewalk Bobby Joe folded up in laughter. "Man, did ya'll see that prick's face?" he howled, smacking his knee. "Sweet fuckin' Jesus, we really got him, didn't we? Some fuckin' nerve, tryin' to tell us to kiss off." He swaggered down the block snickering "Treasury Agent. Hee, hee, hee. I love bein' a T-Man."

I felt more than a bit put off by the plural pronouns, but I didn't say anything. Who knew what might be in his other pocket. All I wanted to do was get back to LA and look for some other job. But there was still time left on the meter, so to speak. Ralph/Rod wouldn't be by for a couple of hours.

We turned the corner and began working the next block. Bobby Joe was still snickering and patting himself on his metaphoric back. There was no one home at the first two houses and then, at the third, a miracle: a couple with three young kids and pretensions, the ones who cannot possibly survive the ravages of reality without a full set of encyclopedias. We were invited in, offered seats on a comfortable couch and served lemonade in frosted glasses that sweated sweet cold rivers of condensation over our knuckles. Bobby Joe launched into *the* sales pitch and lo, another miracle; he was transformed before my disbelieving eyes. Encyclopedias, hell, this kid should go into politics or at least grab himself a bible and a soap box. He was *stunning*.

Up till that moment I had only heard a short snippet of the patented pitch. It was a marvel of fact and obfuscation, a brilliant blend of the sensible and the incomprehensible. Ten minutes later I believed, I did, hallelujah! Praise The Lord! The encyclopedia set was free! No cost. No up-front cash. Nothing. Free. All you needed to do was agree to the simple terms in the contract, to promote the product and be available for testimony. Hallefreakin'lujah!

The fact that those "simple terms" included an obligatory annual supplement that cost about the same thing as putting an extension on your house was buried under layers of flummery. Bahbuhjo was wearing his good ol' boy act like it was a rubbed up moleskin jacket draped round his compact, muscular shoulders. His eyes flashed, double-jointed syllables slid 'cross his tongue like fresh moonshine. The pages of the samples rippled through his stubby fingers and four-color glossies danced across the table. He was on a roll, energized by his thrashing of Mr. Pajamas. He was closing in, oh so delicately, on the magical moment when the contract is brought out for signatures when the door bell rang. Two uniformed representatives of the Covina sheriff's office stopped by to see if "anyone's seen a couple of book salesmen 'round here."

VIII. 1960 – March

In short order I, ruler of heroes, was in the back of a police cruiser, handcuffed and sitting next to a similarly restrained Mr. Campbell. I began playing little mind games, flickering back and forth between feeling like the protagonist in a mystery and the scared little boy who was way out of his league. Since my fantasies have little to do with reality, I went with the first and cast about looking for clues as to how this tale might end. None were forthcoming. They took us to the local constabulary where we were fingerprinted, photographed, and booked.

My life, like many others, has been dotted with moments touching, terrifying, occasionally hilarious. I learned from my father that about the best you could do to arm yourself against it all was to hold on to your sense of humor. I don't think Dad had foreseen how wickedly funny it can be when you toss in a dash of irony. Once we were faced with the glaring formality of our situation, we discovered that Mr. Campbell's little display was totally lost on Mr. Pajamas. Bobby Joe may have thought he put the fear of God, or at least the US Department of Justice, into the guy's heart. He hadn't. The guy was a cop. He was in his pajamas in the afternoon because he'd been on a stakeout for the past sixteen hours. That look of surprise was really saying, "What the fuck? You punks are trying to pull this crap on *me*?"

We were each charged with one count of impersonating a federal agent and one count of soliciting without a license. I expected the first, of course, but not the second. I had underestimated what a little turd my new best pal was. Mr. Campbell, it turned out, didn't have the necessary license to canvass outside of LA. As he sheepishly confessed later, he had been given the money and the papers to file for the permit to work Covina. He pocketed the cash and, as best as I could tell, used the papers to wrap a cheese sandwich.

We were allowed one phone call each. Bobby Joe declined, which I found just one tick up from pathetic. I called Arianna, filled her in as best I could under the circumstances and told her not to worry. "Look, sis," I said with boyish naiveté, "I'm innocent, right? I'll be outta here soon. I mean, what can they do to me? I didn't do anything."

She totally freaked. Cursed up a storm. Screamed about jail time, the feds, lawyers and, "Holy shit, do you know what Dad is going to say when this gets to him?"

"Listen, Anna," – damn, I realized, that was the first time I'd called her that – "it's not that bad. And for God's sake do not call home. They don't need to know this. In fact, I'm beginning to think I shouldn't have called you. I'll be out of here tomorrow. If not, we'll do the lawyer thing." I believed that. I really did.

After they ran us through the arrest ritual, forms, photos, grease on the fingertips, it was too late for anything other than a short walk into the slammer. I was wasted, tired and hungry. Our hosts, however, were obviously deeply concerned about my well-being. They took away my glasses, I guess so that I couldn't cut my wrists. They took away my belt so I couldn't hang myself. They took away my custom Zippo so I couldn't start a fire. They even took away my shoes apparently just because they could. I spent the evening holding up my pants, stubbing various toes, having nicotine fits and enduring Bobby Joe's mutterings about what he was going to do to those "muthafuckas" when he got out.

Eventually I sat back on my rock-hard mattress, propped myself against the stone wall, and cycled through the day trying to drag it back into something I understood. It was so wonky, it seemed like a game. A bit of steeping in a vat of unreality and you go a little numb, nothing feels right and I wondered what Rod/Ralph thought when we didn't show up at 5:30.

It was a slow night, the jail population a mere two and the protectors of the Covina peace decided that they'd caught a couple of raccoons in a cage. They did the sympathetic dance for a bit and then countered with tales of five years in Leavenworth. They found my civil requests for something to eat to be absolute thigh-slappers. Then they discovered they could drive Bobby Joe totally bat shit by calling him "Shorty" and arguing over how tiny his dick must be. I didn't blame them. What could be more amusing on a quiet night than a half-blind college drop-out and an undersized redneck punk who'd left his sense of humor in a vacant lot in Covina? I finally dozed off and slept, unburdened by dreams I could recall.

Morning brought life's next surprise, a real FBI agent – who looked like an extra in a movie. Plain suit a little rumpled, white shirt a little creased, striped tie subtly stained and, yup, the G-man's cliché, a Joe Friday fedora. But clothes didn't make this man, style did. Everything about him, from the odd roll in his walk to the studied jaw line, screamed "B-movie, Roger Corman." I was oddly comforted by this. As every flick-happy kid understood, Corman was a hero right up there with Rod Steiger. One of the deputies said his name but I only heard "Joe Friday" and so he was. Of course, the handcuffs got slipped on.

"Sir," I said awkwardly trying to push up my glasses, which they had thankfully returned, "we don't need these. I'm a college student, not a common criminal." All I got back was a stare which, of course, didn't slow me down.

"I'll just sit in the back of the car till we get there" ... wherever 'there' is. More silence.

"After all, sir, I'm not guilty. I didn't do anything," ... unlike this moronic little fart.

Joe Friday just scowled, tightened the bracelets and pushed me into the back seat of the obligatory undressed Ford. Bobby Joe, who looked ever worse with each new insult, bowed his head and was shoved in after me. Joe slid in behind the wheel, took his gun out with a flourish, placed it menacingly on the seat next to him and launched into a little riff, and it was right out of that movie.

"I can't believe this. Those dickheads got me out to this neck of woods for you two creeps. You shitheads were impersonating Federal agents? You two? Feds? No fuckin' way."

I was caught off-guard. Does J. Edgar know his boys talk this way? Not in the movies, they don't. What happened to courtesy? To innocent till blah, blah? I was also feeling slighted, insulted. If I'd wanted to impersonate a federal agent I bet I could have a done a creditable job.

"You know what," Joe ranted on, "you two shits are gonna get what you got coming 'cause I keep seeing freaks like you all the time now. Punks. Punks and commies. Motherfuckers out to undermine this country and I know commies when I see 'em. You, my pinko friends, are looking at five years in a Federal Penitentiary."

Whoa. Same slammer time the raccoon tormentors used. Was this true? Five long ones the price of a little prank? They, I realized with a vague sense of panic tingling in my gut, really could do this.

Pinko, eh? I rolled the word around on my tongue and reviewed scenes, crystallized images of my father, the leftish immigrant professor sitting in front of the TV watching McCarthy drag *names* out of the intimidated, grill supposed moles, whisper conspiratorially with Roy Cohen whose reptilian tongue flicked in and out of his mouth. I looked over at Bobby Joe sitting next to me behind our very own, real government agent. His head slanted forward on his nonexistent neck, sandy blond hair uncombed, eyes glazing over. He didn't know what a "pinko" was but he was scared.

IX. 1960 – March

At the courthouse the 'cuffs came off and we were led into a large cell, a kind of holding pen where we joined the assorted muggers, junkies and drunk-and-disorderlies waiting to be processed. They had returned my belt, shoes and glasses but not my precious Zippo, the thought of which seemed to have attracted a voice.

"Oy, mate, waun' a fag? For you, only a quarter."

What the hell? I thought. 'Mate?' An Aussie? Here, in the Covina jail?

"No thanks, man," I replied, "You know, I think I'm gonna give 'em up. Besides, I don't even have a quarter on me. Check with the little shit over in the corner," I said, tilting my head toward Bobby Joe, who was looking worse with each passing moment. "He needs a fix of something."

The Aussie, whose name turned out to be Bradley, tossed Bobby Joe a couple of cigarettes and sat down next to me. "What're you in for?"

"Not much. Actually it's all a stupid mistake. How 'bout you?"

"Got into a bit of a spat," he said, smiling, "down at the Tin Hut last night." I looked up and noticed the welt on his left cheek.

"And the other guy?" I asked, nodding toward the Aussie's cheek.

"The other *two* guys," he said, smiling even broader, "are not here right now. I believe they are still in hospital." Which got me to thinking; if I needed a friend in here I could do a lot worse than this fellow.

About a half hour later the bailiff came down and called out several names, among them Robert Joseph Campbell and 'Ekserkses Konsanstukis.' We were led to a courtroom where, so it seemed, we were to be given a preliminary hearing. As the bailiff explained, first will be the soliciting charge. Everything else will wait for later. "What does 'later' mean?" I asked. I got a Joe Friday scowl with a heavy silence for an answer.

The courtroom felt warm and sort of cozy, with cherry stained panels, sober looking judge, court steno, lawyers, prosecutors and various other official looking folk doing official looking things and, to my surprise, about three dozen people sitting on long benches. I assumed from the looks of concern or embarrassment that some were friends and relatives of the incarcerated.

The others? It soon became clear – and obvious. The courthouse was the local proscenium, the one with free admission. There were gentlefolk here on this edge of a parched desert, homemakers, the unemployed, the unemployable, the retired. They woke each vapid morning in The-New-Southern-California-Paradise-In-A-Detached-Stucco-Home-With-All-The-Modern-Appliances-One-Dog-Two-Point-Five-Kids-A-Garage-And-Back-Yard-With-Fence (White-Picket) For-Less-Than-A-Crappy-Apartment-In (God-Forbid) Los-Angeles and crawled into consciousness of a bitter sameness.

All the houses looked the same, as I knew all too well. All the kids skinned the same knee, puked the same bile, pissed off the same teacher. Ipana, a bowl of the Breakfast of Champions, transparent coffee and the morning dump, a fleeting kiss on the cheek of whoever was covering the mortgage, some spittle to hold down the little savior's cowlick as he headed off to school and then, hie your ass down to the courthouse. It wasn't *Search for Tomorrow* or *Love of Life* but there was all this nice cherry paneling, reasonably comfortable benches, air-conditioning and, when the gods smiled on them, a little street theater. Who woulda thought?

The detainees got called up one by one and at first all seemed routine. The D & Ds were sent off with a practiced warning from the judge. A petty felon was arraigned and processed in routine fashion. Then, the first-act closer. I grew up in New York; I'd been steeped in theater. You have to have a first-act closer if you want to draw 'em in. These folks wanted *The Young and the Restless*, they got it.

A couple had been charged with disrupting the peace. Apparently, they had a bit of a disagreement; the ruckus had tumbled out onto the lawn and alarmed a neighbor. The woman spoke first. Her face made me think of neglected gardens, soiled clothing, of abandoned towns wrapped around discarded highways, tangled, dirty blond hair, hasty make-up. The marks of last night were barely there but her cheap rouge couldn't cover the deeper scars from decades of abuse, drugs, booze. I knew that look. I'd seen it in my rambles through the city late at night, in the taverns of Midwestern towns in our wander across the continent, in that bar in Venice, a hollow look that only comes of pain. There are the creases of age, there are the furrows born of joy, of worry, of struggle. Not these. These were dead-end ruts gouged deep in the pale skin of her cheeks, her jaw, her neck.

She let loose a shocker of a tirade. I expected something drunken, incoherent. It wasn't. It was a deep, passionate howl. She had found something hard, sharp at the bottom of the bucket of swill that was her life. He beat her. He'd been beating her for years. She was at the end of a long, unraveling

45

rope. She wanted him out of her life, in the goddamn slammer, *now*. The crowd snapped their fingers and stomped their feet.

Her husband, or whatever he was, countered with considerably less style. "Yeah," he admitted. He did "smack 'er 'round a bit. But," he explained, "she had it comin' 'cause," he'd been told, "she was turnin' tricks on the weekends when she was supposed to be with her sick pa."

Suddenly, she whipped around and cracked him on the side of his face. He swore and, blood leaking under his eye, spit at her. In a flash the guards were on both of them, wrestling them to the floor. The rest of us scattered. The judge threatened to clear the court. The crowd yipped in delight and I truly knew why they were here. I was feeling a lot better. Kafka out; Williams in.

Everyone took five and things slowly returned to normal. The court's business was resumed with the calling of one R. J. Campbell. The clerk read the charge concerning his obvious attempts to circumvent the local laws governing canvassing and solicitation. He bowed his head humbly and pleaded guilty which, of course, he was. The judge issued a fine of $25 which, I thought, wasn't much. The license was $20 and the cost of these proceedings is way more than five coconuts so this was beyond stupid. But, no matter. My goal was to get my butt out of there, not to explain to the county how it might generate revenue.

Bobby Joe sat back down. I looked over and noticed that his feet barely reached the floor. I was next. I stood dutifully as my name was butchered by the clerk. The same set of charges were read out, same time, place, and arresting officers. The judge didn't even look up until I said, "Not guilty."

"Oh?" came from the bench as the judge picked up his head, looking vaguely surprised. "Well then, let's see, hmmm, ... bail is set at $50 and the trial will be held on, hmm .... May 18th" and down came the gavel to seal the deal. A moment's pause and the clerk began to intone the ritual for the next case.

I cleared my throat, rather loudly. "Ahem.... Your Honor," I heard my voice saying, seemingly from afar, "with your permission, I would like to change my plea to guilty." The crowd moved restlessly, like spectators at a Roman coliseum they sensed that something was about to happen.

"Excuse me?" the judge said looking over his glasses, "did I hear you right? You wish to change your plea from 'not guilty' to 'guilty'?"

"That's correct, your Honor." I replied, regaining control and reaching down for my best radio-persona baritone, "I want to change my plea."

The judge leaned toward me, still peering over his glasses, which got me to wondering why he wore them, and said, "Tell me son, in your own mind, do you believe you're guilty of this offense?"

"No sir," I replied, wondering why I was being called "son." Wasn't I supposed to be some kind of miscreant?

"Then why," he inquired with eyebrows raised, odd eyebrows, I noted. They blended gently into each other forming one continuous furry ridge above his eyes but a short distance below his sleek black hair, "would you want to change your plea?"

"Because," I answered, "I can pay that $25 fine but I can't cover the bail you just set and," – I paused here for whatever dramatic effect I thought it might have – "given the last day or so, I would rather be someplace other than your jails over the next couple of weeks." A quiet snickering from the cheap seats.

It was a crystallizing moment. I sensed that I was, finally, in my element with a measure of control restored. I was, I am, my father's son; words are my weapons of choice, my swords, my shields. I could skewer an opponent with a crafty riposte; parry a thrust with my very best *copia verborum*. Demosthenes, Antiphon, my ancestors, give me my voice! Let me rattle and prattle and dance a verbal syrtaki. If the judge was going to let me talk I was going to be fine. Besides, the crowd was on my side now. The new local favorite.

47

"Look, Mr. ...ah,,. Kons..tantakis," stammered the judge tilting his head again in a rather engaging manner, "as a representative of our system of justice I cannot permit this. If a man feels he's innocent I cannot allow him to plead guilty because it's cheaper." A few chirps from folks in the crowd who liked that one.

"Well, your Honor," I interjected, buoyed by being a "man" – if only allusively – "if you could give me a minute I can clear this up."

The judge turned again, looked at me, shuffled some papers, glanced up over his metal-rimmed glasses at the clock on the far wall, hesitated, turned. "Okay," he said finally, "go ahead." My heart started beating again. The Peanut Gallery applauded.

"Your Honor," I began, *basso profundo* now. "I couldn't have been soliciting for this encyclopedia firm because I don't work for them. I'm not on their payroll and I never signed any contract. I went out as an observer. It was like a trial run. I don't know anything about licenses and I never offered anything for sale."

The judge listened, thought, that eyebrow flicked up toward the hair line and back down. He turned to the bailiff and said, "Mr. Burrows, please see if you can check this story."

The bailiff took me off to the side and I got to tell him that he needed more than a phone number. He needed to know that this outfit lived on the sleazy side of the ledger. "Mr. Burrows, sir," I said. "When you ask for Mr. Blackmun make sure they know who's calling 'cause everyone is Blackmun, the guy that answers the phone, the guy that makes the appointment. Whoever's really in charge has this fence set up; you gotta push through it." He nodded and left as the clerk called the next hearing – which received mixed reviews – and I realized I was dripping flop-sweat down my sides.

X. 1960 – March

It was then back to the tank for our group. Bobby Joe continued to tumble into despondency and looked even worse than before. I couldn't stand it. I found Bradley and sat down to chat because I knew that, if nothing else, this guy had a keener outlook on life than ol' B.J. and I needed a bit of boosting. I could hear a distant, rhymeless song, "You do know, don't you 'son,' you really should be scared shitless, …, really." I waited, waited for Burrows to learn the truth, to tell the judge the truth, the unvarnished truth, the exculpating truth, the pure, honest, innocent truth because I really couldn't even think about what my folks were going to say if anything else came out of this.

It took only about an hour before Burrows and a court officer came down to the tank but it felt like three days. Burrows was laughing but he wouldn't say anything and they escorted me back to the courtroom. This time it was just me in the box with a court officer and, off to the side, what I'd come to think of as my fans. The judge smiled and that eyebrow seemed to wave at me, "Well, Mr. Konstantakis, it seems as though your story holds, right down to the elusive Mr. Blackmun. There is no case. The charge has been dropped. You are free to leave."

Cheers from the mezzanine, foot pounding from my groupies and while I was exhaling and a grin was spreading across my face we were all frozen by a sudden scraping of a chair off to the side of the room and a familiar, malevolent voice, "Your Honor...." Joe Friday. Holy shit, I thought, trying to catch my breath. I completely forgot about him and his "five years in a Federal slammer for commies."

I wasn't the only one as the judge and my new best friend Mr. Burrows startled too. "There is," intoned Joe, "a Federal charge potentially facing this *boy*. Why do you think I'm here?" The crowd groaned. One woman actually hissed him. My heart fell down around my shrunken gonads. I could see my sorry ass being dragged off by government goons, handed over to McCarthyish prosecutors, no friendly confines of ticky-tacky land, no hometown crowd.

The judge called Joe over to the bench. I could just make out a few words. "... go ... all this (rising intonation) ... messy ... no way ... save your .... keep other ...." The two conferred for another few minutes, each one draining another month out of my life. As I leaned forward, scrutinizing "my" judge's face, I scanned the morning. I felt strangely upbeat, optimistic. I could hear my mother's sonorous, immigrant voice, the one that nursed me through all those rough patches of childhood, "It's okay, Xerxes, it's okay, you're a good boy, you are going to be fine."

While I waited I thought about my spirited oratorical defense, aided, as it was, by being preceded by a couple of drunks, a fist fight, Bahbuhjo's pathetic mewling, and the fact that his famous encyclopedia firm was transparently run by a bunch of scumbags. My judge, my personal nominee for the next opening on a Federal bench, leaned over and pulled my chestnuts from the fire. "You may go, Mr. Konstantakis." As the officer took me back downstairs I heard a quiet clapping behind me.

It took but a few raggedy minutes to get everything settled. I got back the last of my confiscated possessions, signed several forms and was unceremoniously turned out on the street, free, free at last.

No sooner did I hit the pavement than it dawned on me that I was not in much better shape out here. I was on the far side of town, without wheels and pretty sure that my illustrious encyclopedia firm was not about to send a car out. Then it got worse. I realized that all I had was my Zippo, which I didn't plan to use again, my wallet and a single copper piece. That was it. I held no currency, no coin. I did, however, hold paper, a check, which I pulled out of my wallet. It smelled faintly of cheap leather; it was creased and dirty from weeks of waiting for the day when I would need it. It was from Frankie, for $40, US, a princely sum. It was this check that backed that boast to be able to cover the fine but not the bail.

The monetary value of the check, of course, existed only in the naïve recesses of my post-adolescent mind. It was written on a Ypsilanti, Michigan bank and, unfortunately, was graced with my cousin's real name, Franklin Quasimodo. Yes, Hugo's wondrously complex, deformed hunchback, also an Italian poet, but it was *good* paper – I was pretty sure. To the banks and check cashing services of Covina what it smelled of was rubber. Even the local bail bondsman laughed me out of his office despite an offer of a 25% commission.

I was a newly freed man with money I couldn't spend, a nagging emptiness for I hadn't eaten anything since a soggy pancake the raccoon taunters served us at 6 AM and seemingly but one option – I headed back to the courthouse to *my* beacon of justice, *my* defender of the rights of freemen everywhere, *my* judge.

"Your Honor, sir," I said as I smiled my best shuffling smile and rubbed my left shoe on the back of my right trouser leg and waited for the judge's startled look to fade, "You trusted me, sir; you believed me. And I am grateful. Can you cash this?" I said, reaching toward him awkwardly with the check. "I'm broke and stuck here. I'll sign it over to you at a bargain rate, forty percent. The rest will get me back to my sister's in Santa Monica."

My judge looked at me, over his glasses, like he was gazing upon an apparition, a figment of someone's imagination or perhaps "it" had just arrived from some other planet. There was a painful hesitation. "Look, Mr. Kossantokis, or whatever your name is, I don't think so. In fact, son, you have some nerve." He sounded firm, even angry, like he meant it, but I couldn't quite grasp this and interjected, "But the check is good, your Honor," I said, feeling ever more disoriented with my arm still extended, the check vibrating with the trembling of my hand. "I know it is. I don't understand."

My judge paused, his face flickered between soft and hard, between sympathy and annoyance. Hard and annoyance won. He took his glasses off with a rough twist of the frames and glared at me. "There's no way I can take that check. It doesn't matter whether I believe you or not. Please just leave, now," he said with a dismissal wave of his empty hand. Disbelieving and disheartened, I withdrew and heard a growling "Damn kids."

I stood there, simmering. Santa Monica was on the other side of town and if I didn't get back there soon Anna was going to call our folks. My mother will go weepy and ratchet up the hysteria. Dad will lose that famous even-tempered demeanor. I considered my trusty thumb but I was on a side street well off from the center of things and right now I was working on pushing down the panic surging from my gut. I stalked down the hall from *someone else's* judge's chambers and spotted Burrows chatting with a young man who had all the trimmings of a member of the bar. He smiled and waved me over.

"Well, it's my young friend. Why are you still here?" Before I could answer, Burrows turned and said, "Man, Chris, you missed this one this morning. This kid, nutty name – what's it again, kid? Zero? Exero?"

"It's spelled X-e-r-o but I say it 'Zero' like in one less than one."

"No shit. Okay, kid you can be Zero if you want. Don't matter to me," he said and turned to Chris. "He sure can flap his jaw. Got himself out of a mess. Had ol' Judge Montgomery all twisted up. Didn't know how to handle him."

"He still doesn't," I said, blowing my chance to say "thanks." "And I'm stuck here in Covina, broke and hungry."

"Why?" said Chris. "Give me a quick rundown."

I went through my life as a newly freed man, the suspect but almost certainly good check and my latest encounter with whom I now knew to be Judge Montgomery. As I spun out the tale, it hit me that between these two presumably sympathetic fellows I had a shot at getting at least 75 cents on the dollar.

But, just as I opened my mouth, Chris interrupted. "Xero, how'd you end up here? What did you do?"

I spun out the narrative of the previous two days. Chris clearly got a kick out of it. He kept laughing and tapping Marvin, which turned out to be Burrows' first name, on the upper arm. When I got to the Aussie with the cigarettes he stopped me with a grin and said, "How old are you son?"

"Just turned twenty. I've been twenty-two for the last couple of months 'cause it's easier to get a decent job and a beer when you're 'legal' but, I'm twenty, just twenty."

"Perfect. Marv, let's have some fun. I need a phone and Xero, write your last name down, I'm gonna need it."

In the bailiff's quarters Chris shifted from "nice young man" into "solon from gonzo firm." He called the internationally admired and respected encyclopedia company and ran smack into the firewall surrounding Mr. Blackmun. A "Certainly-but," a couple of "Yes-I-knows" and "This-is-Mr.-Konstantakis's-lawyer" and the genuine Mr. Blackmun – or whoever was ultimately responsible for pretending to be – was on the line. The half-conversation I could hear took intriguing twists that I hadn't thought of which is, I would learn, why people hire lawyers. 'Defamation of character,' was good but the real zinger turned out to be, 'Contributing to the delinquency of a minor.' Ah, good to not be twenty-two anymore.

"Sure," Chris said and, after a pause, "That'll be just fine. Thank you." And hung up.

"What's fine?" I asked.

"Oh, you'll see. It'll be better if you don't know right away. Now, tell me more about this redneck friend of yours, the one our noble G-men still have their meat hooks into."

I told him what I knew, which wasn't much. I found myself hoping he'd take on Bobby Joe's case. He was a pathetic little schemer but after watching how easily he crumpled in the tank and the courtroom I knew he was going to need help. I allowed my heart to bleed for him, a little.

About an hour later a Western Union messenger came in, escorted by the court officer I recognized from the morning, and he was bearing, *mirabile dictu*, a cashier's check for $150. This paper, the local bank readily acknowledged the legitimacy of. Chris refused the fee that I offered. "Look, kid," he chuckled, "I'm doing this pro bono. That check wouldn't cover my standard billing and you'd still be stuck. But I tell you what, kid" – I was getting a bit annoyed with this 'kid' bit but wisely kept my jaw from flapping – "Marv and I'll join you for the very best-tasting steak you maybe ever will eat."

Later Chris drove me to the bus station where I boarded the next cruiser for Santa Monica and, for the last miracle of the day, beat Arianna in the door by a good twenty minutes.

XI. 1960 – March

The next morning I was awakened by the phone which was a little, but not much, better than the dog. It was the elusive poseur, Mr. Blackmun. "Can you fucking believe this?" I whispered to TD who responded with his usual gormless, vacant-eyed look. I listened with amusement to presumably the real Maurice Blackmun who didn't sound like any of the others I'd met so far and who started yammering away the instant I said, "Hello."

"Look, son," he said. – a small step up from 'kid' – "Look son," he repeated himself. "I know you had a pretty rough couple 'a days. Ol' Ralph waited out there a couple hours, worrying 'bout you two. We're real sorry 'bout that. We're kinda worried about Bobby Joe too, but we've got our guys on it and we know he's gonna be fine 'cause he's a good kid and he's tough and he sure as hell can move encyclopedias and we think he's got a future with us, and we care, we care 'bout all our boys but I'm thinking mostly about you, son, 'cause we think you too, yes, you too, have a real future with us."

"Future?" I responded. "Future?" I repeated myself, which seemed conversationally appropriate, but mainly I was marking time till I figured out what the hell was going on.

"Absolutely, we're so sure that I'm gonna do something we never, and I mean *never,* do. We're gonna offer you a paid spot, up-front cash."

"Up-front? You mean, like a salary?"

"Well, you know, the rest of the boys are strictly on commish, so they gotta sell books or they don't earn, but, yeah, up-front is kinda like a salary. You still have to sell books 'cause the up-front is up-front like it's money that we're kind of holding for you against your sales and your commish and let you have if you're not selling too many books at any time. But you do realize that we never, I mean *never*, give a door-to-door salesman this kind of a deal 'cause it's just too sweet."

I felt a wave of seductive disbelief like when Bobby Joe was riffin' with the folks back on Shady Lane. The deal was a can't-miss, the 'cyclopedia set was free, man, free, like the up-front money. Then there was the back-story. Blackmun was apologizing for my troubles; he was offering me a job without screening or training. I had three fast thoughts.

One: The up-front money was bullshit; it was like an author's advance. It helped, I sighed inwardly, to have a mom who was an editor, which had always struck me as unfathomable. She spoke English like it was being scraped off her tongue with a backhoe but she edited narcissistic poets and egocentric philosophers and somehow managed to be more than the frumpy Greek peasant persona she put on display.

Two: A small and mostly irrelevant piece of this rant being shipped my way smelled like admiration. Blackmun was impressed. Pretty much on my own, I'd extracted my still baby-smooth butt out of the mess his cosmodynamic encyclopedia *boy* had gotten me into.

Three: He was worried that I will sue his ass.

I went with the last of these. "Well...," I said, hesitating and hoping it made me sound unconvinced but convincible, "it's tempting. What would the up-front money look like? Exactly what figures are we talking?"

"Well, I can't really say, son. It's hard to say, hard to say, tough to put a figure on it, son."

"How about," I suggested, "we look at what your best *boys* are pulling and we start there."

"Well now, that's a bit more than we were thinkin' and anyway, you're *gonna* be one of our best and you'll be beatin' that real soon in commish, so the up-front doesn't really count for much, you know, like it's your money anyway. It's just to make it smooth, so the job doesn't feel like pressure, so you can ...."

I couldn't take much more. His voice was burning in my ear. The more he flounced around with this ambiguous crap, the more he talked while saying nothing, the more it pissed me off. There were wars being waged within:

"Thank you so much for the call Mr. Blackmun," I heard my father's son say. "I am most appreciative of the offer. You are an honorable gentleman and represent a company with a sterling international reputation. However, I have decided to pursue other avenues in life."

Another Xero, one who had been gaining ground, countered: "Blacknipple, you are a dickhead. Your company is run by cretins and miscreants and you wouldn't give a flying fuck about me if you weren't worried that I might smack you with an expensive and embarrassing suit. So take that set of twenty-two volumes, along with the last decade's worth of annual supplements and stick 'em where the sun never shines."

I gently laid the phone in its cradle and let this petty pleasure warm my soul. This, I mused, was a bit of what Bahbuhjo felt strutting down the walkway, how my sales manager felt hosing me out of my *commish*. It's not bad. A cheap triumph, a small notch in the belt. I finished the syrupy coffee and half-burnt toast – it was always half-burnt, the damn toaster had a busted coil and Anna was too cheap or too preoccupied to buy a new one. The coffee was my fault. I scratched TD behind the ears. "You know," I said, "I don't think I want to be whatever it is that appeals to hotshot encyclopedia salesmen. I need glamour, a little glamour to dress up the summer. Pounding pavements isn't going to cut it."

I picked up the LA Times and flipped right past the front page, didn't even hesitate at the sports section. I went right to the Help Wanted page and joined the circus.

XII. 1960 - Late March

One phone call with a guy whose name slipped by too fast for me and I was on board. Ken Karson Productions, Inc. Easy. Maybe too easy. Wait and see, I thought. Not much else has turned out well. Wait and see.

The next morning, coffeed, toasted and cleaned of TD's slobber, I hopped on the first of two buses to meet with my new boss whose name I got this time, Tony Piccolo. We met on a street corner outside a large fenced-in lot. Tony appeared to be around thirty. He was average in height, average in weight but nothing else about him was average. He felt tight, sharp, vaguely dangerous. He was wearing a black turtle neck and faded jeans over cowboy boots. His eyes were dark, almost black and piercing. His hair was wavy and as dark as his eyes. He took my hand into his and I felt, oddly, that for this moment I was the only one in his world – endearing and just a tiny bit scary. "Welcome to the circus, kid," he said warmly. "I liked your voice over the phone and it's always a pleasure to bring in somebody new."

He liked my voice? What an odd reason to hire someone. Later I found out it wasn't odd at all. Tony took me inside the fence and nodded at the scene. "And welcome to the barn," which I assumed is what they called the large, bare lot strewn with equipment, trailers, trucks, cages, and canvas tents. "It's going to take me a little time to get things organized, so why don't you just wander around and soak up stuff. I'll catch up with you in a bit."

I looked about. It wasn't a circus, not yet. Fantasy's trappings had been bagged, boxed, and crated, shorn of their illusions and humbly wintered over. But the winds had shifted, the days were longer and the place was abuzz. The cast was assembling, the search had gone out for new faces, or any old ones that might wander back. I was, apparently, the first new face, but I knew... I was not "real" circus. I leaned against a pole and stared as though I were looking into a diorama, a kaleidoscope of people and props. For a moment extended, stretched in mental time, I was alone and all before me was unreal, the only customer and I hadn't even bought a ticket.

"Hi there," interrupted my reverie, "so you're the new kid Tony told me about. My name's Doris." I looked down at a chunky, thirty something woman. "Doris," she said again, holding out her hand, and there was a touch of pride in her voice.

"I am Xero," I said with a quick bow and took her hand which was oddly sweaty. "I am delighted to meet you."

"That's the *real* me over there," she said and pointed to a four-color poster propped up against a beat-up Dodge that was sitting unhitched beside a live-in trailer. "I am Roma, few are, even here," she said gesturing at the busy lot. "I tell fortunes, read palms, forecast the future."

I looked more closely at the poster where her whiteface was topped off with a Merlin, star-encrusted hat, planets and stars painted on her cheeks and long dark robes that cascaded wizardly about her feet, and thought, Doris? Doris!? Surely a clown who tells fortunes can't be named Doris.

"You said 'Roma'?"

"Ah, yes, Roma, from Romania and all over. None of these others here are, but some of 'em like to act like it. *My* people, Travelers," she said with a conspiratorial nod at the folks working about the lot, "always kept to themselves. Don't trust no one and they don't trust us. Gypsies, some called us. Folks are scared of Gypsies, not Romani."

"You are a Gypsy then," I said with a questioning tone.

"I'll tell your fortune soon, son," she smiled an ambiguous smile, "You will be amazed, and maybe a little scared."

I looked at her more closely. She was short, full of cheek and rounded in places appropriate. She was decked out in a blouse and skirt of interlocking reds and greens, very Eastern European, bangles and bracelets of woven silver up her wrists, loosely overlapping, jangled with her quick hand movements, a necklace graced with an artfully uneven stone, large hoop earrings, her lobes pulled southward with their weight. A Gypsy? Not a Gypsy? I didn't know. I didn't know why she came over. My bullshit detector hummed quietly as I watched her walk away. I shrugged it off. When fantasy is the norm, it would be so disappointing to find that anyone is what they say they are.

I spent the next hour or so moving about, trying not to get in anyone's way, tuning my ear, getting a handle on who or what I looked like to them. The annoying but obvious truth was that I was a nearsighted, middle-class college drop-out. Do they know this? What do they see? A new recruit? A sucker, a mark, a new best friend? I slipped between two trailers and heard someone snicker "gilly." I was pretty sure it wasn't a compliment. While I stood there feeling ill at ease, Tony came by and said simply, "Come back tomorrow morning nine AM and start work." Whatever the hell that meant.

That night, with a bottle of cheap Chianti and a copy of *The History of European Circuses* that I found in the local library and whose virginal binding cracked when I opened it, I poured my soul into KKP. "They" had become "we."

"We are," I slurringly explained to TD, who was the only one still up and willing to listen, "too small to worry Ringling Brothers or Barnum and Bailey. But we are," I was up now, dancing barefooted about the room, waving my arms in beckoning circles to draw the rubes and the drifters, the vagabonds, the tourists, the children of all ages into the big top, "too big to be just another mud show. We are the honest descendants of the Medieval Traveling Carnivals.

"We are," and I gathered steam, sliding less than gracefully behind the couch which had miraculously become the pitchman's booth, dancing down the midway toward the kitchen calling forth the rogues and the gypsies, the fantasticists, the beguiled and the merely curious, "saltimbanque, a collation of clowns, of jugglers and talkers....

"We eat fire, we defy death, we dance, and sing and, for a while, if you stop and let us," – my voice dropped and I leaned down shakily toward TD whose head was tilted curiously – "we'll do the impossible, strip away the pretenses of your sorry life and, for a small precious moment, we .. will .. set .. you .. free." I had discovered a great truth in that last glass of wine: circuses are subversive, but I couldn't let anyone know, other than the dog.

XIII. 1960 – Late March

~⚬~

I met with Tony the next day and through the lingering headache began to understand the game. It was pretty basic and, luckily, sobering. Everybody tried to squeeze a little profit out of each town they played. Some worked for Ken on salary; some were independent performers who signed on for a season. Some paid for a spot on the midway. Doris turned out to be one of these, her multicolored tent, bedecked with woven hangings and carpets, astral signs and the obligatory crystal ball where the cosmos assembled to reveal its future self to her and her alone was prime real estate, the first place you stumbled upon on your way to the Not Quite Big Top.

Each spring they went on the road, moving along the villages and hamlets up and down the coast, driven by weather, last year's take, whatever vagaries were driving Ken's thinking and whatever deals he'd managed to broker. They did two, three days, sometimes more, in places like Oxnard and Santa Barbara, picked up stakes and headed north, up through the Sacramento Valley, into Oregon and Washington and sometimes all the way to the Sunshine Coast of British Columbia. No bitty villages. No big cities. A very Goldilocks kind of search for the "just right."

But if you're going to travel, someone has to do the preliminary scutwork, set things up before the trucks and tents arrived. Someone's got to advertise, sell tickets, prep the village, stoke the kiddies, sweet talk the parents, con the locals. Tony laid it out over coffee. I was to join one of the advance teams. Before each run, he explained, teams of four or five advance men go into the scheduled towns for planning, ticket sales, and advertising. The operation was built around the classic boiler room. It wasn't pretty but it worked and, well, a job's a job and this is how you join the circus when you're not circus. I left with a copy of "the script" tucked into my pocket and promised to memorize it.

Two days later I arrived at the Odd Fellows Lodge in Oxnard. I took a room in what I romantically thought of as a "flop house." In reality, it was just a small apartment in a boarding house. It was just the right size, a brisk walk from those Odd Fellows and cheap. At nine the next morning I began my new mission: earn an honest living. The used-car salesman bit was a bust. The time spent in Gardena wasn't wasted but I wasn't exactly racking up the big bucks and I never did get around to actually peddling encyclopedias. This was my chance to make good in life, sort of.

I tried, once again, to recall that scale for socioeconomic status. I didn't remember seeing Circus Worker on it, nor Advance Man. I wanted to know whether I was moving up or down. I wanted to be able to tell dad which way I was headed, because he was really going to want to know. I also realized that I had not spoken to my folks since I turned in my get-out-of-jail-free card and most assuredly did not want to. I hoped that Anna kept her mouth shut.

The job turned out to be a total bore. Uneasy, I realized that this kept happening. Why? Was I not listening to the thudding in my ear? Were the apocalyptics too far away? Was I, perhaps, dense as a post? That morning out at the barn I had imagined that I was to be the front man, the agent of adventure, the bringer of joy and wonder to the poor benighted bastards stuck like barnacles in their tiny hamlets. I would be the Aegean Piper to the ragged children, leading clowns and jugglers and tight rope walkers, The Bearded Lady, the elephants, ponies and tigers and perhaps a dancing pig. Nope. The job was exactly what Tony said it was and I understood that crack about my phone voice.

I sat each day at a table, a few feet from four gentlemen of a certain age and stage of decrepitude who seemed very much at home here. We spent the hours from nine till four, with a short lunch break, cold-calling establishments in the area, every freakin' one in the yellow pages which was thicker than you'd think for a mid-sized California town.

I worked the lines, massaged Ma Bell, sent my mellifluous voice down the wires. I'd pick up the phone and sense distant echoes of Bobby Joe, his soft Georgia diphthongs gliding through the company script. Pitch the pitch; don't let 'em talk till I breathe. Do not elaborate. Drone. Get 'em to buy tickets to give to their customers as favors.

"Hi, this is Jimmy Briarman," – no way I could use my real name, Xerxes Konstantakis is not gonna move tickets in this neck of the woods. But "Jimmy," "Jimmy" is America's offering to nominal banality, the all-purpose moniker. The name fairly sheds blandness with each uttering, Jimmy Olson, faithful schnook to Clark Kent, Jimmy Stewart, soothing leading man, Jimmy Durante, unthreatening comedian – "I'm the Advance Public Relations Chief for Ken Karson's circus.

We'll be in town next week, just like last year, and I know you'll be behind us again as we do everything we can to make this a fabulous day for all of the kids of (fill in town's name) .... blah, blah, blah."

So I sold Andriotti's Shoe Emporium fifty tickets at 50¢ a pop. Mark it in the book. Andriotti puts a sign up saying "THE CIRCUS IS COMING, THE CIRCUS IS COMING" and when Marlene buys her runny-nose kid a pair of shoes, she gets two Annie Oakleys. Then I peddled twenty to Gloria's Scarves and Ribbons. Write it up. Another thirty-five to Cosmo's Barber Shop – come on Cos, make it thirty-six, go for forty. I hate odd numbers. No? Okay, book it anyway. I fobbed off ninety to Dana's Furniture, pushed a measly ten ducats to Thee Coffee Shoppee and so it went, though I drew a blank with Dr. Adolpho Fiedler who could not be convinced to dole out a couple of freebies for fantasy for a two-surface amalgam.

Then noon and lunch and I discovered that the thing I needed to do each day was find an excuse not to have lunch with Louie. Louie was a loser. Louie The Loser. It was sad. He didn't want to be a loser. It was just that he'd had so much experience, so much practice, that it was all he knew. Several of the other guys on the team were kind of interesting but they didn't want to have lunch with me because I was a freakin' kid and they were not, at all. Johnny was a retired fireman. He had a nice pension but his wife died and he couldn't handle sitting around a lonely empty house. So he hit the road, in a soft harmless way and turned out he could move tickets. Cliffy was a grifter. He was not to be trusted with anything. I learned real quick that the only thing to say to him is "no" because a conversation with him usually began with, "Hey, man, can you loan me a sawbuck till we get paid?" "No" worked. Connie had done, as he put it, "honest time." He wouldn't tell me what went down so I decided that he'd done five years in Leavenworth for impersonating a Federal agent. It felt right.

That was the gang. And since Johnny, Cliffy and Connie headed out to Mom's Diner every day at noon I was left ducking and weaving, trying to avoid Louie.

It rarely worked, so Louie became my next new best friend. Louie, it turned out, knew he was a loser and he complained about it all the time. As he explained the first time he corralled me into lunch, he grew up outside Des Moines, the baby with two harpies for sisters. Pappy was a drunk but an honorable one who wouldn't hit a girl. So he smacked Louie around whenever things didn't go right, which was most of the time. I sat there and listened patiently. I saw a cowering kid, arm held up defensively over his head whimpering, "Why are you hitting me? Why? I never did anything to you." I had known Louies before. We all have. I could hear that line in my head with its final "you" drawn out, pitch ascending till it's almost a squeal. So I offered to buy lunch. Louie wasn't much of a salesman either.

Four o'clock every afternoon we hung up the phones and hit the streets. We delivered the tickets, picked up the cash and gave each business posters to put in their windows. We carried plenty of extras to staple to telephone poles around town.

And the routine became routine. Up in the morning, blah, blah, blah for three hours. Glare evilly at Connie, Cliffy and Johnny – why, I wondered, do they all have 'y's and 'ie's on their names? Why can't working-class slobs in America have nice clean, chopped-off names? We had Ike (no diminutive there) and JFK (he was John F. not "Johnny" – can you imagine "The President of the United States, 'Johnny Kennedy'?"). And how about Richard Nixon? (well, he was "Tricky Dick" so maybe that counts) – who made sure they never locked eyes with me on their way out to Mom's while I tried to do the same with Louie but couldn't. I was just no good at this little game. Maybe more practice.

I promised myself I would work on being evasive and unresponsive so I could come to feel part of the world I seemed to have contracted into.

Then the first Friday came tip-toeing in. At five, we dumped the extra posters into the nearest trash can and wended our way back to the Odd Fellows hall. Friday was Payday. The week was done and Tony came up to settle things. We were on "commish," a percentage of the gross on our own sales, sign-delivery and poster pasting was part of the deal. That first Friday was a fiscal epiphany. Tony showed up with cash, real US, all-American green. Bills, five bundles, each folded and wrapped snug with a rubber band. I learned that this is how it was done by real men. I vowed never again to put a bill into a wallet. I would, henceforth, fold them over once, never twice, only girls do that when they have to jam them into those silly, snap-up purses, and slide them in a maximally manly way into my left trouser pocket.

I took my weekly earnings and did just that. I didn't count the bills for that might look like I didn't trust Tony. I didn't, of course, but I thought I should act like I did. I would count my "swag," as Connie called it, when I got back to my room – after the dinner Louie had talked me into. He felt guilty because I paid for lunch that day. If I had known this would happen, I wouldn't have picked up the check.

After dinner, which wasn't nearly as dreadful as I thought it would be, and after Louie had headed off to wherever he dragged his lost self in the evenings, I sat on my bed, unfolded my bankroll and counted it. It had looked like mine was a little fatter than the others but I wasn't sure. Hell, I'd never been paid before and I guess the first girl is always the most beautiful, the first drink the most intoxicating. That soft baritone, the gift from my mother that worked so well with someone else's judge, was even better over the phone. I stacked up the bills, fives, tens, twenties. I had made even more than I imagined, a mind-warping one hundred and seventy-five bucks for one week's work. My bankroll was up around ZEP level, and I wasn't nearly as bored with this life as I had been a mere two hours earlier.

XIV. 1960 – Late March

Euphoria has a short life. By Tuesday I had to acknowledge once more the banality of the boiler room. Running through the same spiel over and over had become my version of one of Dante's inner circles, the one reserved for falsifiers, the duplicitous, the impersonators and this thought ran through my head as I introduced myself to Miss Gretham of Gertie Gretham's Smocks, Frocks and Toggeries. Gertie signed up for a stunning one hundred and twenty tickets which was only ambiguously helpful.

When the days closed and after I had openly thanked the last patron of the young, silently told the last denier of children to go fuck himself, after I had nailed the last poster to the last pole and managed to elude Louie and had my dinner blissfully alone with my newspaper and suffered through the fourteenth nicotine fit of the day for I had, true to my word, given them up, life wasn't much better. I took to hanging around in the neighborhood bars, walking along the ocean and sitting on benches in postage stamp-sized parks. All these towns seemed to have these parks, decked out with city flags, state flags, the obligatory Old Glory surrounding a monument to a hometown hero who got sliced up in a glorious war fought in some obscure place whose name our boy probably couldn't pronounce. "Ronald G. Barker, 1922 – 1945, killed in action, Schweinfurt, Germany." Sad, touching, infuriating.

I waited for something, anything, to happen. One evening sitting on a park bench, my uncontrolled mind danced over to the TV in the open window behind me and heard the familiar voice of Nick Adams. *The Rebel*, Johnny Yuma. Damn, I thought. Damn. Yuma just wanders round the country, looking for solace for his wasted soul. Does he end up fobbing off a bunch of four-bit tickets to Mrs. Gretham? Does he find himself wanting to tell the almost certainly caring Dr. Fiedler to go stick his extractor up his butt? No, he pulls into town, anytown anywhere and some extremely cool shit just falls off a shelf. Stagecoach breaks down, mysterious woman shows up in blacksmith's shop; train dumps hero off in high desert plains of Colorado and a ranch war confronts him; horse loses a shoe outside of Albuquerque and deep intrigue follows as a plot to block a widow's inheritance gets revealed in an eavesdropped conversation. Not me. I was, alas, just another migrant worker, an employed drifter.

At the end of the next week, just as we were stuffing the leftover posters into the closet and getting ready for dinner, Tony popped in. "Okay, guys, it's payday," and he tossed a roll to each of us. "It also looks like we've just about used up Oxnard. Time to move on. San Jose is next. Lions this time; Story Road. Like always, I don't care how you get there, I just care when. Monday we start. Nine, as always. See you there, then. Xero," he turned around, "you stay with me."

A flare went off in my brain. Oh shit, what did I do? What does he want? Tony, no matter how sweet he can be, just gives off this "do not fuck with me" aura. I leaned against a table and waited till the rest of the crew got their stuff out of drawers and filing cabinets. I watched as Tony walked out with them. The three hoodlums clumped together leaving poor Louie alone. I could see it, a painful scene in a cheap novel. The three will drive up in Johnny's car, find a rooming house and settle in and the schnook will drag his loser's ass down to the bus station, fumble with his wallet – which is where losers keep their bills – buy a one-way ticket to San Jose and hope he can find a YMCA with a spare bed to dump his droopy butt onto. It was sad but I was content to let Louie dribble his pain onto someone else.

Ten minutes later, Tony came back and put his arm around my shoulder and damn near hugged me. "Kid," – better than 'son' I thought – "stay with me. I know, I know. You sell more tickets than any of those bums but I'd rather have you work with me. Do you want to go on the road? Travel with the circus rather than just doin' all this shit work," he said gesturing back toward the gloomy room with the phones, tangled cords and random slips of paper.

It took me a good five seconds, which is a rather long time in a setting like this, to realize that Tony was not going to turn me in to the FBI, a thought that would recycle through my life. "Yessir, I think that'd be just fine," I said trying to suppress the howl in my sunken chest and still the dance I could feel in my feet.

"And you'll introduce me to Mr. Yuma when we get there, yes?" He laughed – and looked like he understood.

XV. 1960 – Late March

I moved back into Anna and Billy's place for two nights. At first the only one happy to see me was TD, which I was pleased to discover was now his official name, with periods inserted: T.D. We cracked open a bottle of cheap red and sat up and talked, finally. Anna started grilling me like I was back in the tank. But that was okay. It was good to be treated like a normal pain-in-the-ass little brother instead of some creep who slid in under the door and wouldn't leave.

"But it's the *circus*. You're not just selling tickets, it's the real, fucking *circus*," she said looking a bit worried and more than a little intrigued. Just the word seems to weave fantasmic tendrils through the room. She sat there in her cut-off jeans, sloppy shirt and sandals, dark hair as tangled as mine and just kept sipping wine and then suddenly she started to laugh.

"What *are* you going to do? You have oh, let's see, about 'zero' circusy talent. Oh shit, I can't believe I said that. Brilliant. Are they going to teach you to juggle? Walk a tight rope? This is rich. This is so screwy."

"I have no idea, none," I said. "Tony likes me... I think. But look, it's a job. The pay is good, a hundred and fifty a week and they take care of lodgings. I think I'm a roustabout."

"A roustabout? You? Swinging a sledge hammer? Putting up tents?"

"Yeah, I know, I know, maybe the skinniest ever. But, I may get to be Johnny Yuma. Who knows." Billy didn't say much. He just kept snickering. He's okay, my brother-in-law. A good guy, as long as the rent's paid. Easy on the nerves. I thought he'd like to come along.

XVI. 1960 – April

I got to the barn the next day which was, fittingly, April Fool's Day. Everybody was unbagging and rebagging something, cleaning and repairing props and gadgets, polishing the brass fittings on the horses' and elephants' harnesses, touching up the paint on wagons and clown cars, making sure all the rides were ready. Tents got hauled out, hosed down, mildew scraped off, pegs and poles straightened or replaced. Trunks of costumes were stacked up. Jugglers dragged out sacks of clubs, trays of balls and dull swords; clowns unwrapped rubber chickens, bladders, water pistols. The Great Pirellis set up and, satisfied, took down the high wire.

I found myself on the far side where an old log had rolled conveniently against a telephone pole, unslung my duffle bag and pulled out my glove and flicked the ball into the leather, soft from years of being rubbed up with spit, sweat and neatsfoot oil. My nostrils scanned the raw smells, perfumes, fertilizer, cut grass, manure. While I leaned against the pole, absorbing what I could, I sensed a presence at my side. It was Doris. I could feel the warmth come off her, smell the heavy scent she exuded. She slowly ran her long-nailed fingers along my upper arm in a manner that was just short of creepy. "Come with me," she said. "You need to meet people; they need to meet you. You are circus now."

She took me through the lot. First was Ricco of the top hat, the ringmaster and Judy his assistant who will later, she told me with a wink, don a skimpy cheerleader's outfit. Then in quick succession, Persephone, who had this adorable pig on a leash, Laurence who tended to the animals, a seedy looking character whose name I missed but was apparently a clown and endless others all of whom blurred into a spinning kaleidoscope of the improbable.

Ricco and Judy walked me back to Tony's. "You do know," said Ricco, "this could be fun. Tony's told me a bit about you, thinks you got something going for you. Stick with him, he's the best." Ricco was tall, olive skinned with a crooked smile and a quiet confident manner. Judy was gorgeous, which was all that really registered at the moment.

Tony came up and jolted me from my daydream. "Grab your bag and come with me," he said. "We gotta get straight what your job is gonna be." As it unfolded, it was pretty simple. I was now Tony's lackey. I was to help load the trucks at one end and unload them at the other and drive the one holding the food concessions. That "free lodging" turned out to be a bunk in the back of the truck. I could wash up in Tony's caravan when I needed to. When we hit each town, I was to help whoever needed help. During performances I would hawk programs, sell hot dogs, cotton candy and sodas. I will be paid a hundred and fifty a week cash, no questions asked, none answered. "Keep your nose clean, kid, and everything will be fine. Now let's go have dinner."

Which we did and, to add to my delight, we were joined by Ken Karson, the impresario himself. Ken turned out not to be much of a conversationalist. Within a half hour of tucking his napkin in at his collar, he'd downed three double scotches. But little by little I learned about Mr. Piccolo.

He was in his early thirties and had classic street smarts, gleaned from the soft underbelly of America. A delicious mix of contradictions, he was cut from the same cloth as Bobby Joe but the stitching was a lot more secure. For a time he had tried "goin' straight," as he put it, and enrolled at San Jose State.

"I was there for two years, studying languages, Spanish literature. But I never finished. It was like I was a plane stuck in a holding pattern. It didn't feel like me," he laughed. "You know what that's like, hmm?" – one eyebrow arched, lips pinched in. "I was doin' fine. A good student. Kept my nose clean. But I had to get out."

"Didn't git out all that far, kid, 'cause I brought him in with me," said a suddenly awake Ken. "He'd hooked up with some punks runnin' a bullshit carny. Hell, them mothers were nothing but a bunch 'a pimps. Girls givin' hand jobs behind the tent. Sheet. I knew his daddy and I knew he needed to go straight, at least *my* kinda straight."

"Indeed, Ken, you did. I've hated you for it ever since," Tony nodded his head and chuckled.

I leaned forward quizzically, balanced between being enraptured by this tale and wondering why I was being made privy to all this. I'm just another punk kid, but he likes me, which may be good, or maybe not. But it was mesmerizing, the beers and the bullshit, the steak and the potatoes, the tales from someone else's wanderings. Lessons there were here, I knew, memic fertilizer from which I could grow things.

Tony spotted my quizzical look. "Look, kid, you're different. I'm not quite sure what it is but I sniff it. You think and you speak talking-head English. Johnny, Louie, the guys in the other crews workin' other towns, hell, they're all named Johnny, Louie, Connie. They're marginal types; they don't mind taking on a job with no security, lousy working conditions and never knowing where they're gonna be next. Like I said, hang around kid. Listen, learn."

I was afraid to say anything lest it sound wrong, discordant. I just smiled weakly and nodded my head.

"But," Tony shifted gears smoothly, "it's true, I never could escape the draw of the con, the lure of the hustle. Ken bankrolled my dad back when Pop bought a piece of a saloon. He handled a small book and ran a card room in back. The games were honest, but not all the players. Decks were stacked, tourists were fleeced. But that was life."

"He was more than jus' a barkeep," said Ken quietly. "He was a gentleman and honest as the day is long. He was a friend. In my business, they're ain't many who can be both."

"True and thanks Ken," Tony went on. "Yeah, Xero, Pops ran a good room, kept his head down. Paid off those who needed to be paid and kept things as quiet as he could. He carved out a code to live by, and it worked pretty well. 'Make sure you've got your bets covered. Lay off a piece of the action when you get unbalanced. Take a fair vig. No one gets credit. And never fuck your friends.'"

I couldn't help smiling at this. It made me feel strangely comfortable. I leaned back in my chair and looked at them both. One tipping over into old age, maybe sooner than he had planned. A touch of gray, a wrinkle, a line, a crease, a brow furrowed with curiosity and pain. Maybe Ken understood things, things I didn't. Maybe he just saw the same world through other eyes.

Tony lit a Newport and his eyes danced above the sharp cheeks, the two-day beard, the black turtle neck, jeans and shit-kicker boots. There was something very compelling about this guy, quicksilver, elusive, alluring yet distant.

"Tony," popped up Ken, breaking the block of silence that had fallen on us, "deal the kid a hand 'a cards, jes fer fun. I'll get 'em," and he got up, barely. He headed over to the bar moving like an oversized chimp, bow-legged with hands on the back of each chair as he staggered down the aisle between tables. He reached down behind the bar and pulled up a deck of cards. The barmaid just laughed, "My money says you won't get back without fallin' down, Ken," who looked back at her and damn near did. But he grabbed the closest chair and did his chimp bit again, more authentically now, holding the deck in his left hand and using just the knuckles.

Ken fell back in his chair and slid the cards to Tony who smiled and started shuffling. Cards riffled through his hands like old friends. He fanned them, did a couple of one-hand cuts, smiled at me and flashed the bottom card. It was, of course, the ace of spades. "Ever see anyone deal seconds?" he asked me.

"No, but I know about it," I answered. "My buddy Dickless Charlie had been trying to learn it."

"Dickless?" Tony laughed, "Oh, I don't think I want to know," and held the cards out in front of me. I leaned over, my horn rims a few inches from Tony's hands. He showed me the top card and 'dealt' it. Then he showed it to me again. It was still there, on top. He flashed me the second card and 'dealt' again. The top card has still not changed; the second card sat in front of me. Then he showed me the top and the bottom cards and 'dealt.' Again, the top card stayed and the bottom card smiled back at me. My gaze was now focused on Tony's slender fingers; I could not see how it happened. There was just a vague feeling that something wasn't right and a faint swish sound. Tony laughed again. "Don't look for the top card to shift, you won't see it. Check the grip on the deck, thumb toward the front, fingers wrapped around. It's a sharp's grip. The thumb pulls back the top card, just a bit. It's fast. But if you get real close, you'll hear it." A most useful lesson, I thought.

Slowly, I came to see the links between these two. Ken rarely left LA. Tony was Ken's road manager. He controlled the day-to-day operations of the circus, oversaw the advance teams and owned the rights to the concessions. I was beginning to feel that Tony's openness was real and for reasons unclear Tony may have needed me as much as I needed him.

XVII. 1960 – April

I fell into this new chapter of my life. I had really "run away with the circus." The next morning, out on the edge of the barn, I was handed the keys to some serious tonnage – the 10-wheeler that carried the supplies for the concessions, its sides emblazoned with garishly painted candies, pop bottles and a bubble-headed clown with its outsized tongue poised above an ice cream cone adorned with Technicolor sprinkles.

After an hour, filled with several stalls, painful grinding of gears and misjudged turns all accompanied by delighted whoops of laughter from Tony and Ricco, I was dubbed "master of the machine" – and no mere machine, no simple truck. No, this rusting hulk was beyond a conveyor of goods; this fabulously decrepit set of wheels was a messenger of joy and a kid-magnet. Later that day, as I pulled into the lot in the all too familiar town of Oxnard, the waifs emerged, magically materializing on the edges of the show grounds, pint-sized scoundrels, feisty imps, some ragged, some in spanking new Keds. They ran alongside, jumping and yelling and begging for sweets, for what else could a truck like this carry.

Tony taught me how to be a *kid pusher*. We rounded up a squadron of urchins and, with a drop of encouragement and a knowing wink that they will not be stopped should they be seen slipping under a tent flap, we had them dusting off the stands, unfolding canvas, unwrapping pegs and rope and wooden slats and dragging them across the ground's uneven sea of crab grass and wilted dandelions.

When the jump was complete and everybody on site, I indeed swung sledge, helped set up tents and, as instructed, gave a hand where it was needed. In the few hours left before the midway opened, tired and dripping honest sweat, I found a log to sit on, opened a beer and scanned this world off the well-worn path and my vision was graced in ways I could not have imagined.

It was a pig and, as she pranced onto the field, I was transfixed. She was pink and soft with ears like the inside folds of a tulip blossom, her silver-dollar snout angled at the clouds, arrogant and proud. She sported a multicolored tutu of layered crinoline, her spectacular hocks framed by a belt of crushed tulle. She was a pig alright. But I'd heard; I'd seen fleeting images. This was no ordinary pig. This, folks, was worth stepping right up for. She was a porcine masterpiece and she was topped off with a necklace of cheap glass spangles and a bellboy's cap of matching pastels.

As I focused on the pig, an apparition, mirrored in crinoline and tulle, slid into my periphery. Her hands, thin with tiny wrists and supple fingers with long glossy nails, moved in stylized waves and the pig rose on her hind legs, then her front legs, briefly. They flickered leftward and the pig slid up onto my log, laid her chin on my knee and snorted at me, smiled – I swear she smiled – and then with a head nod, sang, after a fashion, climbed back down, rolled over and "died" most convincingly. She was indeed the World's Smartest Pig. She knew it. So did I.

The apparition clapped her hands. The pig jumped up, quite full of life and they bowed together, the pig tucking her left front leg under her engagingly. "Well, my young friend, how did you like that? I am Persephone. We met briefly in Los Angeles. You may, should you decide some day that you are my friend, call me 'Persi.'"

"Xero," I smiled and nodded my head twice. "What may I call *your* friend?"

"Ah, only she knows her real name," said Persephone nodding wisely. "I call her 'Wispy' and await the day when she truly names herself."

I wasn't sure what to make of this tapping of ancient Celtic myths so I sat back on my log. I scanned Persi, from the Philip Morris bellboy cap held tight with a pink ribbon down to the pink slippers all twinned with Wispy, and chuckled inwardly. If she weren't decked out to match that precocious slab of ham she'd probably be a decent looker. In her late twenties I guessed, slim, brown-haired, athletic.

The sight of the two of them each grinning in their respective fashions pulled me into full rumination mode. Persi fairly glowed with a childlike happiness, bland and doe-eyed. She had this goofy smile, with a tad too much lipstick and a bit too earnest a laugh. She reminded me of those infuriatingly happy true-believers who show up at your door, clutching bibles, all white shirt and tie, close-shaven and clean-cut, "We're Christians, ma'am, Christians; doin' the Lord's work."

My eyes flicked back and forth between the two of them; I was in my best pick-at-your-belly-button form now. We are promised the pursuit of happiness – was this it? Happiness, Dad had told me one evening just before I took off, should be slogged for, suffered for. "You can't just grab a hank of 'happy hair,'" he had said with a wry grin. "First you need to be miserable. Pay attention to the miserable, the wretched wise, the ones content in their unhappiness."

I think I understood, a little, but I was feeling a bit put off by all this happiness. I popped out of my head trip and smiled, "I'm curious; why a pig?"

"Why not?"

I kind of expected that. "No, I'm serious. But if you prefer, why train animals?"

"Ah. That is almost right," she chuckled and tapped her fingertips together. "Try again."

I played along. "Okay. Why train animals for a circus?"

"Why indeed.... Good for you, young man!" which was a bit better than "kid." And then out it spun. "Because," she said batting those empty, happy eyes, "Wispy, like the rest, are reincarnated carny folk. They are fated to be reborn here, in the circus, though each," she leaned over and whispered quietly, "will walk its own, God-ordained road. This," she said, nodding sagely, "is why they're so trainable. In each eternal soul is a hidden memory of a clown, a roustabout, a slip of a thing in a fez. I will be the pig next time."

It took a moment for me to wrap my mind around this bit of horse opry theology – then it hit me. This was just perfect. Persephone was in the right game. The damn pig, now firmly fixed in the growing myth I was trying to make of my life, really was the world's smartest.

But I wondered what Persi was going to do when ol' World's Smartest grew up.

XVIII. 1960 – June

The Great Pirellis were the stars of the high-wire. They were also the only wire act so stardom was pretty much assured. It took a while for me to feel comfortable with this middle-aged childless couple, Graciela and Salamon, or Grace and Sal. They were but a few years younger than my folks and I could not get my head around the fact that twice a day they put their lives at risk. Dad would have days when he was feeling really adventurous, meaning that he would actually go out on the lake in Central Park in a rowboat rather than simply walk around staring at the water. As for my mom, well, even the rowboat was a bit much.

The Pirellis were also the only act that always put up their own equipment and never so much as asked me to tighten a guy wire. I was by official job description to be *generally available*, to lend assistance whenever and wherever needed. I had been working steadily, boosting myself up into positions of responsibility, of essentiality. But not here.

One morning on one of those days when by ten everybody hoped the rest of the day wouldn't bother showing up, the three of us ended up sitting together in what passed for shade beside the cotton candy machine. We sat there inhaling sticky sweet vapors from pots of powdered sugar, rolling our cups of pink lemonade across our foreheads and laughing, telling jokes and finally, to feed my ever increasing need to grasp, to absorb this life, Grace started talking about hers.

"You do know... Xero... how in the world did you get that name? What were your parents thinking? Did your dad hate you? I guess you should be happy they didn't spell it with a Z," and she snickered and snickered and finally broke out into a full belly laugh. "No offense, of course."

I took none, though I wondered how she'd react if I did. "I'll let you ponder the roots of my name," I said smiling. "Tell me about yours, your roots."

"Ah, well, you do know," Grace said, "we're just an ordinary couple of hard working stiffs. Really. Some people run grocery stores, some teach. Others rob banks. We dance around on steel wires. My mom, bless her soul," she said and crossed herself, "was a carny. It was in my blood. I first walked a wire when I was three. We traveled everywhere. I grew up mainly in Europe and spent many years in the Soviet Union. Later I met Sal, it was in Romania, yes, love?" she said looking over.

"Romania. Good circus people there," he grunted.

"I know, *we* know," she smiled at Sal, "we're not the Wallendas but, I'll tell you son ('son,' I was always 'son' ... when I wasn't 'kid' or 'boy') we know who we are and, you know, we're pretty damn good."

I was still befuddled. "You are good. You are but ..."

"Well, thank you for that," she interrupted with a laugh.

"But how, how do you handle fear? I've stood under the wire, watched you work that 'double-decker thing' where you're on his shoulders. It scares the shit out of me and I'm down here! You do those flips; my heart nearly stops. You could die, damn it."

Sal laughed and Grace leaned over and touched me gently on the arm. "Dear Xero," she said and snickered again, "we don't do dangerous things, ever. We know where fear begins. There is one simple rule: never cross that line. And don't forget... we're entertainers."

"Something dangerous," interjected Sal, "would be a stunt we're not ready for, one we don't understand. You do what you can and just do that."

"Danger for me, my dear," Grace said with a sly smile, "would be getting up on a wire that someone besides me, Sal or our assistants tightened." That surprised me, even as I realized it shouldn't.

XIX. 1960 – June

The evening was quiet. Everybody was drained and tired. Travelers, circus folk, were outsiders. Adored and admired under the tent, along the midway – feared and scorned when the flaps got tied down and the banners furled. We stuck together, for better sometimes, for worse others. On this still evening I was sitting in the back of my truck watching long shadows ripple across the grass, listening to laughter and song when I heard a gentle "hi" from round the side. It was Judy, Judy of the ring, the skimpy cheerleader outfit.

We had become friends but in a way I did not understand. We spent hours working together but separately like children in parallel play in a schoolyard. We lunched at the same times but someone also seemed to sit between us. We walked along the same straw-strewn paths but always in different directions. She would smile at me, nod, bat her eyes, look away – the link seemed never to be made but the allure was always there, beckoning, rich with tension. If I hadn't been such a dweeb, I'd have known. I bet Tony did... and Doris. It'd been Oracled and Delphied. But not me... for I, whisper, whisper this quietly, do not leak this to anyone, not Harlan, not Frankie, and not Dickless, but the richly moniker'd Xerxes Theodore Konstantakis had yet to round third base.

"Hi," I replied. "What's up?"

"Oh, not much," she smiled. "I just wondered if you could give me a hand, if you had some time."

Of course I could. That was my job, I was to be generally helpful, to give a hand to people in the circus. Judy was in the circus, so, sure, "wadda' ya need, kid?" I felt a need to talk like that since Tony had dumped that "talking-head" crap on me but it was a good cover for I was scared, as scared as I had ever been. Joe Friday looked like just another circus clown right now; true terror smiled back at me from under a cloud of soft brown hair.

"I'm working on moving beyond being just a pair of legs," she smiled. "I need to move out, away from my dad."

"Dad? Who's your dad?" I said, climbing down from my bunk.

"Ricco."

"Ricco's your *father*?"

"Sure. I assumed you knew," she replied. "You don't think I'd get this job on my own?"

"I, wa', huh? I, I never assumed anything. How come I didn't know this? He's your *dad*?" I knew I was sounding really stupid.

"That's why I need an act, to become an artist," she said and she strolled slowly away.

"Oh…" I said weakly as I followed her. "Okay, sure, uh, what're you working on?"

"Gymnastics first, then, you know, a ponger."

"Ponger?"

"Yeah, you know, an acrobat. I'm pretty athletic and got a nice body."

I gulped. I had noticed. I had more than just noticed. I often went back to the moment when I first saw her in the barn, back in LA. Tall, graceful, stunning, as close to the fantasy that I'd tucked away as was possible. She walked with an athlete's grace, long hair in a pony tail or wrapped up halo-like around the crown of her head. She could have been a model, small tight breasts, slim hips, muscular calves.

Symmetry was the word that rung in my head. Everything in balance, small nose set just right, almond eyes with bushy eyebrows unplucked. A mouth set so neatly that it almost seemed wrong. She really needs a mole on her neck, I thought.

"What can *I* do?" I asked, hoping it would be something interesting, in line with the thoughts running untethered through my head.

"Well, I'm working on the trampoline 'cause it's easier to develop moves than on land and I need someone to spot me and, well, I thought you might want to help."

"Spot you?" I said feeling even more at sea than before.

"You know. Watch me. Stay on the side and cover me, protect me if one of my tricks goes wrong. I'll tell you where I'm gonna land. Be there."

So off we went to the back yard, behind the big tent and Judy took off her baggy sweat pants and jacket and climbed up on the mat. She was wearing light green, full-body tights that encased her breasts and wrapped her thighs and buttocks snuggly. A couple of standard moves, a single somersault, a back lay-out, now, gaining height she did a clean double forward. I wasn't much help but that was okay because she didn't need any. She was good. Maybe not a circus artist yet, but she was doing more than jumping up and down and kicking her legs out which was all I could do.

"Okay, hon," she said.

Oh my freaking God, the word swam in my head, did she call me "hon?"

"I've been working on adding a full-twist to the second somersault so I'll be coming down at that end," she said, pointing to the far end nearest the tent. "Set yourself up there and watch, 'cause I have a tendency to over-rotate the twist."

Judy took a couple of preparatory jumps to gain altitude then kicked up hard, high in the air and everything slowed down. She was calling them "somersaults" but that seemed so thin, so inadequate. They were moves of stunning beauty, her body floated. She was planed out, legs tight, toes to a point, arches high. As she turned, her waist was at the center of an ethereal axis, her arms outward, palms flat, fingers pointed to far horizons.

"Now," she said, and time was compressed. I watched, entranced but vigilant. I'd never seen things that way, crystallized so sharply as she rose into the twilight, silhouetted against a three-quarter moon, one clean somersault in a tuck on the way up, then the second where she planed out, her arms spread crucifix-like and at the apex she pulled her arms in, turned and... over-rotated. She landed on her feet but her head and upper body were off line and true to my word I was ready. I leaned over the frame and reached out for her. I grasped her left arm firmly and she spun around and rolled from the taut canvas onto the springs. I had one hand on her left upper arm and the other hand ended up firmly on her left breast. Her face was next to mine, our cheeks touching, barely. I could smell her perfume mixed with honest sweat and it was intoxicating and we stayed like that for oh, most of eternity. She nuzzled my neck and giggled. I was excited, curious, hopeful but.... Was that my mother? Tony?.... Sonny boy, do not deceive thyself, you still be of the untested virginal kind and you do not know what you are doing, you are a little Greek gadjo and she is Ricco's daughter.

But, still, she called me "hon."

Later that evening we ended up wandering through the lot talking about, well, frankly, I do not recall what we talked about. Judy was a couple of years older than me. Indeed, everybody in this traveling phantasmagoria was older than me. But that was good, I needed my elders, I needed my teachers. She was also soft and smart and funny and nearly as tall as I was. We went back to her wagon and found a bottle of surprisingly good wine and lay beside each other for hours. Caressing, talking, kissing. Everything was slow, unhurried. She licked beads of sweat from my arms, curled my dark hair around her fingers, rolled over on me and bit my nose. She stroked me through my clothes. I sat up, leaned across her smooth muscular back, massaged her neck, her arms, worked my way slowly down her back to her buttocks, her legs, feet, toes.

We made love. We had sex. We fucked. They're different. I didn't know that, not then. She kept things slow. I learned. She sat up, her legs bent, knees apart like a Tibetan monk in repose, her light brown hair matted with sweat and semen, firm gymnast's breasts, nipples wrinkled like little raisins. She wondered who I was, how I got here, where I was going. I told her what I could. She laughed, leaned over and tickled me. "So you are a gilly man. I knew, of course. I envy you in some ways. Maybe you will stay. Maybe not. Maybe I will go; it won't be that easy."

I couldn't say anything. There was nothing to say. I stroked her inner thighs and we rolled back over and I slid into her again and we took even longer. It was the only time I was with her alone. Why now? Why this night? Was she my friend? I didn't know. I needed friends but I knew, Tony told me, Tony's dad knew, you don't fuck your friends. Which way did he mean it?

XX. 1960 – July

Tony and I would often cool down with a beer after the last show and shoot the shit. On these nights when the skies glowed as the sun mercifully ducked down into the quiet sea, time slowed. We sat and drank and talked and I felt my childhood slipping away and it wasn't as terrible as I thought it might be.

One evening Tony opened up about his early days trying out one thing and another, living out a less than satisfying Kerouackian existence. "Yeah, kid, for more than a few months I traveled with one of the real dirty carnies, the one that Ken pulled me out of. I just couldn't handle college, too straight, too bounded. I busted out and went with what I found, what we call a 'fireball show.'"

"Fireball?"

"Yeah, don't know where that comes from, but it was a pretty sleazy outfit. Interesting days they were. You know that old Chinese curse, yeah? 'May you live in interesting times.'"

I smiled, nodded and waited. Tony had a story to tell and he wanted me to hear it.

"This one featured strip shows where they really stripped, and, like Ken said, the girls worked behind the tent, ten bucks for a hand job. All the midway games were rigged and we did holler 'hey Rube' to bring in the muscle if a mark got a little hot, and they did."

He pulled up his sleeve revealing a couple of ugly scars. "Souvenirs, courtesy of a jacked up redneck," he chuckled. I nodded and pulled on my bottle.

"We had 'razzle' games," he went on. "Scores keep going up but you never win. Some used a wheel of fortune, other had balls that rolled into a bunch of holes with numbers on 'em. They were all rigged, magnets, peddle-brakes, wires. The best were really seductive. This one night we were really rockin'. We were a couple miles outside of Bakersfield. The local high school football team had just won their big game and everybody was out on the grounds celebrating. I was running a "flattie."

"A flattie?"

"Yeah, it's a wheel of fortune set flat on the front of a booth. Anyway, this local kid was standing there screwin' up his eyes at me. He looked like someone'd just pulled him off a sharecropper's farm. Dirty blond hair, splotchy freckles and a freakin' red neck, a real fuckin' red neck."

"Sounds like he coulda been Bobby Joe's cousin," I said.

"Bobby Joe? Oh yeah, the dwarf who got you arrested."

"He wasn't a dwarf," I laughed. "Just short. And sad."

"Well, this kid," said Tony looking off into the dark with a wistful, slightly twisted smile, "came over and started jawing with me. He was trying to act tough, below the sunburn was this James Dean crap, white T-shirt, pack of Camels rolled up in the sleeve, filthy denims, scuffed boots. Said his team won by four points and he wants to bet on '4.'

"Sure, kid. You got it," I said. "Pays ten fer one."

"Ten for one?" I asked.

"If he wins, and I'm controlling that," said Tony. "He gets back ten bucks. If it's ten *to* one, he gets back eleven. Big difference."

"Really?"

"Really," said Tony. "Anyway, he put up a dollar. I spun. Arrow landed smack on 4. Kid whooped, grabbed the ten bucks and said. 'Okay, man let's do it again.' 'Okay,' I said, 'but you gotta bet both of dem fivers. You can turn 'em into a hundred, ever see one of those?' And I pulled a hundred dollar bill out and put in on the back shelf. Thought his eyes were gonna fall out of his head.

"So he put up the ten bucks. This time the arrow almost stopped on 4 but just slid past on to the 9. Kid lost; he stared at the wheel in disbelief and muttered 'motherfucker.' So I said 'Look kid, that was close. Tell ya what I'm gonna do. I'm gonna *give* you the 9 and I slid in a little tag that said 'winner' on it. 'Now if it lands on 4 or 9 you win and, I'll go one better 'cause that last one was really unlucky, man, unlucky as hell, but since you now own two numbers not one, you gotta double the bet.' Of course this doesn't make any sense but I put a couple of twenties up and the kid only saw green."

"Are you serious? Fucking serious?"

"Absolutely. You don't know yet. Not yet. You will learn..., may learn."

I looked back at Tony, those last two words echoed in my head. He went on.

"So he put up two bucks for each number and I spun and the arrow slid real slow right past 4, past 9 and landed, bang, on the 6. Kid was even more disbelieving.

"I said, pickin' up the money, 'Fuckin' A man, that was close. I cannot believe it either. Look, I'll give you the same deal and I'm gonna give you the 6 to go wit' the 4 and the 9, and what the hell, I'll throw in the 1. You almost got the whole board. Just double up again and I'll pay *you* double.' And I put a stack of bills, maybe four, five hundred, on the back counter where the kid can see it."

"You have got to be kidding me. This is nuts. How stupid are people?"

"A lot stupider than you think, than you can imagine. Greed dulls the mind like any other drug. Anyway, I let him win a spin to keep him around then he loses the next five so I 'give' him a couple more numbers and we keeping doubling the stakes. Soon the kid 'owned' every number on the wheel but the ol' lucky 7 and he had his last dollar on the table. In fact, he'd got every dollar he could raise from his buddies. And the arrow turned and turned, it took an eternity, the leather thong slapping each peg one by one, slowly and it almost landed on the 6, which the kid 'owned' but it just rode over the peg and stopped dead, like a bolt shot through his disbelieving heart on the open 7."

"Wow. What a surprise."

"Yup, real stunner. So I said, 'Holy shit, kid! Can ya' fuckin' believe that? I can't. I sure as hell thought you had a winner. A big one. I'd let you have another spin but I can't, 'cause you then you'd own every number and that wouldn't be fair, would it?'

"Well this one ended up real bad. The kid went nuts. The flush began down around his Adam's apple and flowed right up to his eyes. He hollered something about "fuckin' cheatin' Gypsy pricks" and slammed his shoulder into the front of the booth. I ducked and yelled "Rube" as loud as I could. The kid's buddies, who had started to walk away, turned and stormed the front of the flattie. One of 'em snatched at the cash box. Nobody touches the cash box. I kicked his hand away. He reached behind him and suddenly there was a knife. Two of our boys grabbed him from behind but he was fast. He whirled and next thing I knew, my upper arm was cut open. By now the whole area was chaos. Half the crowd was runnin' for cover, others were fighting with the carny folks.

"A bit later I discovered I was in the back of one of our trucks on my way to the hospital. My arm was bleeding like hell and a huge welt was blowing up on the side of my head.

"That's when Ken showed up. Got me out of the hospital and asked me, no told me, to come work with him. I'm not sorry I did but, you know," and he glanced down at his boots and kicked at the dirt, "there are times when I wonder if it's gonna slide back in on me, when I'm not looking, and I'll have to break out again. It isn't Ken and it isn't my dad. Right now, it's Bobbi and our two girls, the house, the freakin' lawn, that face-lapping mutt we picked up. I think," he paused and a wry smile I hadn't seen before slipped over his face, "I got the real royal hosing. They stuck me in the middle class."

I took a step back and slid this picture of domesticity alongside the other snapshots, Tony on the road, scamming rednecks, taking me into his confidence, telling me what my father never did and probably never could. It made an interesting album.

Circus time for me was time in a teapot; steeped in the life, slowly I was being changed by it. It wasn't just the delightful quirkiness of Persephone, nor the permanent crease left behind by Judy who had resumed her ethereal role, close but never quite here. I think that evening was just something that had to be done....

It was like a summer spider's gossamer web, so fine you didn't see it till the light glanced off in just the right way. It spun itself out, filaments, delicate phrenic weavings of canvas tents, mildewed sidewalls, tanbark, wooden planks, sawdust. It pranced about in garish costumes, with rouged cheeks, white faces, bulbous noses and fright wigs.

And the smells, the mélange of mud, elephant dung, horse droppings and pig shit, cheap perfumes on tinsel-topped chorus girls, the honest sweat of roustabouts, catchers and flyers – all wrapped in a diaphanous net that held us safe, the lost souls of this traveling *fata morgana*.

XXI. 1960 – July

I had my precious Rawlings 'Pro' and the scuffed, misshapen ball I kept nestled in it. I'd had that ball since I was nine. It had cracked off the bat of my hero Gil Hodges and made for my seat, the metaphoric frozen rope. I'd always thought that if a ball ever came that close to me, I'd, well, I'd just catch it. But I ducked, dove under the seat and the ball bounced back and forth between the rows in front and, spent, rolled invitingly over and I scooped it up in that glove and giggled like a little boy who just grabbed a foul ball at Ebbets Field.

We were in Coos Bay, Oregon when the glove, normally lying on my bunk, wasn't. I knew, people lose things, misplace things, trade, sell, barter and loan things. Things grow old and wither away, harden and crack, slink off in despair when ignored, get shelved in obscure places, chucked out with the leftover pizza. But I knew that none of these things had happened to that glove.

A couple of thoughts occurred. Nobody's gonna play with this glove, not while I was around. Nobody's gonna sell it, 'cause it wasn't worth anything to anyone but me. Ah. Of course. I stopped thinking and waited.

Early the next day, Rudy, one of the sloggers who had been following us up the coast for nearly a month, slunk by my truck. "Mr. Xero," he whispered conspiratorially, "Ah know who stole yo' glove. Doris tol' me."

Rudy was just one step up from the lot lice that hang around circuses. He had, however, a talent for sliding along the perimeter, popping up too conveniently, helping just a tad too warmly and, of course, he found Doris who'd been letting him crash in her trailer, raising more than a few eyebrows. My BS detector went off when Doris first oozed across that lot back in LA and nothing since then had stilled its atonal buzz. With the weasely Rudy leaning against the back of my truck, I found myself in one of those intrapersonal scraps.

The Trusting, Ingenuous Xero: Doris is a charming woman who has slotted herself admirably into this collection of wanderers. She tells fortunes with a sly mysterious grace, salves wounds of the psychically scarred, forecasts good fortune for those who have seen little, foresees love for the loveless and riches for the destitute. She is talented and skilled and has taken a poor, lost waif into her protective fold.

The Suspicious, Guarded Xero: Doris is a con artist, a fraud and probably a thief. Her act is as bogus as she is with that phony accent she sports when the pancake goes on. She's been suspected of picking a pocket or two and more than a few bracelets and rings have been left behind after a palm is read. She's working with and on this curly headed piece of jail-bait who may be bowing her strings as keenly as she is his.

This was the circus. Doris was not to be believed. Her manicured hands with those ruby-painted nails were to be watched and all her new best buddies were to be treated with equal distrust. While musing on these matters, I stared at Rudy and had one of those flashes, those illuminating aha's that punctuate the plot-turning scenes in cheap detective stories. How, the thought snuck finally into my cranium, did this little prick know my glove was missing? And why did he say "stolen?"

"How, you little prick," I said in my most menacing voice, "do you know anything about my glove?"

There was only the tiniest hiccup before Rudy said, "Doris tol' me. She said she'd seen one of the locals playin' with it; tossin' a ball around. I knew it wasn't his 'cause he couldn' afford it. And, Mr. Xero, you the only one 'round who's got a neat glove."

That made sense. This "local" breaks into my truck, finds the glove, takes it and then plays with it in front of everyone. Right.

"So," I said, trying to sound menacing, "what are *we* going to do about this?"

"Wu, wu…, well," stammered Rudy while I marked up a tick on my ego that this growly voice worked, at least with insignificant teenage turds. "Well, I betcha I can git it back," he said eagerly. "How 'bout a *re*ward?"

"*Re*ward?"

"Yeah, somethin', like maybe ten dollars?"

"Ten? Sure, ten it is," I said so gently that Rudy looked surprised, like he didn't think it would be this easy. "I really want that glove back – and the ball."

"Okay, Mr. Xero. Neat. So, I'll git it and bring it back. The ball too, okay?"

"No. I got a lot of shit to take care of and can't hang around here. Tell you what, *kid*," – damn, did that feel good – "you get it off that local. After the last show take it to the Pirellis' trailer. I'll leave the money with them."

"Okay, Mr. Xero. You a good guy, ya know." And off he went.

I waited a moment and then followed and, sure as salmon swim upstream, the little slug, grinning like he'd just caught a firefly in a jar, headed for Doris's caravan.

Between shows I took a walk down to the beach. Many of the towns we played were seaside but Coos Bay was special. I spent as much time as I could along the beach with its towering dunes, paths carpeted with crab carapaces and crushed shells, its minimalist trees bent in homage to the constant winds. The sea was alive this day, our last one here. The outcroppings of black rock were speckled with seals; cormorants sat on ledges, their wings outstretched like towels drying on a line; dunlins and killdeer skittered here and there, one quick step ahead of the incoming froth.

But as seductive as the sea was another sound swelled and faded on the shifting breeze, a beckoning of promise, of distraction. The calliope's song, the sound of fantasy, cut through the late afternoon mist and I followed it back, part of a wave of children of all ages, colors, sizes and fashions, to the fairgrounds to top off this near perfect day, to giggle at clowns, ooh and ah at scantily clad girls who somersaulted on broad-backed Percherons, to gasp breathlessly as The Great Pirellis did their not-very-dangerous tip-toe across the ribbon of steel, and to marvel at Ricco's skills, a true Master of Ceremonies, as his ragged but enthusiastic brass band hurled its heart into Sousa marches that never failed to goose the crowd into wild applause especially when it was "be kind to your web-footed friends" and everyone could join in a glorious sing-along.

I smiled as I walked onto the lot. I checked around, saw no one who saw me, walked across the wilted grass of the back yard, over to the beat-up Dodge that towed Doris's digs, opened the hood and removed the distributor cap.

The tent got torn down, the thousand pieces of equipment got stowed, animals were fed, brushed and hosed down, canvas was spooled, beers were opened, hands were clasped, hugs exchanged, accusations tossed about and ignored and it was time to get ready for the next run.

I sat idly in my truck and listened for the sound I knew I'd hear, the cranking of the engine of an old, battered Dodge that would not start. I adjusted the side mirror and looked for the sight I knew I'd see, Rudy sliding greedily along the row of trucks and caravans and buses toward the best kept trailer on the grounds. I knew the script for the next act because I wrote it. Rudy knocked on the door. Grace opened it and said, "Hi Rudy, does Doris need something? Did she send you over?"

"Nope, why would she?" replied Rudy defensively. "I'm here to give you this," and the prized Rawlings, webbing taut and with the honorably scuffed Official National League ball nestled inside was handed over.

"And," said Grace. "I am supposed to give you this," as she handed over a sealed envelope with two pieces of paper in it.

Rudy pulled the envelope out of Grace's hand and sprinted across the patchy grass of the lot, moving straight toward the sound of the Dodge that would not start. Doris was sitting behind the wheel in a sea of consternation and fury. Rudy came up and handed her the envelope. She ripped it open and found a ten-dollar bill and a note that said, "Tony has the distributor cap. There's a $40 service fee."

I spent the next hour getting everything boxed up, secured the cargo and locked down the truck. I cranked its trusty engine into life and got ready to roll when, in the mirror, I saw Tony walking up. He paused, leaned against the door, his dark wavy hair barely visible. A familiar voice snickered quietly, "Good show, kid" and a roll of bills wrapped neatly in a masculine elastic band landed in my lap. I counted it out.

"All forty for me? Don't you get the standard ten-percent vig here?"

"Nah," he said. "The look on her face when she came by for the distributor cap was worth more, so much more. But I'd keep the hood on the truck locked. She's one mean fucker and does not like to lose."

I looked up and saw my boss/friend/father-surrogate skipping (skipping? really?) along, kicking stones, trying to keep them in front of him as long as he could.

XXII. 1960 – August

All was not sweetness and light in KKP, Inc. The circus was also a place to hide, a niche for drifters and misanthropes, a life that let the lost remain that way. One of the clowns, Maxim something or other, was a drunk, a pathetic character who was heading toward the bottom with a sense of mission. Even his act, which took full advantage of his state of permanent loopiness, was getting sour at the edges. He was not pleasant to be around, especially when the wig and mask of rouge came off.

"What's the story with Maxim?" I asked Tony one day.

"Story? What 'story?'" Tony replied testily.

"I don't *know* what story. If I did would I have asked?"

"There is no *story*," he said. "Just give him a wide berth. Don't even talk to him."

"Huh? Why?"

Tony looked back at me, eyes narrowing. "Look, *kid*," and there was a lot of weight on that "kid." "There's a lot of back-life here and it ain't all nice. The details you do not need to know."

"What?" I sputtered. "Look, the guy's a drunk. You don't want me to even talk to him; why the hell do you let him around children?"

"Kids are scared shitless of clowns anyway," Tony replied. "Now you know why."

"But, this is crazy. You tell me to stay away but you and Ken let him go out for two acts every day. You guys are irresponsible shits."

Not a sound. Nothing. Just a look. And a sudden memory of a warning. "Do not ask questions."

I shut up. Tony avoided me the rest of the day.

Maxim may be the one hidden in the circus but many of his kind were drawn to it. At every stop the down-and-outers came by. Guys who needed work for a couple of days to put food on the table or for a couple of hours to buy a bottle of Thunderbird and some smokes.

Tony, probably still pissed over being called a shit, told me I was going to have to supervise them for the rest of the week. He fed me a line about needing to do a run to see what the advance teams were up to. I was pretty sure this was bullshit. I damn near told him so but decided to just suck it up – maybe I was growing up.

It turned out not to be much of a job. Most of these guys were pretty passive and appreciative. They were willing to do just about any job that needed doing, clean up after the animals, drag away the garbage, the shit work that none of us wanted to do. Just gimme some work, gimme some money, let me outta here. Almost all of 'em were damaged in one way or another, usually more than one, alcoholic, tied with ever shrinking rope to some pharmaceutical illusion.

Some were brain damaged, others retarded, but mostly they were the losers in the game, the ones who fell down, got run over, hit by a literal or figurative truck, never saw it coming, saw it coming but couldn't move, tried to move but were too slow, didn't bother to move 'cause life sucks so why bother. Some were okay. Others were creepy, hobos, rail-riders, beards and filthy knotted hair, scars, dead-eyed, hollow-cheeked, tobacco-stained teeth, fingers, lips. Once in a while an eye looked back at me and said, "How did I get here? I was not what I am."

I learned when to look, when to look away. "Clean around the tents, muck the back lot, pile the dung over there, don't touch the girls and don't suck on that bottle till you're done." And etch another line in my memory bank while you're at it.

One of them felt different. We were in Washington, on the Olympic peninsula, when I hired Barney Quinn, a WWII veteran. This broken shadow of a man actually stormed the beaches of Normandy. Unlike most of these *wobblies*, as Tony liked to call them, there was a faint glimmer in his eyes, like maybe someone was home or had been once.

One evening after Barney had raked up the yard and got a couple of bucks for his efforts, I cracked open two beers and offered one to him and we sat cross-legged on rolled up canvas and talked.

"So," I said, "what happened after the war?"
"Docs said I got 'shell shock,'" he said. "Lot of us came back this way. Can't hold down a reg'lar job so I live off a small pension. But I always come by when you guys are in town."

"You like the circus?"

"Yeah, it pulls me outta myself. I can't sleep right, you know. I can't stay awake right neither. Don't make no sense but that's the way it's been for fifteen years. Can't sleep 'cause of the dreams, they wake me. Sometimes they sneak up during the day."

He pulled on the bottle, smiled painfully at me. "How old are you son?"

"Twenty-two," I lied as always.

"No shit. That's how old I was when I signed up to fight the Krauts. Twenty fucking two. I can't ever be that again. I'm about a hundred now and I ain't never gonna get any younger.

"Ever kill anyone kid?"

I tried not to show any emotion but I swallowed hard. I imagine people have had conversations like this but I hadn't. "Er..., huhn, ah, ... no," finally got squeezed out of my throat.

"Didn't think so. Why would you have? Twenty-two and we ain't at war with no one and you don't look like no banger. .... I have. Stuck a bayonet in the stomach of some German kid. Looked like he was younger 'n me, empty blue eyes. I left him lying in the mud and I'm spending the rest of my fuckin' life convincing myself I saved the world."

Barney stood up. "Thanks for the beer, kid. I'll see you tomorrow, yeah?"

For the first time I did not mind being called "kid." I watched Barney walk across the lot. Wasted lives. Depressed, disturbed, demented, depraved, despised. "Fuck a duck," I muttered to the night and headed to my truck.

XXIII   1960 - Late August

We were completing the circuit, heading back south, hitting up other towns, ones more inland. Tony was driving back to LA to meet with Ken to plan the fall run. I went with him and as we cruised along in the Caddy we talked, as we often did, about shoes and ships and sealing wax and whether we had wings.

"Look," I said. "I've been thinking about staying on past the summer," a comment greeted with a troubling silence. I was puzzled. I thought he'd be pleased or at least flattered. But, no, there was just an infuriating silence. He slowed the car a bit and stared across at me, with that raised eyebrow.

"Xero," he said. Long pause.... "Kid," another pause..., "yeah, 'kid.' I know, you hate being called 'kid' but, well, face it, that's what you are. And, you know, *kid*," Unnecessary emphasis, I thought. I've got your fucking point. "You've been playing a sweetheart of a game these past months and I thought you had your head about you. Maybe I was wrong."

"What the hell are you talking about," I protested.

"Xero," Tony kept starting off with my first name, which was more than a little disconcerting. "Xero, innocent little Greek boys don't run away and join the circus."

"Wha, what, whoa, ..." I babbled. "What the hell are you talking about? What do you mean, 'innocent' boys,' 'innocent *Greek* boys'? Jesus, man, I love this life. And what the fuck was that 'little' crap?"

Tony just laughed. I realized I had never seen him laugh, smile yes, chuckle sure, but not let it all loose. But he was laughing now. As he calmed down, he looked over at me again, this time with genuine affection in his eyes. I hadn't seen that before either.

"How old are you kid? Nineteen, twenty?" I'd been peddling the same lie that I was twenty-two and, of course, poor innocent little Greek boy, I thought I was believed.

"I'm twenty," I answered, slightly embarrassed. "But I don't see what difference that makes."

"What's your old man do? Doctor, lawyer, college teacher, something like that, right?" He paused. "How'd you end up out in California anyway, 'cause I *know* you're not from around here. I've been running you through my mind for a while now."

"You've been what?"

"Jesus, kid. You do know you just can't show up on the stoop of a con artist and not expect to get looked over pretty close. So, here's what I'm thinking. I'm thinking you're from the East and you flunked outta school."

"Go fuck yourself," I countered and instantly wished I hadn't.

"Oh, that's good. You do know how pathetic you sound."

I mumbled something incoherent and looked out the window.

"I'm sniffing the breeze here kid and I smell middle-class. Yeah, I saw the elbow patches. I'm getting an aroma, one of those... what'd they decide to call them a couple years back? Ivy schools? Yeah, Ivy League. Right. Ivy."

He looked over at me and started laughing again. "Xero, you should see your face," he said, pounding on the top of the steering wheel. "You did, you got your ass tossed out of some Ivy League outfit. I'm gonna go with some big city school, Penn or maybe Columbia."

Tony looked over at me; I had lost any shot of holding onto a poker face. He smiled, raised that eyebrow again and said, "Gotcha!"

It was done so smoothly I found I couldn't even get angry. Oddly, I found myself laughing. "What the flying fuck is going on here?" I asked helplessly. "I've been careful. I never told you any of that stuff."

Tony just snickered some more. So I launched again, feebly, as I tried to paste my torn ego back into something familiar. "Okay, *boss*," I began, as if that "boss" bit was going to have any impact. "Yeah, my dad's a college prof. He's a linguist. I am, as you guessed, from New York, and, yeah, I got my butt sort of semi-bounced from Columbia."

I paused for a bit mainly to give Tony time to chuckle. "Are you really that good? Or is it that obvious?"

Tony laughed again. "I'm pretty good but, well you know, you sorta got a neon sign blinking over your head. Besides, you kinda remind me of me."

"Is that good? ... Or not?" I asked, not sure I wanted an answer.

"Dunno, kid. Do you?"

We were now on the northern edges of Los Angeles. Tony stayed on the coast road heading toward Santa Monica. "I'll let you off at your sister's, ok?"

"But I thought we were going to Ken's. I was looking forward to this. I was even hoping he'd be sober."

"Very funny. And I suppose you were gonna ask him for a full-time job, right?"

"Well, yeah," I said and I knew I sounded petulant. "I assumed one of you'd have something for me in the off season."

"Xero," first name again, "you've made some pretty good money this summer, all of it in the dark and," he smiled almost evilly, "I suspect you learned about a few other things." That damn eyebrow bounced up again. "Do me a favor, my little wandering Greek, take a long look. This isn't for you. Go home, go away before I stop liking you so much."

Silence now seemed best. We rode up to Arianna's. A part of me wanted to yell at Tony, cuss him out, another to kiss him. I hated being told what to do. I think I was born that way. I drove my parents nuts. My mom said she first spotted it when I was three years old; she said when she tried to help me with something I'd stamp my feet and say loudly, "No, I do it my byself."

I thought of myself as a loner in a communal world with a simple want, to follow my own bent, my own personal gleam, to understand the world on my terms, to dance to the song I sang in my head, boogie to the faint rhythms of drums I claimed I could hear. And I was afraid, afraid I'd never get to do this, afraid I would.

I'd been a lucky little immigrants' son, an innocent child of a quiet decade and I'd been left pretty much alone. But this luxury had spoiled me. "You," a voice whispered in my head, "innocent *boy*, postpubescent *kid*, ungrateful *son* are not supposed to get this lucky. You're supposed to be fucked over. So pay attention."

So I sat there and stewed. But as I stewed I knew I was beat. Tony read me like a roadside billboard. I was so cool; I'd "run away with the circus," really. Maybe, maybe not.

"Thanks for the ride," I said as I dragged my duffle out of the back seat. "If I decide to stay, I'll give you a ring. Love to Bobbi, ok?"

"Sure kid, it's your life. Whatever you say. Be good. You got my number so stay in touch, yeah?"

Part II

XXIV. 1960 – Late August, September, October
❧

At the airport, Anna and Billy were smiling a bit too happily to suit me but I understood. I waved goodbye, stepped onto the plane and was hit with a sense of unease at returning to what everyone else seemed to think was a normal life. I found my seat in the very last row and hunkered down for a solid bout of contemplative navel picking. The threads running through my head all seemed to converge on a singular querulous end: Now what? I heard no answers.

In New York I threw myself into the suffocating, comforting embrace of my mother who smacked me on the head a little harder than I thought I deserved. Tales of my run-ins with the sheriff, "my" judge and Joe Friday had clearly made the rounds. The circus gig seemed to have been reduced to a mere footnote – though not in my mind.

With the surprised blessings of Dean Housemann, I was re-enrolled at Columbia. I found an apartment, a fourth floor walk-up in midtown Manhattan. It was small, drafty, inconvenient and cheap. That last one trumped the others. The folks were footing the bills and I knew the accumulating debt could not be repaid in coin.

They called this West Side neighborhood Hell's Kitchen. It was alive, gritty, testy, rough and felt, so long as I stayed just outside the flow, like a walk on the soft side of danger. It didn't take me long to stumble on O'Shannon's, an Irish pub that felt like it was torn from one of the rougher neighborhoods of Dublin and shipped intact to 9th Avenue. Henry Shannon was the owner and barkeep and I found here the joys of Guinness and the embracing warmth of dark walls, gouged bar tops and scarred floors. Henry's family, I discovered after I'd been there often enough for us to feel comfortable with each other, was indeed from Dublin and originally named O'Shannon.

"Dad dropped the 'O,'" Henry explained one cold, rainy evening when I was the only paying customer, "he said he didn't want people to know we was Irish," his voice classic Noo Yawk.

"You can't be serious," I said, trying not to laugh.

"You dunno kid – can't; you're too young," Henry replied, "You can't believe the prejudice against us was.... hell, still is in places."

"Yeah," I replied, ignoring that "kid" thing that I just couldn't shake, "but, Shannon? From O'Shannon?"

"I know, I know. One day I said to him, 'look Pops, you don't wanna be Irish no more? So, why didn't you just change it to Goldberg?'"

"That," I said, "would really have worked."

"Yeah. He just laughed and said, 'Son, I love my roots, and you should too, so I couldn't let it go. But Americans are pretty stupid so maybe they won't know.' So, when I opened the pub, the 'O' went back up."

I spent much of the first few weeks wandering the streets of my new home. It was another circus with its own smells and sounds. It was New York, Manhattan, where I'd lived most of my life, but this nook felt different. Its texture was uneven, quirky, with its narrow canyons of tenements, four, five stories high, rusty fire-escapes screening crumbling stonework, leaky windows, many with hopeful flower boxes, the street corners anchored by groceries, newsstands, delis, pawn shops, bars.

The docks on the Hudson were magnetic, busy with truckers, haulers, winches and cranes; stuff coming in, other stuff going out. The waterfront gutters were sooty, oil-streaked. Scrawny cats prowled the alleys for scraps. Tough guys, who looked like their job was to look that way and make sure you knew it, sat and stood about in knots.

I walked around trying to be unseen, my blue Dodger's cap pulled over my hair, dirty jeans and engineer boots. It felt familiar, like I was back at the barn and here, as there, I tuned my ear to the language of the street, to absorb its accent, the lilt of Dublin that made its mark on the city's sounds. I saw Bobby Joe in the eyes of local bullies and Irish gangsters. But I was a spectator now; it was all up there on the big screen.

I went home for dinner at least once a week, talked politics with Dad, and ate my mother's food. I told Alkaios how much I respected him and Hanna how much I loved her cooking and really meant it now that I was eating, in an unordered sequence, take-out chicken, pizza and those hideous things called "TV frozen dinners." But I could sense the tension, more with each trip downtown, like it was before I took off on my walkabout. The folks were edgy. I felt my mother's sideways glances when she thought I wasn't looking, like she was trying to peer into the cracks of the façade I'd erected. She loved me, I knew, but she did not trust me. Not anymore.

I was trying. No trips to the race track, no more ZEP. I hadn't even seen Flathead Freddy or Dickless. I had pressed my nose against the glass of Julie's Billiards but resisted its worn, brass door handle. I had been in class on more days than not and was finding that this acting-right bit wasn't so bad. Maybe, just maybe, I could stay on this metaphoric Conestoga. My well-honed sense of curiosity was getting nibbled at by history and political science and I was beginning to wonder if I might not make a good lawyer.

One frigid morning I smiled at the bemused face in the mirror as the heat struggled to make it to my floor. I had a freshly stropped straight-razor in one hand and my newest affectation, a pig's bristle brush which I could not pass up despite its cost, in the other. I acknowledged the face. "You know 'kid,'" it whispered, "this just might turn out to be fun."

XXV. 1963 – March
⁓

I surprised myself, two years of acing courses in politics, math and economics. Even dad was impressed. As spring announced itself in droplets from melting icicles rhythmically pinging on my window sill, I found myself at a social thrown by the Pre-Law Society. I was wearing my new normal life outfit: creased chinos, Columbia tie with its stylized lions, obligatory elbow-protected tweed jacket and tassel loafers with taps on the heels that crisply announced my movements along the polished floors of Warren Hall. I knew how I looked. I felt like a fraud.

The Pre-Law Society conjured up images of a troop of primates on a savannah. Interactions were marked by displays of posturing, misrepresentation and much pompous huffing and puffing. Those months with the circus were the right internship; I knew how to play this game. A dram of suck-up to a noted lawyer brought in to give a talk, a dollop of goody-two-shoes in class, a pleasant "hello" to the department secretary, plans to aid the downtrodden, pro bono, stage-whispered upwind from the very professorial Armin Harmoninsky, Esq., pre-law advisor and, apparently, distinguished legal scholar, and I found myself being treated like a grown-up. Piece o' cake.

I was leaning awkwardly in the 'v' where the two far walls met. This was my observer's shop and I was trying to fade into the flocked wallpaper, the better to take in the room. Harmoninsky smiled and glided across the room to my corner. How does he do that? I thought as I watched this odd man, who was a tad less than six feet, rail thin, with prematurely graying hair, bright gray eyes and an upbeat, if slightly eccentric, disposition come toward me. He shouldn't move like that; he should shamble or stutter-step, not this reptilian, soundless grace. I did what I'd learned to do in these moments of fragility, smile warmly and nod a greeting.

"I think, Mr. Konstantakis," Harmoninsky's voice was as liquid and flowing as his body, "that you ought to consider running for Society President next year."

"Me?" I replied, more than a bit surprised, "Why me?"

"Because," he said with a cryptic grin, "you stand in corners at these little soirées and you are an appropriate head-nodder."

Harmoninsky held his head at a slight angle which made those eyes even more penetrating and a small smile leaked out of him. A soft ominous sound went off in my head. It wasn't my reliable bullshit detector; it was close but the pitch was off. The clenching in my gut said "Look here son, you are in danger, more than in Hell's Kitchen at midnight, for there you can merely lose your life." I tried to return the same small smile and decided I absolutely would not ask Harmoninsky what the hell he meant by that crack. Instead I nodded and said "Well, now, maybe," fairly sure this was what was expected.

XXVI. 1963 - April, May

"Lydia? No one's named Lydia anymore," I said when we were introduced at a Pre-Law party that Harmoninsky had hinted it would be diplomatic for me to attend.

"Sorry kiddo," she smiled at me, "this one is. It's Lydia, Lydia Demerara, and don't even think about saying another thing right now." I nodded and obediently remained silent but I was thinking, *demerara*, sugar, sweet, coarse and brown, the kind that makes your coffee taste obscenely good and makes good rum good rum. As I stood there looking stupid but quiet, I knew, oh yes I knew, this sugar thing wasn't the point. The point was that I was knocked off my pins. Lydia seemed to be carrying around a secret store of pheromones that were twisting up the neural fibers in my brain.

"My folks," she explained on our first date that weekend, while we sipped coffee sweetened with boring, white, processed sugar and shared a piece of pie, "said that the family name started out as something different. Dad said he'd seen some old letters that made him think that back in Palermo it was originally something like DiMonierro. Grandpa Alfonso arrived monolingually in 1903 and somewhere between the ship's logs and his first job it got 'adjusted' and we all ended up dark brown sugar."

"Palermo? Your folks are Sicilian?"

"Yup. All of us. Dad was born here but Mom lived there till she was nearly twenty."

This tale of her name hit me in another, unexpectedly sensitive spot. She's Italian? Demerara? I hadn't thought about it. Why should I have? Now I was. Demerara? It could easily have been Greek, couldn't it? I went liberal, reminded myself how I was raised. Progressive. Diversity is good. Who gives a tinker's damn anyway? Tony Piccolo, I do believe, is Eyetalian and how about those higher-than-life flying Pirellis and Judy, Ricco's kid? My mother had snuck up on me again.

"It's my freaking mother," I screamed inside my head so loudly that I worried that Lydia, font of sexuality, alluring and gorgeous, might hear it. How did she do this to me? How did I let this happen?

Both sides of Lydia's family came from Sicily and she was very Italian, of solid peasant stock, dark haired, full-breasted, hips that hinted of roundness. She had deep, nearly black, flashing eyes behind a pair of most intellectual-looking glasses and a large mouth which she used like a musical instrument, cajoling, laughing, arguing. She was a couple of inches shorter than me but it felt like she was looking me straight in the eye. And she could arch her left eyebrow and speak several languages with it.

"My folks," I said, as we felt each other out, "came over a lot later, 1935 to be exact. It was a good time to get the hell out of there. They were already married. Dad came to teach historical linguistics, which is pretty esoteric stuff, but NYU really wanted him and they did most of the paperwork. So we got to keep 'Konstantakis' which may or may not have been a blessing."

"Where did that 'Xero/Zero' come from?" Lydia arched that eyebrow, which I found also spoke the language of seduction.

"Ah, hmm, well, … my, hmm… real name is Xerxes. Apparently Mom insisted on a heroic name. Dad didn't think it was a good idea for a boy born in the US but, as he told me one day, he realized there was no way to win this one and, well you know, it was just funny enough to work."

"Xerxes?" Lydia smiled. "I like it. Sounds very formal, very bold, vaguely god-like."

"Not a god, not even Greek, a Persian king around 400 or so B.C. Apparently a pretty tough guy, ruthless but mortal. The name translates, unhappily, as 'ruler of heroes.' By the time I started school I knew I did not need this name," I said, looking down at my fingers which had taken to rolling a pencil back and forth like it was some fetish. "Kids are cruel and funny names are like bull's-eyes and 'Xerxes-Jerksies' and 'Hey Xerkoff-Jerkoff' were kind of getting to me."

"I kind of like that last one," Lydia said with an evil smile.

"It hit me one day that it was easier to change my name than keep fighting over it and the sound of 'zero' was just right. Ambiguous, cryptic and, to satisfy my dad, amusing. I like it a lot. And," I smiled looking up at her face, eager and open, "it's a lot better than Ted."

"Ted?"

"Yeah, full name is Xerxes Theodore Konstantakis. The Theodore thing is inserted somewhere in the name of about half of the male Greeks in my generation, the other half got stuck with Nikolas."

"Well, I do think it's cute, if nothing else," she said and reached over and gently stroked the back of my wrist and I knew at that moment that I was finished, done. It was all over.

It may be for the best, it may not be but there wasn't going to be any way to do anything but follow the script. Decades later, I look down at my right wrist and I can almost feel her soft fingers, the sharp edge of her nails tracing parallel illusions along my arm.

More dates followed. I knew it was time to let Alkaios and Hanna meet Lydia. But first there was work to do. Anna and I had learned early that with our folks it was easier to do damage control before the damage. Dad, despite the worldliness and erudition, could be a bit touchy and didn't particularly like surprises, which Lydia just may be. Mom, for all her no-nonsense embracing of life in America, never completely let go of a certain preference for things from the Aegean which Lydia's family wasn't except by a suspect twist on geography.

At one of my visits downtown, I began gently by telling them about my new friend, then let it slip that this friend was a girl, then that she was a really good friend, then that she was a pre-law student just like I was and smart and cute and... I was actually doing a pretty good job; they seemed to be warming up to the idea that their baby boy had a serious girl friend.

"Very nice, very nice Xerxes," said Hanna. "But I have to ask; I know I shouldn't, but I have to. Is she Greek? Demerara? I don't think this is a Greek name."

I was ready for this. I had a well-crafted answer that turned on a discussion of the reach of the Aegean coastline but never got it out. My father interrupted to ask a question that seemed both innocent and odd. "Does she," he leaned toward me, "wear glasses?"

"Glasses? Huh?" I was ready for probing on geography, ethnicity, ancestry, not this. "Why are you asking?"

"Because I've been reading." And I sat back quietly for we had gone down these twisted paths before. My father liked to take little intellectual voyages, adventures into fields he knew nothing about but where he would end up convincing himself that he did. Apparently he had found a new one.

"Genetics," he said. "It's fascinating. If I had a glimmer of this world thirty years ago I ..."

"... would never have become a linguist," I intoned.

"You do not have to finish my sentences for me," he said with a sly grin. He knows, I thought, exactly what he is doing and isn't the slightest bit embarrassed by it.

"Do you know," he continued not missing a beat, "how many common disabilities, little things like a propensity for caries – that's tooth decay, 'androgenetic alopecia' or baldness in men, 'dyschromatopsia' – colorblindness, all manner of things, have a basis in our genes?"

"Well, yes. I did know about baldness," I said running my hand through my dark curls, and noting how few remained on my father's head, "but 'glasses'?"

"Yes. Myopia. Nearsightedness has familial roots. Does Lydia wear glasses?" he asked again, staring through thick lenses at me, his equally myopic son.

To the patriarch, Lydia was going to be the wrongest of wrong girls for his boy. She was as nearsighted as I was, maybe more. I happened to like this. It felt comfortable, familiar. I liked that she was comfortable with it too. Most girls her age had bought into that "boys won't make passes at girls who wear glasses" crap. Lydia was way above this nonsense and I loved it and her for it.

But "Poppy," the identity Alkaios assumed in my mind when he slipped into one of those I-will-screw-with-my-son's-head moods, seemed to be fixated on this triviality. Poppy didn't seem to care if her family had money, prestige, position. He hadn't asked if she was smart, good looking, had a degree, a job, a criminal record, kids from a former marriage. He seemed willing to accept that she was not an authentic descendant of honored rulers of some tiny Aegean island but, just in passing, son, could it be that she is as blind as a frigging bat?

I hadn't thought about the implications of any of this till now because you just didn't think about this kind of shit when you were dating, screwing and arguing constitutional law till

well past midnight, although not always in that order.
Marriage? It hadn't crossed my mind. Kids? Well, if you
weren't married you didn't have kids, at least not our family.
Nearsighted kids? A bit of a stretch, yes? But Poppy was way
ahead, or way behind, but I could see that he'd got his scholarly
glare all set for her.

XXVII. 1963 – May

We came up out of the subway in the heart of Greenwich
Village and strolled slowly, bearing gifts, wine and flowers,
both of which Lydia wisely insisted on. As we walked through
the gateway into MacDougal Alley she was smitten. The house
was nestled among the rows of small homes, white-washed
stucco, brick, faux Tudor, all variations on the stables that once
sat in this Mews. Going home was like walking into a cloistered
enclave in Oxford.

We stepped off the cobblestones and onto that familiar old
weathered wood that tilted gently this way and that, low
ceilings with newly painted walls bedecked with prints,
portraits of the famous and the not so, landscapes from here
and from there, posters and photos of family and friends, some
eminent, most not. There were many old maps, restored and
elegantly framed – for my father was fond of maps – comfy
chairs and scattered rugs with Persian origins and a dark, creaky
dining room table whose wood was as old and uneven as the
floors with mismatched chairs, all of which appeared to have
been carved centuries ago out of olive wood.

To my surprise – and delight – my father was all warmth
and hugs. Hanna was all atwitter. She'd been prepping for this
since I came back from my "wander" as she had taken to calling
it. She wanted grandchildren. Arianna and Billy hadn't given
even a hint that they were thinking along these lines and,

anyway, grandchildren-in-Santa-Monica wasn't the plan. Grandchildren-in-New-York was what lurked behind her bright eyes as everyone got introduced.

"Lydia, I'd like you to meet my folks, Alkaios and Hanna. "Mom, Dad, my 'new best friend' Lydia Demerara."

So the evening unfolded – a martini that drained any lingering tension from the room, a dinner that seemed to have slipped out of a thousand years of peasant culinary wisdom tucked inside my mother and coffee served alongside tiny delicate glasses of ouzo and a plate of crispy, rich almond cookies which she presented with a flourish as *amigdalota* – and my folks got to know Lydia and she them and, of course, a little bit more of me. Then, to my growing sense of outrage, my father dragged the conversation down a not terribly subtle path.

My father – sometimes I think of him warmly, almost a friend, as "Dad," sometimes more formally, when he becomes "Alkaios" and sometimes, like that evening, as "Poppy." He has a rich sense of history and knowledge of civilizations modern and ancient, of languages living, dead and on their way that way. He could be wise, engaging, diplomatic but "Poppy" was never far away. Code words kept sliding into the conversation, clothed in his soft Aegean accent. He said things like, "Well, Lydia, is that really how you see things?" and there was this tiny elongation of *see*. Or "That's one way to look" ... pause ... "at it." Over dessert he picked up a bottle of ouzo and looked through it at her and smiled, "You know, I've always been fascinated by how a thick glass creates these rounded, blended visions. Take a look through this at the flowers on the table Lydia and tell me if they aren't lovely this way."

I knew exactly what he was up to. Lydia didn't appear to. As the evening wound down, my mother, predictably, got out the family photos. Lydia seemed to love every minute of it. It was right out of some sticky, treacle-soaked episode of *Father Knows Best*. She kept laughing and grabbing Alkaios's hand. I couldn't tell whether she was laughing at the photos, at Alkaios and Hanna, at me, at my growing annoyance with my parents or was just having a very good time. Several of the photos were small, taken with a cheap Kodak camera. Lydia did what I do, what we nearsighted have all learned to do. She took off her glasses and held the photos up to within a inch of her nose. Alkaios waited a minute, smiled and said, "Hmmm Lydia, you look even better without glasses."

"That," she said later, "was just wonderful. I adore your parents."

"Really?" I said, trying my very best to raise just one eyebrow though, as always, both of them popped up making me look, as always, not wise, not insightful and certainly not seductive. More like surprised, which I realized I shouldn't be. "You liked my dad?"

"Absolutely. A charmer. Old world, to the bone. How could I not?"

And, of course, I knew this.

XXVIII. 1963 – July

Hanna wanted us to set the date. It was going to get set but I needed to talk. For one, I didn't know all that much about her. Italian, okay. Grandpa Alfonso, sure. Mom emigrated as a teenager, fine. Dad from Brooklyn? I thought this was right but I wasn't that sure. My bullshit detector hadn't gone off but I'd never had to see if it worked in a sea of screwed up hormones. But this crap was trivial. I didn't care where she was from. More importantly, I thought, Lydia didn't know who *I* was.

We were in my kitchen. It was a cool summer night, the windows were open and the breeze whispered in off the Hudson. We had a bottle of ouzo which Lydia had realized was just Greek grappa. She liked using an eye dropper, plink, plink, plink one teardrop of water at a time and watching the swirling milky clouds that formed. She was more sensible, more coherent and more deeply interesting than anyone I had ever gotten close to. Worse, she seemed to really love me. I worried that I was not the person she seemed to love.

"Look, we have to talk," I blurted out, realizing too late that this was a really stupid way to start, like stepping on a land mine. Lydia's eyebrow arched menacingly.

"I'm not what you think I am." Gag, worse. I don't know what I was thinking. She was sure to take that as an insult, which it was. I suddenly wished I were an agent for Interpol or a hired killer or an alien from another planet. Maybe then I could get away with this crap.

What I was, of course, was quite ordinary, a smart "kid" with a probing curiosity, intrigued by legitimacy but unable and unwilling to quell the circus's siren call. She just kept looking at me with a vaguely anticipatory smirk. I decided to try again, another tack. "You remember I told you about that year, when I 'ran away with the circus?'"

"Sure," Lydia smiled giving me some hope. "I loved the story, I'm looking forward some day to meeting Tony or Bobby Joe, if he's not in prison somewhere."

"Well," I pushed forward, "the way I see it, I didn't 'run away,' I went home. That's really me, Lydia. Really. I'm a bum. Oh, I'm smart, I like opera, I read a lot. Hell, I may even be a lawyer some day but, in my gut I am a low-life, a degenerate; I am drawn to the soft underbelly of life."

I paused, stared down at the table top as though inspiration could be found in the lightly speckled Formica, then back at Lydia who continued peering over her glasses at me with that infuriating smirk, brow tightened, her nostrils slightly flared. She said nothing, which I took as an invitation to push on.

"I was happy with circus folk. I'm comfortable with my cronies in the pool hall, the race track. I've been being a good boy but it isn't really me and it doesn't feel right. I've played poker with guys who would steal their granny's social security check to bankroll a game. My best friend at the track is a bookie. That world resting just below the surface is mine. I won't leave it."

I expected that she would now stand up, waver between smacking me for wasting her time or burst into tears, maybe both. But she didn't. She sat there, quietly, that eyebrow arched in a mix of curiosity and threat and it dawned on me that I still hadn't quite grasped what I had gotten myself into.

"So?" she said thrumming her fingers on the table, nails clicking like a car with several stones caught in a tire's tread. "And I'm supposed to be surprised by this?"

"I mean it," I said, a tad louder than I needed to. "This is no bullshit." I got on my feet. "I'm deadly serious. I'm a gambler, a poker player. I'm on the wagon now but," and I leaned down hands on the table trying my very best, intimidate-Rudy voice, "I am just about ready to dive off."

Lydia smiled, reached out and gently stroked the back of my hand and said, "I know. I felt it when you told me about Tony, about the poker games at Zeta eat something or other. You don't think I see your face when you watch a football game, a horse race? I see that look. I *know* that look. And, of course, you've noticed that I'm still here, yes?"

I sat down again, my brow furrowed, eyes pouring confusion and bewilderment into the room. I looked at her closely and waited. After a moment she leaned ever closer. "I do love you, you know. Not in spite of being a gambler or a poker player but perhaps because of it.

"But," and she leaned back against the thin rails of the kitchen chair, "since we've shifted gears, I'll tell you what I am worried about." She was looking back at me, arms folded across her chest. "I'm worried that you won't learn to suffer fools more graciously, find ways to be more honest with your parents. I'm worried," she said leaning forward, "that you won't learn to adjust, to bend with winds and tides you cannot control.

"I, my dearest, have a damn good idea of where I'm going in my life and if you want to join me with your 'degenerate baggage' that's fine. But," she looked at me, alluring and menacing in equal measures, "you better be a fucking good degenerate; I'm not wasting my time with some half-assed one."

I stared at her and realized I needed to start breathing again. I poured another glass of ouzo, sprinkled water in it and tried to read my future in the clouds that swam before me.

"I love you, so much it scares me. Let's go to bed. There's a lot of time in front of us."

I had told Lydia about everything from the year of my walkabout but Judy. I saw no reason to, mainly because I didn't want to hear any similar confessionals from her. But as we made love long into the night I understood, deeply, just how important that evening in her trailer was and would be for the rest of my life.

XXIX. 1963 – August

꩜

Lydia moved into the flat in Hell's Kitchen. Dad wasn't terribly pleased with this "living in sin" thing, as he insisted on calling it. Hanna looked at it as a sign that we were really serious and her Xerxes will make Lydia an "honest woman" before fall – and by next year....

But there was another family to settle with. We still had to run the Italian version of the familial gauntlet. Demeraras had to be appeased; Italians needed to learn to love Greeks. Lydia hadn't told me much beyond the Sicilian ties and that her dad was blue collar. She grew up in Brooklyn, in Bensonhurst, but I didn't really know what that meant. I was born in Astoria, Queens. Brooklyn was where you could not get by subway so no one went there, except to Ebbets Field and then we never quite grasped that we were in Brooklyn. We were just at a ballpark. Then we moved to Manhattan, to that small, quaint house in MacDougal Alley Mews, and Brooklyn was even further away. I liked to joke that it was somewhere in Ohio.

"Bensonhurst," Lydia laughed, "as you will see, isn't anything other than Bensonhurst. But you may soon think you were back in the circus."

She led me to the subway, explaining that it actually continued south, past the Village, over one of the funny bridges that connected Manhattan with Ohio and wended its way to where she grew up and still returned regularly to be amused, loved, charmed and confused by her family, rather like I was by mine – but with less subtlety. We headed off, destination 69th Street just off Bay Parkway. We carried offerings of flowers and a bottle of Chianti, wrapped in a straw basket.

"They call this area 'Brooklyn's Little Italy,'" explained Lydia as we came down the steps from the elevated line. This seemed right as I scanned the shops and stores – *Angelo's Barbershop, Emilio's Pork Store, R. Provenzano, DDS* – and smiled at the group of elderly white-haired women, who sat on folding chairs in front of one of the row houses that formed an impenetrable wall down the street, chattering away in Italian.

It didn't look to me like a place for Greeks or, for that matter, Blacks or Hispanics. But it shared something deep with the Lower East Side and its immigrant Jews, with Hell's Kitchen steeped in Catholic Irish green, with Astoria rich with the culture of my people. Ethnic groups established their turf, poured a new and rich identity onto the streets, the parks, the schools. Over time they moved, were absorbed or pushed off stage and in rolled their replacements. The look, the feel, even the smells would change and yet, at some level, the core remained the same.

The Demerara house was classic, the opening shot for a gritty urban movie. Two alabaster lions sat impressively on their haunches on the low walls of whitewashed brick that framed the steps. Several limestone pots with dying ivy draping over the edges were on the tiny front lawn. The off-white front door had three locks, a "Welcome" knocker and the door bell had a note saying "press twice" and when it was opened I found myself gazing upon a two-foot high crucifix on the wall of the vestibule. Carved in dark wood, Jesus bedecked with a crown of thorns, nails in all the proper places, loins covered, barely, and a touch of red below the wound under the rib cage, it was not subtle – another reminder of the differences along Ionian shores.

The greeting from the Demeraras was as effusive as the Konstantakis' was subdued. I was immediately hugged and kissed on both cheeks which were chucked up like I was a marmoset by an Italian mother who spoke with a flowing Italian accent. She looked like she just walked off the set of a local production of an *opera buffa*: flowered print dress, black hair askew with hints of wispy gray, one knitting needle stuck in from the left, one from the right, glasses hanging from a mother of pearl chain around her neck, a throw around her shoulders and, of course, sensible shoes.

An older sister, Selma? Selena? looked me over like I was a piece of pork, wondering whether I needed larding or had enough fat on me for her sister. Rosalia, the youngest, eyed me like I was, verily, that slab of ham. A brother and an uncle (I thought, I'd lost track), smacked me on my upper arms. And then, Papa. Papa slowly hauled his blue collar self up out of his chair which, like the matching sofa, to my horror and confusion, was entirely encased in clear plastic and rolled across the shag rug and stood silently in front of me. I wondered if this was how a slave, fresh off the boat from West Africa felt, on the block, naked, in front of a buyer. "Strong enough, 'boy?' Enough endurance, 'kid?' Good enough for our family, 'son?'"

The Demeraras spoke a version of English I was only vaguely familiar with. Many words began with a "dih" sound oddly akin to the Dublin that filled the air at O'Shannon's, others had slippery vowels that I'd heard from Abe Vigoda or Jimmy Durante and still others found their anticipated endings chopped unsympathetically off. But, to my surprise, Lydia spoke it fluently. I finally understood what my father meant when he talked about linguistic "code switching."

Lydia's sister Rosalia, the assessor of high grade pork, was the youngest remaining girl in the house and had claimed for herself the role of princess. Big brother Luigi, the only boy, was an auto mechanic with a local Chrysler dealer. I had visions of Frankie, only with a DA haircut and pegged pants. The oldest of the four, Selma, was a part-time beautician and adored in the family for it was she who had blessed the clan with three point five children. She was alone among the Demerara siblings in her fecundity and she was worshipped and I began to understand some of the sideways stares I was getting from momma Tessa who appeared to have, just perhaps, noticed that I was rather nearsighted.

Papa, who was introduced as Sabato or Sabbie, was, as advertised, a blue collar kind of guy only blue here meant cop. "A cop in Bensonhurst," he said to me, "is basically a hood who managed not to get a rap sheet before he applied for the job." As Sabbie told it, when we were on the second bottle of Chianti, "Too many of the guys I've collared are high school buddies." This line had become almost a cliché but I nodded sympathetically. It was clear he meant it. "Dere," he gestured with his glass at unnamed felons, "but fowa de grace of de holy Gawd of my fathers, go I." It was the Bensonhurst version of dinner with Tony and Ken with Abe Vigoda playing the lead.

As the evening wound down, Luigi opened up and I got a glimpse of why Lydia was comfortable with my hibernating degeneracy. Big brother may grind valves and solder mufflers but this was not how he paid for that Caddy out front that he proudly dragged me out to see. It turned out that Luigi ran a little sports book out of, of all places, the race track. Most of his customers were local horseplayers, the track a business annex. As he explained, he just tossed off the garage one or two days a week and headed out, paid off winners, collected from losers and, of course, put down a couple of bets.

"But look, man, like you gotta know, I'm not connected," and he paused and bent over conspiratorially toward me as I tracked a finger along the smooth polished fender, "but, well, I know who is and who ain't and I'm careful to make sure that those that are, are kept happy. We are Sicilian and we got roots."

He was, as he told me while we leaned together against the Caddy, part of an office because he needed the cushion against a serious hit on his bankroll. "If I get unbalanced," he explained, "which can happen if too much action comes in on one side, I gotta lay off some with another book or call on my office. Offices are like insurance companies. They give you a bit of protection but you do not fuck with them."

"And the office?" I asked, leaning back on the fender, "Lucchese family, yeah?"

"Oh, you know."

"I know. They leave you alone?"

"Too small. They like being the backup in case I get hit hard they know they can leverage. So far I've stayed away by stayin' small."

"And your dad?"

"My Dad? Course he knows. Shit, man, he's my Pops," Luigi chuckled slyly, "He really don't like it much, but what the fuck's he gonna do? Arrest his kid?"

So we were bound in life, in blood and in Bensonhurst, Sabato the cop, Luigi the small bookie and me, the edge-walker. I knew now why the Italians lost the war. And I thought a singular thought, "Fuggedaboutit."

XXX. 1964 – February

Six months later, with all hatchets buried or well-camouflaged, we gathered to plan the nuptials. Sabbie reserved a private room in a restaurant in Bay Ridge – neutral territory. It started well. Our parents traded compliments, toasted good fortune and did their best to understand each other's eccentric ways of butchering their shared language. Then slowly a new identity emerged. They turned out to be control freaks and worse, thieves, all four of them. By the second glass of wine they had hurled themselves into plans for the wedding, their plans. How big, where, when and, of course, how much.

"Sigh," sighed Lydia when she realized what was happening. "We," she whispered quietly, gently stroking the back of my hand, "are getting married, but it isn't our wedding any more. They," she nodded at the four of them huddled together, "hijacked it."

But the real shocker was when parental joy got shanghaied by history. As the evening grew long, floating on a stream of neutral French wine, minor nuisances seeped out from under ancient, unstable formations. I stared in disbelief as ancestral grudges, nurtured by two millenniums of shuttle invasions from both sides of the Adriatic, leaked out.

My mother was reminded of Mussolini's invasion of Greece in 1940 for she lost a cousin in it – which until then I knew nothing about. Tessa didn't realize this petty little war had happened but took a different slant on Mussolini maintaining that he hadn't been such a bad guy since he had made Italy important again. I watched Lydia's face when this one popped out of her mother. That left eyebrow was arched in a blend of amazement and disappointment and I knew she was, perhaps literally, biting her tongue.

Sabato, it became clear, was not particularly fond of foreigners, except the one who shared his bed, and winced when Hanna's prominent accent made her hard to understand. My father, of course, knew far too much about these primal squabbles, the treaties made and broken, compromises ripped asunder, gods, myths and recipes borrowed and stolen, and retreated into a pained silence.

They ordered another bottle of wine and headed down the rabbit hole, to the nub of it all, the Schism of 1054. None of us, except perhaps my father, had thought about the implications. Rings on the right hands? The left? Will they be exchanged outside? In the vestibule? At the altar? With bearers? Without? Vows? No vows? And who will officiate? Lydia and I watched in dismay as the history of Southern Europe was replayed in a cozy restaurant in Bay Ridge surrounded by Norwegians, Germans and Poles each burdened with their own ethnic mistrusts.

Alkaios emerged from his silence and suddenly blurted out a bizarre rant on traditional Greek Orthodox weddings. "It's *our* way. It's an important ritual. It's how we got married. It's how our daughter *should* have gotten married. It's how our son *will* marry."

"Poppy" was back, drawing a line in the Eastern Mediterranean sand.

"Dad," I said, "I thought you felt that rituals like these were unnecessary, even primitive. Are you serious?"

"I am, Xerxes," and I knew we were all in trouble. Hanna often called me that; Alkaios never did, only Poppy.

"I have a role here," he said. "I'm the elder of my clan." And I knew then why Anna and Billy eloped.

Tessa, who had been sitting quietly since that peculiar defense of El Duce, suddenly cleared her throat, "You heathens," she said in what was awfully close to a wine-fed snarl as her accent got richer and elongated vowels started appearing at the end of words, "abandoned our'a Pope, broke'a from the righteous ways and'a besides, your church isn't'a really Greek and *we*" – I wondered if she meant all Roman Catholics or whether she'd taken on a royal veneer – "object to you'a calling it that."

Sabato interjected angrily, "My Tessa is right. Our family isn't gonna sanctify no marriage not done the Roman way."

Lydia fell against me in open-mouthed shock. Sabbie backing up his wife was something she'd not seen before; her mother sprouting a set of serious cojones was equally unprecedented and that "sanctify" coming from her father was the topper. She started to laugh. It began small, with a snicker, grew into a noisy giggle and pulsed out of her with a raspy nasal outburst so loud that the whole table stopped.

"You four are hysterical!" she blurted out. "I've been sitting here listening to this insanity – ancient civilizations, crazy tug-boat wars over islands, oil, lands, women, egos, who the hell knows.

"Guess what, *patres familias*," she said, staring malevolently at Alkaios and Sabato, "and *matres familias*," she added glaring at our mothers bound together in obfuscation, "I'm taking back my day. Me and my good friend here," she said chucking me gently on the jaw.

"We're going to have a 'joint' wedding. Two priests, one in a well-turned collar, celibate and devout to keep you, my dearest parents, happy. The other," and she paused and nodded at Alkaios and Hanna, "black-frocked and bearded for those from the peninsula to the east. And frankly I don't care if they get squirrely about sharing the pulpit. They will act right and ecumenicalism will mark this day, *our* day."

A welcome silence fell and my father started to laugh. "Lydia," he said leaning over and giving her an awkward hug for he had to reach across me, "you are quite wonderful, and you're right. Thank you. I agree. I hope you all do. We shall heal the Great Schism, if only for a few short hours." Sabbie nodded in assent, lifted his glass and toasted the mediated solution. And I was, once more, amazed at what had graced my life.

XXXI. 1964 – November

Fall was ebbing as the beauticians and the linguists, the cops and the small bookies, the editors, princesses, mechanics and a couple of maybe-some-day lawyers assembled for the reclaimed day. Anna and Billy flew in. Frankie arrived with the same girl friend. I liked that. It's hard to imagine a couple lasting that long based just on a blow job.

Forgotten cousins and uncles and aunts whose names all blurred into each other poured in through revolving doors with presents and envelopes and hugs. Bensonhurst opened its gates and from it spilled Lydia's friends and relatives and, of course, a couple of wannabe gangsters from down 68th Street courtesy of Luigi. Henry Shannon – who I had recently discovered already was one – and his wife Janice were the representatives of Hell's Kitchen.

Only Tony was not there. I wrote to him but never heard back. I called him. No answer. I called again. No answer. "Just as well," I said to myself but didn't believe it.

Lydia and I sat at the head table to see and be seen. I had my ring on my right hand to mark my Eastern origins, Lydia on her left to heal the Mediterranean divide. Her siblings Luigi, Rosalia and Selma with her brood and blustering spouse had set up camp on one side of the spacious ballroom surrounded by the Bensonhursters all speaking that rollicking argot, that crafty, fractured language that had spilled out of mean streets, bars and clubs and improbably made its way into America born by a generation of actors and comics who knew just how heartbreakingly funny life was.

I scanned tables, smiled at how well-programmed we all were, like some cultural anthropologist wrote the damn script and we all just skittered around playing our assigned roles. The boys all had pompadoured hair, smoothed and tapered with fine-tined combs they tucked into jacket pockets; young girls sat awkwardly with emerging bosoms protected by ersatz pearls, hoping to be noticed, hoping not to be; children in unlikely suits and ties tippled sneakily from half empty glasses on their way toward adulthood and the knowledge of pain.

Greeks lined the other side. As resolutely as the Demeraras embraced the working class ethic of Bensonhurst, so the Konstantakises cleaved to middle-class intellectualism and the professions. Our side of the hall was dotted with physicians and lawyers, professors and editors, businessmen in their own tuxedoes and, thankfully, a mechanic or two to keep everyone honest.

Some of my clan still spoke Greek. I liked this. My folks had hurled themselves into America and made English the language of the home. Dad said it was so that they would become truly fluent and meld into their adopted land. Arianna and I never learned Greek, which was just idiotic. How in hell could a linguist raise monolinguals? The only times I heard Greek in the home was when they didn't want us to know what they were talking about. So I sat there catching snippets, the vaguely familiar cadence, the language that seems to have no special tone, no vibrant quality. German rasps, French glides on tightened lips, Spanish is quick, its phonemes densely packed. Greek? ... Greek sounds like English you can't understand.

The celebrations, as ecumenical as the ceremony had been, rolled on with but a deaf ear to language or dialect. We toasted each other with ouzo and grappa and danced ethnic dances. Italians snapped their fingers over their heads as though they'd done it all their lives. Greeks hugged anyone close and threw manly fists glancingly off elbows and shoulders. Greeks toasted the future, children, the sea, learning and glories past and maybe to come once more. Italians drank to family, the soil, honor and vengeance. Lydia and I looked at each other tiredly.

At that moment there was a sudden, unnatural hush like all the air had been sucked out of the room. It was one of those random moments where silence punctuates cacophony, a chancy instant where everyone seems to inhale at the same time and an eerie quiet forestalls talk. All stopped to listen for the thing that does not happen. But this time it did, for a rant not foreign to anyone in the room, except perhaps a few still suckling at the breast, was heard from the corridor behind our table. It was drenched in anger and steeped in alcohol.

"What the fuck are you doing, you little prick," snarled a female voice quivering with rage. Lydia and I recognized it instantly and with shared distress: Janice Shannon.

"This cannot be good," I said, for anything out of the ordinary that involved Henry was worrisome. Henry, I'd discovered, was part of the Irish Mafia that controlled their patch of Midtown turf. You didn't run a restaurant or open a newsstand within several blocks of O'Shannon's without buying protection. It was Henry you bought it from for only Henry could protect you from, well, Henry.

I liked the guy and spent probably too much time downing pints of stout and digging as deeply into his gut as he would let me. Lydia liked him too for he was clever and worldly. He was very protective of Janice whose condition was not uncommon in bored Irish spouses with access to cheap booze.

Lydia looked up and said, "Shit. I hope she's pissed at Henry and not someone from my side of the aisle."

That first outburst raised a few eyebrows but it wasn't close to what followed as Janice's voice grew louder and as she turned shakily around, it carried directly into the now deathly silent ballroom, "An' fuck your whole family, bunch a' greasy fuckin' Dagos."

"Nope, not Henry," I grimaced as I rushed into the corridor just as a disheveled Janice was aiming an awkward kick at a teenager with a badly fitting tuxedo, a flushed face graced with pimples and eyes that flickered back and forth between embarrassment and rage.

She whirled unsteadily around at me and screamed, "He grabbed my tit, that fuckin' Whop. I'll kick his fuckin' Dago ass back to fuckin' Italy."

The kid was Lydia's cousin Sal and he was, alas, a greasy piece of street scum. He probably thought he could cop a feel from a drunken broad at a wedding.

Sal whined weakly in my direction, "Like man, she was comin' on to me, bendin' over and showin' her bazooms."

The three of us stopped to breathe and for one tiny slip of time there was utter calm. I stood there my eyes darting between the quivering Sal in the middle of the corridor ostentatiously adjusting his tuxedo jacket with that outward flicker of his arms, thumbs downward, that teenage punks seemed to think was threatening and the wobbly Janice leaning over, hair disheveled, the top of her dress askew, thinking how to handle this when all choice was removed.

Luigi was first through the door followed quickly but unsteadily by Selma's husband and two more pimple-faced adolescents from the Bensonhurst side of the hall, as tuxedo jackets were shed and switch blades suddenly sprouted from hands. Luigi pulled Sal off to the side. One of the offended Demerara clan turned menacingly at Janice, switchblade held pointedly at her face. "What'd you call him? You whore, you fucking Mi...."

That was all he got out because Henry, who had come around the corner from the rest room, blindsided him and plowed his shoulder into his lower back. The knife skidded across the floor. Henry rolled the kid over, pulled his head up by his hair and hit him full across his left cheek. Luigi shoved Sal away and jumped onto Henry's back and Janice took off her shoe and awkwardly, drunkenly swung it at Luigi's head.

The next wave arrived a few seconds later and, predictably, it was made up mainly of Greeks, one of whom tackled the hapless Sal who was shrinking against wall where Luigi had left him. Others milled around shoving anyone who got close and making odd growly noises and other mostly empty threats. These late-comers didn't seem like they wanted a real fight but felt somehow obliged to act like they did.

I like to think of myself as pretty good in a crisis but there wasn't a lot I could do except yell, "Stop it!" and "What the hell are you all doing?" which was pretty useless and couldn't be heard anyway.

While I was bleating impotently, Sabato appeared in the doorway and I wondered if the plans I had for my life, nascent, still ill-formed, might be disappearing. As he moved into the corridor he reached down, pulled up his right pants leg with its elegant, satin tuxedo stripe and levered a pistol out of its ankle strap. His face was red with wine and dancing, anger and ethnic insult. It was a face that wasn't pretty at the best of times and these were not those.

"Hold it right there," he bellowed and fired one shot into the arched ceiling. Everyone in the corridor froze. I glanced around. It lasted but a second, maybe two, a somewhat artless simulacrum, a secular pieta, black tuxedoes, white shirts, Janice's oddly virginal white dress, Henry astride the kid, fist raised, all in unmoving stone. A light plaster snow fell upon us as Sabato reached into the inside pocket of his tuxedo jacket with its shiny lapels and double-folded handkerchief in the breast pocket and pulled out his wallet, flipped it open to reveal his badge.

I had one of those out-of-body, out-of-time moments; the 8-track cassette in my mind reran the tape. I was back on a blisteringly hot day in Tackyville as the puffed-up Bobby Joe waved a shiny piece of fabricated officialdom at a guy who turned out to be a cop. Ah, yesss, but of course. He *is* a cop. And I instantly felt so much better and the room returned to living, embarrassed, flesh.

Sabbie may have had a bit too much to drink but he was a pro and there aren't many things as intimidating as a large man with a badge and a gun when you have neither. Luigi, bleeding from a cut inflicted by Janice's high-heeled shoe, headed to the men's room. Henry stood and let the kid with the now reddening, swollen cheek up. Sal slunk back further against the wall, Sabbie smiled and said "That's better. Thank you all for your cooperation. I think I hear music. Shall we join the party?"

Lydia, in the meantime, had gone over to the band and said, in a voice that could command a brigade of marines, "*Hava Nagila*, play it, now, loudly!"

"What? Why?"

"Because it's Jewish. We've got Italians, Greeks and the Irish ready to restart World War II. Play something Jewish, for Christ's sake," which was pretty funny although no one was quite in the mood for the joke.

And so they did and Lydia grabbed the hands of the two closest children, pushed several women to their feet and into the middle of the ballroom. A hora. They danced around in circles, stamping their feet on the beat and making as much noise as possible. And it worked.

XXXII. 1965 – April, May, June

Living with a spouse wasn't quite like living with a lover. Why? What's changed? Nothing? Something?

We were in the same apartment, wearing the same clothes, blindly following the same daily rituals of the toilet, meals, time together, time apart. We sported a couple of ridiculously expensive gold rings, worn in touching ethnic symmetry; there were various legal documents sitting in a drawer which, I assumed, would eventually get lost as neither of us was very good at keeping track of things stuck in drawers. Even our names were the same.

"I'm keeping Demerara," she had said. "It's mine, sort of, but I've decided I'm not getting pushed around in the name game like poor old grandpa Alfonzo."

"Wise move," I retorted. I'd expected this since she came home with Betty Friedan's *Feminine Mystique* in her bag. "It'll probably save you considerable embarrassment. But we could have some fun here you know. Do that hyphen thing that seems to be going 'round. Wouldn't that be a hoot?"

But names aside there was no doubt. "Married" *was* different. It had a boilerplate feel. Thoughts like "So this is the way married people live," or "Here's the script sweet'ums, now you be a good boy and do your part," nagged at me. Why was this? I reflected back on scenes of my folks as I grew up, of Anna and Billy as I watched them together, other married friends. I saw commonality, overlapping sketches, shared rituals as though they were all caught up in the same social vortex. I knew, even then, that we'd be pulled in, funneled through the narrow bottlenecks of middle-classness. I thought it was maybe okay – if I could continue to fool myself into believing that I actually was making the choices.

Over time, as Lydia and I racked up the days and fell into automatic routines, I discovered that there were other tiny dramas in the theater of the espoused. Back when we were living in sin (thanks Poppy), I had remained immunized from the family of dust bison housed under the bed. I didn't see dirty dishes or care if the windows were opaque from the grunge that floated up from the rough streets below. But with nuptials tied, rituals fulfilled, when legitimacy was a mantle we'd wrapped about our shoulders, Hanna snuck up again. I found myself washing floors, vacuuming, swirling a brush in the toilet bowl and, worse, worrying about these once-foreign niceties of domesticity.

Then odd things began to happen. Is this some plot, a female game? No one said anything but a gentle and relentless metamorphosis of our little fourth-floor box was clearly occurring. I had always kept the utensils in a drawer next to the stove. Suddenly they were in one by the sink. T-shirts, once folded with arms atop each other and creases down the middle, were popping up in drawers folded square with arms inside. Pencils were moved. Funny colored staples and pins held notes on tack-boards, themselves having appeared unbeckoned, hung on the wall by the fridge. I decided to say nothing for as long as possible.

"Marriages call for compromise," Alkaios said. We were having a rare lunch together, down in a tiny Village bistro. He smiled with a grave nod toward the kitchen as though Hanna were back there.

"But does the 'guy' do it all?"

"Maybe, maybe…. Maybe she's compromising too but you don't know. But maybe too it depends on where you live," he said. "Before you married, when you two were, you know, 'shacking up,'" and he laughed quietly, "you were in *your* place, so maybe she didn't want to move *your* stuff. Now it's *our* place, so she's just moving *our* stuff, which means, of course, *her* stuff."

Time passed. I grew accustomed to forks and spoons on the left of the sink where, I realized with some annoyance, they were easier to put away after being washed, to notes tacked on now-painted boards that kept us from missing appointments and saw the benefits of T-shirts folded just so. But I had limits.

The gnaw du jour was trivial but had wormed its way into my consciousness and sat there waiting to be paid its due. Towels. Lydia had a thing with towels. She washed them, regularly, usually once a week but sometimes more often. Then she had this other thing with sheets. She didn't wash them. Oh, she did, but far less often, like once every two weeks, often longer. This little quirk drove me crazy.

"Why do you do this?" I asked her, finally one day, knowing, oh I knew, that this almost certainly wouldn't go well. Lydia had reasons for the things she did, reasons for the things she didn't do and they always were reasonable, although outsiders often lacked the delicacy of mind to grasp why. I, of course, was an outsider.

"Because I like clean towels," she said which should have put an end to it.

"Do you not like clean sheets?" I asked.

"Of course," she said. She knitted her brow and adjusted her glasses to glare at me. This was a signal, what in poker we call a *tell*. Time to fold – except I was like a demented Ann Landers now. I couldn't stop.

"Towels," I said, "are really clean things. They hang on racks, air circulates around them and their job is to dry off bodies that have just been washed," I paused and waited. She said nothing. I continued, sounding like someone making a speech, not having a conversation. Lydia raised that eyebrow again but this time left it up there, hovering above the rim of her glasses.

"Sheets, on the very other hand," I pushed onward, "are horrifically dirty. We lie on them for hours, sweating, drooling, dribbling bodily fluids on them. We nap on them, fart on them, fuck on them. The cat deposits fur, fur balls and, oh yeah, she farts too."

"I don't see sheets," her eyes narrowed dangerously, "I see towels. I'm awake with the towels. I'm asleep with the sheets."

"That's just silly," I responded. "Dirt doesn't care if you see it."

"Fine, you do the wash from now on." And she opened her paper all the way. I could no longer see her face. The conversation was, quite clearly, over.

I lost this hand in the lover-to-spouse poker game. I lost more than one hand. A week later I ran out of clean underwear. Lydia, true to the literalness of her threat, was no longer washing anything. There really wasn't anything to do. I made a note to myself to remember to thank my father once again for teaching me how to laugh at life.

XXXIII. 1967 – February

❧

"So, I'm pregnant," smiled Lydia as I started to open the brown wrapper with the take-out roasted chicken – we were both in Columbia law school now and law students don't have a lot of free time. I wrapped my arms around her and rocked from side to side, the hug I learned from my mother. I hadn't heard three nicer words since Tony's "Good show, kid."

"Well, that was sweet," smiled Lydia. "A girl worries about these moments. Guys, you may have noticed in your wanders, can be real assholes when it comes to kids."

"Ah, but not this 'guy,'" I grinned, pleased to have made it all the way to *guy*. "I think we will have brilliant children, savvy, sneaky, blessed with Eyetalian and Griik heritage."

"And," she said laughing, "they will be blind as little mole rats. But," she said turning a somber eye at me, "we need to think of serious things."

"Serious?"

"Yeah, serious. Money."

"Money?"

"Money. My scholarship is being revoked. I am going to have to drop out."

"What? Why?"

"School policy is that 'preggers' women are not permitted in the classroom once they show. They consider it unseemly, like it's a banner that announces 'I've been fucked.' The only one backing me is Harmoninsky and he seems to be a minority of one. I will worry about suing them later."

"That is beyond stupid. It can't be true."

"It is true. Surely you don't think I haven't pursued every angle here. But we need to focus on the more immediate fact. There will be another mouth to feed and it won't be take-out chicken."

"Cute, but this has nothing to do with poultry, does it?"

"I've been thinking," she said, "about approaching my folks. They were there before when I was broke."

I looked over at her. She looked vulnerable. Is this what pregnancy does? Or poverty? Or, more likely, no longer being in control. I waited to make sure I understood; Lydia not in control was new, different and, as I had learned in those days in the circus, *different* should never be reacted to without thought.

"No, and not mine either." I said after a sensible silence, "Not for a penny. That's too deep a hole. It's been dicey enough when it's you and me but we can't let little Moley become ensnared. We will do this on our own."

Lydia paused, wrinkled her brow and looked over at me. "I hate this, you know," she said. "I hate that you're right as much as I hate the rightness of it. But I'm glad you said it. There are far too many open manholes down that road."

"*Man*holes?"

"Oh shut up. Go talk to Henry, get a beer. Let me stew for awhile."

"Well, look at it this way; it's just another small step on that metaphoric road I like to think I'm on."

"And that is?" she raised that eyebrow.

"Becoming a grown-up. I won't be late."

I wandered into O'Shannon's and perched on my favorite stool, down by the short hall that led to the men's room, where I could see the room in one sweep of my head and watch Henry run one sweet bar. No matter how busy it got or how slow it was, Henry always seemed to have things moving at pretty much the same speed.

"Janice okay?" I asked as Henry slid a pint of Guinness over the bar to me. "It's been some time since I've seen her." Thoughts of Lydia evoked thoughts of others' wives.

"Ah, Janice. Indeed… Janice. She doesn't get out much these days." And he paused, washed a couple of glasses, served two locals the next round he knew they'd want, wiped his hands and smiled painfully. I was intrigued to see such vulnerability in a guy who was, when you stripped away the cover, the genial smile and iconic apron tied around his hips, one dangerous son of a bitch.

"Piece o' work, ain't she?" Henry looked down, then up, then at me. "I think," he twisted up his mouth, "I think I got it in its proper place. I just kinda look at the things she does like each is just another of the small nails she's been drivin' into me for near twenty years. I am," he said with a mix of frustration and resignation, "just waitin' for her to kill herself. I don't know when but it won't be pretty.

"But you," he said raising his head and pushing a smile onto his face, "are bursting with something so let me have it."

"Lydia is pregnant. *We*, are going to have a baby."

"No shit! Congratulations. That is so good to hear." Then he bellowed, "De kid 'ere, and his more than lovely Eyetalian wife are gonna have a baby. And you bums are all getting a drink on the bloody house. And," he said laughing, "when's the last time this cheapskate Irishman did *that?*" And the celebratory crowd, few of whom even knew me or Lydia or gave a shit, cheered the happy couple and their budding mole rat – but mainly the free drink.

"I will have that other Guinness but what I really need, Henry, is work. We're gonna need cash, folding stuff, moola. Lydia's taking a leave from school. She won't be working."

"How about doin' what most kids do, hit up your folks."

"Nope. That money would cost too much."

"So," said Henry, looking a tad suspicious, "you wanna do this on your own? That's real noble but what can you do? You're smart kid, but you got no trade. Smart all by itself ain't worth shit."

"Ah, hmm, yeah. Well, I used to punch up pocket change playing poker but I don't see that as steady enough right now. Need someone to tend bar?"

"No, not really. But, poker you said?"

"Yeah, poker. I played a lot in school and put in a short apprenticeship in lowball, back when I was in California. Haven't played a hand since then – being a good boy."

"No shit? Well then," smiled Henry, "how about dealin'?"

"Dealing?"

"Yeah, a dealer. I discovered I need one, one I can trust. It's a hell of a lot steadier than playing. Can't lose on that side of the table."

"Ah," I said nodding my head as if I knew what Henry was talking about. I knew there were underground games around because, well, this was Hell's Kitchen. But I didn't know what Henry obviously did. An ambiguous queasiness bloomed in my gut. I took another sip to buy time; turned on my stool and looked at Henry, the latest satanic, patriarchic figure I'd pried out of the woodwork.

"Deal, eh? Well, why not. Why the hell not. When do we begin?"

"It ain't *when* kid and it ain't *we* neither, till *I* know you know what you're doin', okay?" said Henry, snickering with that blend of affection and contempt he was so good at. "Come by tomorrow, around four and we'll get a look at just how stupid you are."

"Tomorrow? At four? Aw, come on man, I gotta class on contracts that starts at four," I protested, although that class seemed to have lost some of its allure in just the last couple of minutes.

"Fine, feed your family your way. I won't have any trouble findin' someone to do this. I'd like to have you for a bunch of reasons but," he smiled and paused, "let's not fool ourselves. Here, lemme get you another, on the house," and he pulled another pint.

I looked at the glass, hesitated, looked back at Henry. "That's fine.... It's okay... boss. Four it is," I said, trying to sound as tough as I could. I sipped from the frothy head of the Guinness, its tiny persistent bubbles, its singular dark grainy flavors, and smiled. There was – what's that cliché? – "a shift in the cosmos."

Tomorrow, like all tomorrows, would be different from today but this one, perhaps, more so. I felt like I'd just skidded off the road into a ditch. I needed to sit a while, make sure all the stuff that used to work still did. Nothing seemed obviously out of place but, still, I felt disoriented and wondered what my professor was going to think about that empty chair in the room. I leaned on the polished bar, stared at the rows of bottles that dressed up the richly framed mirror on the back wall. The circus was back in town. I could sense its tug, drawing me back from the beach, through the sand dunes. I could hear the calliope's siren song, distant, faint, weaving through small openings in the cacophony of 9th Ave.

XXXIV. 1967 – February

Who knew? The card room was just above O'Shannon's, past the men's room, through the "Employees Only" door, up a flight of stairs. Two tables, their brushed green felt bathed in diffuse light from green-shaded lamps that hung from twisted, cloth-covered wire. We were greeted by the familiar sounds: chips being riffled, cards shuffled, the typical banter of a card room punctuated by grunts of "fold," "call" and "raise" and, of course, by smoke. The room was enveloped in a toxic fog. It seemed that just about everyone was sucking on a fag, chomping down on a cigar or spitting brown glop into a cup and the guys sitting around looked an awful lot like the mugs back in Gardena.

One table was a low-stakes game, the other high and high, as Henry explained, could get very high, "when the right people are around."

"You're here, kid, to deal this game," Henry said nodding at the nearest table where one of the players was flipping cards to the others and using a suspicious grip on the deck.

"There's been too much cheatin' in this game and we gotta fix things."

"Cheatin'?" I said and realized I was dropping my g's.

"Yeah, usual shit, false shuffles and cuts, markin' cards, dealin' seconds."

"Like that?" I whispered, tilting my head toward the guy holding the deck in a manner familiar to me.

Henry stared at the guy and winced. "Oh, fuck it! I'll 'fix' that later. How the hell d'ya learn to spot shit like that? I like that, a lot. I like you, kid."

"Well, I had a good teacher. I'll tell you later."

"You... ah... can't *do* that shit, can you?" Henry said with a look that poured hope and worry into the same expression.

"Nope, just how to spot the grip and that 'somethin' ain't right' feel that all but the best let slip."

"Ah, good, good." nodded Henry as he turned back to me. "You know, shit's been goin' on here. A couple of guys was winning just a little too much and a little too often and, well, we had a bit of a mess last week," he grimaced and glanced down at the wood floor next to the cashier's table where there was a dark reddish stain. "I don't need shit like that in here."

"What," I asked, trying not to look bothered by the implications, "the hell happened?"

"That, you don't need to know and will be better off if you don't," which, of course, made me want to know even more. But having learned a little something about this life from Tony, I merely nodded.

"Okay, so let's go sit over at the side table. I wanna run you through a couple of hands. Seven-stud, $2 - $4 stakes, so let's start there."

And we did. It was weird and a little embarrassing. Turns out that playing the game doesn't mean you know dick about how to run it. Scoop up cards, always facing away so that no one thinks you're doing anything fishy. Shuffle with cards flat on the table – minimum three times, four max. Place deck down. Cut onto the cut card. Hold deck "honestly." Antes from everyone. Deal. Two cards down, one up. Lowest up or "door" card has the 50¢ "force" bet, anyone can "complete" the bet to $2 and anyone else can raise another $2, three raises max. In stud, from fourth street on (each round of cards, I discovered, is called a "street"), the best board cards lead the betting. Bets on the first two up-cards are $2, $4 on the others. The seventh, or "river" card, is dealt face down. Rake each pot, 10% up to $3. Someone will spell me for a bit every hour or so, so's I can pee, grab something to eat.

Two hours later and Henry turned me loose. I was now an official denizen of the NYC underworld. My pay? Nothing. I worked for tips, or "tokes," in the street slang. No wages, no deductions. It's all in the dark, which was fine as I was comfortable with the dark, in its many forms. On the way out we stopped to look at the game at the high-stakes table, which was playing $10 - $20. "Here," said Henry, "a good dealer can expect a $1 toke, pretty standard, more if the pot is heavy. But," he laughed, "don't expect nothing like that back there. But, fuck it kid, it's a good start, yeah?"

Alas, it was anything but good. The regulars were pissed at Henry for bringing in a dealer. But since it didn't do much good to be pissed at Henry, they were pissed at me. The less-than-honorable didn't like that it neutralized their scams, the honorable wondered what had been going on before and they all saw that this tipping crap was gonna cost them. It wasn't exactly the gravy train.

And there was all that shit that kept happening. Guys folded out of turn, bet out of turn; they called out bets and then claimed they didn't mean to. A couple of characters were real "angle-shooters" and pulled crap like acting like they were going to throw their hands away to induce action and then called or raised. Others "shorted" the pot, "splashed" the pot with their chips instead of putting them out where they could be counted. Some even tried stealing chips from the pot and others would toss in bills in bunches which were difficult to count. Cash played but Henry preferred chips or "checks," as he called them; they were easier to count and that way the cash stayed in the drawer, where Henry liked it.

I staggered home after my first night sometime after 6 AM. The sun was just creasing the eastern sky with its unwelcome rays. My back hurt, my wrist was sore and I could feel calluses forming on my thumbs from all the shuffling. My eyes burnt and everything from my clothes to my hair stunk from tobacco smoke. I was exactly $14.25 richer than when I sat down. A paltry sum for ten hours of abuse.

XXXV. 1967 – March

I'd been putting in five, sometimes six days and/or nights on the job. I'd been doing more than "jes fine." On the evenings when I got to deal the big game I was taking home $100, $110 sometimes more. I'd developed a patter, a talker's style right from the carny. I riffed and spun. Call the cards, "4 of hearts is low, bring-in's on you, sir." Smile. Control the action, "Kings a pair; it's your action, my friend." Nod. Let 'em know what's happening, "That's a raise from the dapper gentleman in the Joe Friday fedora, twenty rutabagas to call."

I dealt fast and smooth. The game was tight, fair and honest and they appreciated it. They were getting in a lot more hands than when they were doing their own dealing. The bickering pretty much stopped and cheating became a lost art. The tokes were drifting up; hell, a buck wasn't unusual and every now and again a redbird got tossed to me. Tap it twice on the table, give effusive thanks and into the old left-tit pocket it went. And no one was taking out taxes.

It didn't take long before Lydia got comfortable being married to a law-school drop-out, her degenerate aborning. The cash this bum was bringing home was a nice balm and formed a solid fence against parental control. But she'd had these odd pains in her side the last day or so.

"Don't know, just don't," she said grimacing one evening as we cleared the table after a late dinner on a rare Saturday I had off. "It only started really hurting yesterday. I keep wondering if it's my appendix."

"Hmm," I muttered, "I know that one. I went through it when I was ten. But it wasn't just pain. I was sick as a dog and couldn't keep anything down. What do you want to do?"

"Sleep."

Two hours later sleep still sat across the room mocking her. Lydia's pain increased and she rolled over. "Hon, I am very good with pain. In my family you had to be 'cause no one ever really gave a shit. But this is different. This is very not good."

In the ER at Bellevue we got the usual. Fill out these forms; sit over there; wait. Wait, indeed, in pain, in cheap, blue, industrial, vinyl-covered chairs, back to back, double-row upon row aligned on linoleum someone was at least trying to keep clean. It was 1:15 in the AM but it was still Saturday night and Saturday nights in midtown were special.

The room was filled and everybody was in pain. Physical pain, mental pain, emotional pain, pain from knowing what was wrong, pain bred of ignorance and worry. Everyone waited. The kid bleeding from a stab wound on his upper arm, the pregnant woman for whom the ER was the local gynecology clinic, the wizened, crippled creature in the corner eating out of a box of laundry starch licking white powder from her fingertips, the drunk who fell, his face a mess of bruises, the prisoner handcuffed to a chair, one eye swollen shut and two bored cops standing guard.

They all waited; each withdrawn into their own cocoon of private pain and as I sat casting about the room, it morphed into a cinderblock tank with a wall of bars and an assemblage of assorted lowlifes. I blinked once or twice and lined up the palpable pain I felt against the dispassionate curiosity of the manchild I once was.

A half-hour later Lydia hit on the way to end the waiting. She grunted horribly, the blood drained from her face, now chalk-white and mottled, shivering, she started onto her feet and fell onto the woman in pain on her left in a dead faint.

Ripped out of my Covina reverie, I leapt up, grabbed her as she rolled over and slowly lowered her onto the floor. Nurses and orderlies who turned out not to have been too busy doing other things rushed in. Everyone was ordered out of the way and that included husbands, drunks and cops. Lydia was bundled onto a stretcher, strapped tight. Blankets were thrown over her and she was wheeled through metal doors with frosted glass. "You," a gruff orderly said to me, "stay here. We'll come get you as soon as we can."

I spent the next four hours tilting between worry and frustration, rage and concern and being ignored by the clerk who was visibly annoyed by my peppering her with questions like "What does 'as soon as we can' mean?" If this is what growing up involved, it was beginning to look like Peter Pan was on to something.

With the sun streaking in through the window bringing hope to the few remaining dolorous souls, they came back for me. They led me down a maze of antiseptic corridors lined with stretchers and IV poles looking like steel hat racks and rolling tables bedecked with pans and gauze and tweezers and here and there a scarred bench upon which sat all the peoples of the world linked together in pain and into the office of, said the sign, "Dr. A. P. Bolling." To me this could not be right, for the sandy-haired fellow who took my hand warmly and offered me a seat could not have been more than twenty years old.

"Ectopic pregnancy," were the first two words out of this youth. I squinted myopically at his name tag and, indeed, it said "Dr. A. P. Bolling."

I knew I looked confused.

"You look confused," smiled Dr. Bolling. "It was a tubal pregnancy? You know, yes? Baby was growing in her tubes."

"Yes, I know," I replied. "I know. I'm tired. I assume she's still alive or your first words would have been, 'I'm sorry.'"

"Ah, yes. Alive, very much so. She will be fine but it was messy. The tube ruptured, almost certainly in the waiting room; she lost a lot of blood. The surgery went fine. The recovery should go well too. But it will be a while.

"But there is one complication."

"Complication?" I said, feeling a sudden swirl of anxiety.

"Yes. There will be no more children."

"More? There aren't any yet."

"Ah. Well, then there will be no children. We had to remove the affected ovary. The other is wrapped in scar tissue that was probably there from birth. She won't have any untoward consequences other than the sterility. I'll be here for the two of you if you ever need me."

And the "real world" got yet a little more real and a lot less alluring. As I sat and rocked slowly back and forth, I came to like the "kid" posing as a gynecological surgeon when it was so obvious that he was a twenty year-old dropout who had run away with this singular circus.

XXXVI. 1967 – March

"Hi."

"Hi."

"How're you doing?"

"Been better; will be better. I do want to get the hell out of here which I take as a sign I'm mending. You know the hijackers were here this morning. All four of them, together. Can you believe that?

"Yeah, I know. My mom told me they were coming over. Henry sends his love and best wishes. He'll be here later today. Without Janice."

"And you will not believe who else wandered in. Armin."

"Armin? Harmoninsky?"

"Yup," she said. "Why do you sound surprised?"

"Why Harmoninsky? I thought we left him behind with the rest of the Columbia crew," I said with a touch of annoyance.

"Because, love, he has been the only one of that crew who has stood behind me, the only one defending me."

"I understand," I said which was a total lie. I had no idea they even talked. "So what'd he have to say?"

"Well, he asked about you."

"Me?" I said.

"Yes, you. You're in for some surprises. He's been paying attention to you, to me."

"You're being cryptic."

"Well," she said, "I suspect he'll find you. I told him what you'd been doing since vanishing from his sight."

"Oh, shit. You didn't."

"Ah, but I did. Cross examined me, he did. He is, as he put it, not the slightest bit surprised. I think he'll stop by O'Shannon's sometime later this week."

"He will *what*?"

"Stop by," she said. "I told him where you were working. He was, as he told me, when he was young and not quite so proper, a reasonably serious poker player. He won't sit in an illegal game, for reasons screamingly obvious, but he does want to chat with you. And, speaking of you, how're you doing?"

"Me?"

"Yeah, you."

"*Me?*"

"Yeah..... Am I caught in some weird feedback loop here? Yeah, you!"

"Why me? You're the one they did the slice and dice thing on."

"Because, bozo, no blind mole rats."

"Ah, yes. No bats, no rats. No, I'm not alright but, of course, I am."

"You do know there's an upside here," she said.

"Up?"

"We won't have to worry about birth control."

So I sat down and very gently hugged the best thing in my life. We sat together without talking for a long time. Finally, Lydia wiped a tear off her cheek, smiled and said, "I think we need to get away."

"I've had the same thought."

"California?"

"I've had the same thought."

"What should we do there?"

"I can play a little lowball."

"I want to get back to school. I lost a semester and that hasn't made me happy. I want that degree. I want that life and, anyway, you're probably going to need a lawyer one of these days."

"Why do I have the feeling that you're way ahead of me here?"

"Because I've had a lot of time to think this crap through and somehow, well, you know, I suspected you'd be on the train with me. And, dearest one, just to stretch the limits of your disbelief, Armin has already begun working on a transfer to UCLA for me."

"Armin? Not 'Harmoninsky,' 'Armin!'"

"Yes, Armin. He'll be 'Armin' for you too soon. He is, as I'm discovering, full of surprises, little secrets he keeps in a drawer along with those silly bowties."

"I cannot wait," I replied sarcastically although I had to admit I was intrigued. "I'll give Anna a ring when I get home. We can start there. I suspect none of the shanghaiers will be happy but, well, let the winds blow as they will."

XXXVII. 1967 – March

"Take a break, I'll deal for a while," Henry said tapping me on the shoulder after I pushed the pot to the drunk in the 3-seat and pocketed the quarter toke. "Some character stopped in and asked for you. He's downstairs."

Gotta be Armin, I thought, sure hope so anyway. Indeed, as I turned past the men's room I spotted him looking just like he did when I last saw him, tall and graceful, bedecked in classic academic garb: tweed jacket, striped shirt, bowtie, wire-rim glasses, hair tousled just enough to seem unattended and those intense gray eyes.

"This, Professor, is a surprise," I greeted him with a slightly embarrassed smile. "I hear you've been told about the corrupt and depraved existence I live."

"Xero," grinned Harmoninsky as he slid gracefully between tables with his hand outstretched, "it is so very good to see you. And, please, call me 'Armin.' I cannot bear the 'Professor' label, surely not here."

We found one of the more engagingly scarred tables in a corner and ordered a pint of Guinness each. I sat back and scanned Armin's face and hair and realized that he looked younger than I had thought he was and, yes, even a bit more vulnerable, more human.

I flashed back on a day when I was a grade-schooler and I spotted my teacher at the market. She was wearing pants, a sweatshirt and had a cigarette stuck in the corner of her mouth. I stopped, stared, then when she turned, in a panic I ducked behind a display of canned peaches. How could this be? It was all wrong. What was she doing here? People shop here, not teachers. Regular women wear slacks and sweatshirts, not my Miss Maple. And she was smoking! It was an appalling, illuminating moment. I had assumed that Miss Maple just vanished at 3:00, like a fog that dissipated in the slanting rays of the afternoon sun. But if she was here, on a Saturday, buying and smoking, what else did she do? Did she have sex? Children? Did she drive here? Ride a bicycle? Did she ever cry? Get scared? I shook my head and smiled inwardly at the vision and outwardly at the obviously very human Professor Harmon... er, *Armin*.

"Lydia said you might stop by. But why? Why me? I've reverted to being a bum. I assumed you'd just chucked me on the ash heap with all the other drop-outs."

"Ah, well, yes and no. You did blow us all off and I am not happy about that but, well, I've liked you from your undergraduate days. You and Lydia. You two slipped through my protective fence. I have done a terrible thing. I have stooped to care."

As the pints arrived, I looked at this willowy man and began wondering what Lydia meant when she said he had secrets tucked away.

"Care? Why?"

"I don't really know. It began early on. Remember when I called you an 'appropriate head-nodder?'"

"Of course," I answered. "One of the more amusing things I've been called."

"A professor doesn't always know when he's getting through or when he's lost the class. I learned early on that the sharp students are those whose reactions are appropriate. You frowned when I was being obtuse and nodded when I made a good point. You became my barometer of how the class was going. It was important then; that was the first undergrad course I'd taught.

"Plus, both you and Lydia have an intriguing independence that I liked – so many of our students are painfully sycophantish. They all want to get into law school, then they want to be on the Law Review, then they want references and internships and jobs and God only knows, judge's robes or partnerships. It's all quite hideous. It was a delight to discover two sharp minds that basically didn't give a rat's ass what I could do for them except teach them the law."

Rat's ass? The words echoed off the dark paneled walls of O'Shannon's. Did, Professor Har ... er, Armin just say *rat's ass*?

"How did you get into law?" I asked, looking for a simple hook onto which this conversation could be hung until I figured out where it was heading.

"I started about as far away as you can get. I was a dancer, still am, I guess. I majored in music and dance. Later I turned professional and toured with a company out of Chicago." And I now understood the fluid grace he walked with.

"After a time, I came to two epiphanic moments. One, I wasn't really good enough. Two, even if I had been, the pay stunk. So, off to law school I went. I haven't regretted it for a moment.

"But, I think I'm more interested in you right now. What are your plans in the great utopia on the other coast?"

"I don't know. I'll look for a job or," I chuckled quietly, "pretend to. I'm not ruling poker out, of course. It is a surprising world in there, up there," I said tilting my head toward the stairwell. "Lydia has, as usual, much better-defined plans. I understand you've been helping her with the transfer."

"Indeed," said Armin. "The dean called. He's an old friend. She's in. She is going to make a wonderful attorney."

I looked at Armin. I flashed back to the way Lydia talked about him and just a tiny whisper of jealousy danced across my brain and must have exited onto my face.

"Oh, no!" blurted Armin when he saw the look. "No. I would actually be far more interested in *you*." And I felt my expression shift from suspicion to surprise.

"There are reasons why I was drawn to dance," he went on, diplomatically ignoring my look. "I am – I believe the vaguely pejorative term bounced around these days is – a 'faggot.' It's not an easy thing to be in my position. I maintain my role as a largely invisible member of a secret legion, which I trust you'll preserve."

I nodded, feeling relief intermingle with the tolerance I'd been taught and thought I'd learned. But, then, I'd not actually had to be tolerant in the sexual orientation domain. Gamblers, sure. Con artists, grifters, no problem. Homosexuals? Closeted queens? Sigh. Okay... so long as we have an understanding.

"Lydia said you had surprises, we're up to two now. Anything else?"

"No. Nothing special, just friends in California who may be able to give you a hand. The law school connections have already been made. There's a real estate agent who knows the Los Angeles area and, well, as crazy as this is going to sound, a bloated old homo who, very quietly, owns a piece of the Normandie card room in Gardena, in case you end up looking for a job in that 'profession.'" And in Armin's tone, 'profession' was wrapped in a good lawyer's ambiguity.

XXXVIII. 1967 – October

⤐

We had made the coastal shift. Lydia was into the grind at UCLA. I'd been wandering the legit world looking, half-heartedly, for a job. But until one could be dragged out from under some rock, I'd been playing poker. A couple of weeks at the low-level games were a rude reminder of life in Gardena. The games were unimaginative, tight and moving up to the higher stakes tables would be folly. It's a bankroll thing. If your 'roll can't take the hit of a losing streak – and these babies pop up all the time no matter how good you are – you can't risk it. If you "git broke," as the local pros put it, you're unemployed till you can raise another stake. I didn't even like thinking about "gittin' broke." The tokes back at Henry's were looking pretty good.

I realized I was going to have to use Armin's contact, which threw me into a bind. That old "my-byself" thing came bubbling back and knowing how idiotic it was didn't make any difference. I didn't want to have to impose and, even more, I didn't want to be obligated. But if I didn't, it'd be an insult to Armin and, well, we needed money. I got out the card Armin had given me. It had the phone number of one Bowie Blatinmann, pronounced, Armin had said, with the accent on the second syllable, Blat*in*mann.

"Well, *hello* Mr. Konstantakis," came back over the phone and the voice was rich, almost flowing. "Armin said you would…, no actually he said he 'hoped' you would call. And so you have. We should meet. Can you come to the Normandie around seven tonight? I'll be at the $20- $40 lowball game. We can have dinner."

"Not a problem. I know where it is, but how will I know you?"

"Oh, let's just say 'it'll be obvious,'" said Bowie with a rich chuckle. "I assume Armin gave you the 'bloated old homo' line. He likes to say that, God knows why."

At seven I wandered into the Normandie and found indeed, a "bloated old homo" but not one I expected. I assumed Bowie would be a sweet quiet fellow, maybe another ex-dancer gone to seed for his voice on the phone was warm and soft. Nope. Another curve ball and I must admit I was coming to enjoy these *maybe not* moments.

Bowie wasn't exactly bloated but he was big and he wasn't that old, maybe in his mid-forties. The shoulders and the upper arms, however, told a tale. He sat like a man who was once an athlete, maybe a body builder, and everywhere that Armin sported tweed Bowie donned leather. But all that cowhide was just the beginning. Bowie's body was an exceedingly large canvas upon which artists skilled and amateurish had worked. Old tattoos, their colors faded with time, their edges ragged with the lines and creases of age and sun adorned his hands, fingers, arms. His neck was covered with rich, colorful ink, a many-cultured collage of images from Asia, North American Aboriginal art and Welsh myth all flowing downward under the black T-shirt and up the back of his shaven head. A salt-

and-pepper handlebar mustache hung down Yosemite Sam-like nearly to his shoulders. Like he said, "Obvious."

Bowie rose from his seat with surprising grace, took my offered hand into his own soft and forgiving one and said, "So, this is what Armin has sent my way." And he chuckled as he racked his chips.

Presentation aside, Bowie shared traits with Armin: intelligence and loyalty. He had promised his old friend that he would help and by the time dinner was over, I was offered steady work as a prop player at the Normandie. "Props," Bowie explained, "get games going and keep them going if the tables get short-handed. You play with your own money but we'll pay you minimum wage. If you lose more at the game than you make, you just chalk it up to a bad day at the office. If you win, the money is yours.

"A prop's life lacks several things and glamour's one of them. You're going to get stuck in a lot of low-level games and you're going to get shifted when the table begins to fill up. But it's an honest living. Armin said he thought you might want to go legit; this gets you half-way there." A handshake, wine glasses tapped together and I was back, officially, in Gardena, like I thought I would be – though not exactly in this role.

No matter, I hunkered down, to follow the script, see where it might lead. The cast of characters hadn't changed much in seven years. It was still a rock garden and the sixty-something biddy with the lethal cane, all gnarly hickory, was still sitting at the curve of the table, still looking to crack someone's shins if they even glanced at her the wrong way.

I propped diligently, doing what I thought was best for the club, the things I had learned at Henry's. I was pleasant at all times to everyone. Played tight, ABC poker, nothing tricky, nothing fancy. When I won I was gracious; when I lost I was gracious. I realized I was learning important lessons. Respect everyone no matter badly they play or horrifically they act. Stay calm no matter how weird things get and pay as much attention to myself and my emotions as to the other players.

Being Bowie's friend carried a mixed message, as Bowie was a mixed message writ large. He was wealthy, physically imposing and eccentric. He was also, as I was to learn, an amazing jazz pianist and a partner in a music production company. He evoked curiosity, fear, envy and admiration in equal doses and a bit of this slopped over onto me. I was accepted at the tables and treated with respect. I also got occasional sideways glances that made me feel uncomfortable in a genderish way. These, I learned to live with.

XXXIX. 1969 – February

Time crawled by. As I felt more comfortable in this life, I propped less and, with Bowie's support, slowly adopted the role of true professional. "It's pretty simple when you cut away all the bullshit," he said one day. "Win or lose, soar or crash and burn, it's all on you, your decisions, your actions. You want real crazy," he laughed, "try the recording business."

My life settled into a loosely structured routine. Time became less relevant. Lydia was either in class, the library or a book. I slunk into bed at hours unrelated to the movements of the heavens, got up at odd times, ate, hit the head, showered, smacked a kiss on Lydia's cheek – if she was there – and headed for Gardena.

I joined the parade of the damned who crawled the crowded, chaotic, roads of LA. I would emerge from my cocoon, sniff the air and curl my lip at the brown sludge that hung in the reluctant breeze. "Smog," it'd been dubbed, a witch's brew of toxic crap that billowed out of a million tailpipes. Hazy, malevolent clouds of it, crackling with ozone and littering everyone's lungs with shit-brown particles. It was a good place to be indoors, in an air conditioned card room breathing good ol' tobacco smoke.

I crept into self-imposed isolation sprinkled with quixotic efforts at introspection and little forays into amateur anthropologist mode. I was fascinated by this community. The serious poker players, the ones grinding away to make ends meet, didn't give a shit about much but poker. The rest of the world reciprocated. Few outsiders cared or even thought about them (us?), which was fine. It was like dealing for Henry. Real world stuff felt like something others did, down the block, in an office, behind some translucent curtain. Oddly, I found that I wasn't missing things – music, movies, philosophical novels, sex. I loved Lydia. She loved me. There wasn't much time for the love to overlap. Even family faded away. Anna and Billy might as well have been back in New York and my parents... it was best not to think about them. An interesting time.

Some days were rife with humor, others marked by pathos. I saw more cheating than I liked and tried to stay aloof. I watched friendships form and break, saw intimidation, annoyance, bullying, sexuality, anger, even true passion at moments. Poker is a cruel game, chance is fickle, the cards follow no laws but those of the mathematics of large samples and your life, son, no matter how long you plant your butt in that seat, is a small sample. You are a ten-to-one favorite and all your money is in the pot and you can lose – will lose – often enough to break your heart.

Once in a while I'd think about living some other, maybe "legit" life but it was always followed by the now banal truth, I just didn't feel like a legit kinda guy, not any more. I slowly moved up to higher stakes. I was doing okay, enough to pay the rent and cover expenses. Lydia's tuition was getting racked up in student loans. I refused to worry; Armin said she'll make a hell of a lawyer. I knew she'd be a hell of a whatever she decided on. Tomorrow would just have to take care of itself.

In my drift into non-legitimacy I found myself embracing a new identity: mute urban hermit. I'd always been able to not-talk but I had to work at it. This new self, this not-talking self was different and as it took hold I was surprised to find that it felt as comfortable as the old persona, the one who could barely refrain from "flapping his jaw" – an idiotic line that still conjures up a near-hallucinatory memory so distant and unreal that there are moments when I wonder if it really happened or I read it in a book and only thought it was my life.

As I was not talking I had more opportunity to scan and observe the array of characters who regularly hunkered down at these tables. One in particular caught my attention, a thirty-something grinder whom I knew only as T-Bird Tommy. The moniker came from the Thunderbird that he upgraded the day the new model hit the showrooms. We kept running into each other at the same clubs at the same times, like two predators who knew when the young and weak came down to the stream to drink. We always acknowledged each other but never exchanged anything but friendly, distant nods until the afternoon of the sticky palm.

It was mid-afternoon at the El Dorado and the $10 - $20 limit lowball game was about to get underway. I headed over, saw T-Bird sitting down and promptly took a seat across the table. I did not want someone aggressive like Tommy acting right after me; it can be unsettling. Besides, across the table I could look at him, study him.

The table soon filled up and the game was rolling. Nothing terribly interesting happened for some time. No matter how glamorous or fatalistic Hollywood has tried to make a poker game appear, most of the time not much happens, kind of like the circus or a used-car lot or pounding the pavements of Covina.

Another thing the flicks miss is that every poker game has a rhythm. It emerges unbeckoned, unannounced, formed by local custom, sculpted by the random events that just happen to happen that day. I worked at sensing what form the table was taking and then playing against it. If it was aggressive and loose, I tightened up and looked for opportunities to trap the overly enthusiastic. If it was soft and tight, I widened my range and became a bit pushier. But like all cultures, it could change as it adjusted to the currents of chance and the vagaries of those very human players sitting there doing what they do.

The game this day had started slow, relaxed. First to act – "under the gun" – raised; everyone folded. Again. And again. Then the opener limped, it got raised, everyone folded. Another baby pot. And so it went. Open-raise, fold, fold, fold – like the violin section obediently following the flicker of a baton. Then there was a minor variation on the theme. T-Bird open-raised, the next player re-raised, it got folded back to T-Bird who made it four bets and stood pat. The other guy took one. Bet, fold. Done. Tommy was now up a couple of coconuts.

And we ran up and down this metaphoric corridor for an hour or two maybe three, maybe four but no one seemed to notice for one of the peculiar things that a poker game can do is compress time, fold it into a tiny sliver of itself.

"How can you," Lydia once asked me, "sit there for ten hours, ten fucking hours!"

"Oh, was it that long, sorry I was late. Never noticed."

Then without warning it changed. A contested hand emerged, sprung up like a weed in the driveway, a pimple on your inner thigh. You can't predict these things and shouldn't try. The guy on my left opened the pot. Next player raised. Tommy then re-raised, the next player cold-called three bets and the original opener capped it. Everyone called and out of freakin' nowhere there was a large molehill of chips sitting alluringly in the middle of the table. Everyone drew one except the opener who stood pat. There was a flurry of bets, raises, calls, re-raises, calls... and... in a moment, a tiny insignificant moment in any larger, more meaningful world, three fairly ordinary citizens were out a decent chunk of change and one equally pedestrian fellow was stacking up a whole lotta chips, feeling pretty good about almost everything and likely beginning to think he's a great poker player instead of just another slob who got lucky.

I'd been a spectator in this drama. I glanced over at T-Bird, who had just bled off more than a few chips, and saw that he was looking about carefully. Hands like these can change the nature of the table. One or two of the losers can go a little wonky, start pushing weak hands to try to recoup. These are the true fish, the ones who cannot fathom the unfairness of it all nor grasp the cruelty of the game. They just lose it; they go *on tilt* and a player in this state resembles nothing so much as a three-legged pin-ball machine.

I scanned the table, forming educated guesses about the others. I was curious about the fellow sitting on my immediate right who'd dealt that hand. Pretty ordinary looking guy I hadn't seen before. The others I knew. There was Toby, a construction worker just off the job and still wearing his tool belt, who was now stacking a small mountain of chips, a dentist whom everyone called "Doc," T-Bird, of course, who looked just right with his cowboy hat pushed back a bit on his head, silver bracelets with jade insets on both wrists, light blue shirt tucked into his jeans and a stunning pair of hand stitched cowboy boots and Charlene, the omnipresent gray-haired harpy on Social Security who could be the tightest player I had ever seen and one of the more eccentric. I never heard her use "I" and rarely the absent pronoun. She never said "call" or "raise." It was like she was an observer commenting on her own behavior. It was always "Charlene calls" or "Charlene folds her junk" – and when it was "Charlene raises," I realized I had to pee.

So this new guy, dressed in a starched, black shirt with jade buttons, didn't stand out. He was mainly neat, very neat. His hair was combed carefully, his pants creased sharply and he kept cleaning his glasses. But his chips were a mess. Unlike most players, he didn't keep them in neat columns. Some were stacked, some not and those that were, were in uneven stacks. He seemed to be winning quite a bit but he wasn't winning that many pots and it was hard to tell how much he had on the table. My BS detector buzzed gently and I watched Mr. Neat, carefully.

Neat was also sweet and helpful and on his deal he would push the pot to the winner with a smile. Then I noticed something odd. Just before it was his turn to deal, he would put his left hand in his pants pocket. And a loud "bingo" went off in my head. The guy's a snatcher; the messy chip stacks are to disguise how much he's got in front of him. I was dead sure that there was a tube of resin or something sticky in that pocket. I waited. It took about an hour for the right moment. Neat dealt. I won the decent sized pot and when he pushed the chips over I reached out, grabbed his left wrist and twisted it over. There sat a red $5 chip and a greenie worth $25, stuck to his palm.

Caught as cleanly as a fly in a web, he just sat there utterly silent. I held onto his wrist, hard enough to hurt. Several of the others jumped to their feet, Charlene grabbed her cane, raised it menacingly and bellowed "*floor*." Two blue jackets arrived quickly and justice was meted out, in the club's immanently fair way.

The shift manager, with a tag that announced him as Romeo, looked at the upturned palm, shook his head several times, each accompanied with a "tsk, tsk." He turned to me. "Did y'all you see what he bought in fer?"

"Sure did. Four hundred," said Charlene.

"Fine," though from Romeo it sounded like 'fahn,' "everyone hyah agree?" asked Romeo.

Nods all around.

"Fahn," said Romeo and he counted out $400 and put them in a rack in front of Mr. Neat.

"Have all ya'll been here since he sat down?" he asked.

Again, nods all around.

"Fahn," he repeated. "Makes it easy." Romeo took the remaining $550 or so in chips, divided them into even stacks and distributed them to the other players. Mr. Neat was then escorted off the premises and we all knew we would never see him again, certainly not in any Gardena poker room. Simple, clean, painless.

The drama was over. I was ahead a couple of hundred so I racked up and headed for the cashier. As I waited I heard a sly whisper behind me, "Sharp eye, kid. Wanna have dinner?"

The first word that leaked through my defenses was, of course, "kid," and I bristled. Then I realized that it was the near-legend T-Bird who was standing behind me. "It's on me 'cause, like the rest of those dodos, I owe you."

I picked up my money, turned, found I could still smile and said, "Sure. I'm Xero K., by the way, and you, I suspect, are called 'T-Bird Tommy.'"

"Indeed. I know who you are Mr. K. I have for some time. Let's have dinner. Surprising as it may seem, there's a steak house a couple of blocks over that's very good."

I folded the bills, wrapped them around the others in their elastic embrace and walked out with Tommy, pleased to note that there was no buzzing in my head.

XL. 1969 – May

Tommy and I had been on the road for nearly a month surfing the vagaries of the world of poker where justice was a no-show, luck fleeting and fickle, and the spoils belonged to the skilled, the patient and the stable. Tommy's newest set of wheels didn't hurt either.

I'd thought Lydia might try to scotch the trip but she didn't. "You need to find a circus," she laughed. "Besides, it's time for me to line up a real job or an internship. I wasn't planning on paying much attention to you for the next couple of weeks anyway."

We shared the driving. I felt like I had been canonized, ushered into a very small, select group. Not many even touched the leather seats of one of T-Bird's T-Birds let alone wrapped their hands around the red, gently ribbed steering wheel and got to push that baby heavy-footed along the winding coastal road, top down, radio blasting, the sun dazzling off the ocean. I flashed back on similar, more innocent days on this road in a white Cadillac and wondered, as I often did, what had become of Tony.

If there was a card room we missed, I can't imagine where it was. We drove, played poker, met up with Tommy's friends from this cloistered world, drove some more, sat up nights drinking, talking. Stories got traded, lives were unpacked and examined. It pulled me out – a bit anyway – of the shell I had crawled into.

We were in one of the newer rooms in Oakland when the floor brought Tommy a message. We were playing *North California draw*, a tough game and to be honest, I was having trouble getting the hang of it. Three blinds $5 - $5 - $10, guts to open and it played no limit. You can burn off your bankroll in a hurry here and I wasn't terribly happy being in this game – torn between needing to learn and battling the nagging sense that I may be the fish. I was relieved and intrigued when Tommy handed me the note. There was a private game that evening arranged by some guy named Lorenzo and Tommy and "his friend" were invited.

"Xero, compadre, we must go, for many reasons. Rack up and let's move." Tommy had shared snippets of his life as one of poker's road warriors, first in Texas and now here. To me they were like Tony's stories of scams on tour boats or grifting in sleazy carnies – amusing but someone else's life. I experienced no fear, quailed from no danger; there was no tug of anticipation, no surge of adrenaline. It wasn't my bankroll on the line, not my ass sliding quickly behind the wheel and gunning it out of there just in case that scummy bastard in the torn leather jacket decided he's got another way to get his money back.

I looked at the note again and smiled. I remembered my first rollercoaster ride – the car clearing the cusp of the initial, benign ascent, the look down, the mix of terror and euphoria that hits like a shot of over-proof rum tossed down neat. You know what's coming... maybe.

When we got outside, Tommy handed me the keys. Navigating off an old map we made our way, not to some dive, but to what turned out to be Lorenzo's house. Through the entry gates I looked up at an ostentatious, architectural hodge-podge with windows that looked like they came from a British manor home, squared-off columns in front and turrets seemingly hammered onto each wing. It was a fashion statement, a trophy house that isn't a home so much as a poke in the eye to every delivery guy, housemaid or gardener who came by. So much for dark and edgy.

I negotiated the curving, brick, crosshatched driveway at the head of which we were greeted by a middle-aged man in a cashmere sweater over pressed jeans and white tennis shoes. "I'm Lorenzo," he said sporting a slight Italian accent and a hundred-dollar hair cut. "I assume you are Mr. K.," and he offered me his hand and, "you," he smiled warmly while glancing first at the hat and then the boots, "are most certainly T-Bird Tommy. Your old friend Maury, who is downstairs, recommended you. Glad you're here; we were getting tired of playing short-handed."

He led us between the double, curved balustrades, past an enormous kitchen and down the stairs to an elaborate basement complete with a wet bar, mini-kitchen with a buffet spread on the counter and a custom-made poker table. We were greeted with all the little details of an upscale game, a dealer, a thirty-something blond with teased hair, decked out in a white shirt with a black string-tie and name tag announcing her as "Sam," a waitress who could be Sam's younger sister and a set of custom chips, each with a bright yellow **L** embossed on it.

I was a bit out of sorts, a feeling that'd been growing since I realized what part of town we were in. This wasn't the back room of some pool hall or the local Odd Fellows Lodge. Road gamblers were supposed to be "on the road." This place may be on a "road" but it was in a zip code I hadn't been privy to before. I wrapped myself even deeper in my insular, urban hermit persona and became very attentive.

Around the table sat five men, all giving off waves of influence and money, except for one, whom I assumed was Maury. The others were introduced as Herschel, who said in a classic accent straight out of Brooklyn, "Yeah, yeah, Herschel, Schmerschel, you can call me Harry," and he shook our hands warmly and vigorously; Arnie, who was deeply tanned, his thinning hair elegantly combed backward, sporting yellow linen slacks, silk socks and tasseled loafers, which were just a bit too familiar; Sarge, who sat with the erect, no-nonsense bearing of an ex-marine; Sal who had that cheesy "I'm your best friend" smile of someone who owned an automobile dealership; and Maury, who sat there looking like what he was, a professional poker player, baseball cap, blue shirt under a black leather vest, sunglasses and a most unexpressive face.

I probed the room and... a revelation! It's ZEP, time-shifted. These were the captains of commerce, of the military-industrial complex, the wheelers, the dealers, the ones with the family legacies, and their spawn were Dickless, Flathead and No Name.

We were going to be playing alternating rounds of 7-stud and hold 'em mainly because neither game was allowed then in California's card rooms. Stud at $40-80 limits, hold 'em at no limit with $5 and $10 blinds. I'd learned to like stud back in those Hell's Kitchen days but I hadn't played a hand of it since. Hold 'em was a game Tommy and I had been working on since the old Texas rounders brought it westward. I didn't really think I understood it yet but I doubted that these guys did either.

Tommy and I each bought in for 2,500 bananas – yeah, bananas. Sometimes to me they're rutabagas or coconuts, even zucchinis. By this time in my life I had given up on *dollars*. You say a word often enough and it starts to sound like nonsense so I decided to do vegetables. I sat down and was pleased to note that Sam held the deck honestly.

We went back and forth for some eight or nine hours and the sun was just winking in through the row of windows up near the ceiling. Everyone was tired. Sarge said he was ready to call it a night. Arnie was a bit in his cups. He'd been hitting cards and the Chivas he'd been using to celebrate his success had woven its ethanolish magic. Sal looked like he was about even, maybe up a couple of bucks and poor Herschel, who had to reload twice, was the big loser. But he was still upbeat and I had come to like him. It was a rare thing, a thing to be relished: a guy who gets his ass kicked and maintains his composure. Most of Schmerschel's pain came from two hands where Arnie sucked out on him.

Arnie had shown himself to be an asshole. He kept yapping about his furniture business, the three new stores he'd opened, his money, stocks and his damn country club which, he let slip, barely acknowledging Herschel's existence, was "restricted." I'd been toning down a desire to get him. Targeting someone at poker is usually a mistake. If you get the guy in your cross-hairs, fine. If not, not. Not surprisingly, Tommy and Maury were still sharp; days without sleep were part of the routine. "Last round, hold 'em, okay guys?" announced Lorenzo. "I'm tired, we're all beat, some of us pretty bad," he snickered at Harry who just laughed gently. "Shall we kick up the blinds to $10 - $20?" Lorenzo was down at least two grand himself and, like so many, was willing to chase his losses.

I was up a bit over a dime. But I was tired. It would suck to blow off a four-figure win at this point so, even though I hate defensive poker, I settled down, ready to fold anything even remotely troublesome. But life, as they say, is under no obligation to cooperate. On the scheduled next-to-last hand I looked down at two black 8's. Arnie raised to $65 and everyone else folded.

I felt a subtle up-tick in my heart rate. Flop a set here and maybe, I thought, maybe we could felt this prick – or maybe not; it is poker. I was in the big blind and put out another $45. Sam dealt a mildly coordinated board: 6♣, J♦, 4♣. Not bad – one over-card and some weak draws. My first thought was did Arnie there hit any piece of it? His opening raise most likely was two big cards like K, Q, or A, Q. He hadn't done anything tricky all night. The odds were he missed and if he didn't have a pair bigger than eights, I was in decent shape.

I checked. Arnie promptly overbet the pot, pushing out two stacks of redbirds. Two hundred into a pot with only $140 felt, well, just wrong. If he had a big pair or something like A, J, or a set of 6's or 4's, he wouldn't be trying to push me out of this pot, he'd be trying to keep me around. It didn't make a lot of sense, so I slid $200 out.

The turn card was an almost certainly irrelevant 2♠. I checked again and Arnie quickly bet out $600. I was now close to certain that Arnie had nothing. He'd got himself committed to trying to steal the pot and trapped himself. Of course, if I was wrong I was gonna "git broke." So I called again and hoped another overcard didn't hit the board. The pot was now over $1,700.

The river was another deuce and Arnie shoved all-in – without a second's hesitation. "Count it," I said. I wanted to hear his voice, watch his hands. Arnie ticked off each stack and said, "Thirty-one hundred plus, more than you, *sucker*," and that "*sucker*" thudded into my brain.

This was the first real test I'd faced in this game that would soon capture the imagination of every poker player in the world. I sat back, thought, looked at Arnie, thought some more, realized that I should have raised on the turn but too late for that now. The room was silent. Sam sat motionless. I watched the sun set the smoke and dust in the air dancing in flickering gold and brown motes and ran through the hand again, ran through the whole session.

Arnie had had a good night up to now. Everything about the way he'd bet this hand felt wrong. He could have a monster, pocket Aces or a flopped set and just hoped that this kind of thing would happen, but then why overbet the flop and the turn? If he'd thought at all about my hand, he probably put me on a flush draw. But then, why the all-in? That didn't fit either 'cause I wouldn't call any bet with a busted draw. No, the only thing that made any sense was Arnie's holding A, K or A, Q and running a big, three-barrel bluff.

"I call," I announced and, although I didn't have to, I turned up my 8's.

Arnie saw the 8's and leaped awkwardly to his feet, knocking over his chair and spilling a glass of Chivas on the table. "What?" he screamed, "How the fuck can you call with that shit? You're a fucking moron." The vein in his neck was bulging, "An asshole, a fucking low-life scumbag." Lorenzo went over and tried to calm him down only to get pushed away. "You," he said glaring at me, lowering his voice as if a sneer could accomplish what yelling didn't, "are a fucking punk, you couldn't carry my jockstrap you low-class loser," and he flung his cards at Sam, like it was her fault, and they landed, face up, A♠, K♠. Everyone decided that that was the last hand.

As we cashed out, Tommy smiled, "Breakfast? And it's on *you*."

"This is not a problem," I grinned at him. "Maury, join us?"

"That would be my pleasure Mr. K."

I peeled two hundreds off my roll; handed one to Sam and the other to the waitress who turned out, of course, to be her sister, Sienna. "We've all got 'S' names," she explained, "one brother is Sewell, the other Sirus and the youngest is Serena. Parents had no imagination."

"But," I said, "doesn't it take more imagination to come up with all those names with the same first letter?"

"Hmm, never thought of it that way," she replied as she folded the bill up twice and slipped it into a small, leather snap-purse. "And thank you, Mr. Xero."

"You know, guys," I began while slicing up the slab of fat and gristle sitting between two runny eggs and burnt hash-browns, "there was a moment in that last hand...."

"Indeed," said Maury leaning toward me, smiling, "you wanted to crush his nuts, didn't you."

"It surprised me but, yeah," I said.

"How'd it make you feel?"

"Feel? Jeez, Maury," I laughed, "what are you, a freakin' shrink?"

"I was a psych major which, trust me, helps in this crazy game. But that's as far as it went."

"Well," I said, "to be honest, I don't know. Yeah, I wanted to see him go ape shit. I guess..." and my voice drifted off.

When I looked at Arnie counting his chips, I saw only a pompous, overbearing dickhead, heard him call me "*sucker*," and found a focused deadly desire not to just win the hand, get the money, but, yeah, "crush his nuts." The clarity of this was shocking but worse was the realization that I liked it – yet I could not completely silence my father's softly accented voice muttering, his tongue clicking "tsk, tsk" only it sounds like "tszk, tszk" – it's coming from over there, behind the potted palm on the plastic stand. "Poppy" was, *in absentia*, messing with my mind but this time, maybe, he had something to say. I was, of course, just another confused "kid." Maybe I hadn't suffered enough and didn't deserve to know who I was – am.

So I sat there trying to find something edible between the ribbons of gristle and runny egg yolk in what was supposed to be "steak and eggs" and wondered how I got here. Self-discovery was supposed to be illuminating, uplifting. You find out who you really are. Cool. If this epiphanic moment was supposed to be one of those, where the wraps on my soul got peeled back, just a bit and a sliver of that "self-aware" crap everyone in California was looking for nodded back at me, it wasn't. It was delivered in a plain brown wrapper stamped *fragile*.

XLI. 1969 – May

I persuaded Tommy that it was time to head back to LA. I'd stayed out of Lydia's way long enough; it was time to be back in it. We headed south on the scenic route, as close to the Pacific as possible. "Let's stop at my place first," said Tommy. "I want to get this," he smiled patting the bulge in his pocket, "in a safe place. Then I'll get you home."

He pulled the T-Bird into the driveway of a sprawling stucco house, turned off the motor, stopped dead still and said, "Xero, gimme your 'roll."

"What?" I blurted. "Why?" I thought, no way. He isn't gonna rob me. Not after what we've been through!

Tommy stared at me, unflinching, cold as ice, looked in the rear view mirror, tilted his head backwards and said, "Give me your 'roll. Now!"

No one had ever talked that way to me before and for maybe the first time in my life I did what I was told. I pulled out the twelve grand or so strapped up tight in two bundles with wide elastic bands and gave them to Tommy, turned and watched as the peaceful trip – except for disconcerting moments of self-illumination – found its ending.

A dark blue station wagon careened down the street and skidded to a halt by the curb. The doors flew open and three kids jumped out. They looked like teenagers with de rigueur leather jackets and bandanas tied around their heads but the two who climbed out of the front seat had guns stuck in their belts. Tommy looked at me and said, "Stay out of the way, in the car. Don't move one fucking inch. We've played this game before."

He got out, walked slowly down to the end of the driveway and stopped. The kids came over in that stalking, menacing style that the local hoods ripped off from Chuck Norris. The first one, who was clearly bossing this triumvirate of thugs, pulled the gun out of his waistband and snarled, "Jes' like last time, fuckface, gimme the fuckin' money and no one gets hurt."

I felt a lot like I did back in the corridor at my wedding, calm but useless. With the rear plastic window of Tommy's rag top framing the scene, I watched. I saw but could barely grasp what happened for it was so fast, so lethal that when I told Lydia about it, it took longer to describe than to happen.

Tommy walked up to the first hood and pulled the three wads of bills out of his pockets. "Like last time?" But he didn't hand them over. He stopped, smiled and dropped them into the gutter, into the storm drain where the curb cut sloped down to the street.

"What? What the fuck are you doin'?" yelled the kid and he leaned down toward the drain. "What th..." he repeated with a mixed look of horror and bewilderment on his face but only got the first part out for Tommy used this split second to close the gap between them. He pivoted on his left foot, "Oh my, just like Norris," I said, I think out loud, from the safety of the front seat as Tommy's right foot caught the kid full in the face. His gun skidded across the driveway and the kid crumpled, blood streaming from his nose. Spinning onto the other foot Tommy drove a beautiful, hand-made Lucchese boot into the second hoodlum's crotch and I swore I could hear a horrible squishing sound. The kid hit the deck grasping his nuts with both hands and screaming.

Suddenly the two guns were in Tommy's hands and the other manchild was on his knees with his hands over his head crying, "Don' shoot me, don' shoot me, please. I don' wanna die."

"Go inside and call the cops," Tommy called out. "The keys are in the ignition."

When I returned Tommy was standing over the three of them. "These motherfuckers," he said, "robbed me before.

"I know what you punks do. I know who you are and where you hang out," he sneered. "If anything like this happens again, to me or any of my friends, I will find you. You may think you're tough but you're way outta your league."

We all stayed there, framed in this otherworldly montage until sirens were heard coming down the street. A squad car and a police van screeched up to the curb and four cops jumped out. It took but a few minutes for Tommy to explain what happened and for me to verify it.

Tommy turned the guns over to the cops who nodded, asked a couple more questions and took lots of notes. They 'cuffed the kids, put them in the van and took them away, leaving just the squad car and its two officers. The elder one turned to Tommy and said, "You know sir, this looks bad. It looks like excessive violence and, since it seems like two of these kids are juvvies, we may have to bring you in for more than the usual. Besides, no one has verified that there was any basis for a robbery here or before."

Tommy just smiled and walked over to the gutter, pulled back the grate and there, to my astonishment, was a chain hammered into the pavement. Tommy reached down and pulled it and up came a small steel basket with our bankrolls, a little soggy but intact.

"Those hoodlums watch my house and the houses of other high stakes players. Sometimes they follow us home from card rooms; sometimes, like today, they hang around waiting." Tommy said, turning to the cops. "This isn't the first time they hit me. And before you ask, no, I didn't report that one. I built my little 'safe deposit' box."

"You put that down there?" asked the young cop looking surprised.

"Yup, good idea, eh," he said with a wink at me. "But," he said turning back to the two uniforms, "I understand the danger you and your partner were in. This will balance things."

And he peeled off, to my horror, ten bills from one of my carefully strapped 'rolls. The cops paused, for a terrible second I could see myself being dragged in for attempted bribery. Covina flashed before my now thoroughly screwed up brain. I could see "my" judge, gavel raised, sentencing me to decades, nay lifetimes in cinderblock tanks with steel benches and dented toilets and there is no way, no way I would be able to piss in front of all those miscreants and my bladder would swell up and burst and I would die, pathetic, leaking urine on the floor of a cell surrounded by punks and gang bangers who laughed and called me a "pussy."

But, no, no drama, no tank. The cops took the bills, squeezed them, the slimy water running over their hands, got in the car and left. Tommy then pulled the rubber band off his similarly soggy bankroll, counted out five bills, gave them to me with my two soaked, smelly rolls and smiled. "Too bad it rained so hard last night. I thought I set that cage up to be above water. Shall we go have dinner?"

XLII. 1969 – July

Lydia had spent the month efficiently. After sifting several offers she chose a junior position in a local firm that dealt mainly with union issues and community organizing efforts. The pay stunk but everything else was *just right*. Armin came out for a visit and it didn't take long for us to realize that he arrived with a plan. As he raised his glass in the first of the celebratory toasts the "meddling professor" appeared.

"Lydia, congratulations on the offer but...."

"But?" and that eyebrow went up.

"Yes, 'but,'" he said, clearly not noticing.

"Ah, I see," she said. "This is the 'but' that comes after, 'some of my best friends are black, gay, communists... *community organizers.*'"

"Yes it is but I don't mean it to sound quite like that. You still don't know how good you are, do you? We might have started with a judicial internship. We still could."

"I don't think so, Armin, and why was that 'we' in there?"

"Huh? Did I say 'we'?" said Armin, looking uncomfortable. "I didn't realize that. Look, I just want you to do well."

"Well, that's nice," said Lydia. "But the 'we' thing is, well, weird."

"Oh, Christ," and Armin let out a long sigh, the one of spurned mentors and disappointed parents. "Look, okay, okay, it was. You're right... sorry. But the 'but' still holds. You could go almost anywhere, even teach."

"See, you've done it again. 'Teach' like in 'what I do.'"

And he sighed again, slowly this time. "I'm sorry. It just keeps leaking out. Long ago you two slipped past my defenses. I care, damn it."

"I'll carve out my own career," she smiled. "I do love you and I'm pleased you're a part of my life, but don't try to make me you."

"I'm not, I'm..."

She cut him off. "Yes you are. But that's okay; I don't blame you. I'll probably do the same thing some day. But it won't work. I don't want to be a judge. I want even less to play the professorial game."

I watched with an inward smile. Armin looked like someone who thought his towels were being washed too often.

"I've already taken the job. The thing that surprises me now is that you're surprised. So stop trying to make me what I'm not and what you, if you ever take off that silly bowtie and look inwardly, aren't either. More wine anyone?"

"On another issue, Armin," I said. "We heard there was something they're calling a 'riot' recently in The Village. What do you know?"

"Indeed," said Armin anxiously jumping on this new topic, "they've been dubbed the 'Stonewall Riots,' after the gin-joint where it all erupted. I wasn't there, not the first night."

"That makes it sound like you were the second," said Lydia.

"I was. I wanted to see what happened. It wasn't exactly my kind of place. It catered to drag queens, hustlers and junkies. Bowie was; he still feels comfortable in that world. 'The faggots revolted, finally,' he said. They took over Christopher Street, most of the Village. With tears in his eyes, and when you see tears in eyes like those they get to you. He said, 'You couldn't believe it. All those beaten, wounded queers. Together. And no one looked lost anymore. They were just beautiful.'

"It's got me thinking. I may," and Armin paused, his eyes downward, "I just may come out of the closet. I… *we*'ve been too proper, too establishment and it hasn't worked. How can I stay hidden?"

"Armin," Lydia said, "this time '*we*' is fine, but are you sure? The world is a pretty screwed-up place. Why do you think I chose this firm?"

"I'm in a privileged place," he said, sitting upright, trying to look confident. "A law professor with four books and dozens of law review pieces. I'm hard to hurt."

"You can be hurt," said Lydia.

I sat there feeling a pleasing tension. I was a poker player who had become perhaps a bit too comfortable with that world. I'd spent the last couple of years hanging around with some very odd characters, breaking bread with them, drinking in dark bars, traveling, trading stories true and self-consciously crafted. I liked being with them, the reserved, the gregarious, the tolerant and the bigoted. I embraced them and struggled not to become them. I could live, I knew, a life divided.

As we talked it became clear that Armin had been hiding in plain sight for years, in the "proper" homosexual-rights movement doing quiet, didn't-really-notice-I-was-here-did-you? work for the various bloated homos who got pulled in because they said "hi" to some swish in a bar who turned out to be undercover and had their overweight, oft-plundered butts dragged into the local precinct for no other reason than they could because "You're a cock sucking faggot and that's all we need to know." But did they know he was a closet queen himself?

"Bowie is in New York?" I said. "I hadn't seen him in some time and was wondering."

"Indeed. He moved there a couple of months ago. I assumed you knew. His production company has branched into New York. Plus he wants to see if there's anything new in the jazz scene. He was there, didn't get arrested and, feeling like he'd failed, came over to my place. We went back the next night and got to witness the truly weird and wonderful."

"I assume you also managed not to get arrested," I smiled.

"Oh, I stayed away from the real action and had on my most conservative bow tie," he said winking at me. "The police arrived in force but with a hesitancy – like they didn't know what to make of it, what they should do. The Village was out, leather boys, drag queens, dykes and femmes."

"You're making me wish I'd been there," said Lydia.

"You would've loved it. There were lots of straights. Maybe they have gay children, maybe just saw injustice. Someone had a bull horn and starting hollering into it and the police began grabbing anyone they could, stuffing them into vans and police buses. Discretion seemed wisest and we left. But there's no doubt who will win this war."

"War?" said Lydia, arching an eyebrow.

"Metaphorically speaking, yes. Things are changing. I feel it. You will too for this will rip across the land. I'll sum it up for you, it's 'no-more-mister-nice-guy' time. I'm comin' out."

I smiled and nodded assent for the stance and for Armin's dropped 'g.' Maybe things were changing and maybe he wasn't really upset with Lydia's choice.

XLIII. 1974 – September

Lydia got *the* offer, the one she had wanted so much she almost couldn't admit it: partner in a firm staffed by hopelessly naïve utopians, childlike idealists who specialized in civil rights, in San Francisco where said rights were moving to center stage.

Looking back I had trouble putting any "texture" on those LA years. Lydia was carving out a career, but for me it was a blur of poker games, dinners with friends and family and long evenings bitching about how messed up everything was. Raucous political donnybrooks punctuated the many gatherings in our house and my social conscience was certainly getting sharpened. I guess we were just having a bloody good time.

With the move I felt a burden lift, one I hadn't realized I'd been carrying. My old lady, I smiled inwardly bouncing that idiotic line around in my head, is gonna be bringing home a serious paycheck. Playing poker is, as the old line goes, "a tough way to make an easy living." It had become a grind. Hours were money and money was the full and total sum of the life. Like that month Tommy and I spent on the road – except for Lorenzo's basement, I never saw the inside of anything other than a poker room, a restaurant or a bar. Pathetic.

The chance to relax also gave me time to reflect on change and I noticed some things had happened while my attention was elsewhere. For one there was this annoying patch of skin on my head which used to be blanketed with curly Aegean hair. I felt violated. Lydia thought it was funny. I also noted that

Lydia's hips and breasts were doing their Italian momma thing. "Look at Tessa," Alkaios had said with a laugh, "because that is what Lydia will surely look like." I didn't say anything; instead I worked out what I thought were clever ripostes about gravity and stored them away for when I would need them.

As fall crept in and the mist and fogs rolled in from the bay, Lydia cranked it up on behalf of the descendants of slaves denied life's basic rights, campaigned against wage standards geared to genitalia, filed briefs for those having the poor judgment to have last names ending in "-ez" and defended the homosexuals who had, as Armin predicted, taken to the barricades across the land. She was as happy as I could remember. I hadn't seen this glow in her eye since the day she found out she was pregnant. Children, I saw, could take on metaphoric forms.

We bought a house in Oakland. It quickly became a crazy mix of Konstantakis and Demerara, with olive wood chairs and overstuffed sofas – thankfully without plastic slip covers – framed maps on the walls, family photos on shelves and tables. Lydia finally had the office she had pined for and she turned it into a total mess, piled with papers, accordion binders strewn about the floor, her desk covered with legal pads, their pages bent, folded, dog-eared and stained with brown, wrinkly circles from neglected coffee cups. She swore she knew where everything was and what was on each scrap of paper and in each drawer and no one, except for the cat, still nameless a year into our lives, was allowed in.

"That cat needs a name," I said. "I went through this before. A dog called 'the dog' because no one took the time to name it is silly. Same for cats."

"Ah," she smiled. "You do realize that Persi was right. True names are sacred; they capture the essence of self. The naming myths give fair warning to the reckless."

"Reckless? It's reckless to name a cat? You are not serious."

"I am. I'm content to wait for her to reveal hers."

I didn't know whether she was joking or not although I had to admit, this was a better reason for being nameless than simply having no one who cared. So I named her T.C. but we were the only ones who knew. She let me know that was fine.

Finally settled, we threw ourselves a little party to warm the hearth and anoint our new lives. Anna and Billy drove up and Armin flew in. I had claimed the kitchen; it was my way to redress my karmic balance from all those take-out chickens. I had on the "Hell's Kitchen" apron I'd bought on a lark. It'd been stuck in a drawer till the storm-drain day when I decided that there could be more useful and less terrifying ways to spend my off-hours. My offering was a seafood risotto and I felt utterly full of myself as I accidentally dropped slivers of scallop on the floor for T.C. who let me know that was fine.

Two bottles of wine later and we were talking about kids, which wasn't easy for any of us. I have no idea how this toxic topic ever wandered into the otherwise upbeat evening. Lydia couldn't have any. Sabbie and Tessa were more or less quietly disappointed but there wasn't a hell of a lot they could do about it. At the time I didn't think Anna and Billy wanted any, which turned out to be wrong in a revealing way.

"I guess I've pretty much come to grips with this, but it took a while," said Lydia. "I'm not Selma and Momma Tessa will just have to be satisfied with the brood in Bensonhurst. If she wants more she can work on Rosie. She won't say a word to Luigi. I think she's terrified that he might actually disperse his genes into the world."

"In a truly screwed up way, Lydia," Billy said, frowning, "you've gotten yourself free from the heavy stuff. Hanna knows there's no sense pressuring you two, so we're getting it all."

"Really?" said Lydia.

"Well, she tries to be gentle," he said, "but it keeps coming up. We don't even want to call them anymore."

"The weird thing," said Anna, "is I'm 'getting on' and we've been thinking it might be cool to have a baby, hell, maybe more than one. But it feels less like 'we want a baby' and more like 'Momma won.'"

Armin leaned forward and smiled, "There is a delicious irony here. You don't know, of course, but I have a son." And the room grew very quiet. I looked over at my friend, Lydia's intellectual guru and laughed. "I'm sorry, Armin, I shouldn't treat this as funny but it is and for the moment I'm going to believe this is true."

Lydia leaned back in her chair, "Indeed. It's hard not to laugh."

"Laugh as you wish, both of you. I've never mentioned it because it's well, kind of private and more than a little out of character. In fact, I have two children – there's a daughter."

"All right," I said. "No one move. And, *you*" as I turned to Armin, "don't you utter one more word till I get back." And I headed off to the kitchen for a bottle of ouzo, five glasses and an eye dropper.

Armin tossed down a chilled glassful, let the aromatic essence of licorice swirl on his tongue and stared aimlessly out the window. He looked like an actor assuming a role, the teller of tales.

"I grew up in a small New Hampshire town," he began, still gazing out the window, "tight and buttoned down as you can get. We did all the things we were supposed to do. Climbed hills we called 'mountains,' swam in ponds we called 'lakes.'"

"Sounds idyllic," said Anna.

"Superficially, it was. We were blessedly normal. My parents were solid, middle-class with all the strengths and foibles of the breed. Dad taught high school and Mom stayed at home and overcooked pot roast. Aron, my older brother, was killed in action a few months before Hiroshima. Life was not the same after that."

"Your brother was killed? That is horrible," Lydia said.

"Yes, in a campaign in the South Pacific. It still hurts in a distant kind of way. It hit my parents far harder though."

"Oh Armin, I am so sorry," said Lydia as she reached out to touch the back of his hand that was now clenching the arm of his chair.

"It was rough. Dad pretty much withdrew, largely into the school. Mom found the classic solace of the small New England town: she became a secret alcoholic."

"Secret?" Billy piped up.

"Well, more I guess like 'quiet.' She'd wait till after dinner. Then it was gin with lemon slices till bed – usually we carried her. She used to take the car and say nothing. After she died, I discovered she'd been driving to liquor stores in neighboring towns. New England village gossip can be brutal.

"As the new number one son, I felt I had obligations. I went to UNH to prepare for a life of some normal kind but, more importantly, I married Dotty, the girl down the block."

"You were married?" I said. "This is getting more and more interesting. I feel like I'm back in O'Shannon's with Henry doling out secrets."

"Oh, yes, married, I was 19, Dotty 18. It was very traditional. Tuxedoes, white church, white gown, many white people. Confetti, rice and toasts to the next generation."

"But," I leaned forward looking at his eyes which had moved back from the window and were fixed on the empty ouzo glass, "you're gay."

"I didn't know that then. I tried to be a good husband. Bowie and others say they knew from the time they were kids they were homosexual. I didn't. I knew I didn't fit in but I didn't know why. I hated the arm punching and macho antics of the locker room, the dating, the dance halls. But there was no other identity to cling to, just that of the small town New England and its middle-of-the-road ways. I did my duty and the result is Horst."

"How did you feel during all this?" asked Lydia. "Playing a role? A fraud? I don't mean to sound cruel but I've wondered if I could pretend to be a lesbian. I don't think I could."

"It wasn't easy but I wasn't *pretending*. I was just confused. Slowly it became inescapable. There was no other answer. I tried to hide it but it just kept growing, like an infection I'd caught but fought off until my immune system weakened. I found I wasn't alone, not even in small-town New Hampshire. 'Secret assignations,' as they call them, began to occur, it became harder and harder to live the lie. So I stopped lying."

"Interesting," said Lydia. "You've come out more than once, yes?"

"I guess, but it was more like moving from one small closet to another. Dotty did not take it well. We split immediately. My father tried to accept me but really couldn't. Mom, well, even a well-practiced alcoholic can't survive two and a half bottles of gin."

Nobody said anything. Lydia wiped a tear from her cheek. Armin took a deep breath, staring out the window again.

"I moved to Chicago. Switched to dance and theater and began to feel like me for the first time. I met Bowie there. He is, as Xero knows, a brilliant jazz pianist with classical training. He was playing the clubs around Hyde Park, did keyboard for the university's dance theater and was on his way to becoming one of the city's biggest record producers."

"That's where the money comes from, yes?" asked Anna.

"Yes, and there's a lot of it. That's how you can buy a good sized piece of a Gardena card club. We lived underground, largely out of others' sight. We made quite a pair. It felt comfortable, safe. I danced, we did drugs, had far too much sex and yes, Xero, we had a regular poker game," said Armin, smiling now, the cover restored.

"Poker eh?" I said. "You mentioned this once or twice. I kinda thought you were kidding."

"Nope. Sounds funny, doesn't it. A bunch of faggots, sitting around a table, smoking mother nature and playing poker, like 'we wuz nawmal, reg'lar guys.' Why do you think Bowie bought into the Normandie? He was the best of us."

"*Wuz, nawmal?*" said Lydia. "Like in Bensonhurst?"

"Yeah, wuz and reg'lar. Like in South Side Chicawgo. Well, that's about it. You know the rest... or as much of it as is relevant right now."

"Dear Armin," Lydia said while refilling everyone's glass. "It is, if you pardon me, a wonderful story. I was expecting much worse. Do you see Horst? And didn't you also say 'daughter?'"

"I do. Not as often as I'd like. I'm still a bit unwelcome back home, Ivy League law professor notwithstanding. I get up there when I can and Horst comes to New York from time to time."

"The daughter?" said Lydia.

"Ah, yes. I am not avoiding her. It's just that I have no idea who she is, where she is or even her name. I merely know she exists. Bowie got in touch, said a lesbian friend wanted to have a child and did he know someone smart and good looking to donate some sperm. He said he volunteered and got laughed out of the bar.

"So I did it. I think it was an ego thing. I got a cryptic note telling me that it was a girl. That is all I know although I admit I have a lingering hope that someday a young woman will walk into my office and say, 'Hi Dad.'"

XLIV. 1992 – June

She, I thought as I glanced back over my shoulder at Lydia, is having too much fun. She was sitting there, one of the legions of unappreciated legal laborers, defenders of the downtrodden, the abused, neglected and despised and now the head of the San Francisco office. Her hair was tousled, glasses slid down her nose and she looked suspiciously at a bunch of legal-sized papers folded back at the stapled top and muttered.

"You would think," she said while I fussed at a pot of brown sludge that could, with luck, become a demi-glace, "that us poor slobs who hurl ourselves into this level-the-playing-field racket would get some respect."

I smiled at her, sipping carefully from the edge of a wooden spoon and looking suspiciously at the pot. "You know, only an idiot would do this. I could buy a jar of this stuff for less than the ingredients cost and end up with a better sauce. But," I said looking back at her, "I respect you."

"Since you have to say that, it doesn't mean crapola. But I'll take what I can right now. I'll tell you what, baby snooks, we're in a very distinct minority. You know how you, like everybody else, is convinced that guy Lippenham is a mobster because he defends Mafia dons? Well, everybody who bothers to think about me assumes that I'm some bimbo lesbian hooker commie because so many of my clients are."

"Yo, kiddo, you could'a been a contenda. You had class, babe. You wuz good. All youse had to do was what our favorite commie homosexyoooul perfesser wanted fer you."

"Yeah, but we knew, that kind of life, that kind of money is too expensive. But, to tell the truth, I've come to like being a bimbo commie. It gives me a little edge. Did I tell you? After my guy got acquitted yesterday the moron pretending to be a prosecuting attorney called me a 'nigger lover.'" I can't remember when I felt prouder."

When not in the kitchen, I would still curl up inside my cocoon. I played poker but not as often. I'd taken to reading the densest novels I could find and rummaging around in my psyche. I felt older, which was okay; I was. I had, along with most of my cohort, survived decades amusing and terrifying. Vietnam, Watergate, the collapse of the Soviet Union, Reagan's voodoo economics and all of it salvaged, barely, by hard rock and the Rubik's Cube.

Time had made me ever more follicularly challenged and, like my father, I had put on weight in predictable places. Lydia continued on her way to looking an awful lot like Tessa, which

I was very, very careful not to mention, not to even hint at, not to even think lest the thought leak out. The house in Oakland swung back and forth from the high-decibel hermit's cave when I was alone with the Stones at full volume to scenes only a bit this side of insanity when Lydia's many connections provided a running supply of politicians, lawyers, drag queens, community organizers, transvestites and prostitutes of all possible genders. A reasonable life.

One late summer evening, while Lydia was developing the defense for two young black twenty-somethings locked up for "assaulting" a police officer, which was what it got called when a black kid talked back to a white cop in Oakland, I decided to wander over and see what kind of action there was at The Palermo, the new poker club that had opened a week back.

I liked to look around a new room before I sat down. I hung around the perimeter, leaned on the rail and checked out the crowd. I recognized some of the faces, local grinders who had stopped by, checking for contributors. A new room brought new faces, locals, who thought they knew this game but rarely did, tourists who wandered in looking for some action. Without a steady supply of these donkeys, life would have been even tougher for these guys, all of whom were trying to scrape a living off of the same green felt.

Leaning on my elbows I scanned the newness, tables still clean, their taut felt coverings bright virginal green, unmarked by cigarette burns, spilled drinks or sweat, chairs with even, straight legs and smooth cushions, the sound of newly minted chips being riffled, the familiar clatter strangely comforting, dealers with smart black pants, white shirts and bolo ties.

A vaguely familiar face, one of the road warriors, spotted me and let the corner of his mouth tighten in what I took to be a smile. We knew. We could pick each other out across a room, in a restaurant, a bar – conspecifics, a nuthatch singling out another in a cloud of chickadees and finches. It was a small fraternity and this life, like the one inside Hesse's Magic Theatre, was "NOT FOR EVERYBODY."

These not-everybodys tended to be loners, they tended to be men. The few women in this world seem divided into those who used their sexuality, loose tops, convenient bends from the waist, gentle touches, open-eyed smiles and, once in a while, a little of that "Ah don' know nothin' about birth'n no babies" fluttering innocence that worked so well, and the others who had withdrawn into shells, the Charlenes, mean and unforgiving, who seemed to distrust their sisters even more than the men, their natural adversaries.

This world was unlike all others and yet the same, a Frankie kind of life. Everybody was doing it "my way" and all the "mys" were different and yet all the same and, like peddling ducats for Ken or swinging sledge for Tony, it was all in the dark. There was no dress code here, there were no contracts, no unions, no deductions, no taxes and there were no pensions, health coverage, social security.

In those days I lived a cash-in-the-pocket life. I walked around with wads of hundred dollar bills wrapped up in rubber bands, jammed into the pockets of my jeans. I had others stuffed into drawers in the house. Occasionally I made deposits in bank accounts under Lydia's name and pretended that the future would treat me kindly. I always kept a couple of twenties loose or in my wallet. When paying for dinner or the groceries it was unseemly to peel a hundred off a fat roll. Outside the clubs everyone freaked when they saw one of them and if you were not careful nasty people might notice.

I leaned back and drifted into one of my nostalgia-dusted reveries. I conjured up the vivid memory of that afternoon in Housemann's office. Who knew we'd be here? Who knew we'd be happy to be here?

I moved my head down a bit, as if I were talking to a curious child before me. But there was only the curved, white railing. I'm Alkaios's "son," I told the smooth rounded balustrade, Tony's "kid," Lydia's "guy."

How many of these bozos – I abandoned the rail, looked about the room feeling a bit full of myself – have an Ivy League degree or care about civil rights? Have lawyer wives, gay friends? Can cook? An answer was heard, a small, mouse-like voice below the railing and it whispered, "And what'll that buy you here, asshole?"

I acknowledged the mouse and while I chewed over these matters I felt a presence behind me and a heavy tap on my shoulder. I froze and waited for it was never wise to react quickly in these settings. A voice, rough but commanding, whispered in my ear, "Sir, would you be so kind as to accompany us."

Code. The greeting to bums and cheats and sharps caught dealing seconds, snatchers with chips stuck to their palms. It was always delivered in the most pleasant manner, often with a thumb nail raked across your upper back, "If you would..., would you be so..., could you please..." but it was not a request any more than the state trooper who leans down and says, "Sir, would you please step out of the car," is making you an offer which you may refuse or decide to comply with, but a bit later. The next stop was always the office in back. Sometimes the folks there were pleasant and forgiving, sometimes decidedly less so, but all too often the end was the same, barred from the club. And if they decided to flash photos of your face around, from all the others in that neck of the woods. For a playing pro being barred was death.

I was confused and more than a bit pissed. These guys are just flunkies so I knew not to ask why or plead my case. I assumed that they'd got me confused with someone. As we walked across the carpet waiting for its first coffee spill, I wondered, as I had on so many occasions, if there was an FBI agent waiting for me.

The manager's office was classic, small with industrial-strength, all-weather carpet, a little nook off to the side to keep coats and a six-pack, obligatory photos of celebrities and a couple of bookcases stacked with binders and folders. The desk at the far end was cluttered with papers but its chair was empty.

The larger of the security guards pointed to the chair in front of the desk and they left me to ponder my fate.

"Hello, *kid*," came a voice, one so familiar, with its singular stress on "kid," that it collapsed decades into a shrunken fold of time. I leapt to my feet and turned to find the last person I would've guessed would be standing in the doorway. Tony Piccolo was alive and well and, fer cris'fuckin'sake, appeared to be the manager.

We stopped and stared for a lingering second as each took in the other. Tony was as he had been, as he should be, with just a little new flesh on the image I'd kept with me for so long. His hair line was, like mine, retreating, though in his case it sharpened the edges of his cheeks and his forehead. A black turtle-neck still wrapped his torso though now it was cut a little looser to cover a bit of a paunch and, as befitted his role, it was under a fine wool suit jacket, the pocket of which displayed a buffed up brass tag that said, "Tony P., Manager."

We fell into an embrace that closed generations. Tony felt younger, almost like a contemporary. When you're twenty, anyone in the neighborhood of thirty seems so old, as though the shadows cast by the years embodied wisdom. When you're in your fifties, sixty something is just another drinking buddy.

"Spotted you leaning on the rail, looking like you were sizing up a mark," he said leaning back to take me in. "Hope you didn't mind the 'escort' I sent. I simply couldn't resist. Besides, I wasn't totally sure you were you; it's been some time."

"Well, I probably should be pissed. Maybe later I will be. But not now. Now I am just so fucking happy you cannot imagine. How did you end up here? What about the circus?"

"This gig here, *kid*," Tony said with a knowing grin, "*is* a circus, as I suspect you know."

"Oh, yes, I know. We've been in the Bay area for some time now. I play poker and cook; Lydia defends the downtrodden. You will have to meet her some time soon. Did you not get the wedding invitation?"

"I did, but too late. Bobbi and I had split. She got the kids, the house and pissy about my mail. Later I wrote but the letter bounced. I guess you had moved, out here. I'd always hoped there'd be this day where our paths crossed again."

"And the circus?" I asked.

"That's a tale for a drink and dinner which, given that I'm running this joint, will be comped."

XLV. 1992 – June

Sucking on a lemon twist pulled from his martini Tony began, slowly, quietly. "About three years after you left, Ken's wife died. It hit hard. He was, as you saw, a bit of a boozer and he tossed himself seriously into the bottle. There wasn't much anyone could do. I tried because I cared for him and I owned that piece of the midway, you know, the concessions. But everything was falling apart. Scheduling got messed up, advance teams were stealing, we'd get to a town and Ken wouldn't have made the right arrangements.

"Then it got worse. Doris had been sucking up to him and he started listening to her. Over the next winter me and Ricco went to his place in LA to try to talk to him, warn him off her. We were too late. She greeted us at the door. With those cheap bangles on her wrists and a really mean snarl she told us to get the fuck outta there and leave her and Ken alone.

"The next year was a total mess and it didn't help that Bobbi and I weren't exactly living the American dream any longer."

"The others? Ricco? Grace and Sal? Maxim?" I asked.

"Ricco and I are still friends. He's in LA, got a little band. They do weddings and stuff. Grace and Sal took a gig with an outfit in Europe. Haven't heard anything since they left."

"And Maxim? The guy I wasn't supposed to even talk to?"

"Okay. Time to 'fess up. Maxim was Ken's brother. I couldn't tell you then. Ken woulda freaked. I hated having him around. I worried every day, that he would do something weird, something that could wreck everything. I worried every time we sent him into the tent, onto the midway. But he was Ken's. Ken protected him, gave him cover. I had to also."

"And?" I said.

"And, like I said, 'was.' When Ken dumped himself into the bottle he found Maxim had already set up living quarters there, down at the bottom. He died soon after. No one misses him. The saving grace is he never actually molested some kid."

"None you ever heard of," I said and regretted it.

"Yeah, none we ever heard of," he echoed and paused. "None we ever heard of," more quietly this time.

After an appropriate moment, I leaned in and asked, "Judy?" I felt myself flush slightly and hoped Tony didn't notice.

"Ah," Tony tilted his head knowingly, "Judy. Yes, Judy. Well, after a time she went back to school. My old stompin' grounds, San Jose. She hooked up with a pretty good guy who has a small hardware store in town. Ricco's now a grandfather twice over. She's teaching school there. Kinda like it should be, yeah?"

"Yeah," I nodded, thinking that was exactly right.

"Next thing Doris and Ken got hitched which is when we found out, and I know you're gonna love this, that her real name is Daciana which I discovered originally meant 'wolf' or 'wicked.' And that turd Rudy was now living with them. There was no way I could have her as my boss or that little fart underfoot. Ricco bought me out."

"Daciana? Hah!" I exclaimed. "My BS unit went 'bong' the moment I met her. 'Wolf?' 'Wicked?' Oh man, it fits. So well it's almost eerie."

"Ken lasted about a year under her care. When they found the will it was decades old and still listed his first wife. Suddenly everything was wrapped up in legal bullshit and red tape. Ricco tried to take control of operations but Doris was like a cornered badger. She was everywhere, messing with everyone's mind, filing law suits. There weren't any kids so the court gave her the damn thing, minus the concessions.

"Two years later it collapsed. You can't have a psychopath run something like that. It was just as well; an era was ending. Everybody scattered and I've lost track of everyone but Ricco."

"But how did you end up here? In a poker club?" I asked.

"Well, I bummed around for a while. Then an old friend who had some connections got in touch. 'Did I want to work in security?' At first I didn't but nothing else was on the horizon so I went along and ended up at a card room in San Jose. I found I liked the life. Worked hard. 'Did good,' as they say and they kept movin' me up. It's okay. It's got a little pizzazz, a bunch of fun characters and it's easy. Pay's not bad either."

"Do you," I asked, "not miss the con, the game, the mudshow side of life?"

"I do – but I don't. The 'don't' wins out. You get older and the carny starts lookin' like what it really is, an illusion, a thin veil pulled over pain. Except for Ricco – and you, but you don't really count, sorry 'bout that, you were just 'passing through' – no one in the crew was stable or honest with themselves. Every piece of fantasy or fun was balanced by pain, self-doubt and fear, fear of life, fear of a reality hangin' there, outside the tent, behind the rubber chickens and prancing ponies. At the end of the midway, Daciana was waiting for you.

"But," he said, leaning back in his chair, "I am as happy as a newly fucked monkey to see you. And, to make sure I do not lose you again, I want you to come on board."

"Whoa, what did you say? Come on what? Where?"

"On board, here, at The Palermo. Join me. Run away with the circus, one mo' time."

"You've gotta be kidding," I said. "You were the one who pushed me out of the carny, practically laughed me off the big ol' wheel. Something about getting my, 'nice-Greek-poppa's-boy ass back to some Ivy joint' was how you put it."

"Hmm. That sounds familiar. I see it had no impact."

"Ah, but it did. I went back. I finished, even did one year in law school and am still a middle-class kid, a wandering Greek gadjo, looking for enlightenment. I just play a lot of poker. But what do you want from me?"

"Well, the suits offered me this job when it suddenly opened up. I was supposed to be the Head of Security. So, I need a new one. Want the job? Just think how much fun it could be. For one, you'll be the boss of those two ex-wrestlers who escorted you in."

"But I don't know anything about security."

"You didn't know dick about the circus either but that didn't matter. Besides, you got what I need, smarts and flexibility. And, the old boy network still operates around here, and I got a lot of clout, old 'boy.'"

Two days later I unbent. Life finally caught up with me and Lydia couldn't stop laughing. "Legit! You're going legit. A salary, a contract and they'll be taking out FICA. The IRS is going to go nuts if anyone there ever sits down and looks at this. 'Where'd this guy come from? How come he's getting paid like an executive when he's never earned a penny before?' Good thing you're sleeping with an outstanding lawyer."

"Very funny but, guess what. I'm tired of living on the fringe. I want to pay taxes."

"I wouldn't say that too loudly, certainly not in public. It's un-American."

"Yeah, then they oughta really love poker players 'cause damn few of 'em even file. But seriously, I need to learn how the system works, from the inside. There's an awful truth that has been adawning."

"And that is?" she asked.

"I'm bored."

"Bored? With poker? Hah!" she laughed. "When did this happen?"

"It's been sneakin' up on me.... Jack Straus, one of our finer degenerates, got to the heart of it. 'The game,' he quipped, 'is long stretches of boredom punctuated by moments of terror.'"

"Sounds like a lot of things, like going into court."

"Court? Really? That's hard to see."

"Oh, you think my life is just a series of fascinating cases. You watch too much TV. We've been together what, a hundred and ten years now and you still have no grasp of what my life is like."

"That's not true – though the 'hundred and ten years' thing was pretty good. But this isn't a boredom contest. I'm just trying to make a point."

"It better be a good one. I'm not big on 'my pain is more painful than your pain' bull."

"Look, I know, I do. Everyone's life is mostly tedium with little slivers of excitement. Suppose you did nothing but traffic offenses. That's it. Traffic. Parking tickets, speeding, DUI. Once in a while it's some butthead who ran down a little old lady crossing against the light. You would wonder, 'Why am I doing this? I'm smart, skilled and I'm bored to fucking tears.' This defense rests." Lydia just sat there snickering... and raising that eyebrow. I think I won that one. Who the fuck knows.

XLVI. 1992 – July, August, September

The club was new, the building was new and there were problems. My first move was to set up a two-safe system. In my briefings I got the inside dope on a couple of robberies at other card rooms and made sure the cashier's cage only kept a small portion of the drop. I hired Manny, a sharp, funny guy from San Diego as my Assistant but I was stuck with the holdovers.

One was an ex-cabbie, another a retired cop and then, of course, there were the two goons who first greeted me. To a man, they were old, slow, fat and had lost whatever edge they might once have had. But, that was okay. Poker's a good teacher; you can't change the cards, you just try to play 'em right.

It was an interesting phase-shift. Regular times at work. Up in the morn and hi ho, hi ho, it's off to work we go. I bought a couple of suits and a bunch of no-iron shirts and dug out my old Columbia tie, the one with the stylized blue lions resplendent on a yellow background. I wondered what Housemann would think if he saw me standing in front of a poker table all decked out in Ivy finery – assuming he was still alive. I even hammered out a note for him:

you thought I'd never grace 'er
was sure I'd disgrace 'er
but I've always embraced 'er
the cartoon Columbia lion

I discovered I had a head for management and surprised the hell out of myself. I got my guys involved in the operation, including my "escorts" who thought it was funny me being their boss. I made a point of going to them for advice so they didn't feel like I was pushing them around. I started working on plans to redesign the layout. I wanted to move the cage to a more secluded, protected spot, away from the front door. I settled into my new identity, and the relaxed lifestyle and quiet nights that seem to be carried on its winds.

Who knew? – Point. How long? – Counterpoint. How long, I wondered, before I am bored to tears?

On one particularly quiet evening, a couple of months into the routine, I found myself musing on clichés. My life, like everyone else's, has been full of them. I didn't think they were clichés; no one does when they're yours. I liked mine. They meant things, personal things. They were comforting, like the fuzzy blankie I carried around as a child holding its impenetrable armor up against my frightened wee self. Some I crafted myself; others were borrowed from people who had wandered into my life. "Don't fuck your friends" was a good one; I got it from Tony's dad. I liked its ambiguity. "Cuteness counts" was another. I think I made it up, courtesy of a two-toned Nash. I had gotten in and out of trouble with it over the years. Clichés should be useful.

Then there was this one, "Be wary of quiet nights." It came from my dad. He said he grasped its importance back before they left Greece, when things were stirring across the continent and quiet didn't always mean peaceful. Silence pulls you in, layers of false comfort wrap about you and you stop looking over your shoulder.

I took a stroll outside. The evening had been very quiet, graced with soft breezes marred only by a wafting of stale cooking oil from the fried chicken joint across the street. Somebody was playing Buddy Holly and the beat of *It Doesn't Matter Any More* slid down from an open window across the greensward to the south of the parking lot. Sounds travel well on sour air in a quiet evening. The street lamps came on; it was between cuts of the Holly record. I stood on the steps outside the club waiting for Manny to take over so I could get a cup of decaf before heading home.

From nowhere a humungous black van pounded over the curb and into the parking lot, tires screaming. It whipped around the perimeter and headed for the front door. At the last second, the brakes slammed on and it ground to a halt and out stepped one scary-looking son of a bitch. He was a good 6'4" and went at least two and a quarter. Black porkpie hat, three maybe four chains around his neck, shades, black leather jacket, black sleek pants, black cowboy boots with thick black heels, the kind that angled down just a bit for style and he carried a large black leather sack. Only things not black were his face and hands, pasty white like he was afraid of the sun.

He stalked over to me, grabbed me by the shoulder, shoved me up the steps and onto the porch. He pulled what looked like a cannon out of the inside pocket of his jacket and said, "Down motherfucker, down. Now. All the fucking way."

I found a lot of imported Italian tile to cover and lay there waiting to see what was up next. We didn't have the kind of security to deal with this. On this quiet night it was just me, Manny and two uniforms, Larry and a part-timer. "Poor fat Larry," I muttered under my breath. "He shoulda stayed with the taxi company."

Manny was just inside the door. He ducked into a side room and called 911. I rolled over onto the cement abutting the door and watched as "Porkpie" moved across the room with surprising grace; like some feral animal, he seemed to skim over the carpet.

He fired one shot into a planter holding an artificial palm tree and it exploded in a sea of terracotta shards. Players and dealers scattered. A poker table got upturned. Chips rolled everywhere, cash floated on the currents from the air conditioner. He went over to the cage, leaned menacingly on the counter with the gun through the cage window. He slid the leather bag in and said, "Y'all just fill that up, sweetie. Now. Real fast."

Donna, who was handling the cage, knew what to do. She knew why I set up two safes. Difference this night? Maybe fifty, maybe seventy-five thousand. Donna moved to the "robbery" safe.

Porkpie leaned in through the window and whispered, "No, love, the other one. Do not fuck with me." Donna startled, looked at Porkpie and went over to the back cabinet, opened the real safe, dumped a shit load of cash into the bag and handed it back. Porkpie snapped the bag shut and backed out.

When I saw him coming out, I jumped to my feet and, bent over for cover, ran for the service entrance at the far end of the lot. He saw my fleeing butt and apparently he did not like it at all. "Hold it right there, dickhead," he yelled and suddenly 'pop' 'pop' 'pop' and the pavement around my feet exploded. I dove into the bushes that lined the side of the building and rolled over to get as far out of the line of fire as I could. I felt blood running down off my cheek.

I was sure I had bought it. I flashed on Lydia and wondered who she will end up shagging after I'd died, which was truly bizarre but I really didn't have a lot of control over my brain at that moment. A few seconds later I realized that it was just a gash from the pavement shards and Lydia will be spared the ugly, insensitive lugs who would follow in my wake. But the lunatic with the cannon was still stomping around the parking lot. A bunch of guys streamed out of the club. Gee, this is great, I thought. Half these idiots probably think they're gonna be some kind of hero and take him down. The others looked like they're trying to decide between a stroke and a heart attack.

Porkpie turned around on them, slowly raised the gun and fired two rounds into that sweet nautical scene painted on the ceiling over the entrance and pink and aqua plaster rained down on them. Manny started screaming, "Get back in the club. Get the fuck back in!" And they did.

I was still in the bushes and the crazy motherfucker with the .45 was stalking around the rows of cars looking, looking... for, what? For me? Why? None of this made any sense. Nobody held up a poker club alone, without backup. It was just crazy. They will get him. There gotta be four, five dozen witnesses; there's the taping system. But this was one crazy guy. I looked over and saw Porkpie slap a new magazine into his gun.

Then, as suddenly as when the van jumped the curb, the cops showed up taking the same route. Waves of 'em streamed over the curb and onto the lot with great screeching of tires and howling of sirens. They blocked the driveways, clogged the escape lanes. I crawled down the side of the building where, unbelievably, I saw Manny doing a frog walk up from behind a bush.

Manny was a fortyish, balding Mexican with a pencil mustache and he was waddling toward me like an undernourished Sumo wrestler. The whole goddamn world was blowing up and this nutball snuck out the back door so he could be right there, up front, in the crossfire. I started to laugh. Crazy laughing. Weeping laughing. Like it was funny, which it was, in an otherworldly way. The two of us were crouching along a stucco wall, sheltered, barely, by a badly pruned row of boxwood bushes. We were scared shitless and were giggling like schoolgirls, with tears running down our faces.

About a dozen cops jumped out of their cars, everyone had a gun the size of a Louisville slugger and they were all pointed at Porkpie who stood there like a tree trunk with his legs spread. He looked like he just walked out of a really bad movie, all in black, with a black pistol in one hand and a black bag full of cash in the other, streaks of red and blue lights crisscrossing his body. His back was to the cops and for a second or two he didn't move a muscle. Then slowly he raised the gun so it was right up next to his white chalky ear.

This isn't real. This is a movie. They're making a freakin' movie and Tony didn't tell me. But then I felt the blood trickle down off my chin.

One cop yelled out, "Drop it, shithead. Drop it now. On the ground. Down, motherfucker or you're gonna die."

Porkpie actually smiled. I was close enough to see his face. He held the gun up to the side of his head and said, "It's a good day to die."

He let loose a volley of shots back over his shoulder at the cops and took off. He was in the fire zone maybe twenty, thirty feet from the arc of cops. It was like a fireworks factory just went up. Pop, bang, zig, zap. It wasn't just a movie anymore; it was a comic strip. The cops all dove when the first shots rang out. Rolling around on asphalt, jostling each other for safety behind squad cars, behind open doors, they scrambled to their knees, their feet, took the stance, gun out, support wrist, fire. Unbelievable. Nobody hit him.

He tore-ass out of the lot, across the main boulevard, four lanes of cars swerved and hit their brakes and he dodged and weaved his way to the corner where a couple of kids were sitting in their Chevy eating the last couple of pieces of fried chicken.

He ripped open the side door and pulled the guy out and jumped in. He pointed the gun at the girl and suddenly it was a hostage situation. Manny and I had come out from behind the bushes and could see the whole thing. Porkpie was sitting there pointing his freakin' cannon at the girl's temple and, I swore I could see what he was saying. He was telling her to just finish eating the chicken. I don't know how she could swallow but she got it down. Porkpie flicked the gun at the steering wheel and they drove off.

The cops were in a total jumble. No one seemed to know what to do. Two of them ran out into the street, waving guns and arms, stopping traffic. Two others ran over, grabbed the kid and threw him up against a car and started to scream at him. Because the girl drove away, I guessed, they thought they may have been Porkpie's partners or something. The kid looked like he was going to puke. He crumpled on the pavement and started to shake and cry about his girl friend. We heard him calling her name, "Cindy, Cindy, Cindy," he kept saying, rocking back against the car door. A cop shouted at him some more and someone yelled, "Fuck him" and off they went. Everyone jumped back into their cars, sirens shrieking, lights ablaze they peeled out of the lot, forced their way onto the street and took up the chase.

They didn't have a chance. Porkpie and Cindy were long gone.

It was a long time getting back to what passed for normal at The Palermo. I hated the next couple of days. Everyone was swarming around the place. Photos, TV interviews, local press, cops looking for evidence, assistant DAs looking for angles. I tried to keep it clean but the press liked it juiced up. It got juiced because the poker junkies were full of tales of their heroic actions. Even Larry showed up on the evening news. Later I discovered he was in the washroom through most of the action.

It took a kidnapping in Oakland to get them the hell out of my hair and, finally it all wore off. I got an increase in my budget. They also now saw the wisdom of my plan to relocate the cage. I was not sure I wanted it, any of it.

As for Porkpie? They never caught him. A short while after they disappeared he dumped the girl. Later that night there was a holdup at a convenience store a couple of miles away. A guy dressed all in black wearing a porkpie hat was caught on the store's taping system. He also traded in Cindy's Chevy for the counter kid's pickup. The next day he robbed two banks within a mile of each other and that was it. Nothing more. He just fell off the edge of the earth.

I had a cliché for the rest of my life. I also began trial-running a new series of thoughts. Perhaps I've had enough of California, of this life, legit or not so.

XLVII. 1992 – September

A week later the bravado after that not-so-quiet night faded leaving unsettled feelings. I kept flashing on me and Manny cowering, damp-cheeked behind a bush. The scar forming on my cheek carried hints of mortality and I couldn't shake the weird part, the son of a bitch knew we had two safes.

Then there was Armin who, since emerging from his sometimes comforting sometimes stifling closet, had launched himself into civil rights law with an emphasis on gender and sexual orientation issues. "We shall see," he wrote to Lydia in a long letter, "just how close we can get to actually becoming real people – in the legalistic sense, of course. Warmly, Armin."

There was something very provocative – and familiar – in that "we," but it was the postscript that was classic, where he snuck it in, the zinger to ensnare Lydia, the only one that would work. "I almost forgot, I've been asked by the New York branch of the ACLU to recommend someone to develop an approach to gender and sexual orientation issues. They want to form the basis for the next decade's efforts." And I felt another tendril snake its way into our lives.

Then the phone rang.

"Hello, Xerxes," a familiar but rarely heard voice said and it sounded weak and weary and I felt a jump in my heart rate. "It's your dad."

"I know. Hello, father dearest. You sound less than wonderful. Are you alright?"

"I am. Your mother is not."

"Oh." I sat down. I'd worried off and on about this message, this phone call, letter, telegram, carrier pigeon, which, now that I was over fifty, I knew for a certainty I would get.

"She had a heart attack. It's sort of serious, but maybe not. She's in the hospital. We'll know more in a day or two. Funny, I always assumed it would be me."

"Okay, Dad. We'll be there as soon as we can. Lydia will have to change around some meetings but it shouldn't be a problem. I'll call you as soon as things are firmed up. But, more importantly, how are you?"

"I honestly don't know. When I worried I worried about how she would get on without me. I haven't thought about how I might get along without her. Strange, yes?"

"No Dad, not strange, not at all. But no sense worrying now. We will, as Lydia likes to say, 'jump off that bridge when we come to it.' We should be there by tomorrow evening. Did you talk to Arianna?"

"I called you first. I really don't want to go through this again. Could you call her? If either of you want more information, she's at St. Vincent's. They don't seem to have a Greek Orthodox hospital here," he said with a familiar up-tick in his voice which made me feel a bit better.

"Well," said Lydia when I relayed the message, "the stars are aligning aren't they, though I can certainly imagine more engaging ways."

XLVIII. 1992 – October

The funeral was arranged quickly and efficiently. As much as I wanted a rollicking wake, a celebration of life that my mother's death should be, I knew I wouldn't get it. And I didn't. The church felt leaden and a little phony despite its size, its vaulted ceilings, iconographic windows, statues and an admittedly wondrous marble apse. I noted, yet again, how much darker our Christ was than the one claimed by those to the West, his hair and beard a rich brown bordering on black, less groomed, eyes shadowed, sadder.

But there were customs to be observed, things that must be said, gestures that must be made. Among the assembled were relatives and friends, lawyers in tailored suits, editors, colleagues of Alkaios's, all sacramentally bound with a complement of secretaries, mechanics and a poker player masquerading as an executive in the security racket.

Some mourned genuinely, older women, damp handkerchiefs clutched in arthritic hands, wisps of gray hair seeking release from black head-scarves, some in groups of the like-minded making deals, rearranging relationships, acknowledging loss. Others lamented obligatorily, glancing quickly through texts looking for clues.

I hadn't even thought about most of them since our wedding. It still looked like a gathering of an Aegean society of the bespectacled and mostly successful – with a few whose image was compromised by tell-tale creases in pants and dresses. This was good; it helped keep the room honest. Frankie was there with the old girlfriend-now-wife and two budding mechanics in ill-fitting suits. A brief embrace and I could tell my cousin's attendance was reluctant. He was not close with Hanna who never released the delusion that he was responsible for her son's slide into degeneracy.

Like at our wedding, Greek, with its soft phonetic grace, flowed along the halls, echoed off the tile in the restrooms and murmured its way along the carefully carved wood of the pews. I stood, obediently but reluctantly, off to the side of the open casket. Alkaios, next to me, looked, frankly, like shit. He seemed to have aged a decade in the last week.

"She went fast, Dad," I tried. "It's what she wanted, what you want for yourself."

"Yes, of course. But it isn't death; it's the lack of life. Death is easy. Over. Done. What's left behind is life without life."

"Your research, Dad. Hold to that. It can be the thing that pulls you through, always has."

"Work? The shine's gone there too. My new book? It's lost its heart. Who really cares about vowel shifts in ancient Sumerian?" he said and walked off toward a clump of well-dressed relatives, men and women of an age, distanced by money and caste from the wispy-haired scholar whom they embraced awkwardly.

Looking out over the eerie lifelessness of my mother, I realized there was another source of suffering, the guilt that can no longer be relieved, the past insults, the gifts unthanked, birthdays forgotten, books unreturned. The room was awash in emotional debts, left with no possibility of repayment.

She was my mother, my Hanna and she slipped quietly through the byways of my mind leaving little crumbs of understanding, small trinkets of love, even smaller, almost imperceptible triggers for guilt, shame, fear, desire and loyalty. I wished to mourn this Hanna for she was mine, not the numerous other, burdened Hannas whom I was content to leave for others. I would have much preferred to celebrate life at this death. I felt very Garbo'ish.

I looked up and saw Armin gliding toward me, his arm tucked under Lydia's. He embraced me warmly, "I am sorry Xero, I'm sorry for you both. How are you holding up?"

"We're okay; well, not really, but we are," Lydia replied.

"And Alkaios?"

"We worry mostly about him," I said quietly. "He is alone in a large and unsympathic city."

"Perhaps," and there was a small but rich pause in Armin's soft voice, "he needs family." I saw that beckoning glint in his eye. It was a follow-up to that postscript. I looked at him, back at Lydia, leaned back a bit to take them both in and knew my life was about to take off again. Here comes that big mother of an 18-wheeler. It's still got the same lethal grill and towing all that ambiguous cargo, all those boxes stuffed with fears and hopes, plans and illusions. I could hear the rattling chatter of its air brakes as it slowed down to pick up the kid, standing there with his thumb out.

Part III

XLIX. 1993 – March

We'd slipped into California young, unburdened, ill-formed, pliable. Now we were middle-aged and none of those things. The plaster sets, creases in brows and jackets become permanent. I knew I'd miss Tony but not that "legit" job. The move was tougher for Lydia. She would be on the same do-goody stage but with a different cast. New relationships would have to be formed, new lines of influence and power identified, aligned, new links of trust and support groomed. The east coast was not the west coast. Obviously. For one, there was no legal poker in the city.

We bought a TpFl-2-BR/2-BA, EIK, LgTr, RvVw condo with almost as much room as our house in Oakland. It really had some sweet views of the Hudson from the windows there on the western edge of the only neighborhood we considered living in, Hell's Kitchen. Some funny things had happened while we were otherwise occupied. There wasn't much "kitchen" left in it and it sure as hell wasn't "Hell." It had been remodeled, rezoned and we had our pick of euphemisms: *Midtown West* (Lydia), *Clinton* (me).

Lydia, who'd been working for months long-distance on policy, deciding on what legal roads were best to travel down, now had to tackle what Armin insisted on calling the "buggering bureaucracy."

"The State of New York," she said angrily yanking the cork out of a bottle of cabernet, "on the off-chance that you don't know, does not have open reciprocity with the state of California. That translates into they're not making life easy."

"Easy?" I said. "You expected 'easy?'"

"No, I never expected 'easy' but I reserve the right to be pissed off."

"What the hell's 'open reciprocity' anyway?" I asked.

"Ah, well, the bar has spoken," she smiled, dipped in a small curtsey, wine glass daintily at shoulder height, and shifted into windbag, harrumphing lawyer mode, "*You,*" she whirled pointing to an empty chair "may have *pro hac vice* status for individual cases but you..." and Bensonhurst slipped in, "will need tuh be fawmally admitted to the Noo Yawk State ba' to be a legal fucker of citizens and other miscreants in a mannah appropriate to de State.

"Which is pretty much it, except for the 'fucker of' part."

"I'm assuming that pro hac thing is lawyer tawk fowa temp'rary," I tried in Bensonhurstese.

"Close enough," she laughed.

"So you gotta write the bar exams again."

"Yup, it's back to the books. It might be fun; who knows," she laughed. "I've got to meet with Armin and a couple members of the board about this and get started. Isn't there some circus around here you can go run away with?"

"Ah, always the circus. I have a more limited quest, to see if Henry survived gentrification."

I closed the door behind me and stepped into the elevator, finding it hard to grasp that I now actually needed one to get in or out of my home. I walked out past the doorman whose presence was even more disorienting. I headed uptown, sniffing out the land, trying to get a feel for what had changed and what hadn't.

They may have renamed the neighborhood, buffed it up but still it exuded a familiar edginess. The old tenements were still guardians of the sun, their fire escapes scars along their outward faces. There were fewer rust spots on the sidewalks, more plants on landings and flower boxes readying for spring. The corners were where newness wasn't subtle; apartment houses had sprouted, condos, bristling with balconies graced with glass, coffee shops, boutiques, restaurants and book stores. It made an odd mix. The streets were busy, the gutters clean and almost everyone was younger than me.

I walked up 9th Ave., feeling the chilly breeze off the Hudson, to see if, by some ridiculous fluke, there still was a rough and tumble Irish pub on the corner. As I approached the intersection my heart picked up a tick for there it was, the ancient, sun-bleached sign in the window still announced that this, friends, was an "Irish Pub" and overhead the crackling neon faithfully beamed out *O'Shannon's.*

I walked in, felt my soles embrace the uneven floor, slid onto an ageless stool at a familiar, if darker and more scarred bar and looked at the seventy-something gent down at the end, near the corridor to the men's room, his hair wispy and straggly with hints of its former rusty colors, a white apron double wrapped about his hips.

"How about a pint of Guinness, my man," I called out and waited a second. As he turned I smiled at the wrinkled Leprechaun face with its sharp green eyes and large ears and added, "You do still have it on tap don't you, you poor excuse for a barkeep."

Henry stopped dead, put down the glass he had been drying, and stared in disbelief. "Xero? Holy shit. Is dat you? Really? Jeasus, Mary and fuckin' Joseph," he said and I was snapped back decades as Henry's classic Noo Yawk landed soft and forgiving on my ear. "You're still alive. Not only alive. My God you look so good. I can't believe this." And he came round the bar to hug me.

"Well, thank you my old friend," I said returning the hug. "It's just as good to see you. I was worried, you know. We've moved back and we were afraid that the tides might have swept you away."

"Back?"

"Yup. Down on 48th in one of the new high-rise condos. We just got our stuff in from California a couple of days ago and still haven't unpacked. Haven't found the bottle opener yet so I thought I'd take a stroll and see if I could find a Guinness on tap, at the right temperature, you know, the only way an Irishman would have it."

"Back. You're back, you smooth-talkin' Greek, my best dealer, ever. You're both back." He kept squeezing my upper arms. "I couldn't be happier. Tell me what's gone down. Whassit been, man? Damn near twenty-five years?"

"Damn near. I'll fill you in later but tell me what's with you and ..." And I paused and tried futilely to raise one eyebrow, "Janice?"

"Dead." And he sat on the stool next to me. "Long gone. Nearly twenty years ago. Made it longer'n I gave her. Totally fuckin' drunk one night. Grabbed a girl friend's keys and took her car. Lost control on the West Side Highway and rammed it into a stanchion. Quick. Best that way. I've wondered, you know," he said with a soulful look, "like maybe she wasn't all that drunk."

He walked around the bar and pulled two pints. "I missed her in a weird way for a month or two. Like when a cut heals over you miss not having the scab to pick at. But then I grabbed hold of solitude, my best friend since. I am happy alone, alone in a sea of people.

"And, in case you missed it all, you got out at the right time."

"Right time?" I echoed.

"Fuckin' right," he said. "And those tides? Well, the ones here swept in a lotta shit."

"Tell me," I said sipping from the glass.

"It started a couple of years after you two went west," he said, leaning over the bar conspiratorially. "It was dicey, man. We got 'gentrified' but not till we got free from the gangs."

"Gangs?" I said.

"Yeah, gangs. Xero, there was an awful lotta stuff going on below the surface, stuff you didn't – couldn't – have seen."

"Like what," I said.

"Well, you knew I was part of what they were callin' 'the Irish Mafia.' I did a little protection, you know, to keep my place here. But we were basically the good guys in a not so good world."

"Part of a gang?" I asked.

"Not really. Just that I'd been around for so long that they let me do my thing. But then the whole thing blew up."

"I heard something about this," I said. "But I never understood."

"It wasn't real complicated. It had gotten weird. Crazy Billy O'Donneghy went berzerko; then dem Eyetalians started stickin' their fuckin' noses in, guys wuz gettin' killed seemed like every other week. The mayor's boys and the FBI moved in."

"The feds? Really?" I said. "I didn't know this part."

"Interstate shit brings 'em in. I did a lot of duckin' and weavin' man, a lot. I paid and paid and held my breath. They missed me. Too small, I guess. An era has ended. There are no mourners," he said and paused.

"And there's no card room upstairs and that I do miss. But it isn't worth the aggravation and, frankly, I'm not sure I could work with these real Mafia clowns. They do things diff'rent than we did." He smiled, leaned back and looked at me. "And that's it. So, how 'bout you?"

"Well, as nutty as this is gonna sound, I've been thinking of opening a card room," I said and watched Henry's eyes narrow. "But not right away. I'm planning on enjoying doing nothing for a while. I have books to read and shows to see and, of course, a stake to raise. But I plan to pick your brain. You were my teacher. I learned a lot dealin' up there," I said, gesturing upwards with my head. "I learned more since. I need to learn even more to do it right."

"Are you sure? This ain't no picnic. It's not exactly 'sanctioned' and, like I said, there's still a lotta wise guys who need to be kept happy and palms that need silver and from time to time a couple of 'em are gonna turn up sportin' badges which means they gotcha from both ends."

"I know," I nodded, "or at least I do theoretically. Things will have to spin themselves out. Lydia doesn't know what I've been thinking yet. She'll give it her best 'what the fuck are you doing?' bit. It's good for our relationship to have one of these every now and then.

"Henry," I said, leaning down on the bar, "I am a man with limited choice. I'm a gambler, a poker player. I know the game as well as anyone – not just how to play it, but how it's played. The Mayfair, I hear, is still drawing 'em in and, well, maybe they need a little competition."

"No shit. So that's what you been doin' all these years. Am I ..." and Henry paused and smiled, "your pappy?"

"Oh yes," I said with a chuckle, "one of several, if you don't mind sharing. You taught me how to deal but, better, you let me learn, learn how to run a game, run a room. The future is not sitting at the green felt but owning it. You were also the wise-ass Irish gangster who once said to me... and let's see if these words ring true, 'you're smart, kid' the 'kid' part I know is right, 'you're smart kid but smart by itself ain't worth shit.'"

"Don't know if I said it but I sure coulda, 'cause it's true. You're smart, I'm smart. I don't look it an' don't talk it but I am. But without being a whole mess o' other things, I'd be cleaning up that cesspool over there," he said nodding toward the least appealing room in the building, "'stead of owning this joint, the building above it and the two on either side. I'm behind this bar, been here for freakin' ever, 'cause I like it. I like the bums that hang around, I like you. Liked you then, I think I'm gonna like you more now. We're both pretty smart, yeah?"

L. 1995 – October

〜

"I've been having these odd pains," Lydia said rubbing her now Tessa-shaped abdomen and my brain fired a dozen terrifying

Roman candles into the ceiling. "Don't know, just don't," she said grimacing. "It only started really hurting yesterday."

Why, I wondered in fear and worry, do people keep hitting the play-back button on my life's recorder? I rolled over and said the only thing I could, the same thing I said thirty years ago, "What do you want to do?"

"Sleep," Lydia said, for what else was there to say. This time she slept, fitfully.

"It hurts," Lydia said the next morning over breakfast sitting at the kitchen table surrounded by the usual sea of paperwork, her hair a delicious, seductive mess, her bathrobe slightly askew with a hint of breast exposed, which drove me nuts and had since we first met. Decades had rolled by and still she could turn me on with a flashed nipple.

"But it's different from last time. I'm bloated and peeing all the damn time. It feels like woman crap but different women crap. I just don't know. The pain is new but the rest of it's been going on for some time."

"How long?" I asked.

"Couple of weeks, maybe longer, maybe a lot. I know I should have said something but I figured it'd pass, like gas or any of the other annoying intrusions in my life."

Two weeks later, after examinations, tests, X-rays and a biopsy, we found ourselves back at Bellevue sitting in the office of, who else but, Dr. A. P. Bolling who still, annoyingly, looked like he was an intern who should be catching barf from some junkie in the ER instead of being the Head of the Ob-Gyn unit. I'd been sure he was going to run away with the circus. Maybe he did.

"Well, Dr. Bolling," I said, "Where are we?"

"First, please, call me Paul. It's much less awkward."

"Paul? Well, that's the 'P' part," said Lydia. "What about the 'A?'"

"Ah, that. Well, I think Xero and I share something," replied Bolling as he smiled in my direction, "a tradition-bound Greek mother. The A is for Adonis. Now don't laugh. 'Xero' is short for what, 'Xenophon?'"

"Good guess," I laughed. "It's 'Xerxes.' We're not distant cousins, are we?"

"Probably not, but we need to get to the heart of the matter. The test results are back, Lydia. The news is not good. It isn't the worst but it isn't far off. Sorry to be so blunt but you two, I suspect, prefer it that way.

"It's a tumor and it's malignant. It's in the other dysfunctional ovary. It's operable but that will not be the end of it. It's metastasized, malignant cells are in several other places," and he leaned in toward Lydia, "the usual ones in these cases, your bladder and bowel."

I looked over at Lydia. Fear and anger swept across her face. I merely felt numb. I looked down at my hands. They seemed to belong to someone else, small, far away. I'd been confused and anxious for weeks. Lydia refused to worry. "I'll worry when there's a need to," she said last night. I didn't know how she could do this. Maybe she wasn't. Maybe she was just putting a good face on it. I think I can grasp a bit of what she felt, an illusory sense that if you don't know for sure that you're dying, you're not.

"The standard approach," Paul dragged me back to uncomfortable reality, "is surgery then follow-up chemo. You're a tough broad if I may put it so crudely Lydia, but it isn't going to be easy. You need to know this before we start."

I sat unmoving as rivers of fear and nausea ran through me. I had tried to prepare myself for this moment but it turned out to have been no preparation at all. So I did what I did when shit came my way, I sat and waited for the next card to be dealt and tried to be ready, ready for anything – for anything will happen, it always does.

"Okay," Lydia said in her best tough broad voice. "So we know where we are and we know what we have to do. So, we do it. When do we begin?"

"Soon. As soon as we can. You're a Stage III now. There's no way to soft-pedal this; there will be discomfort, nausea and pain. Pain is the great leveler. The great are made humble. No one is immune. I'm unusual in this game and, frankly, you're lucky you got *me*," Paul chuckled and held her hand. "I've studied pain management. I am of the new school. We'll keep the dragons at bay if you wish. It's up to you. You'll want to balance the clarity of pain against the mental fog of opiates."

LI. 1996 – April

"You know what makes you old, hon? Pain." Lydia grimaced over a late glass of wine as the clock on the shelf chirped the arrival of another day of struggle. Another day, one that dragged us into a tomorrow like yesterday, like the first day six months and ten metaphoric years/decades ago of treatment. "Pain makes you old. Bolling got part of it right; pain makes us all peasants, but he missed this part. I was young, much younger than I was. I never thought I was young; I just was. I didn't think about being old. I just assumed it would creep up on me some day, sit down and say 'hello, may I join you for a while?' But your old 18-wheeler hit me. I got old fast, too fast for wisdom to catch up."

There wasn't anything to say, anything that could be said. I sat beside her, put my arm around her shoulder and let her lean on me. Leaning on me was so different. I loved it; it scared the hell out of me. She loved me, but she was never dependent on me. Now she was. I used to think I wanted this. Now I knew I didn't. But it was too late for this tiny revelation.

"It hurts all the time. You know when it's best, or least worst? When I'm bitching about it to someone. I've discovered bitching. Isn't that a hoot? My dad would go nuts. 'Take like a man,' he always said. 'Dad, I'm not a man,' I would say. 'Don't

213

make no diff'rence, take it like a man anyway.' So I did. It didn't really work but I was too young to know. This, of course, is one more reason why I love you. You let me complain. What more could one ask of a friend?"

The end came quickly. It was as if she died but left behind the pain. Between me and Luigi, the only one of the Demeraras I felt even slightly comfortable with, we hastily made arrangements with Battaglia's, the mob-run funeral parlor that would be Lydia's barge over the Styx. Yes, the Styx, my river, for she was my Lydia, of them but not with them.

I stood off to the side in the chapel scanning its iconic walls bedecked with their pale, wispy-bearded Jesus, slim, beckoning Virgin with those little rounded titties under a shawl impossibly fine for the wife of an innocent furniture maker. Poor Joseph. He kinda got chucked on history's slag heap. His son (foster-son?) ends up the freakin' savior of mankind; his wife the embodiment of perfect innocence – and him? Shouldn't being the most famous cuckold of all time make you special? I leaned against the wall at a slight angle, hoping it made me harder to see.

I spotted Luigi, his hands gripping the back of a pew. He had crafted himself well, greasy hair slicked back, eyes darting, slight hunch in his shoulders, heavy in the gut, hips. Soft whispers were exchanged with two guys doing their best Al Pacino thing. He said he wasn't connected before; he sure as hell was now. He was, he said, still running that book, which meant he was in tight with the mob. There were no independent bookies in Brooklyn, not any more.

I tracked over to Sabbie. He looked old. He was having trouble grasping that he could lose his daughter before his wife. He looked over, plucked me out of invisibility and shook his head slowly, the edges of his mouth turned down in a grimace. He started to move, stopped, shrugged his shoulders, a sign of mutual suffering.

A voice pulled me toward the back door. Selma and her Emilio or whatever his name was – I couldn't remember – were whispering heatedly. Luigi saw me and slipped up quietly. "That prick is shtuppin' some broad over in Bay Ridge, some fat, sloppy-titted cunt. I'm tellin' ya man, we ain't gonna stand for this much longer." And I felt that revenge thing from the toasts back at our wedding oozing out of Luigi.

Tessa, by the coffin, was the day's cliché. She had reverted to Italian. Small wail-sounds emerged from her as she and a sister, their heads wrapped in black shawls, rocked rhythmically. Her black dress seemed to suck the light from the room. Her pain was compelling. It resonated in my chest like a hammer. I understood. I just wished she would stop wailing.

The priest moved to the altar. I dutifully took my place at the center of those who were supposed to be suffering the most. My mental camera pulled back, long view, it shifted to a fish-eye lens, someone cued the dissonant, edgy music and I heard Abe Vigoda's raspy, breathy over-voice: "Yeah, dat's right. You got it, 'kid.' They're fucked up. This is the way it is here. But listen close. Do you hear it? It's faint, a low-pitched continuo. I can, but then I'm just a figment of your imagination. So, lean forward and listen:

"He's just a lousy Greek faggot who messed up Lydia's life. She coulda' been a real hot-shot lawyer in some spiffy firm, not workin' with queers and niggers. Fuckin' Greek bastard."

I sat next to an aged but still spry Alkaios and understood truly my father's sense of emptiness. The priest droned, glory to the Lord, reverential confusion about God's greater plan — naked sounds that slid through me, making no impression, those arcane vestments as marginally symbolic as Maxim's white-face and rouge.

You never knew her, never knew me. Three decades in faithful loving duality, howling separately at moons and fools, bad beats and benighted judges, at losses on the felt and in the courts, all smoothed over. A martini, a jug of cheap wine, a flashed nipple just to show she still had it and I could still get the old flag to fly and most, not all, certainly never all, the woes and sufferings of our worlds would slide away, lost in the luxury of that extravagant down duvet we wrapped our separate but linked selves in. Like Alkaios said, it's the life that goes on that's tough.

LII. 1996 – April

That evening Armin sat across from me in my living room. I kicked awkwardly at an empty wine bottle – which obediently rolled off toward the wall – and pried the cork out of another. A small, sad smile formed on his face, an unwelcome empathic mirror of my pain. "Xero, maybe we should go out, take a walk. It's a nice cool evening."

"Oh, no. Don't you pull that 'you'll feel better later' crap."

"I didn't say that, I said take a walk."

"Crap. You're just being diplomatic. I don't want to feel better. I want to feel like shit. I want to roll around in my misery."

"Losing a loved one will do that, you know."

"Losing? You said 'losing,' like that empty vessel of a priest. 'We lost Lydia, Lydia moved on, Lydia passed.' How come no one dies anymore?"

"It's a euphemism. It makes death easier," Armin replied.

"I don't want easy," I said softening my voice. "I don't fear death. It's just sleep without waking. I fear life with light. I don't want light; I want dark. You knew her, in some ways as well as I did. She was remarkable, different, special."

"She was," he said.

"But she didn't want to be special. She honestly didn't believe she was. Now how special was that?"

Armin merely raised an eyebrow.

"One day I said, 'Lydia, don't you see the paradox here? You say you're not special. You pillory me if I even hint that you are. But you're alone in your thinking. Everyone else thinks *they* are, so, simply by not thinking you are, you are.' You know what she said?"

"I suspect she told you to go fuck yourself," Armin said with a smirk.

"Ah, see. Like I said, you knew her as well as I did.

"What about me? I think I'm special. I'm certainly an anomaly. An intellectual gambler who, in case you care about this kind of old fashioned stuff, never 'shtupped no other broads,' as Luigi would put it – despite thirty years of opportunities. Lydia told me I had to be a good degenerate. I was. I am. It made no difference. She fucking died anyway."

"Xero, really. You're upset. Can't you…"

"Don't," I whirled around wobbly, "don't, please, ..., don't try to stop me. I need to do this. It is pure selfishness. Your role, because you're my friend, my best friend – I don't know how that happened but it did – and because you may have loved her as much as I did, is to listen. I know you're hurting too. I know," I said softly. "You can rant later, tomorrow. I'll be there."

Armin poured himself another glass, nodded and sat back.

"I have days, you must have them too," I said pacing around the room, unsteadily, "where I think I've got life by the short and curlies, then I wake from a nameless dream, drenched in sweat, knuckles white on the edges of a sweat-soaked pillow and I know. Nope. Wrong again.

"You've met Tony. Did you know he's been a practicing Buddhist for some ten years? But I'd watch him, in the club, our house. There are beasts curled up in his closet, under the eaves of his dark, leaking attic. Does his little gig work? Dunno. It's like the hallelujah Freudians. They sit in their comfy chairs, stroke their gray beards and nod, 'ach so, yah, und how does zat make you *feel?*' Your answer doesn't matter, of course."

"Do you really believe this?" Armin laughed. "That well-trained analysts are frauds? Mr. Naturals?"

"How do you do this?" I laughed. "How do you know who Mr. Natural is?"

"I'm well read," Armin said with an evil grin.

"Frauds? I don't know," I said. "Fraud requires motive, mere ignorance won't cut it."

"Perhaps," said Armin, "but you seem to be saying that psychoanalysts, Buddhist monks, the wise of the world, don't 'get it.'"

"What?" I blurted. "You mean *really*? Not a chance."

"Xero, you're hurting. But..."

"Okay," I said, holding up my hand. "I'm not trying to be arrogant. Maybe the better question is, does the cover story work? Fuckin' A it does.

"Why do we say 'fuckin' A' Armin? Why not 'fuckin' B' or 'shittin' A?'" I looked shakily over at Armin. "Surely someone must know. Perhaps a psychoanalyst. No? Well then, another life mystery."

"You don't think," he said. "That Tony's come to grips with these fucking As and Bs?"

"Ah, good question," and I smirked at Armin. I couldn't recall him using the F-word so freely before. "At best he clings to a comfortable illusion. Don't you?"

"Perhaps, perhaps I do. I admit I wonder about others," he said quietly, his head tilted, eyes narrowing. "Do you?"

"I used to. I don't anymore," I said, flicking my hand dismissively toward the ceiling. "True understanding is personal. It's acceptance, balancing suffering against joy and being at peace with yourself."

"Do you believe in God?" asked Armin.

"I used to. I may again, but I doubt it. I listen to those who do. So much of what they say is fuzzy, obfuscatory and self-contradictory and when you call them on it, they smile like some slippery psychoanalyst or a Siddhartha wannabe."

"You're serious."

"I am. Do you want to believe in a God who drowned everyone on the planet but one family because he was pissed off? The greatest mass murderer ever?"

I stopped, paused. "It's almost tomorrow Armin. What will tomorrow be for you?"

"Tomorrow? I hav..."

"You don't have to answer," I interrupted. "I was really asking myself."

"You do know you're getting to be a pain in the ass," said Armin with what I took to be a grin.

"Yeah, I know. I'm almost done. Look, I'm a poker player. That's what I do. It taught me something... important. How to wait for the last card."

"Really? Are we back in that 'poker mirrors life' bit?" Armin said.

"We are. The last card is like the question answered. Long ago I learned never to ask a question unless I was prepared for all possible answers. You want to survive in poker, in life, never ask for anything but the last card. It will pop up like a circus clown, a Roma grifter or... a Judy."

And I felt Armin pick me up, drape my arm over his narrow, dancer's shoulder and deposit me in bed and I heard him leave alone into the night and it was cool and it was pleasant and I know he hated it.

LIII.   1996 – May

⤳

"Get ready for another one," Armin said with pain in his face. We were in his apartment and he had just opened up a bottle of white.

"Another? Why do I think this isn't good," I responded, half question, half exclamation.

"It's not. It's Bowie. He's dying. Kaposi's sarcoma."

"What? Damn. Oh, Armin, are you okay?" I said.

"Yes, no. It's tough, not a total surprise but still...."

"Yeah," I said. "not a surprise. I've worried about this too, how could I not, given what's going on? AIDS?"

"Uh huh. He found out last year but didn't want anyone else to know. Sympathy isn't high on his list."

"Sounds like him," I said. "This cancerish thing, I hear, is a common side effect."

"Side effect?" said Armin. "Yes, I guess. Only now it's the main effect."

"This is so weird," I said. "You look at him and you think nothing could hurt him, move him off any path he's on. I have this rich fantasy life, you know. I like to wander around, figuratively, in dreamy states where all kinds of nutty things are okay, like you have a wombat walk into a room with a huge cigar and say 'anybody got a blow torch so I can smoke this mother.'"

"I like that one."

"Thank you. Well there's one where I sneak up behind Bowie with a crowbar and hit him as hard as I can across his back just, you know, to see what he'll do. There're a bunch of variations but in all he just rolls the shoulder nearest to the blow, flexes his back, twitches his neck and just walks on. Tiny little microbe, eh? 'Irony' doesn't get close."

I paused. "What about you?"

"Oh, I'm fine," said Armin. "Bowie and I became far better friends when we stopped sleeping together. And, I've been on my own since."

"Really? I guess I'm both surprised and not to hear this but my mind does many weird things thinking about sleeping with Bowie, wombat-level things."

"He didn't always look like that," said Armin. "The tattoo thing started soon after we met and he just kept getting more outrageous. He said he got a kick out of watching folks freak out. But I loved him. I still do but sleeping with him had an edge."

"So, in a funny way," I said. "We both ended up with the same sexual preference, self-gratification."

"Touch of irony, there, no doubt," he laughed then looked at me seriously. "Xero, I know you didn't choose to be alone and it hasn't been easy. I did. We queers are a thorny bunch. We've been marginalized, despised and feared. It gets to you. You start wondering if you aren't sick or depraved or a stain upon the species. It sneaks into who you are, who you think you are. So many of us are damaged and it is hard to have a stable relationship with a damaged man. So I play with myself when I feel like it. It is a lot easier and it turns out to have been fortuitous."

"Again, I am not surprised. But there's always tomorrow; no one's taken vows. Anyway, where is Bowie?"

"At home. I'm going over tomorrow. You're welcome to come. He'll be pleased to see you. You're one of a very small group, straight men who are comfortable around bloated old homos.

"Now, ready for one more?"

"One more?" I said. "Everybody's already dead or dying but you and me."

"Not death. Even worse. Money."

"Money? Well, I know you're fine, law school salary – I don't want to know what you bill per hour. I'm fine. Pop's okay too. So, what's up?"

"Well, you're actually going to be more than 'fine.' You are, or will be as soon as the paperwork is done, a rather wealthy chap," he said.

"What the hell are you talking about?" I asked.

"Well," Armin said, hesitated, began again, "Well, in addition to the assets you shared, Lydia had a life insurance policy. You are the sole beneficiary. It is," and Armin dropped the old 'pregnant pause' in here, "for one million dollars." And he sat back and waited for the eruption that he knew was coming.

My jaw dropped, a spectacular array of emotions must have slipped in rapid succession across my face. I know what I felt: amazement, anger, delight, fury, embracing warmth, suspicion, respect, distrust, alarm, fear – each I felt flicker for but an instant to be replaced by the next.

"Interesting," said Armin. "You claim to have a poker face at the tables. Before me is an open, ingenuous, jaw-dropping tell."

"Tell? What do you know about tells?" I said, trying to be menacing.

"You forget," he said, grinning at my blustering. "I've played a lot of poker."

"She never *told* me! She did this without telling me! How could she?" I was on my feet, stalking around the room, shaking my head, staring out the window, running my hands through my thinning hair. It was a crazy, disorienting moment.

"You do know, this is a fucking insult, a slap in the face?"

"I see that," said Armin. "A piece of it anyway."

"Do you see?" I asked angrily. "That she was saying 'oh poor Xero, poor baby boy can't survive without me bringing home the bacon.' Can you even grasp, for a second, what a kick in the nuts this is?"

"That," said Armin, "is a narcissistic response. Might it cross your tiny mind that she did what normal humans do, look to the future of their loved ones?"

"What do you know about narcissism?" I said. "You're supposed to be a lawyer, not a shrink."

Armin merely smiled with that infuriating, engaging grin... the one he'd been using since we met. I turned back toward him, "You might as well have told me she had seventeen lovers or was a drug addict. I'd be less surprised and less bewildered. She never, ever told me!"

"Well, yes, that is right. And I never told you either so when you're finished railing at her ghost you can shift your anger over here. When she raised this a couple of years back I agreed. I arranged for the premiums to be taken from her paychecks so you wouldn't find out."

I turned around, stuck my hands in my pockets because I just didn't know what else to do with them and walked slowly around the room. My hair was mussed from raking it with my hands. I walked past a mirror and saw my face. It was that of a sallow, olive-skinned, middle-aged Greek who has spent too much of his life inside card rooms – and it looked confused.

"Okay," I said, trying to stay calm. I walked around some more. Armin just watched passively, waiting. "Okay. I've told you before that poker is a mirror of life. You always laugh and I know you think I'm just trying to elevate a game, to give it some mythical status. Well, of course I am, but there's truth in clichés.

"You play the cards you're dealt. You can't change 'em. You try to make the right decisions, but you have to know who's dealing, and," my eyes narrowed and I looked intently at Armin, "how they're holding the deck."

"She never told you," he began, calmly, "for a number of reasons. One was she didn't want to see what I'm looking at now. But the truth is, and if this doesn't keep you up tonight nothing will, she worried, as you guessed, that the skills that maintain your life style would fade and if she weren't around your old age would be something less than wonderful."

"Armin, I loved her. I always will but right now I'm glad she isn't here. It would get ugly. And," I looked at him accusingly, "how could *you* do this to me?"

"Ah, well. It wasn't easy. Obviously it isn't now either. I promised to keep quiet about it till this moment. She knew how you'd react. She also knew that if you found out you would try to neutralize it and she didn't want the fight. If you want her words, pretty much as I recall them, they were, 'fuck him and his ambiguous ego. I don't care if he screams at the moon for a week when he finds out. Just don't tell him till you have to.' So that's where we are. And since Lydia's no longer a target, feel free to excoriate me for as long as you wish, although I have a meeting at nine tomorrow."

I looked at him. I'd run out of things to say, so I sat down and waited.

"You," he said after a time, "are soon to be ushered into the world of the millionaire. Get ready for it. Money is very crazy stuff. If you've never had much, you're in for surprises. I'll help with the legal parts; I'm the named executor. The rest of the choices are yours. Just like you like them."

LIV. 1996 – August

I was standing in front of a nondescript baker's storefront on 9th Avenue with questions and doubts in my mind. The bakery wasn't any more; in the shaded window was a small sign that said, "Hibernian Social Club - Opening Soon." I knocked. The door was opened by a large, dark-haired man who nodded and pointed to the back room. Funny, I noted, the wise guys here were looking more like Lydia's relatives than Henry's Celtic cronies.

In the back, my escort introduced me to Artie Mondessini but not to the other two nervous looking men who sat along the side wall, their chairs propped back on hind legs. They were quietly paring their nails, both of them so focused that I wondered if there was a plague here seeding finger nails with some fungus. Artie got up from behind a large wooden desk graced with the *Daily News*, a couple of photos of kids and a middle-aged woman with beehive hair, two statues, one of the Virgin and the other of Jesus on the cross and a lethal looking dagger that I hoped was a letter opener.

He was a classic "five-by-five" guy. Square body, square head, square jaw. Even his hand, which he offered in a genuinely friendly way, had thick stubby fingers that triggered memories of Bobby Joe. The rest of him evoked no memories for I'd never met anyone quite like Artie, at least not in the flesh. His hair was black, combed over an emerging bald spot. He wore a sharkskin suit that rippled when he moved, a yellow tie and a blue shirt with a white collar so large that it cut the knot into a small chevron. All sorts of extras adorned him, ruby stickpin in the tie, pinkie ring with a circle of diamonds around a center stone, silk pocket hankie.

The guy was a living cliché. The whole joint was a cliché, my escort standing off to the side of the desk with his legs spread in a Porkpie-ish way, the two hoods on the tilted chairs scraping moss, the room bare but for a couple of photos on the walls, magazines and posters in little piles and three sofas around a coffee table. I went 'poker.' I was afraid I'd start laughing and probably get the shit kicked out of me. But I couldn't keep my imagination in check and... I was in the casting office for a Roger Corman flick. "Wha'? You guys need a minor league gangsta? A Mafia street-thug who's hopin' to get made? Hang on, 'hey, Artie, I got a spot fer ya.' Give dese guys a ring over in Hell's.... Oops, sorry, in Clinton..."

"Pleased to meetcha, Mr. K.," Artie said. "I'm gonna call you that 'cause I got no idea how to pronounce that weird fuckin' name you got. What're you, a fucking Russian?"

"No, it's Greek. My folks are from there. I was born in Queens."

"Okay, Greek's okay. Queens even better. Have a seat," Artie said gesturing at a swivel chair in front of the desk. "Henry said you were lookin' to do some card shit. If so, you need to talk to us," he growled pointing at his chest.

I didn't say anything. I was still working on suppressing the urge to snicker while wondering about this first-person plural bit.

"So, what're you thinkin'?"

"Small to start," I said, after taking a deep breath which Artie smiled at. I figured he took it as fear, which was maybe good, maybe not. Who the hell knows what works with these guys?

"I've got plans for five maybe six tables, more than what Henry had, a couple will be small stakes stud and the new game hold 'em. I want the others mid- to high-level. They could go big, could be any game. It'll depend on who's in town, who's flush and who's looking to play. I'll spread what they want."

"What's the drop? What percent rake you gonna use?" asked Artie.

I was a bit surprised by that. But I liked it. Maybe, this clown knew something about how to run a room.

"We'll rake 10% – max three dollars a hand. The drop? Don't know for sure," I said.

"Got any guesses?" Artie asked.

"Sure. Based on what I've seen around town, I figure maybe eighty dimes a month; maybe nine hundred, a mill a year – if we last that long."

"Hmm," Artie said. "Hmm," again. "You really think you can pull that much out? Here? In Hell's Kitchen?"

"Yeah, but that's gross. You gotta take expenses into consideration; five, maybe six salaries, always a guy covering the door, a couple of room managers 'cause we're gonna run fifteen, sixteen hours a day three-sixty-five."

"Okay, okay," said Artie. "So, yeah, it could go that high then. You know, we gotta make sure you can cover *our* expenses."

"That's why I'm here, Artie – that's why we're talking."

"Okay," said Artie, "anything else I need to know?"

"No, nothing much. But I want to do this right. I'm gonna have a small kitchen with cookies, fruit, sodas, coffee – and waitress service – you know, like for call-out delivery, pizza, sandwiches and stuff."

"What the fuck?" Artie blurted out learning forward against his desk. "You wanna run a freakin' health club? You were making sense. Now you're not. I thought you were gonna run a fuckin' card room, not no pussy cookie joint. Hey Big George," Artie laughed and looked back behind him, "this fuckin' Greek faggot wants to have fuckin' cookies.

"How 'bout warm milk?" Artie turned around to me, pursing up his lips like he was talking to a little kid. He started laughing so hard he could hardly breathe and started making little snorty noises.

I again reminded myself I was not in a movie. I scratched the scar on my face and smiled. "Yeah, I know. Sounds stupid. But you know, it only sounds stupid 'cause no one's done it that way. It'll work. I know what these guys want. Give 'em a clean, safe room with drinks and snacks, a good-lookin' broad to take orders and set up delivery meals and they will come. And no booze. You get booze you get trouble. I do not want trouble."

Artie was still laughing but he'd toned it down a bit. He looked back at George, "Think this could work?"

"Could."

"Okay, Xero. Henry said to call you dat. Xero? Is that a fag name? How the fuck'd you come up with that? No, don' tell me. I wanna guess," and he started laughing again punctuated with those little piggy snorts. "Lemme think about it some more okay? I gotta work out an estimate on the net. You stop by Henry's later in the week. Remember, if we do this, you wanna go 'clean and safe?' That's fine. You take care of the 'clean,' we do 'safe.' That's what we do. We keep things safe. Maybe we talk later, maybe not," and he leaned back in his chair and picked up the *Daily News*.

Big George escorted me out with the same gorilla-like grace with which he escorted me in.

LV. 1996 – August

～

"Henry," I said. "I thought you said this Artie-guy's name was 'McMahon.'" I was trying to sound pissed but I couldn't help laughing. "That was not a brogue."

"Oh, sorry. Jeez, didn't think that through. We call him that 'cause when him and his friends moved in they were takin' over from us Irish. So for a joke I gave 'em that sign in the window and nicknamed him Artie McMahon. Stuck a 'mick' onto the 'M' part. He's a lot of fun, ain't he," Henry said with an evil grin.

"I think he'd be 'a lot of fun' if I were watching a movie," I replied. "Are these guys for real?"

"Yeah. I think Artie's seen The Godfather too many times. He's a cartoon but there's a lot of shit in the other room and he can call on it if he needs to. Mainly, I try not to laugh when he stops by. And watch out for George; he's not as stupid as he looks.

"But they are here and they ain't leavin'," Henry went on, running a towel around a dimpled-glass mug. "This part of Midtown may be lookin' good upstairs, where you got your condo, but down here and over by the docks, it's still a jungle. It's like in the wild, kid; you knock off a bunch of scary fuckin' meat eaters you leave all the meat sittin' around. Pretty soon some new scary mothers show up 'cause there's so much good food jes' goin' to waste."

"Henry, my friend, you have a way with words. But I didn't realize you were so in sync with the theories of Charles Darwin."

"Darwin, who the fu... oh, yeah, that guy who thinks we came from monkeys. You know, maybe he was right. I think back on those years trying to survive around here and monkeys comes right up close. You knew a little bit back then but only a little. You worried me then kid," and Henry couldn't help snickering again, "I felt I needed to protect you, 'cause you wasn't ready to know."

"And now?" I asked.

He didn't answer. He just looked at me, a little crease forming on his brow, between his sharp green eyes. "So, yeah, monkeys. But not the cute ones, no baby chimps in circuses. Not these guys. Toward the end, what was going on around here with the Westies was fuckin' nuts and none of us had much choice. They were dangerous but it was still profitable workin' with 'em, so I did. We did 'protection' pretty good."

"And you didn't have to pay yourself off."

"Cute. Cute. I like that. Yeah, being in the protection racket saved a good chunk 'a change when I opened.

"But that didn't mean shit. No, the serious part was that we didn't have nothin' like the organization Artie's guys got. O'Donneghy worked on fear. Cross me, motherfucker and you're a dead man. Effective but limited. Artie's guys are different – they weave fear in with loyalty."

"Loyalty? Really," I said.

"Yeah, really. His boys are scared of him, and you better believe he's not all that comfortable when it's his Capo on the phone. But he wants to be respected more than feared. The freakin' Eyetalyians it turns out are smarter than us Micks. Funny, eh?

"Anyway, you wanna work around here," he said picking up a glass from the sink and wiping it dry, "you gotta keep Artie happy."

"What does a 'happy Artie' cost?"

"Depends. You can negotiate a little. If you want you can go on the market 'cause Artie's family isn't the only one trying to work this area since it got opened up."

"You mean play one family against another?"

"Well, it ain't as scary sounding as that," said Henry, "but, yeah, I could get you another 'interview' if you wanted."

"No, I think I am already beginning to know too much. What kind of a deal would you expect if you opened back up?"

"Well, for what you want, I bet you guys could shake on a dime a month. That should keep Artie happy."

"And how do I keep you happy, old friend?" I said with what I hoped was a nice balance between suspicion and warmth.

"Me? Hah. That's easy. You just stop by once in a while. Tell me some bad jokes and remind why I run this bar. And someday," he said lowering his voice, "I'll tell you about that stain on the floor upstairs. Yeah, I saw your face. That's when I knew you didn't know shit from shinola. Some day... when you've paid some more in dues."

Henry stopped, stared at me squinty-eyed; he kept wiping the glass he'd had in his hands for what seemed like forever and said, "Look, kid, yeah, sorry but you're still 'kid' to me." He leaned down on the bar, his face grooved with a lifetime of joy and fear, sadness and bravado, love and loss. A wise, aged and dangerous Leprechaun, he reached out and, just for a second, put his hand over mine in a manner that sent pangs of remembrance through me.

"You lost," he said, "the best thing that ever walked into your life. I liked her. She was a classy broad – for a lawyer. Street smart and people smart. And she liked a beer and a shot and a good joke. It sucks. I lost a fucked up alcoholic but I loved her in my own way. You lose someone special, it's gonna hurt. It's gonna hurt for a while. But, it'll stop. It will. I found peace alone. You'll find it too. Dunno where or how. Just keep wanderin' around, look in the light, peer into darkness. It's there."

LVI. 1997 – August

Sheldon and I were leaning on the counter, grinning. All tables alive, all seats full, chatter and laughter, chips being riffled, the TVs on the walls flicking the stock prices, the football scores, today's game. "I have," I said without realizing I was talking out loud, "run away with the circus yet again."

"Huh? What circus? What're you talkin' about?" said Sheldon.

"Oh? Sorry. You know, man. The circus. Big top. Clowns, jugglers, elephant shit. Never mind. Sheldon, do me a favor, talk to Idaho Bob. See if you can get him to keep his elbows in.

scrum."

"Huh? Scrum? And what the fuck's rugby? You okay, Xero?"

"Sheldon. You're an idiot. Tell Bobby to push his chair back a couple of inches. Maybe that'll work till Linda gets here. We gotta get him off the tables and on the door where he's supposed be. I love the crazy bastard, but he is the worst dealer in the world."

I had my card room. Finally. Artie had received the first month's payment for his "services," permits to operate the Ivy League Lounge were filed and the proper licenses were hung, framed, on the wall of my office. The renovations were completed on schedule and under budget and all relevant palms were graced with silver.

Before I opened I'd spent several months playing in the clubs that were operating around town, getting a sense of what the city's underground had spawned since I last worked in Henry's. I hated what I saw.

"How do you even know about these places?" Armin was laughing over lunch. He was enjoying this, I could tell. "How do you find them? How do you get in?" he went on. "Did Henry get you a 'free admission' pass?"

"No. No passes, no tokens. But it's surprisingly easy. You want to find a poker room? Put down a bet on this Sunday's game? Score some dope? Get laid? Well, maybe not you, that was just a generic sleazeball question. Start by hanging out in a sports bar, Midtown is good, so's Bay Ridge in Brooklyn but, believe it or not, Wall Street is best."

"Wall Street?" laughed Armin. "You're kidding."

"Nope. Think about it. Think who works there, what they're into. Start by talking up the Giants, Knicks, Yankees, whoever's playing, hell even the Mets'll do. Pretty soon you'll have two or three new best friends and know all you need. That's how I found the first room which, big surprise, was in

Little Italy, the others from there. That's also how I realized how badly I wanted to run the right kind of room.

"What I saw was dispiriting – not a word you'd be likely to hear in one of those joints. They were terrible, far worse than Henry's. They stunk of smoke. Cheating was common and, to me, obvious. I watched one guy set up the deck using an overhand shuffle – if you ever see one of these do not sit down in that game. Then he hopped the cut and, wow what a surprise, two aces hit on the flop and a third spade on the river. I couldn't believe what I was looking at and could not believe the guy was gettin' away with it."

"Uh," said Armin. "I understand some of that but what's the point?"

"Couple of possibilities. Probably he had a partner in the game and he's setting up a cooler where some poor slob gets all his chips in 'cause he's flopped a set of aces then the spade on the river gives the other guy a flush. That's likely but you can't pull stuff like this too often; folks notice and some of the folks who notice are not people you want to notice you.

"Besides the cheating, there were guys selling drugs and the feel of these joints was just ugly. What really got to me was I saw maybe two, three women in all my visits. I knew what I needed to do and I could, thanks to Lydia and her million dollar insult."

"And now that you have," said Armin, "I promise to be an enthusiastic supporter. I am, as you have surely guessed, getting a small vicarious charge out of this. It's like a safe walk on the fringes of 'the dark side.' I'll offer legal counsel should it be needed."

"Oh, it will. You'll have to bail me out of jail when – not if – I end up there. It'll happen because we're going to be successful."

"Of course," nodded Armin. "I'll start with some non-billable advice. If they want to get you they'll use whatever route is open. When they put Al Capone away it was for tax evasion. Others have been convicted, not of the true crimes they committed, but for trivialities like illegal drugs on the premises, firearms violations, even operating without a license."

At this I snickered, "Oh, I know all about that."

"Huh? How?"

"Come on, Armin. I was married to a lawyer. All renovations were done with proper permits. The club is registered with the city as a private chess and bridge club. And I recently had a most interesting discussion with the local defenders of the realm. I stopped by the local precinct yesterday for a chat. Two representatives of vice will meet me at the club in the morning. I want them to know that we're about to open and not have to find out through unreliable channels or rumors."

"Luckily, I've got a meeting with the head of the undergraduate law society at ten – otherwise I'd be tempted to join you," said Armin with a smile as he finished his coffee, left a twenty on the counter and left.

LVII. 1997 – August

"Look," I said to the two cops, "We're opening in a couple of days. You'd know we're here within a week, so I thought I'd show you myself."

"Opening? Opening what," said the one with the sergeant's stripes.

"A private club, The Ivy League Lounge. You don't get in without a membership card unless a member vouches for you. We're gonna be playing games, chess, backgammon, bridge, maybe a little poker. There's no booze allowed, no drugs, no guns, no nothing. We're not even gonna allow smoking, except in the air-vented space behind that screen."

I stopped and looked at the two of them. Bewilderment marked their faces. I went on. "We've got free food," and I opened the door to the small kitchen, "fruits, cookies, soft drinks, coffee and take-out service. Over here's the TVs, all brand-new wide-screen, a couple of comfy chairs and a small library. We got professional dealers; they get paid a salary. I'm takin' out taxes including FICA. They get tips too but that's between them and the IRS.

"Any time you got a problem, call me," and I handed them my card. "I don't need anyone knocking down doors or busting up the place. You call, the door will be open. Do we have an understanding?"

"A what? An *understanding?*" The sergeant looked at me in a manner that rang those Covina bells. "You want us to okay an illegal gambling joint? Are you nuts? I should arrest you right now."

"First," I said calmly, "you can't. Second, I don't want you to arrest me any time. There are reasons for thinking that this club is legit. Bridge, poker, chess, they're games of skill. Read the court records from the '40's when this got ruled on. I have. I also have a very good lawyer. It won't be worth it for either of us."

"You are fucking nuts, aren't you," said the other cop which gave rise to another Joe Friday moment. What is it with these guys and manners? "You're gonna open a illegal joint right here, under our noses and you want us to okay it?"

"No, not okay it. Just not bother us, because we won't be bothering anyone. In fact, we're doing the city a favor."

"Favor?"

"Yeah, favor. This club will be as clean as your kitchen table at home. When you have 'clean,' it keeps out 'dirty.' There are some very dirty places operating in this city and they are run by ugly people. There's only one other 'clean' club, the Mayfair." And Stripes looked at me like suddenly we understood each other.

"You know this," I said after a pause. "I know this. A place run above board is the best thing for you guys. Trust me." And, apparently, they did, at least they both left without saying anything more.

The next week we opened. Within a month I had to squeeze my office into a closet so we could add three tables to handle the action. The circus was back, the midway was open. The Great Pirellis were setting up in the corner, Persi was workin' that pig and Ricco and Judy had the crowd in the back room enthralled. I smiled and hoped that Doris wouldn't put in an appearance.

LVIII. 1997 – October

"Xero, we got a problem," a worried sounding Sheldon whispered to me. It was nearly 4 AM, three desperate stragglers were sitting in the $15 - $30 limit hold'em game, Marty, who'd been losing his ass for the last couple of weeks, months, years, hell all his life was sitting between two local grinders who were gonna keep playing as long as the ATM was open. Idaho Bob was dealing, which should have been enough to make any sensible poker player rack up and head home. He misdealt so often that Sheldon started calling him "bring 'em back Bobby."

"Problem?"

"Yeah, problem. Big one. There's these three guys who haven't cashed out yet and the racks are full. It looks like we're over about two dimes."

"The racks are full? That can't be." If the racks were already filled with chips then there were more chips out in play than people bought. Bad things can happen in a poker room, some to players, some to owners. This was bad for owners, for me.

A hour later I shut the game down. The three of 'em bitched but knew they had no choice; it was my football. Sheldon and I counted up the outstanding chips and, as he guessed, there were two thousand more out there, in play, than people bought in for. I had to dig into my pocket to cover it.

After everyone had left and we could see the unwelcome sun sending snippets of its rays along the edges of the blackout curtains lining the windows, we ran through the video record. It was a pretty shitty taping system. I'd picked it up cheap from a local bodega that was upgrading.

But, even grainy and streaky, there it was — or at least we were pretty sure that it was there. And "it" looked an awful lot like Marty slipping into the back room. The time marker said 8:50 PM, just a few minutes before the evening's tournament. "Hectic" described the place at this time every evening and Marty clearly recognized it. We checked out the chip trays in the room and, with a closer look it was clear, the bottom drawer had been pried open, the lock was twisted and two grand worth of chips were missing.

The next evening I confronted Marty who, of course, went bat crap crazy. He screamed at me, accused me of picking on him 'cause he's Jewish, of making up shit, of having no decency, of being a donkey-fucking asshole of ....

"Look Marty," I said, "I'm not gonna get into a fight with you but we got you on tape."

"Tape? What tape? What the fuck are you talkin' about?"

"The place is monitored, Marty. Don't tell me you didn't know this?"

"What? You don't trust us? You're fuckin' tapin' us?"

"Of course I am. Look up. There are cameras all around. Do you think I'm stupid? It's like any casino. Everything's recorded. I got you going into the back room just before last night's tournament."

And Marty looked around, obviously for the first time. "But you got no camera in the back room," he said peering down the hall.

"That's true. I didn't think there was a need for one. I now see that was wrong."

"So, you got nothin' on me. I was just taking a quick look to see if you had another toilet in there. I needed to take a leak."

"Marty, I'll keep it simple. You see if you can find two grand, somewhere. I'll give you two weeks. They can be in chips, cash, gold bullion, whatever, and we can forget this. If not, well, one reason I don't get into fights is because I got guys who do it for me. Guys you do not want to meet."

This last remark, of course, was greeted with a heartfelt "go fuck yourself" from Marty who stalked out.

"Why don't you just bar him?" asked Sheldon, smirking at Marty's flabby ass as he left.

"For the same reason Artie and Big George don't break legs any more. I bar him I have no chance of getting back the two grand and I lose a customer, a good one. He's a fish and fish bring in players and everybody posts the juice."

Two weeks later I had seen Marty but I hadn't seen any cash, chips or bullion. So I made a visit to Artie, the first other than the monthly envelope drop. As before, I was met at the door by Big George. I wanted to ask him if his first name was really "Big" but the guy just didn't seem to have much of a sense of humor. In the back room the same two lugs were sitting along the side wall and Artie was, as before, behind his oversized, Jesus-blessed desk which today was covered with reference works of the trade, the *Daily Racing Form*, the *Daily News* and, hell, I guess he was trying to keep up with what was going on in the world, *The National Enquirer*.

Artie leaned back in his chair and smiled. "So, it's my favorite Greek faggot, Mr. K. What do you want, asshole?"

"Well, thank you for your usual warm and effusive greeting Mr. M."

"'Effusive?' what the fuck's that mean? Don't you go fuckin' around wit' me."

"Sorry, Artie, I cannot escape my education. It follows me like a bloodhound sniffing, looking for old socks. It means 'enthusiastic' or close enough."

"Okay, that's okay then. But do you need something here? From us?" he said, pointing to his chest in that familiar way.

"I think so. Yeah, I need you. I'm having a problem with a certain gentleman who has ripped me off to the tune of two dimes. I'd appreciate it if you, you know, would look into it."

"Okay," said Artie. "Gimme the info."

And I did. I waited a week, then two, then three and nothing. Marty came in two, three times a week. He played, lost most of the time, sneered at me when he arrived, when he left and he flipped me off if he thought I wasn't looking.

A month later I strolled over to talk to Artie again. I was amused to see that there was a new sign in the window announcing that this was now the Clinton Chapter of the Italian-American Anti-Defamation League. Big ushered me, as always, into the back room which had begun to take on an eerie redux quality. The same two hoods were sitting with their chairs tipped backwards on their rear legs along the wall to the left of Artie, still paring their nails. Big took his spot just behind Artie where he stood with his legs apart, radiating nasty shit.

I had one of my back-flashy moments, to Miss Maple smoking in the market on a Saturday. Do these guys exist when I'm not here? Do they sit there perched on those stupid chairs tilted back at just the right angle so they don't slide away from the wall? Does Big always stand there behind his boss, probably figuring out how to get his hands on this piece of cheap-ass turf?

"Artie, my friend, how have you been?" I said.

"Me? I'm always fine. How's your Greek faggot ass? Tell me, Mr. K.," he said, "are all you Greeks ass-fuckers? By the 'Greek way' we mean up the ass. You know? Of course you know," and he snickered with his usual swinish snort, leaned back in his chair and waited for the snicker, graced with the same snort to echo from the tilted chairs along the wall, and I had a fleeting, ephemeral glimpse of Wispy sitting in the far corner smiling as only that porcine wonder could.

"I'm fine. It's good to know that you spend so much time worrying about my people. My wife was Italian. We often wondered whether her people understood us. I still do."

"Was? Was Italian? What the fuck you talkin' about? You cannot cease to be Italian."

"No, but you can cease to be."

"Ah, uh, like that, eh? Tough, man. Tough. I'm like real sorry. Didn't know. Forget that ass fuckin' thing. What can I do for you today?"

"A couple of weeks ago I asked you to look into this guy Marty."

"Yeah, so what?" said Artie.

"Well, nothing's happened," I said. "I'm still out two grand and Marty is still playing in the club, pissing people off, scamming my games. I don't like it."

"You don't like it? Well what the fuck's that got to do wit' me?"

"Artie, I pay you to cover me, protect me. I need about two thou' worth of protection and I may need more tomorrow, metaphorically speaking."

"Look, asshole, I don't know what that fuckin' 'metafor' thing is but I think you made a mistake. I don't provide no 'help.' You ain't payin' me to help you; you're paying me not to hurt you. I ain't hurt you yet. Don' do nothin' to make me want to. And, by the way, asshole, the juice is now fifteen hundred. You guys are doing some pretty good business there. You think I don' know? I know." And there was a snicker from one of the chairs.

"Yeah, Sonny," said Artie turning around. "Put on the other hat and them cool fuckin' shades." I looked over at the two hoodlums, Artie's stage props, as one of them put on a Yankees hat, took off his jacket and slipped on a pair of aviator shades and, son of a bitch, it's "Eddie G." a guy who'd been in the club a number of times and was not a bad poker player.

"Like I said, I know. Now, Big George, show this ass-reaming Greek the door. See you later, Mr. K. Stop by when you got something, anything you wanna talk about. I am always here for you," and I could still hear him snickering as Big closed the door behind me and I knew I was out two thousand coconuts and, well, life's like that. A grand to keep a couple of cops in LA happy. Two grand here, another there.

But maybe, I thought, it's time to get a better taping system.

LIX. 1998 – November

Horst and I were arranging cheeses, laying out grapes and strawberries in artful interlocking spirals while Armin and Sarah fussed in the kitchen. Horst and Sarah and their twins had moved to the city and brought with them the baggage that vaguely estranged sons with proper wives and two teenaged kids carry. As pleasant as he was being at the moment Horst pissed me off. He was smart and outgoing, in a word, *charming*. His public face, that confident air, felt like, well, a bluff. But he was Armin's son and we all were bound in a union that could only be broken at great cost.

"Well," said Armin, "I have two toasts to make."

"Two?" said Horst.

"Yes, two and to different people. The first is to me," he smiled and filled the glasses. "I would like to toast my own day for, as of this morning, I've used 'em up."

"Used up what, Dad?"

"My allotted years, the ones the actuaries assigned me," said Armin.

"It's your seventieth," I said. "How about that! You do *not* look it." Armin smiled and adjusted his bow tie.

"They also," I said holding up my glass, "let you know, I hope, that the odds say you now should suck another decade and a half out this vale of tears. A toast to the bonus round, like on Wheel of Fortune."

"Wheel of Fortune?" said Armin looking confused.

"Armin," I said grinning, "you are a hoot! The only answer you'll get from me is 'never mind.'"

"I'll tell you later," said Sarah looking a bit embarrassed.

"The second toast," said Armin, ignoring Sarah, "is to you Xero for the room is a rousing success and I cannot wait to get into court to defend you. Success in domains like this, as you yourself have said, is a richly mixed blessing."

"Success? What success? What *room?*" asked Horst looking like his father contemplating Wheels of Fortune.

"You don't know? You've known Xero for, what, close to a year now?" Armin said looking at Horst. "He owns and manages a rare thing, a thing to be treasured, admired and, of course, condemned, an underground card room run without mob control, without paying off the cops, without liquor or smoking or violence. I applaud the accomplishment. I worry about it every day."

"Well, then, I guess," said Horst, "a toast to Xero's, uh … success." And that pause rung that well-worn bell of mine. Time to kick it up a notch.

"So, Horst," I said. "How're you doing in the world of the day trader, still floating on the clouds of all those dot-com start-ups?"

"Actually, it is a bit weird when every obscure IPO takes off like a goosed waitress."

Sarah cringed. I looked over at Armin who was wearing his best poker face. "It's a bubble," he said. "You know what happens when they pop. What little I know about boom and bust cycles is screaming 'get out – now.' Sarah, what do you think?"

"I am utterly with you, Pops," she said and Armin bristled. '*Pops?*' My God, I thought, where in hell did she come up with that?

"I keep telling him," she said. "Get out while we can. We got lucky. Invest in something stable like real estate."

"You all could be right," Horst interjected. "But I want to ride the wave for a bit. It isn't," and he turned and looked piercingly at me, "like gambling."

"Oh, really?" I said. "What do you call 'gambling?'"

"Well, what you do, playing poker. And casino games, slot machines, you know, that kind of thing."

I smiled at Horst. "You know, we finally met a year ago and I've come to like you. You remind me of your father, except for the arrogance."

"Arrogance?" said Horst, drawing himself up and looking like a British actor doing his best Bertie Wooster, "I don't know whether to be offended or pissed."

"You shouldn't be offended when someone tells you the truth, but pissed is fine."

Armin leaned back in his chair, folded his hands behind his head and a very sneaky grin slipped onto his face. He looked at Sarah, who fell silent and seemed puzzled.

"Xero," said Horst. "My dad likes you. I don't get it. You say you're a gambler and now it seems you've stepped outside the law. I respect him so I'm going to resist the desire to tell you to go fuck yourself."

"Good," I said. "You might make a good poker player yourself."

"Huh?"

"Horst, you're a gambler. We're all gamblers. You think that gambling is just something people do in casinos, racetracks. It isn't. Every vaguely interesting choice we make in life is a gamble. If you don't have some piece of you on the line, some slice of your precious life at risk what's the point?"

"Are you nuts?" Horst said. "What I do is called, in case you've not heard the term, *investing*."

"Investing is gambling," I said, finishing off my glass and reaching for the bottle. "It's just another euphemism. Horst, you *invested* in a start-up – you gambled. You *invested* in a college education – another gamble. Got married. Ah, now you're a real high roller. If that one goes south, there goes half your wager." I stood up and glanced over at Armin who was, only partially successfully, suppressing a grin, his jaw lowered just a bit so that the bow tie was mostly obscured and he was peering over his glasses. Laughing at this sight, I turned back to Horst who had fallen strangely silent.

"These are all *games*. Some you can play for profit, some you can't. In poker you dance with the cards, in business you swing with the customer base, adjust with their hopes and dreams and failings and confusions. Same with the stock market, commodities investing, real estate and currency ex…"

"What?" interjected Horst, his voice sounding strained and in a higher register, "You can't really mean this. Playing poker isn't anything like trading commodities. You…"

"Right there," I interrupted. "You're wrong. They are, in fact, very much the same."

"That's just crazy. How can they be the same?"

"You trade, you pay your broker. If your trades break even, you lose money. I play poker, I pay the rake. If I break even at the game, I lose money."

"I'm sorry. What the hell are you talking about? There's nothing the same here."

"Ah, but there is," I said. "You pay your broker on every trade you make. I pay the rake on every hand I win. Make smart trades and you beat the 'vig,' the broker's fee. If I make the right decisions I cover my game's 'vig,' the house rake. There are professional poker players; I was one for thirty years. If it's just 'another gamble,' like you seem to think, I couldn't have done it."

"But," said Horst, "the stock market has historically gone up. Poker games don't."

"This is true but irrelevant. It's because of the generally improving state of the economy. If the economy goes in the toilet, the market follows. Yeah Horst, you're arrogant because you've been looking down your nose at me when you should be looking straight across the room, right in my eye. Okay. I'm done. You're free to tell me to go fuck myself."

Armin broke out in applause. "That was bloody good fun! I knew there was a reason why I always watched your head, when it nodded, when it fell off to the side. Horst, pour yourself another glass of wine and don't say another word until you have finished it. Xero, pass me a slice of toasted baguette and make sure it is buried in that goat cheese you found."

"No, I still don't agree," said Horst after the required spot of silence. "I still think you're an idiot for slinking along in the legal shadows."

"I may be but that's my business," I said. "I think you're an idiot for staying in the dot-com game. It is going to crash and it is going to take down a lot of people. You can invest in my poker room. We'll drop about one-point-five this year, maybe more."

"What?" said Armin and he turned so sharply his wine sloshed over the rim. "By one-point-five I assume you mean one and a half million? From a poker room in Clinton? Maybe more?" He stopped and smiled, "Gross or net?"

"It's still Hell's Kitchen and, gross. I'm readying myself for when Artie kicks up the juice again."

"Artie? Who's Artie?" asked Armin.

"I'll tell you later. Horst already thinks I'm a lowlife bum, I don't want to give him any more ammunition."

"But a million and a half?"

"Wait till next year. We're adding two more tables and the tournaments are big. More wine anyone?"

LV. 1999 – June

"Xero, the safe's missing." It was Sheldon, that unmistakable voice, a baritone with a layer of whine, straight out of Brooklyn and a guy I would trust with my life.

"What? Hang on, let me get my glasses. I can't talk on the phone without my glasses. And no, that doesn't make any sense but it's 10 AM, a truly obscene hour. And what do you mean, the safe is missing?"

"I mean the safe is missing."

"Sheldon, you're a sweet guy but you are not exactly an Einstein. I assume you mean the money is missing, you know, the money we keep in the safe."

"No, you pompous ass, I'm nowhere near as stupid as you think. I said 'the safe' and I meant 'the safe.' The safe is missing, all hundred or so pounds of it. Gone. Zippo. Just some dust left behind where it used to be and the distinct shading on the floor."

"Shit," I whispered into the phone. "Okay, gimme an hour or so. I gotta wake up, pour some caffeine in me. It's tough to lose a safe."

By noon we were in an empty poker room scanning through tapes. "It'll be here, I'm sure," said Sheldon. "We've got the joint pretty well covered now."

As we ran it there he was, one of the hot shot pros, a guy with a bit of an attitude who'd been playing at the club a couple of times a week, shooting off his mouth, doing the shades and hoodie bit, riffing and bullshitting and there he was crawling under the desk in the back room and inching the safe onto a wheelie luggage carrier. On a tape from the stairwell he was, with no-little effort, lowering it, presumably still filled with the last three nights' drop, probably a good fourteen, fifteen Gs, down the stairs, one step at a time, till he was out of the camera's range.

"Motherfucker," I said.

"Motherfucker, indeed," mirrored Sheldon. "So now, whadda we do?"

"I think I need to have a chat with Rollie, Mr. Hot Shot Rollie. Could it be that he is dumber than I thought? That he didn't know we've got the place covered?"

It took a week before I got my chance. Rollie came in around ten when the high-stakes game usually got rolling. I pulled him aside, steered him down the hall into my office, closed the door and turned around. He looked a bit nervous but was trying to cover it with outrage. "What the fuck are you doing, man. Ninny called me, said a couple of fish were in town. I need to get in that game."

"Look, Rollie," I said, "I don't give a flying fuck who's in town. I pulled you in here to let you know that I am a real fan of situation comedies."

"What? That's it, dude. You've lost your fuckin' mind. Situation comedies? Get the fuck outta here."

"Nope, haven't lost anything but I like looking at videos and I just happen to have a very funny episode on tape. Wanna see it?" I asked, leaning toward him.

"You're startin' to worry me, man," said Rollie uneasily. "I know this place is grooving and you and your partners, whoever they are, are like printing money but your grip on reality, like maybe it's slipping?"

"I used to be in the circus Rollie," I said. "I know a clown when I see one. Come over here." And I pressed 'play' to reveal a young, twenty-something kid in wrap-around shades and a hooded sweat shirt covering part but not all of his face dragging a dark and obviously heavy box out from under a desk.

I looked at Rollie who was looking back and forth at the screen, his hands, his feet and up at me.

"There's more. It's an even more interesting 'situation' and even more of a 'comedy.' Check this out." The monitor now showed the same guy with the box strapped to a metal airport-style wheeled cart, lowering it down the stairs leading to the street.

"Now who could that be?" I said. "Is it possible, just remotely, that it is some thieving prick who thinks he's making a living playing poker but actually he is a fucking low-life crook? Maybe you recognize him?"

Rollie sat there silent for more than a few seconds, the first time I could recall him staying quiet that long.

"I dunno what the fuck is gettin' you in this hissy fit," he said finally. "That's me, sure. And that's also my suitcase."

"Oh, I see, you routinely walk around with a hundred pound suitcase."

"Yeah, this time. 'Cause I just got back from Vegas and I had all my shit with me."

"And it just happened to be under my desk?"

"Yeah, that's right, dude. Idaho put it there for me. Said it'd be safe."

"Rollie," I said. "I could, no I *should*, kick your thieving butt outta here. But I have a terrible character flaw; I don't like fights. Here's the deal. I will, for now, believe that was your suitcase and not my safe. I'll also believe that you brought heavy gifts back from Vegas. So, you go back to *your* suitcase. Lighten it by some fifteen thousand give or take a couple of C-notes and bring it here. I'll swallow the cost of the safe which I'll henceforth believe I had misplaced – otherwise things can get messy."

"Messy?" said Rollie. "You threatening me?"

"No," I said quietly, "merely warning. I hate messy. But if I need it, it's there." Of course, while this was coming out of my mouth a voice was chuckling in my head…. Artie's voice. I knew I had no "messy," just a three-bet bluff.

"Look, Xero," he said, "I like you. If nothin' else you got the coolest name. I like this club, this room. I'm feeling kinda put upon here 'cause you think so badly of me. If I took your fucking safe and if I was really a lowlife thief like you think, I'd bring it back but I can't 'cause I don't have any safe. All I got is my suitcase with a bunch of gifts from Vegas for a couple of my buddies."

"I'm gonna start to lose my patience," I said trying, I suspect unsuccessfully, to sound dangerous. "My safe goes missing, my taping system picks you up after we've closed when no one is supposed to be in the building and you think I'm gonna believe this crap about a suitcase?"

"If you got a problem with me," he sneered getting up and walking toward the door, "why don't you just call the cops. That's what honest guys do when they get ripped off. If you're not gonna do that, just move out of my way so I can get the fuck outta here."

The next morning my phone rang, and of course, it was even earlier than the day before and, of course, it was Sheldon. "Xero, we got a lead."

"Lead?"

"Yeah, Julie, the shylock, is pissed 'cause Rollie's been muscling in on his racket."

"How's this a lead? Julie knows he can't do business in my club. No one makes book, no one sells drugs and no one does the loan shark thing."

"Yeah, that's right and he wasn't. That's why he's pissed. Rollie's been loaning money at rates that even Julie would be embarrassed to charge. And, guess who one of his customers is."

"Sheldon, please," I said. "it's early. I haven't had my coffee and my brain is still on hold. I'm not guessing. Tell me."

"Idaho Bob."

"Idaho Bob? Our Idaho Bob, *my* Idaho Bob?" Bob was one of my favorite characters and he really does look like a very large sack of potatoes. He's not the sharpest knife in the rack but deep down one of the most decent people I've known. He did what I needed done, kept things quiet and orderly. This news did not make me happy. "Okay, I'm awake now. I'll be down there as soon as I can."

"On your way there's something else to ponder."

"Ponder?" I said startled.

"Yeah, I know what words like 'ponder' mean, *Boss.*
Maxine said she's pretty sure Bob arranged for Rollie to hide in
the back room the other night and told him how to get out
without setting off any alarms. She'd seen them together a
bunch of times and said it didn't look kosher."

Two hours later we chatted with Bob who denied
everything – that he'd borrowed any money, that he even knew
Rollie, that he owed him anything and, of course, that he knew
anything about any safe. We weren't surprised. So we let him
stew and waited.

That evening Rollie came by to play in the nine o'clock
tournament. I pulled him and Bob aside. "Look guys, I know
you two are responsible for my safe going missing, along with
the fifteen or so thousand rutabagas in it. We're gonna have to
work this out, here and now."

"Look, man," said Rollie and unlike last time he was now
looking like he wanted a fight. "You accused me before of
being a thief. Now you're bringing Bob into it too. You really
are a scumbag, you know."

"Rollie," I said, "I'm gonna give you one more chance. I've
got a guy who is a private detective who does lie detector tests.
Let's let him decide who's a lying thief and who's a scumbag.

"Here's my last offer. You bring back the safe with the
fifteen Gs and I forget everything. No one knows but you two
and Sheldon. If you didn't take the safe, convince me. Pass the
test. If you do, both of you, I will apologize publically and
swallow the fifteen thou'."

"Fuckin' A, man" said Rollie with his best wiseguy grin
and I wondered yet again where that stupid line came from.
"Bring on your deeetective, your priiiivate eyyyye. I wanna see
your face when we're done and, man, do I ever wanna sit there,
on that nice soft couch you got out there and listen to you
apologize. In fact, motherfuck, I'm gonna write the speech for
you," and he started that inner-city ethnic split finger hand
roll, thumb out, pinky out, stab 'em down toward the floor.

"Whatever you want, Rollie and by the way you do know how stupid you look.... Bobby, you've been with me since I opened, how 'bout you?"

"Er, uh, ... fine with me... I guess," and he glanced briefly at Rollie, looked confused and more than a little worried.

After they left Sheldon turned to me. "Are you sure you know what you're doing? Who's this private dick guy? Does he know what *he's* doing?"

"Yeah, I know a guy. Lydia used him once or twice. Does he know what he's doing? Actually, no one does. There are reasons that they're not admissible in court, one of 'em being that psychopaths can fool them. Bobby isn't a psychopath, just a poor bastard down on his luck. The real scumbag in this little drama may very well be. I'm playing the only game we got left; I'm gonna gamble. Isn't that what we do here?"

Two weeks later I got the report from the deeetective. He's sure that Rollie and Bob did it, that Bob set it up to pay back the loans he couldn't cover and Rollie stole the safe. To knit the fabric up tight, Maxine, whom Sheldon insisted also be tested, passed with flying colors.

That evening Rollie came by looking full of himself and putting on his best swagger. He walked over to me and said, "I heard your little dickie boy got back. So, now you know I'm innocent and you're a lying prick who owes me a public apology. I have your speech here," he said waving a couple of folded up pieces of paper under my chin, "and I will stand here while you deliver it to these fine people," most of whom had actually stopped their games and were staring at us.

"Nice try but it won't work," and I handed him the report. "I want the safe with the fifteen thousand in it. I want it back here within twenty-four hours or I call in my muscle who will extract fifteen Gs worth of pain."

Rollie looked at the first line in the report and went off on a rip of insults that was truly creative. The whole room stood dead silent for the entire rant and after Rollie ended with an assault on my physical appearance, my intelligence, my ancestors and their presumed sexual habits he stormed out the door. The room erupted in applause. I did the only thing left. I laughed and joined the applause for I knew I'd never see him again, certainly not here.

I gave Sheldon and Maxine ten percent raises and Idaho Bob an ultimatum. Pay back three grand of the money, either up front or, if he can't, stay on and work it off. Bob almost broke a rib thanking me. Then I left a message with my accountant about what recourse the owner of an outlaw card room has when he gets ripped off. I was pretty sure I already knew the answer.

So it goes, the trickster who keeps popping up took another curtain call. Hell of a business I was running. I was shelling out a thousand – no, make that fifteen hundred – a month to Artie for protection that didn't protect squat, had a top-drawer taping system to provide clean, hard, useless data, was weighted down with a shit load of knowledge about law, evidence and testimony gleaned from Lydia and Armin and what was it all worth? What was that old line, something about 'a bucket o' warm spit?' The one thing I did know was that pushing card rooms underground was stupid, for all the obvious reasons that no one seemed to appreciate.

I decided to take the next day off, stay home and watch reruns of *I Love Lucy*.

LVI. 1999 – August

Then I had a different day. Despite my fondness for clichés this one really was different – although there were familiar elements. It was a soggy summer day, a standard-issue mid-August "Three-H'er" of a day. I wasn't in any of the places I like to be, home, the club, O'Shannon's enjoying a pint. I was sitting on a dented bench in a "tank," one of the holding pens on Rikers Island, feeling old and scanning the Covina reruns being projected in my head.

On the way in, peering through the bus's grubby, chicken-wired windows, I tried to do my usual step-outside-the-current-river-of-shit bit and engage in a little fantasy. Like Armin once told me, "You can, you know, re-form reality, mold it, shape it on the lathe of your imagination. There isn't an introspective faggot alive who hasn't learned how to do this."

I gave it a shot. I contemplated the outcroppings of rocks and the stumpy trees scattered haphazardly between the Stalinesque buildings, trying to make sense of the place. It was just flat out ugly. An island in the western end of Long Island Sound which, for reasons I never grasped, New Yorkers call a river. Barren and boring. I tried mentally sketching in an art deco arch at the head of the causeway; I stuck a marina over there with a view of the towers of Manhattan, carved a bicycle path along the water, painted in upscale condos, organic green grocers, Starbucks. Sorry Armin, it's hopeless. It is what the morons turned it into: a dormitory for the unsavory, the unlucky and the stupid.

This little island voyage, of course, was not unexpected. I'd known with a certainty bordering on absolute that it would happen. A scant two days ago it was around eight o'clock, when the action usually starts picking up. Maxine was in the cage and monitoring the feed from the camera on the door.

"Oh my God, Xero, take a look at this," she said staring at the screen.

"Holy shit!" I said leaning over and squinting. "Is that who I think it is?"

It was. Mr. T (for Trucker) Jones, the best point guard on the planet was on his way up the stairs, escorted by Joey Blue Eyes, the only black man I've met so graced. Joey, it turned out, was a buddy from the early days, back when Trucker was just a glimmer in a scout's eye. Mr. Jones had heard about us and wanted to play a little poker where it was clean and safe, if not exactly sanctioned. We'd gotten bigger than I imagined.

But, no matter, Mr. Jones had to buy chips like anyone else, stack 'em at the table like everyone else. Poker is the great equalizer. The cards don't give a shit who you are or what you can do with a round ball son, so have a seat.

The room, of course, went totally ape shit. Paper and pens emerged from pockets, autographs were sought, testimonials begged and, of course, cameras sprouted at the ends of arms. Everyone seemed to have a camera, or a camera phone. One of them had a flash and with that burst of photons my gut tightened. There was an unhappy place that one of those photos could lead. Here.

Two days passed without incident and for a brief, fleeting moment I thought that maybe we dodged a bullet. No such luck. One of the guys who took a picture just happened to know someone who knew someone else whose brother worked for a guy who knew an agent... and bingo, Simon "Trucker" Jones's face landed on the "do-you-believe-this-shit?" page (I think they actually call it "Page Six") of the *Post* with a couple stacks of redbirds sitting in front of him and a wired pair of ladies winking back at the lens. Do not embarrass us was the rule in the city. The uniforms did not like it. The mayor liked it even less. And early this afternoon my friends from the local precinct were knocking on the door – thankfully. I guess my little piece of inner-city diplomacy had some effect.

So there we were, me, three of my dealers, Ninny, Phil and Joey Blue Eyes who started the whole fucking debacle, Sheldon and Idaho Bob. Linda, Maxine and the girls were on the other side where, as I was to discover, things weren't much better. I think it's nice and progressive that all were treated with gender-neutral shitiness.

The tank was, well, a tank, a familiar tank. Decades had crawled by marked by marriage, death, elation, fear, despair and a couple of fleeting self-revelatory moments but tanks didn't seem to have undergone any notable changes. It was still cinderblock walls, bars across the long end and an uninviting toilet inside a flimsy stall, though the wooden seat was replaced with a chaotically dented metal one – an upgrade that could've been a cultural shift or just geography.

Naked bulbs in wire cages hung from the paint-chipped ceiling. It was crowded and there was quite a tableau spread before me. There must have been thirty of us, some slouched in corners, others slept on the floor curled up in child-like repose, a few talked softly in small, conspiratorial clumps, their voices rich with hissing sounds. The drunk and disorderlies were mostly leveled by hangovers, the druggies were in various stages of unhappiness, a thin, nervous twenty-something paced anxiously, dangerously.

I was shaken out of my state by a tap on my shoulder and a surprising voice. "Oy, mate, waun' a fag?"

"Huh?" I replied, thinking, 'Oy *mate*?' an Aussie? On Rikers? – and Jung's crap about time and coincidence started banging around in my head.

"A fag. Three bucks, jes' for you, mate."

"Three bucks?" I tried to garnish it with a touch of hometown outrage. "Fer one freakin' cigarette? No thanks," I said, shaking my head gently. "I gave 'em up long ago. Your name isn't Bradley by any chance?" I asked.

"What? Nope, but pretty good guess, mate. It's Bailey. Why are you asking?"

"Oh, you reminded me of someone I knew long ago. But if you're peddling smokes, try that poor bastard in the checkered shirt," and I nodded toward Ninny who, unused to sitting around in large, dank cells in the bowels of city jails, looked distinctly twitchy.

The Aussie took one look at Ninny and handed him a half-smoked butt, "'ere mate, no charge." And Jung smiled quietly.

Ninny whirled around on his bench along the far wall and bleated pitifully, "What are we gonna *do*, Xero? I don't need no record. I already got a place in Atlantic City. They won't let me deal if I got a record."

Ninny was whining again. I hated it when he did that. Everybody did. I couldn't wait for the guy to get a job in AC.

"We, my pathetic friend," I said, "are going to sit here and wait for Armin to take care of the legal stuff. Take a nap."

"Who the fuck's Armin?" said Ninny.

"My lawyer and, unless you've got a better idea, yours."

"Cool, man. I always wanted to have a lawyer."

"Ninny. Take a fucking nap," I said wearily.

But there was no sleep for me. I maneuvered my butt around trying to find comfort for its unfortunate shape in the bench's many dents and took a mental wander. I'd been on this carousel before and I knew you don't always get the brass ring. Armin would come in the morning. We would all be released, brought back later for the usual ritual and given some trivial sentence. It arched over the idiotic. I honestly did not care. Didn't give a raccoon's butt... yeah, "raccoon" – "rat's ass" was starting to sound boring. Mainly, I wanted to crawl into my own bed.

LVII. 1999 – September

⠂⠶⠄

Two weeks passed – the first two days of which I spent cleaning the tracks in the subway. Community service. It was actually a lot of fun. I got to work with a couple of street-savvy kids who were caught with a couple of doobies. We picked up all kinds of crap and joked about almost everything. They seemed to get a kick out of shoveling shit (literally) with a professional gambler.

I was now, more or less officially, a recidivist. I was surprised at how little I cared. Those "Joe Friday" spasms that used to sneak up on me had finally faded and I was looking forward to getting back to my life – my version of community service. I left the place shuttered for what felt like the appropriate amount of down-time.

Henry said to treat it like a mourning period after a less-than-beloved aunt dies. You really want to open but can't violate social protocol. That's not how he put, of course. That's my translation of "Just keep your freakin' ass low for a couple a weeks. The cops know when you're back in business. Give 'em a break or they'll bust you again."

So I spent a fortnight drinking Guinness, struggling with impenetrable novels and playing poker at the Mayfair. The mayor's boys only hit us; they left the other clubs alone. When we unsealed the doors our crowd came back and the club took on its usual ebb and flow when I had another different day.

It was late afternoon, the usual down time. Only two tables were going, both $2 - $4 limit hold 'em, lowest stakes we spread. The buzzer went off and Joey checked the video. "Xero, a *small* problem is coming up the stairs," and the way he said "small" made me turn quickly to the monitor. It wasn't small, at all. It was Earl, back again. Earl was a local black dude who might've given Bowie a run for *small* and he wasn't a welcome sight.

"Let him in. I'm gonna ride on him tonight."

"You want me to call Idaho?" asked Joey.

"Nah, let him have the evening off. I'll see if I can't get Earl to tone it down a bit."

For the most part, my run-a-tight-ship-brook-no-nonsense style worked, but not with Earl. Cortez, one of my regulars, had vouched for him. After a couple of sessions it became clear. Earl was rich and a truly awful poker player. In poker, like the rest of life, if you've got money and are moving it around, voluntarily or reluctantly, people will cut you more slack than you deserve.

Four or five evenings of putting up with Earl had tested my tolerance levels. He physically intimidated other players, made crude jokes, hit on my few women players and even put a move on Linda. One night he damn near got into a fight with

Cortez who was supposed to be his buddy. Earl may be hemorrhaging cash at the tables but from my end of it he was just another customer whose pots were getting raked the same as anybody else's regardless of race, gender or overall shitiness. There was a fine line I had to walk.

About three hours later the "Barry" moment put me over the threshold. Barry was a school teacher. A totally sweet guy, lived in Brooklyn, told me his grandmother taught him poker. After his wife died he became a regular. He'd come by one or two nights a week, play a little low- to mid-limit hold 'em and lighten up the room with his quiet grace. He'd struck me early on as someone I wished I had as my teacher. Barry transcended chalk and small wobbly desks. He had a passion for ideas and loved kids, all kinds, all ages, all everything. Barry had become my talisman. If I could attract and keep the Barrys I'd go to my grave satisfied.

Barry and Earl were heads-up in a big pot. I missed the details but Barry apparently hit a miracle card on the river to take it down. Earl leapt to his feet and erupted with a fuselage of obscenities and threats of bodily harm that startled even the most hard-bitten in the place.

The room grew deadly silent. I walked over to Earl, who stood a good three, four inches above me. I saw the anger in his eyes, winced inside and suddenly I found myself making maybe the biggest bluff of my life. I looked up and said, very gently, "Shut the fuck up and sit down. Act like a grown-up and not some pussy who can't take a punch in the gut. You wanna play in my club, act like someone I can respect."

Earl did not sit down. He just stood there, sweat beads forming on his forehead, his right fist was clenching and releasing rhythmically. Ten, fifteen seconds scrolled by excruciatingly.

"You don't know, do you?" I said, narrowing my eyes.

"Don't know what, honky," he sneered.

"You don't know if you can take me. I was a Golden Gloves champ," I lied. "You wanna go, we can go. Right here," I said pointing to the floor.

"You may take me; you may be in for a surprise. But if I take you, you are never gonna live it down. Everyone will know this pot-bellied Greek faggot whipped your nigger ass."

Earl flinched, just a tiny one, but I saw it. I leaned back a shade to give him a chance to do the right thing. My heart was pounding. I could almost hear it. Since opening the club I'd taken to wearing all black and was glad I put on a turtle neck that day. It covered the throbbing vein. I wasn't a hood, a bouncer, a fighter. I was Xerxes Theodore Konstantakis, son of an immigrant scholar, a misplaced, out-of-shape pacifist, armed only with the oratorical skills of my ancestors. I had just shoved all my chips into the pot and was waiting for the big lay down and hoping I didn't puke.

Earl stared at me for an endless ten seconds then, slowly a smile slipped from the corner of his mouth. His fist unclenched, his upper body relaxed. He gave a small snicker, reached out and chucked me on the upper arm, rather gently and said, "You know, I could wipe the floor with your sorry white butt but I think I like you. You Greek ass lovers just might be tougher than you look." And he sat down.

I turned to Ranjani, the waitress who had taken over running the kitchen and said, "Get Earl a two-day chit for dinner from any take-out he wants. He is my new best friend here."

The next day over lunch with Armin, I related the moment. "I honestly don't think I've ever been so scared," I said.

"It does seem, well, a little out of character."

"It was, but what is so interesting is that, in retrospect, I had no sense, none at all, of planning it or thinking it through. It just erupted out of me, like some id-driven impulse – pure reptilian brain."

"Yet it was the right thing to have done, yes?"

"Ah, right because he mucked his cards. If he calls, I 'get broke,' as we gamblers like to say, and, yes the double entendre was intentional."

LVIII. 2000 – July

"Mr. K."

That, I knew, was Ranjani. She was the only one who called me that except for Artie when he was getting ready to insult me or jack-up the juice.

"Yeah, what's up?" It was 4 AM and I was locking up the cash and chips in a safe that was now bolted to the floor. Ranjani was washing the dishes and putting away the last of the small buffet that she had introduced as a way of dressing up evenings when we held a tournament.

"Oh, not much, what subway do you take home?"

Oops. I don't need this, I thought. I do not need temptation. I stopped and looked at her from my somewhat awkward position, kneeling down in the corner of the back office room. "Actually, I don't, not when it's this late. I have a limo picking me up in about fifteen minutes. If you need a way home I can have him drop you off."

"That would be great. Thanks. I'll get my coat."

I watched her move. She had an athletic way of walking and I wondered if she, like so many kids in the city, was an actor or dancer, a star-in-the-wings waiting on tables, waiting to get discovered and the one-word chant "What?" "What?" bounced around in my head. What the hell's going on? She cannot possibly be interested in me. I didn't know what was happening; it all just leaked out so unexpectedly. I fell back on the tried and true. Go mum, kid. Watch, carefully. Look for tells.

In the back of the limo, Ranjani smiled, "You do know that I need to talk. Can I come over to your place?"

"Talk?"

"Yes, Xero… and I know, I usually call you Mr. K. but Xero is what you are now."

"Ranjani, you are being very cryptic. You are also young enough to be my daughter and I don't really like seeing that look in your eye."

"Xero… I like the sound of that," she said and patted my knee. "You're a very good poker player and a wonderful boss but you don't read women as well as you read the guys at the tables. I want to talk to you. That's all. You're far too old for me anyway," she chuckled and I felt a wave of relief interleaved with a slice of annoyance. I didn't like it when sandy-haired twenty-somethings with sharp, gray eyes were way ahead of me.

"It's important and it isn't what you're thinking."

When we got to my building, I felt even more annoyed at the twenty-four hour doorman than I usually did. If you want to get hijacked by the local gossip gamers in my building there's no better way to do it than to walk in at this hour with a pretty young woman on your arm. But I knew, there's nothing to be done for it. If I said anything it would just make it worse so I turned my best nasty half-narrowed-eye stare at Gordon who actually was a pretty decent guy. We stood there awkwardly waiting for one of the damned elevators both of which, of course, were on the top floors.

Ranjani lowered herself tiredly onto the far end of the couch. The drapes on the west-facing windows were open. The lights from the high-rises lining the Jersey shore danced on the shifting currents of the Hudson, their reflections moving sinuously between the buildings that seemed to be sprouting every month in this once rough and tumble neighborhood.

"Wine? Beer?"

"A glass of white, or anything, anything you have would be wonderful."

"There's a chilled bottle of pinot gris. Sit for a bit, I'll be right back," I said while walking into the kitchen and feeling even more at sea.

What's going on here? Ranjani had managed to get me into a spot that I hated and avoided with a skill honed over the years. All that time in circuses, literal and figurative, I'd learned many ways to stay outside the uneven flow of the connivers, away from the awkward reaches of the devious, the grifters and scam artists, the Dorises of the world. Ranjani didn't feel like one of those crazies; there was something very honest and sincere about her.

I'd liked her from the moment I hired her. She'd come to me and asked if I needed someone to run the kitchen. She'd played in the club a couple of times and then, quietly, she approached me with the idea of setting up a small buffet on tournament nights and, oddly, I said, "Sure, yeah, that would work," and it did.

I realized, as I poured the wine, that I'd let her slip under my guard. I remembered, with an inward smile, how Armin had laughingly told me and Lydia how we, too, had slipped past his. The memory brought a sharp reminder of loss. It was okay, okay. I didn't want to forget, not yet.

"Now," I said standing beside the dining room table and handing her her glass. "You said you needed to talk to me, talk."

"Xero. Sit down, please."

"No, I think I'll stand," I said with false gravity, "I like my mysteries on my feet."

"Fine, just don't drop the glass. Xero... I'm Armin's daughter."

"Okay, that was good advice. I think I will sit down and I think I'll listen carefully while you do more of this talk thing."

"The story is long and yet not," she smiled and sipped her wine. "I hope I finish before this," she said holding up the glass in a toast-life movement, "puts me to sleep.

"I grew up in Boston, a single child in a lesbian family. Mom's partner was from New Delhi, in case you've been wondering where the 'Ranjani' came from. They split and Mom moved to New York. She died of breast cancer three years ago and among the many things she left me was a letter.

"'If,' it said, 'you should ever decide you want to know who your biological father is, track down a linguist at NYU named Alkaios Konstantakis.'"

"No. Really? My *dad*?"

"Uh huh. The note went on. It said that she didn't know who but she had a name, 'Armin,' that he was gay and that Alkaios could help.'"

"Okay, like maybe that glass of wine is screwing up my brain. Your mother knew that some gay dude named 'Armin' whom she never met was your biological father – the sperm donor. How? It doesn't make a heck of a lot of sense. And how'd my father get in here?"

"Well, there's another piece that ties it up. Mom was an editor and a translator and she often worked with your mother, Hanna. They became friends and talked about a lot of things. I assume that in some conversation my origins came up."

"Ah, of course," I said. "My folks knew about Armin's 'seminal' adventure."

"So I found your father, happily retired, and that's when I found out about you – and Lydia. I am so sorry. It must still hurt."

"It does but it's okay. In a strange way, one I learned from an Irish bartender, I'm holding onto the pain for a while. It's cleansing."

"Well, your dad confirmed that my father's name was 'Armin' but that's all he would say. Of course, there might be more than one homosexual sperm-donor named Armin, but when I pushed, he just smiled and said, 'I think my son should tell you the rest. He's the one who knows what needs to be known.'"

"That sounds like Dad."

"He told me how to find you and, frankly, I was as surprised as I've been in my life. A professional poker player? Running an underground, therefore illegal, card room? You can imagine all sorts of things were swimming through my head. It was starting to feel like I was caught up in the plot in a seedy mystery: unknown gay stranger linked up, somehow, with a gambler whose widowed father is a professor of linguistics and whose deceased wife was a civil rights lawyer."

"This is getting better and better. So, how'd you find me?"

"Well, your dad told me where the club was. I didn't want to just show up and confront you. Frankly, the 'degenerate gambler *cum*-gangster' image was overshadowing all the other stuff and I wanted to find out if I could trust you. Alkaios told me to say that 'Sheldon sent me' when I got to the club and it worked."

"My dad does pay attention. I regaled him one day about Sheldon, the stupidest smart man I've ever known."

"I stayed low," she said. "I played a half dozen or so times – at the lowest stakes and lost, of course; it is a devilishly complicated game – and watched. Then, when I thought you might actually be a human being, metaphorically speaking, I started talking about the kitchen and my ideas for the food service and, voila, you hired me, which was good 'cause I needed a job."

"And now," I said, "you will want to know about your father."

"Not quite. Not right away. In the past couple of months, I discovered something. The quest has begun to transcend the goal. I'm having too much fun and, it's like an orgasm, the longer you can delay it the better."

I narrowed my eyes, reached for the half-empty bottle and tried not to let my mind run away without me. I don't need any new best friends, not now, not at my age... and not with Armin's daughter, no matter how remote that daughter-thing actually is.

"Fine," I said. "I'm happy to continue the fantasy voyage. So, tell me, how have you been living?"

"Off a small inheritance and, lately, tips – or 'tokes' as you seem to like to call them. Working in the club has been terrific. But it's time to move on."

"On? You have plans?"

"I do and they are set, as of last week. I auditioned with Donna Tarfarin's Dance Company and was offered a spot. I join them next month. I am, I hope, on my way in that world."

"Dance? You're a dancer? Of course you're a dancer. You move like a dancer and, not to give too much away but, as my Hanna, my salt-of-the-earth-Greek-peasant of a mother used to say, 'you came by it honestly.'"

"Do you want to know perhaps a little more? I think I need to say a few things, to draw out the drama. Not too much, though. I'm a big fan of Goldilocks."

"Xero, sorry, I'm tired too. Goldilocks?"

"Yes, Goldilocks, as in 'just right' or here 'just enough.'"

"Okay, tell me just enough," she said through a yawn.

"Your father and I are close. He was a dancer. He isn't any more, but that's okay. He still moves like one with a liquid grace that startled me the first time I saw him. He's complex, rich with contradictions but consistent in his standards. He's not a gambler, well not in the usual sense, but he embraces my life. He savors the vicarious trip along the edge of legitimacy. I think it gives him a bit of a tingle. I do think you'll like him."

"I'm getting the sense that I just might. A sense I got from your father too," she said.

"And that's it for tonight," I said and rose creakily. "I'm off to bed. You can stay if you wish, the extra bedroom is off down the hall. I hope you do for we still need to talk.

"One last thing," I said. "A bit of stage direction. When Armin told us about you, he said, 'I have a hope, a lingering hope that one day she'll pop her head in my office and say, 'Hi Dad.'"

I was almost asleep; the sun was leaking under the bottom of the drapes when the covers of my bed were pulled back and a warm dancer's supple body slid in and wrapped strong arms around me. We fell asleep like that. It may have been the most peaceful, deep sleep I'd had in nearly two years.

LVIX. 2000 – July

"Professor." It was Shelia on the intercom, "Your friend Xero is here with a young woman. She didn't give her name but said you were expecting her. Should I send them in?"

"Of course, Xero always gets past you. But I wasn't expecting anyone today."

Officially retired, Armin was grateful that the university let him keep his office and have a small piece of Shelia's time. Before, when they were still paying him, Deans and desperate students, fellow lawyers and consultants all had legitimate claims on him. Now it was just him, Shelia and the chance to do some serious writing.

"Good afternoon, Xero. And you? A friend of his? Do I know you? You look vaguely familiar."

"I think I was supposed to first knock on your door but Shelia opened it. But I do know the script: 'Hi Dad.'"

"Hi 'Dad?' Hi *Dad?*" said Armin, his voicing rising and looking bewildered.

"Yes, 'Dad,' as 'dad' in biology, in absentia."

"Oh dear, oh dear. You are... you really are?"

"Ranjani Winstone, an early 'test tube' baby, and, I do believe, your only daughter. Could I have a hug, please? And then we should go somewhere. There are *so* many things to talk about. And before we do you should know I slept with Xero last night."

"Armin, that is true only in the most flagrantly false manner possible. Don't listen to her, she is devious and clever..." I paused and looked at the two of them in an embrace that seemed both genuine and a little tentative, "a terrible combination. I didn't know they could code those in genes."

"So, tell me about your life," Armin said as we settled down in his living room with the usual trappings: wine, various cheeses on toasted baguette slices.

"It's straightforward. Emma Winstone wanted to be a mom. A gay man, apparently you, donated sperm and the usual nine months later, me, Ranjani. I grew up with two moms, for a while anyway. Emma was a free-lance translator and copy editor, warm, supportive, a little fragile but she held us together when Noma, her ex-, left. She nurtured and protected me. I realize now that she was more than a mom; she was a companion, a friend. You both may actually have met her."

"What?" I leaned forward. "Met her? How?"

"She was at your mother's funeral. They were friends."

"So," said Armin, "I missed the chance to say 'hello' to... to what? My partner in procreation? The mother of my daughter – neither of whom I'd met?"

"It is odd," said Ranjani smiling at us both. "But no one knew then. Three years ago she died. She left me a small amount of money and some stock which is how I've supported myself till now. I just accepted an offer to join Donna Tarfarin's Dance Company and that's pretty much it."

"A dancer. This is so interesting, so oddly satisfying. A dancer. That's how I began too. I'll tell you later. But how did you find me? For years I've hoped you – or whoever 'you' would turn out to be – would."

"Mom left me a cryptic note about how to find you if I ever wanted to. I didn't until recently. Living surrounded by women gives you a certain slant on things and, well, I guess I just didn't think much about fathers. I wondered from time to time if you were still alive, whether you were a bum, a druggie… who knew."

"Of course, of course," said Armin. "I never thought of this. How pathetically narrow of me. You don't know who your father is. There are no obvious bounds on what or who he might be."

"It was unsettling," nodded Ranjani. "I felt I needed to protect myself and didn't want to risk inviting an idiot into my life."

"But Xero? How did he get in the middle of this? He takes delight in surprising me but, well, this one has taken him to new heights."

"Thank you," I said, shaking my head. "But I had nothing to do with this. I was a pawn in a game being played around me."

"Like I said, my mom knew Xero's mom, Hanna, from sharing editing duties with a publisher. They became friends and something she said one day must have alerted her to the possibility that she and Alkaios knew about your role in this. I know, I know, it's all so insane, so unlikely that I couldn't get my head around it for the longest time.

"I tracked down Alkaios who is still sharp as the proverbial tack. I loved his mysterious refusal to give me anything but the code words to get admitted to an underground poker club."

"Wait a minute. You've been playing poker? In *his* club?"

"I gave you fair warning, Armin," I said.

"Yes," said Ranjani. "A bit. You understand, I didn't know who to trust; I had to find out. This underground card club thing didn't do a lot for the image of you forming in my head.

"Once there, I found Xero. I slipped under his radar using the usual, boring female wiles. He didn't even notice. In fact, he was such an easy touch that I actually slept with him and he never touched me, not once."

"This is true," I acknowledged, "devious *and* clever, like I said."

Armin looked back and forth between me and Ranjani. He seemed to be wondering what to do, what to believe – or maybe it was more like what he should do and what he wanted to believe. Ranjani had just showed up, out of nowhere. It was clear he still couldn't get things in focus. I watched him try my old trick. He pulled back, physically, just a bit and tried to focus on the obvious.

"You're a dancer," he said finally. "This is most familiar and, my goodness, I see myself in those eyes. You look more like me than Horst does."

"Horst?"

"Ah, yes, Horst. He's my son."

"Son? Oh, this is rich." said Ranjani breaking into a laugh. "My father is a gay man with at least two children. This just keeps getting better. How many other half-sibs are awaiting my arrival? Did we share the same test tube?" Her voice seemed to dance and I realized how easily that could have been nasty. It wasn't.

"None. Horst was conceived in the most mundane of ways," said Armin joining in the laughter. "I was married when I was very young. There are many homosexuals in traditional marriages. Few of them are happy. Many of them produce offspring. You'll meet Horst, eventually. I hope you'll like him.... I hope you'll like me."

"Oh I do already. Since I had, as you said, no 'obvious bounds' on what or who you might be, finding myself sitting in a Central Park West condo with a with a gray-haired legal scholar wearing a hand-knotted bow tie is, well, ..., let's just say it's outside the bounds of any fantasy I had conjured up. I have to go now. I have a rehearsal tomorrow morning. I'll call you. There is so, so much to talk about."

LVX. 2000 – August

It was getting late, well after we finished dinner. One of the marks of this friendship is that Armin lets me cook in his kitchen, which is more fun than driving T-Bird's convertible. His kitchen would make an upscale SoHo chef hyperventilate but unless I come over it's almost never used. Armin said he'd become an "urban forager" – too busy to bother with pedestrian things like cooking your own food.

We'd washed up everything and between us knocked off a bottle of a pretty good red. I was enjoying the one-acter in front of me. Armin, who'd had a head start with a martini while I was cooking, was drunk. Not totally smashed but way past the buzzed he usually stopped at. He got up and walked unsteadily toward the kitchen, "I'll get another bottle but you're gonna to have to open it," he said.

'Gonna?' echoed in my head. Gonna? I watched him navigate the corner of the table and barely make it through the door and had visions of Ken doing his chimp-walk.

Things had been unsettling for the supposedly retired, laid-back Ivy League legal hotshot. First, he was woken up unceremoniously by my 'you-got-one-phone-call' call from Rikers. Then Ranjani appeared evoking a medley of previously untapped emotions which he obviously didn't have a clue what to do with.

I looked at him, weaving his way back into the room, his head clearly spinning with regrets, hopes, doubts, hints of obligations, questions about responsibility, all of it kicked up a couple of notches by a half-bottle of that red whose nose, he announced loudly, kept getting better with each glass.

"Xero, what am I supposed to do now?" he said.

"I assume you're talking about your newly unveiled daughter, not the fact that you are now officially my 'mouthpiece.'"

"You, hah, you're easy. You and that, that gang of Runyonesque characters traipsing along in your wake."

"Runyonesque? Well, I guess that fits, but they all use contractions you know."

"You should do a show, a black comedy. That Sheldon is a dead ringer for the Sparrow character in *The Man with the Golden Arm*, Ninny I've got in the chorus of *Guys and Dolls*, Idaho Bob is Lennie, just hand him the script... he can read, yes? ... and Linda, hah! Yeah, I know she's a dealer, cards, poker, but hooker with a heart of gold? You do realize you're running a stable of clichés?"

"Of course. My life is bound up in clichés. I'm still looking for George Hanson."

"George who?"

"Hanson, the Jack Nicholson character in *Easy Rider*. Just crazy enough to fit right in. Anyway, what's the likely outcome here? The drama-queen in me, pardon the expression, wonders if they'll mine the data base and discover my Covina escapade. Strike two. Xero, the recidivist."

"Covina?" Armin said, wrinkling up his brow. "Covina? In California? Reschidivist? That didn't sound right, did it? *Recidivist*. Ah, good."

"It doesn't matter. It's too long a story to tell now but I had an interesting brush with *the law* back in 1960. I used to get a creepy sense that they were still watching me, waiting for me to open my unrepentant soul to them so they can put me away for good, in Leavenworth."

"Leavenworth? That's nowhere near Covina."

"Geographically that's true. Metaphorically it's just next door. And, luckily, you are too drunk to understand that and probably won't remember it."

"My God Xero, I am drunk, drunk as a skunk, couldn't find the bloody corkscrew but I still know the law on pokah."

"'Pokah'? 'Pok*ah*?' You said 'pokah?' That's even better than 'Gonna,'" and it hit me how much fun it was being the sober one in the room. Armin just grinned so I sat back to listen.

"The case," Armin continued, "was a half-century ago — judge said it wasn't illegal to *play* poker in New York. The crime was providing the accrout... accroot..., *accoutrements* ... for the game and, this, this is key, to make money from providing such provisions. There, that's better, 'providing provisions.' Hah!"

"It made sense," I said. "Otherwise all those games by the old proverbial kitchen sink would be illegal and every frat house would be filled with criminals... not that they aren't anyway."

"But it is merely a misdemeanor, which is why you got two days 'community service.' You know I coulda pretended I'm a real criminal lawyer. Done the plea-bargain thingy and got you only one day." And Armin started laughing and to my amusement, sniggering in a high-pitched 'heeee' sound on each inhale.

"Rikers Island, really... *heeee*. I do not, well, did not, *do* Rikers Island. I was a professor, on an endowed chair. *We* do not *do* Rikers. I hadn't been there before. God. What a dump! ... Pace, Bette Davis. *Heeee*.

"But," said Armin shifting gears and lowering his voice, "this escapade is not what's threatening to burn off the calming mist that had wrapped itself around my life; the game changer is Ranjani. You waltzed into my office with my mythical daughter, pulled flesh out of some milky glob in a test tube which was all I knew of her." He fell silent.

I sat quietly, leaned forward and said softly, "And?"

"And, I loved her. Instantly. She moves like I move. It is eerie. I have a daughter. I've always had a daughter, of course. But I didn't really. Not till now. I think... no, that's not really right... I don't think I'm thinking, not at this moment, not the way I'm used to." And he leaned even further back into his chair, his head almost disappearing into its soft cushion. I sat there, caught up in amusement over Armin's inebriation, in concern for his bewilderment and deeply satisfied to see both. There wasn't anything to say, so I sat there grinning.

After a bit he roused himself, leaned forward, his elbows on his knees, palms upward, "Tell me, please. I don't have to do anything, do I? Except care. Do I? Can I? Will she even let me? How about Horst? How do I tell him? He'll be furious at me for keeping her a secret from him."

"Never told him, eh?" I said. "That's funny."

"No," Armin said. "I never did. Didn't think it was his business. Besides, there was no reality there, till now. Was that wrong?"

"Dunno," I said. "You told me and Lydia – not to mention Anna and Billy. That, I think is interesting."

"Well, you wouldn't have cared so it didn't matter much. I was in a revelatory mood. And I was havin' fun."

"We did care, you know," I said.

"Different kinda care. Safe. Do I care what Horst thinks? Not as much as maybe I should. But I still don't know what I'm supposed to do."

"You aren't," I replied. "There's no 'supposed to' here and, luckily, there isn't anything *to* do. The work's been done, the cake is baked. Just enjoy her and be happy that she turned out so wonderful. Anyway, she's the next bridge."

"Bridge? I'm having trouble sitting upright. Do not do your enigmastic... enigmagic, oh hell, *metaphoric* thing with me."

"Sorry, I don't mean to be difficult. But it's pretty simple, I think it is anyway. You had a bridge for a long time, Bowie. He carried you over fears and lingering insecurities. He cleared the way when your shields, the elbow patches and bow tie didn't play that well, the clubs in Hyde Park, the Village, the jazz world."

"Keep talkin'. I like the bow tie thing there, *heee*.... But you're being serious, aren't you. I think I can handle serious. Pour me another glass and we'll see."

"Yes I am. Bowie deserted you. Selfish bastard, he went ahead and died, so I became the next second banana in the ongoing saga of Armin the I-Think-I'm-Out-of-the-Closet-Dancer-Lawyer-Guy."

"Hang on for a second," he said. "I think I need to get..." And palms on knees he pushed himself up and I saw Alkaios in that move – an old man's move – wandered back into the kitchen and started rummaging around in a cupboard smiling vacantly, like someone who knew he was looking for something but couldn't remember what it was. He picked out a cracker box and looked at it blankly and nodded at me. "Astute. Very. I do hate it when you're right you know."

"Lydia used to say the same thing, warned me not to make a habit of it. But, you know, you must know," I said looking at Armin who had made it to the door frame which he grasped holding the crackers, "every half-assed-decent drama has a third act and the last scene before it is sometimes called the 'bridge' scene."

"Ah, we're really shuffling metaphors now, aren't we? I've lost track."

"Yes, we are and I do believe I can hear Ranjani's cue. She does seem to have arrived at a most propitious moment. I am heading home now. It's late. You're going to pass out soon and I'm tired, more than just tired. I can feel one of those really off-pissing headaches that have plagued me the last couple of weeks coming on."

LVXI. 2000 - Late November

⤳

"Armin."

"Yes?"

"Armin, it's Xero."

"I know. I'm barely awake but your voice is distinctive. What's up, usually not you at this hour."

"Are you free this afternoon? I need you to meet me at O'Shannon's."

"O'Shannon's? Why?" he asked.

"Because Henry's there and I feel comfortable there. Right now there is not much to be feeling comfortable about."

"You are being cryptic."

"I know. It isn't deliberate, not today. Today I need simpler things, a top-drawer lawyer who is a good friend and a good friend who is, or was, a gangster. Can you meet me there, around four?"

"Yes, of course," he said. "It'll be good to see Henry. He always looks at me as though I was some nerd who wandered in the wrong door, looking lost. I think it's the bow tie."

"Henry does not get the Boston Brahmin thing."

"Hmm. I'll see you there."

At a tad past four the wind, cold and nasty, nearly tore the door out of my hand as I walked into O'Shannon's. Christmas was but a month away. The bar was gearing up for the holidays, strings of lights were wrapped around the painted columns, ceramic Leprechauns dressed up in Santa Claus gear were stuck randomly along windows, ledges and the back of the bar. It is, I thought, probably festive but I wasn't feeling that way, not in the slightest. I sat down beside Armin who was already at the bar, looking worried.

"Two Guinnesses, Henry... no, make that three. Pull yourself one and join us at the table in the corner, where it's quiet. I need your counsel as much as Armin's. We need, first, to talk about stains on the floor."

"Stains on the floor?" Armin said as we walked to the darker of the two corners at the back. "Stains?"

"Henry knows. It is time to tell me, us, what the stain was from."

"It was a long time ago," said Henry leaning on the table top and looking old, tired but wary. He nodded at Armin and looked back at me, his eyes pinpoints and still sharp. "You were still a student and a curiosity around here. You needed work. I offered you a spot in the room 'cause we had a couple of scumbags hangin' 'round. I told you it was 'cause of the cheatin'. Well, that was true and I liked it when you spotted it. I knew I'd have someone I could trust."

"But it wasn't just cheating, was it?" I said.

"No. The real trouble came earlier, from a bunch of gypsies; called themselves the Roma. They got in through one of my Micks who'd gotten sucked into some scam they were runnin' and was up to his fuckin' eyeballs to one of 'em. Then they brought in the others.

"It got real nutty, man, and not just the cheatin'. They started selling stolen stuff, watches, rings. Then fake shit, make-believe Rolexes, zircon 'diamonds' and they began buyin' in with counterfeit bills. I had to throw one of 'em out one night when he got into a shouting match with one my regulars and threatened to kill his wife. Not him, his wife. Like this was some kind of tribal threat. I didn't know."

"Why didn't you just bar them when the shit started?" I said.

"'Cause I didn't know what I was dealin' with, how many, what backin' they had. I didn't wanna start a gang war. Besides, there's always the business angle. These gypsies weren't real good players and they were pulling in others and, you know Xero, you run a room, you're rakin' every pot. But I did toss this Romanitsky, or whatever the fuck he was, out the door and held my breath. He'd no idea what he was getting into. The guy he threatened was one of us, well, 'us' back when we was 'us.' He was one of Billy O'Donneghy's guys."

"O'Donneghy?" said Armin. "In all innocence, I have no idea who this is."

"The Westies," I said. "Irish Mafia. Very bad people – I hope you are not offended Henry – very dangerous."

"Offended? Not a bit. I knew from the start what I was in and who they were. Survival was what I was interested in. I was good at it. I still am. I'm still here."

"When are we talking about?" asked Armin.

"It starts way back, way," said Henry. "The Irish gangs moved up here from Five Points maybe a hun'ert years ago, but the real crazy shit didn't start till the '60s. The cops had pretty much cleaned things up but to me – and that Darwin guy Xero likes so much – it was clear what was gonna happen. Survival of the fittest, right? They got rid of one bunch of assholes but didn't replace 'em with some good guys and so, in walked a bunch of very bad guys."

"Okay, I think I see," said Armin. "Not exactly how the history books would put it, but I get it. The 'very bad guys' were 'your guys.'"

"Yeah, in a way, a baby-kinda way. I'd been a minor player but once you play the game you cannot stop, not till someone turns out the lights. I worked with 'em when I could and stayed low. I had a small protection angle which they took a piece of. They liked to play poker and more than a couple of 'em used my room – which kept me tight."

"So, some of the guys I was dealing to were part of the Westies?" I asked.

"Yup. Including the guy you spotted dealing seconds. I had a chat with him. Nothin' serious. He was a minor punk."

"I'm glad I didn't know at the time," I said.

"Yeah, prob'ly. But you're right, Xero. Billy was very bad. In fact he was totally fuckin' crazy. But, back to that night – after things settled I noticed that this gypsy guy had left his fancy leather jacket behind. His wallet was in it. I took a look, to see if I could get some kind of lead on him. This prick had eleven different driver's licenses under at least six different names, and three social security cards, all different. I had no idea which one was him, if any."

"Ever find out?" I asked.

Henry ignored me. He fell silent, looked warily at Armin, down at the scarred wood. "He came back the next night," he said softly, "to get his jacket. I had it with me, here, downstairs in the bar. I wasn't gonna let him back up. But some guy was hollering for a refill and when my back was turned he slipped up and, well, Billy was up there. So we had that stain."

"I know," said Armin very quietly, "this happened a long time ago. I've come to like you Henry, but 'a stain' doesn't really cover much ground."

"Well, I've come to like you too which, frankly, surprises the hell outta me, but let's just say it was red, okay? And, don't worry, this is strictly confidential and since it is over turty years now I am pretty sure there will be no evidence. We have... *had*, ways to deal with this stuff. Mr. Roma ended up in the Hudson, along with the jacket and the wallet. No one seems to have missed him. His friends never came back." Henry paused, leaned back and looked at me with those piercing green eyes.

"And now you know Xero. And now I need to know why you asked. And why we are all here sipping Guinnesses like we was a cheery trio of Irish gentlemen."

"Because my friend Barry, a school teacher and one of my favorite characters in the funny world I live in, was shot last night. Not in my club, in one down on Houston. It'll be on this evening's news and, well, it's ripped out a piece of my heart and I need to talk and I need help and you two are the only people left in my world I can talk to about this shit.

"The Houston room got hijacked," I said. "This is a small world. The news moved fast and, I think, without too much embellishment. What these guys were doing taking down that club is beyond anything I can imagine. It makes no sense unless it was part of a family war or these guys were from, oh hell, I don't know, Romania? Houston Street's room is Gambino family turf, Gotti's people."

"Uh, uh," said Henry. "Are they fuckin' nuts? This won't stop here, not if Gotti's involved."

My head was killing me. Over the last couple of months the damned headaches had been increasing in frequency and lasting longer. I turned toward Armin. He probably didn't have a headache in the usual sense but if he looked confused when Ranjani walked into his office that was a pale glimmer compared with the bewilderment that had settled on him now. My dear friend, my quiet intellectual homosexual dancer lawyer friend was used to reading and writing about miscreants and their evil deeds but was clearly knocked off his pins when a very bloody reality was played out in real life. He leaned down on his elbows, lowered his head in a way that oddly mirrored Henry's move, like he was in this movie too, with us, a co-conspirator. So much of my life has felt like that. I live it, I lived it, but often it seems like it's all happening out there, scripted.

"You're right," I said. "It won't end here for some. For others it is done."

"Do you know how it happened?" asked Armin.

"All I know is apparently three thugs came in. They were wearing ski masks and were armed, big time. They took all the cash, and there was a fair amount, counting what was in the till. As I got the story, one of the locals tried to play hero, tackled one of the robbers, a gun went off and Barry took one in the chest. A couple of hours ago I heard he died on the operating table in the ER.

"Guys, I closed down the club this morning. They'd have busted us today anyway; better that they find an empty room. They're gonna shut up every one in the city. I'm selling out. I can't take this. As long as the idiots insist on keeping this game illegal, as long as they force it underground, this shit is what's going to happen. I've tried for years now. It's only cost me one small turn in jail and, frankly, that was more fun than anything else with Aussies with cigarettes popping up in unexpected places. But, no more."

"That sounds right," said Henry. "What can I, we, do?"

"Henry, you, as my hoodlum friends like to say 'knows guys what knows guys.' The room drops close to two mill a year. Let the word out. Talk to Artie. I'll let it go for a lot less, ten percent over what I paid for the space and start up. They can reopen in a couple of weeks, months, after things die down a bit. I'm throwing in the regular and new email lists and my phone book. They're worth as much as the actual club.

"I've got a real estate agent looking for a place for me in Atlantic City. Poker is booming there. I just hit sixty and I've gotta work out how to use the rest of my life. Beside the metaphoric headaches, the real ones are beginning to bother me, like right now. I think it is the stress.

"Armin, I need you to help me with the legal shit," I said and I started rubbing my thumbs round and round on my temples and screwing up my brow. "It's not – God it hurts – at all clear how one sells what looks like a legal business on the surface while everyone – shit Henry you got some aspirin or something – within the realm of the interested knows it isn't and still manages to get the cash out and, of course, pay the appropriate amount in capital gains ta....." and as that sound slipped out of my mouth I felt the blood drain from my face. I felt cold and clammy. Later they told me I turned an ashen gray, a slight whitish slip of spittle collected in the crack between my lips and I slid off the chair with a grace I rarely displayed, rolled onto the floor and shook violently.

LVXII. 2000 – December

I shifted my chair so I could see out the window, onto First Avenue. Bellevue, the vortex, pulling me in yet again. I was wearing pajamas decorated with donkeys that Lydia had given me years ago, refusing to say whether they were political symbols or marks of a losing poker player, a richly embroidered robe that Ranjani had brought me just yesterday and a Mets cap to cover my head, now shorn of what was left of my once dark Aegean curls. I waited for Armin to say something. He didn't. So I filled the silence.

"I remember when we were living back in Oakland," I said. "It was one of those wonderful evenings with Lydia and the amazing, crazy-quilt collection that clustered around her. I was panning the room with my mental camera which, of course, was a cheap 8-millimeter camcorder. I was the director, carving reality, tweaking it so it fit 'just so' and I realized it had a title, 'It's a Reasonable Life' – with appropriate debts to Frank Capra."

"Indeed, it has been," Armin said nodding, trying to look hopeful. "I assume you have signed yourself on as screenwriter." He knew he had a role to play here. You can't sit across the room from someone who may be dying and not have one.

"Not yet. First comes the novel, then the screen play – which some other clown may have to write. I feel fine right now, just some lingering weakness on my left side. The headaches have abated since the first itty-bitty aneurysm burst. That cold fish of a neurosurgeon, Romason his name tag says, told me they will come and go till they do the big ones. But for the novel I need to play with this 'Roma' thing which keeps sneaking in through the stage door – starting with Doris."

"Roma?" he said. "You're being cryptic again. Who is Doris? You've mentioned her before."

"Sorry. I keep forgetting that I still haven't told you the whole story. Doris was a grifter. I met her in the circus where I ended up that summer before I met Lydia – and you."

"This story, I'm looking forward to."

"It's in the book but I'd rather tell you in person, over wine and cheese. In so many ways that year was a defining one," I said.

"Really? How?"

"Mainly in setting boundaries – for life. No matter where Lydia and I were or what we were doing, in my head I was always circus. I got a degree, put in time in law school but I never really left the circus. Tony was my benchmark. Him you know. Doris you don't and should be happy about that. There were others, so many. Each left a token behind, their own device. I used them to mark the 'out-of-bounds' line. Except for Judy. Ah Judy... she was my Mrs. Robinson."

"Judy? Xero, why am I beginning to sound like a one-word question machine?"

"Because you don't know and that isn't your fault. It's funny, my holding all this back from you. I think it's because it was mine, so 'mine' that it's hard to share. Even Lydia never got all the details from that year."

"I understand," smiled Armin. "I've got a few of those tucked away too."

"Okay, short version, Doris... Doris became a most useful metaphor, the gypsy dybbuk. She was a fortune teller, a pickpocket and a very convincing con artist. And, of course, Doris wasn't her real name. She gave my old bullshit detector a real workout.

"I first met her," I said and I guess I had that far-away look, "when she slunk across the uneven tufts of weeds and dirt at the back lot of the carny in LA."

"'Slunk across the uneven tufts of weeds and dirt!'" Armin laughed. "Even you don't talk like that. Are you writing?"

"Yeah, I guess I am. It's the 'reasonable life' thing. Sorry. I'll try to stop sounding like a screen play. Anyway, Doris claimed to be a gypsy, said she was from Romania. Sure sucked me in. Only later did I discover that 'Roma' has nothing to do with Romania."

"But it stuck, yes?"

"More like it just lurked below the surface, till Henry's gypsies triggered it. Then, to top it off, this pale-skinned, cadaverous character who looks like Basil Rathbone shows up with 'Roma' in his name."

"So?" said Armin.

"So? So nothing. It doesn't mean anything except that it gives me an excuse to rename him."

"Huh?" came from Armin.

"Rathbone, Basil. Look, if a guy who looks like that, who never even cracks a smile and into whose hands I'm going to have to put my brain pops up, I have every right to dick around with his name.

"*Basil,* yes," I said turning back to the window, "I like that. I think this is what he shall be named in this book I'm trying to finish."

"Book?" said Armin, looking ever more confused.

"Jesus, Armin. I've been dropping hints so heavy you'd think one of them would have landed on your toe. You don't think I'm going to let this life run by without someone writing stuff down. I have an ego, you may have noticed. You're in it. If you don't like the you that's there, tough shit. You'll have to write your own.

"In this maybe-last chapter he shall be *Dr.* Basil. He says the headaches will come and go. Aneurysms do that and mine, of course, are special. Turns out there are two others and they are big, ugly motherfuckers.

"I do love it," I said, turning back toward Armin, "when docs tell you you're 'special.' It's like being on Sesame Street only here, when it creaks out of the humorless mouth of Dr. Basil, it is merely shorthand for 'interesting case, there's a conference presentation here.'"

"Morbidity doesn't become you, unless you're writing again," said Armin. "I've got to go now which is too bad. You appear to be ready to launch into one of your better rambles. You can recover by watching some enriching daytime television. I believe Oprah starts in a bit."

"The fact that you know who Oprah is, is as wildly improbable as having two children."

"Fooled you again, another Mr. Natural moment. I get bored too and well, she is special. But I'll be back, after dinner and... after *Wheel of Fortune*," and he let out as close to a 'whoop' as he had in him.

"Ranjani will come too, with Alkaios if he's up to it. We're doing Christmas a couple of weeks early and here. I called Henry and even Horst, who seems more comfortable sharing me with Ranjani than I expected. The whole gang, some of whom have never met each other will be sneaking in. See what you do? You bring together the best and the brightest, dancers and their queer daddies, linguists and gangsters, the flotsam and jetsam."

"Ah, yes, my special skill; 'flotsam and jetsam,' whatever the hell 'jetsam' is. Armin, do you think anyone knows? Do you think anyone has actually ever said 'jetsam' without 'flotsam' two words earlier?"

"You just did."

"Damn. You're right. I feel so special. If I bring them together, it's like a fight in the schoolyard or a messy collision in midtown. Only, once again, Tony is missing."

"Only temporarily. Ranjani and I tracked him down. He left your old club some years ago. He retired and now sits around waiting for his old friends to have brain surgery. He'll be here as soon as he can. And he said to tell you that 'Larry was found floating under the Oakland Bay bridge.' He said you'd know what that means. I don't and you are barred from telling me."

"No shit. So it was Larry; who the hell would have guessed. Now get outta here. I've got writing to do and who the hell knows how much time I've got to get all the words in the right order. Order, Armin, order," I said smiling as best I could and thrusting my right hand up, elbow bent, index finger toward the ceiling, "is important in so many ways. I find I am a word machine, they pour out of me. The struggle is getting them in the right order."

LVXII. 2000 – December

That evening Ranjani, with a large knapsack hanging over her slim dancer's shoulders, came in with Alkaios. Armin and Henry arrived a few minutes later with a carved wooden box in Armin's arms and a large brown bag in Henry's and Horst and Sarah followed with a tray. Ranjani pulled out three bottles of an outrageous Bordeaux. I knew I should not be tempted by it but, frankly, at that moment I didn't give a raccoon's bottom about what *Dr.* Basil wanted me to do – or not do. Horst pulled the corks and set them to breathe on a metal rolling table more used to gauze and bags of saline solution. On the tray were seven wine glasses and a spread of wondrous cheeses that expanded each time Armin reached back into his box. A pile of crisp water crackers sat in the middle of the bed and I wondered about the crumbs pressing into my thighs when finally I would crawl into it. It's good, I thought, to worry about such things.

"First," I said. "I want to offer a toast to my clever friends who have managed to smuggle this feast, including stemware – Ranjani, you continue to astound – into this uncertain place. If this turns out to be my last supper, it's a beaut."

"And a toast to you, my son," said Alkaios, his voice still strong, "to the unknown future and to a life I did not expect." And he paused for a bit, turning around with his glass held as high as his arthritic shoulder would let him, his eyes sharp and clear. "This yet unfinished life has been, well, so damn funny in so many ways it almost defies imagining. Thank you Xerxes."

"Thank you, father. I did try, you know, in my own way," I said. "And please Dad, keep pouring that stunning red, where did you get this? And what did you pay for... oh never mind, I don't want to know....

"You all know I really did run away with the circus. I know it's a cliché but at the time I was sure no one had ever experienced anything like it. A belated apology to you, Dad. It didn't occur to me, not for a second, that it was more than a little worrying for you and Hanna.

"The circus became my perfect existential trope. Beauty, glitz, clowns and music, wire acts, flyers and catchers, barkers and fortune tellers but pull back the canvas flap, just enough to peer inside. There someone's running a scam, some clown is heading toward a brutal alcoholic abyss, the advance teams are stealing and the lot is strewn with marginal bums and hobos. In the end they took it down and the rag pickers came and stripped the carcass clean. Just like my poker room.

"There's a will Armin," I said turning to him. "I wrote it myself. It's been witnessed and signed before a notary. There's a clause in it that says whoever buys the joint has to keep Sheldon as manager and Idaho Bob on the door. I learned a little from Lydia. I sure as hell hope you won't have to read it but you should know that you're the executor. Dad, this is toughest on you but you do understand. One of us will have to bury the other.

"You don't know Paul Bolling but he stopped by this morning. He operated twice on Lydia. It was quite wonderful of him but not exactly settling. Every time he shows up somebody either dies or is in pain. But, he means well.

"He said he'd talked to my surgeon who is, indeed, a humorless robot but, Paul said, he has the things we need, magic hands, an ego the size of The Bronx and he knows his statistics. There are two more aneurysms. He will try to clip them both off without killing me. I do like it when alternatives are laid out starkly.

"As he told Paul, it's 'a coin flip.'

"Funny, that's a poker player's term for situations where your odds of winning are about 50-50. They happen all the time, a pair against two overcards. So, flip a coin my friends," I said holding my glass high in a toast to tomorrow, "heads I'll buy the wine for the celebration. Tails and you poor bastards are going to have to take care of all the annoying details."

Arthur Reber is a cognitive psychologist who spent a half-century studying human intuition. He's an elected Fellow of the American Association for the Advancement of Science, the Association for Psychological Science and the Fulbright Foundation. He's also a dedicated poker player and expert on gambling. He lives in Point Roberts, WA in semi-retirement with Rhiannon Allen, Obediah Jones and Burney Blue. This is his first novel. His website is www.ArthurReber.com.

Made in the USA
Middletown, DE
02 August 2015